# Gloria Wolk

Bialkin Books
Raleigh, North Carolina

Cover and interior design: Æonix Publishing Group, Ridgefield, Washington, www.aeonix.com

Editor: Sandi Gelles-Cole, Woodstock, New York

*Accidental Felon* is a work of fiction. Names, characters, places and incidents are the products of the author's imagination or are used fictitiously. The opinions expressed are those of the characters and should not be confused with those of the author. Every case mentioned, every court ruling, every news story cited, is real and accessible on the internet. The author has chosen to change the names of people who completed their sentences, but these cases are internet-accessible by using the correct search terms. Other than these exceptions, any resemblance to actual events, locales, or persons living or dead is coincidental. Through legal consulting and research the author acquired many transcripts. Since they are not protected by copyright, she adapted excerpts where appropriate.

This is a work of fiction.

Library of Congress Control Number: 2012903042
ISBN: 978-0-9652615-5-5

First edition published by
Bialkin Books
14460 New Falls of Neuse Rd. #149-247
Raleigh, North Carolina 27614
Toll free: 888.798.BOOK (U.S.)
Fax: 815.572.9707

Printed in the United States of America

Dedicated to
Dick Allen, Connecticut Poet Laureate
and in Fond Memory of
Norman N. Goroff, M.S.W. (1925-1989)
J. Raymond Pichey, M.S.W. (1924-2009)
Mentors and Friends

# Prologue
# Victims and Victimizers

BLAKE ARCHER, VICE PRESIDENT of Archer Life Settlements, was in Fort Lauderdale, Florida, presenting a sales training conference for new recruits. Standing six feet tall, with a surfer-bronzed and runner-toned body, he resembled a tall Tom Cruise. With his banter and practiced charisma, Blake was a popular presenter. And his message promised wealth.

His audience, five hundred insurance agents and securities brokers, sat at linen-covered tables in the Grand Ballroom of the Ritz Carlton. Two thirds were men, about half were age forty or older.

Standing at the side of a large pull-down screen, Blake clicked the remote to a new picture. "Okay, guys and gals, you asked about the legality of an insured selling a policy, and here's what you tell your clients: The U.S. Supreme Court allows an insured to sell his or her own life insurance policy. It's like selling a house or any other property."

He nodded as he scanned the faces of those sitting at two front tables. "So," Blake continued, clicking to the next screen, "if Mrs. Jones is insured for $1 million, she has the right to sell the policy. We will pay her six thousand—just like that." He snapped his fingers. "It will cost her nothing. She never pays a premium. She pays nothing. Nada. Zip. Now is that a good deal, or what?" Blake saw a hand raised. He pointed to the man.

"Who are the investors? After Archer buys the policy, I mean. What if Mrs. Jones is worried about being killed for the death benefit?"

"Tell her we sell to investors in Hong Kong. Wealthy investors. Very wealthy investors." He clicked the remote, looked at the screen, and saw it was a diagram. "This gives you an idea of the profit to you. First, you sign up a senior for new life insurance. Once the policy is issued, the insurer pays you a commission. Most insurers pay fifty percent of the first year's premium. Say your applicant is seventy years old and the death benefit is at least one mil. The premium will be in the neighborhood of sixty thousand. That's thirty thousand in your pocket. One sale. Think about it." He paused to allow the audience to react. "Do less than one a month and you have an annual income in excess of three hundred thousand. And that's for starters."

Blake clicked the remote to a new screen. "You bring this new policy to Archer, we agree to buy it and we pay you a commission." Someone in the audience whistled. Blake reached out his arm and pointed his index finger at people in different parts of the room. "Here's a question for you folks. What will Mrs. Jones do with that six thousand?" He paused to allow the question to sink in. "What about selling her an immediate annuity? Or a Long Term Care policy? Or an investment?" He shook his head up and down. "With any of these sales, you get another commission. Commission plus commission plus commission. Think you can live with that?" He grinned broadly as the audience laughed.

As the room quieted, another hand went up. Blake nodded at the questioner.

"Six thousand is not enough for an immediate annuity or a Long Term Care policy, if Mrs. Jones is seventy years old."

"Exactly!" Blake shouted triumphantly. He began walking the length of the room. "That's why, once Mrs. Jones sees how easy it is to make money, she will be eager to apply for a half dozen policies. Now she spends the money on products that pay additional commissions to you."

Blake clicked to the next screen. This one showed profits to the fictional Mrs. Jones. The next screen showed profits to the agent who solicited her. He saw another hand go up.

"What if Mrs. Jones can't qualify for $1 million death benefits? None of my clients is wealthy."

"How many of you have that problem?" Blake looked around at the raised hands. "Well, I am here to tell you: It. Does. Not. Matter. Wealth does not matter. We've been doing this for five years. The insurers do not verify the income statement you submit with the application."

Blake pointed to a woman who was mumbling to her seat companion. "Care to share that with all of us?"

"If the insureds are not wealthy, they can't afford six figure premiums. Even if the policy is sold, they have to pay the first premium, don't they?"

"We have that covered." Blake turned toward the screen. He clicked to a new frame. "Either the investors pay or we use a premium finance company. The finance company pays premiums as a loan. The loan is repaid with interest when the insured dies."

Another hand raised. "You're saying any senior can get a bunch of policies for $1 mil and more, even if they have no assets?" Blake nodded. The woman continued her question. "Won't the insurance companies catch on? Too many policies issued to people who are worth nothing?"

"Guess what," Blake answered. "Insurers did not check the Medical Information Bureau when we were buying policies from insureds diagnosed with HIV or AIDS, and they don't check now. They don't check the bankruptcy courts. They don't check the address of the insured. That's why million dollar death benefits have been issued to people in subsidized housing."

"Not all insurers," the same woman continued. "Not the company where I work."

Blake nodded a few times, as if digesting her remark, then asked the name of her company. "Aha! They head the list of companies to avoid. Just take the life insurance applications to another company. We have a list of," he cleared his throat for emphasis, "friendly companies." The audience chuckled.

Blake returned to the front of the room. "To sum up, every time you sign up someone, ask for referrals—relatives, friends, neighbors. Ask if they are members of a church or senior club. Once you exhaust your client list and their referrals, we turn to the free lunch or free cruise. Then you can recruit seniors you never met before. And speaking of free lunch, I see it's time for our gourmet lunch. We'll meet back here in an hour."

∾

Breathing noisily, gripping a cane with one hand and a FedEx envelope with the other, Frank Candless shuffled into the kitchen. He watched as Emma took a chicken from the oven and placed it on top of the stove. He waited until the chicken was safely settled before speaking.

"I signed the papers."

Emma froze, her hand on her heart. She turned toward him. "Please don't, Frank."

"You know there's no choice, no one left to lend us money. Once I mail back their FedEx, it's a done deal."

A tear rolled out of Emma's left eye. Ten months earlier they almost sold Frank's life insurance. At the last moment they stopped. Despite his frail health, they were not ready to give up hope. Emma still was not ready.

"I'll contact the bank to ask them to delay foreclosure," Frank told her. "I'll tell them we expect the money within weeks."

Emma shook her head but could not speak. Frank continued. "You have to sign, too, Emma. You have to give up your beneficiary rights." He withdrew the page from the envelope, placed it on the table, handed her a pen.

∾

Vito Capone sat at his kitchen table with a pen, three applications for life insurance, a bag of potato chips, an empty bottle of Heineken's at his elbow. He struggled to remember which versions of his social security number he used the last times he applied for life insurance. Frustrated, Vito pounded the table with his fist. The bottle jiggled but did not fall. He swore aloud, knowing it was his own damn fault that he could not remember, knowing he had scrambled the numbers so many times over the years he could not be sure which combination to use for these applications.

Hell, he mumbled. I'll use Jimmy's.

For good luck he wrote his son's social security number on the biggie, the application for $250 thousand in death benefits. Luck, he muttered. He needed luck to get a policy with such a large death benefit. Insurers would demand a blood sample, and probably a paramedic exam. Vito laughed aloud to think of the Oops! if they knew what his blood would tell them. Well, they would get a stand-in—Angelo. Since falling off a ladder and hurting his back, Angelo could not work. And his brother looked enough like him to use Vito's driver's license as ID.

The problem was Angelo might demand more than the last time. Greedy bastard.

❧

Jeff Minor was pumped up after the Fort Lauderdale sales conference. His newspaper ads lured investors like catnip for starving cats. When the receptionist buzzed to announce the arrival of his ten o'clock appointment, Jeff hurried to the door of his office. He was tall, wide-shouldered, his hair clipped close to the scalp, the same as when he was the town's football star but in his forties he kept it cut close to hide the balding. Hurrying, his belly jiggled over his belt. Jeff tried to ignore it. He would scarcely be recognized if he attended a high school reunion. Which is why he did not attend any.

He greeted Mildred and Harry Santori, a couple near his age with two teenagers. The first time Mildred phoned, she asked about the newspaper ad. "What is this best investment in a century?" He told her he was all out of inventory but would put her on a list and contact her when his company had more.

Pretending to run out of inventory was one of Jeff's favorite tactics. When people believed they might lose an opportunity, they acted fast.

Mildred must have dragged Harry here. Harry stepped into the office, looked around, and accepted the invite to take one of the visitor chairs at the desk. Mildred smiled brightly, as if she expected to be crowned prom queen.

"So," Jeff said, clapping his hands as he took his seat, "I told you I would contact you as soon as we had more inventory. These are going like hot cakes. I have a long waiting list after you folks."

"Mildred showed me your ad. What's it about?"

"It's about life insurance policies. You invest in the death benefits of people who are dying. These are people who used up their last dollar and have nothing left to keep a roof over their heads. Nothing but their life insurance. It's worthless to them unless they sell. You buy the policy and become their Guardian Angel. You ease their last days."

"Got it. But what makes it a good investment?"

"Let me ask you a question so we can make a comparison. Do you have money in CDs? IRA? Mutual funds?" Mildred said yes to all. "What kinda return are you getting—two percent?"

Harry frowned. "Some are minus," he admitted.

Jeff's face broke into a broad grin. "That's why this investment is so hot I can't keep inventory. It's as safe as CDs and money markets. The big difference is—get this—a return of fifty percent."

"No way," said Harry. Mildred grabbed Harry's hand. "See, I told you," she said.

"Yes, way," Jeff told Harry. "Warren Buffet invested in these, that's how good it is. You can't lose."

"Explain about the fifty percent returns," Harry said, disengaging his hand from Mildred.

"Say the insured has a death benefit of one hundred thousand. You buy it for fifty thousand. When the policy matures—the insured dies—you get the full hundred thousand. You are paid directly by the insurance company. No risk. High yield. Can't beat it."

Mildred looked ready to sign. Harry still looked grim.

"What's the catch?"

"There is no catch."

"There's always risk. What's the risk?"

Jeff sat back and folded his fingers. "Oh, I understand what you're getting at. Yes, you're right. You're a pretty savvy investor, aren't you? Lots of people never ask that. Well, here's the problem. If the insurance company goes belly-up, you won't get paid immediately after the insured dies. That doesn't mean you won't be paid. You'll just have to wait longer." Jeff leaned forward. "That's not likely to happen here. Other companies, maybe, but not here. Our supplier is strict about selecting policies from companies rated A or A-plus."

"I didn't know that could happen to insurance companies," Mildred said.

"Let's say, against all odds, it did happen." Jeff shifted his gaze back to Harry. "There is a solution. It's called the state insurance guarantee fund. Every state, by law, has a guarantee fund. If an insurance company goes bankrupt, the other companies have to chip in to pay their claims. So, bottom line, even though you may have to wait, you will be paid. Not immediately. But you will be paid."

Jeff asked if they had other questions. None. He asked how much they had in CDs—could they handle a fifty thousand dollar investment in order to get a one hundred thousand dollar return?

"I just thought of another thing," Harry said. "How long do we wait to get paid?"

"That's up to you. You choose the life expectancy. One year, two years, five years, all the way up to ten years. In fact, you could stagger the life expectancy and get several policies, each with a different pay day."

"Each one costs fifty thousand?"

Jeff laughed. "No, sorry, I did not make myself clear. Some policies have death benefits of as much as five million." Jeff felt like laughing again, when he heard their gasps, but he restrained himself.

"We can't afford something like that," Mildred said.

"Well, you can buy a piece," Jeff told her, then looked at Harry. "With policies that large, unless the purchaser is a Wall Street company, we sell fractionalized shares. You could buy, for example, three percent. And have other investments go to policies where you are sole beneficiary."

Harry's brow was furrowed. He looked down. When he looked up he had another question. "We can choose the life expectancy?"

Jeff repeated, "You can choose one year, two years, out to ten years."

"If we go for one year, and the insured lives two years, what will the return be?"

Jeff opened the folder on his desk. "Here's a chart that shows the returns." Jeff turned the chart around so that Mildred and Harry could read it. He knew he had them. "Do you have IRAs? Yes? Good. We can transfer your IRAs from the current trustee to one who specializes in viatical and life settlement investments."

"And what company did you say is selling these?" Harry asked.

"Star Spangled Life Settlements. They buy most of the policies from the top viatical and life settlement provider, a terrific company licensed by every state." Jeff told them to go home and think about it. Unless they had more questions, he had a long list of people to call. As they stood, he added, "You need to know that if you do not act now, you'll be bumped to the bottom of the list. Then you wait for new inventory."

They signed.

After he walked them to the door, shook their hands, and congratulated them on their wise decision, Jeff returned to his desk. The commission was twelve percent of the checks the Santoris had written. Their CDs would be cashed out. He failed to remind them of the penalties for early withdrawal, but they should know if they read the bank's brochure. Their IRAs would be converted. One hundred fifty thousand. Eighteen thousand commission. Not a bad start to the week.

❧

Three times Carly called Ethan to breakfast. He slowly walked downstairs, barefoot, his Spiderman pajamas getting short in the legs. He saw his mother at the sink, her back to him, and he remained at the foot of the stairs, head down, black hair tumbling into his eyes.

"Your egg is cold," Carly told him as she turned. Her mouth fell open. "You're not dressed! You want to be late for the school bus? I don't have time to drive you."

Ethan clenched his fists. The ten year-old was nearly the mirror image of his mother, the same emerald eyes, slightly lighter bronze skin, tall for his age and pencil thin.

"I'm not going to school," he said quietly. Unless Ethan screamed, his voice never had inflection. Carly blinked quickly, straining to keep her tone soft. She asked why, and nearly lost it when he told her, "The teacher said she would have a surprise today."

Ethan did not like surprises. He loathed surprises. Ethan's world needed to be consistent, predictable, routine. Life did not work that way, Carly knew, but she tried to make Ethan's as consistent and routine as possible. Try humor, she reminded herself and was unable to call up anything. Failing that, she said, "Maybe the teacher will bring a jumping frog to class. Maybe cookies. I'm sure it's something nice. Tell me, what kind of nice surprise would you like it to be?"

He did not respond. Frustrated, her voice rose again as she told him, "No way are you staying home!"

They were at an impasse. She pointed to the stairs and ordered him to march upstairs right now and get dressed ASAP. Again, the wrong way to handle this. Ethan stared at nothing, his fists clenched, fighting a meltdown. Geez, she realized, he had more control than she did.

Her brother stomped downstairs, his strawberry-red curls disheveled from sleep. Carly looked up as Ben pounded down the last two steps. He, too, was barefoot, wearing only jockey shorts that revealed pale skin that never tanned. Her kid brother, stomping as if he was still a teen, Carly thought with annoyance. Instead, she grumbled, "You sure make a ton of noise."

"Crappy morning again?" he said. "Thought you changed your job."

"I did. But I still have to get to work on time. And I still get phone calls from people who are dying, people I know. I hate to tell the receptionist I won't take their calls." She turned away from Ben and walked into the living room, wringing her hands. "And I must get to work on time. I want a leisurely ride. I need a leisurely ride."

"I dig it. Like, I wanted a few hours of leisurely slumber."

Carly apologized. Her brother worked nights; this was the middle of his sleep time. Ben told Carly to go on to work, he would stay with

Ethan. "Maybe, after a few more zzzs, we'll go to the beach to look for tide pools." Ethan's head jerked up with surprise. He reached out to "high five" his uncle.

If Carly was clever she would have said, Surprise, Ethan! You get to go to the beach. But she was angry and frustrated, some of the anger directed at Ben for turning Ethan's stubbornness into a celebration. If Ethan stayed home, he should be bored, not doing something he greatly enjoyed. But what more could she do? Carly grabbed her purse, her cell phone, her keys, and dashed out of the cottage. Her truck waited in the driveway.

# Chapter One

CARLY DROVE HER DODGE RAM double cab to the end of Blue-bird Canyon Road, stopped, and turned right onto Pacific Coast Highway. Once past Main Beach PCH, with two lanes going north and two lanes going south, paralleled the shoreline, sometimes curving, then straightening, then curving again. The route never failed to lift Carly's spirits. When calm, the blue ocean stretched like a blanket to the horizon, sparkling in sunlight. Today there was an incoming tide, foam-capped waves chasing each other ashore. A perfect early June morning, Carly thought. With temperatures in the sixties, her window was half down, and a salt-tinged breeze drifted into the cab, fluffing her short hair.

Carly's radio was tuned to zippy, bluegrass music, tuned low so as not to block the excited chatter of seagulls as they spotted breakfast. Carly took a quick glance at a large dark blot—a pelican—circling the cloudless, cerulean sky, and smiled as she returned her gaze to the road and the poky car ahead of her truck.

The Pontiac with a Michigan license plate had to be tourists. Tourists who refused to move out of the passing lane. Tourists who forced her to keep braking. She flashed her lights. Carly cursed them under her breath and flashed her lights again. "Get the hell out of the ocean side of the road," she mumbled.

Another half mile and she flashed her lights again. Again they ignored her. Carly was ready to scream. Coupled with anxiety about getting to work on time was the lingering guilt for dealing so poorly with Ethan—as if she did not know better. As if she had not been trained to help him. And now the tourists.

Carly flashed her lights again. The car ahead continued to plow along at its leisure. Cars on the inside lane were passing her and the sluggish Pontiac. She watched as a dark blue BMW, a red Chevy, a florescent green Kia passed her truck and the poky tourists, before shifting back to the left lane and speeding on. With mounting frustration, she put on the blinker, glanced behind and to her right, and quickly changed to the inside lane, slowing as she came too close to a rusted Ford pickup. The pickup's brake lights glowed and Carly tapped her brakes. The pickup slowed more. She tapped her brakes again. As the distance between them increased, an arm reached out on the passenger side of the pickup and tossed something from the window. The pickup sped up, putting yards between them.

Carly's mouth fell open. The thing thrown from the pickup was small, pale in color, and looked like a baby.

A quick glance in the rear view mirror to be sure no car was close and Carly pulled her truck onto the grass. She jumped out. Her slim heels dug into the earth and grass as she walked to the thing that lay in a tuft of uncut weeds. With a gasp she saw a baby. A baby dog, a very young one.

❧

By the time she pulled into the small office park off Jamboree Road Carly had a new problem, a veterinarian problem. She glanced at the dashboard clock. She would have to make up lost time during lunch.

Carly parked at the far end of the lot and hurried to the second steel and glass, mid-rise building, the one with the huge metal sign, Archer Life Settlements. Everything was lit by a southern California sun that glowed from cloudless, blue skies. At Archer Life Settlements, sunlight spun rainbows on the glass. Rainbows, usually a symbol of hope, but not here. Within those walls, death was welcome. People died, and her employer's profits increased. People died, and she had a pay check. Much as Carly deplored this work it paid better than similar jobs anywhere else. The work was stressful but finances were a bigger stress.

Carly was nearly at the door when she heard an agonized growl, a wounded monster entering the parking lot. A quick glance confirmed the source of the abominable noise—Blake Archer's red Ferrari convertible. He treated his newest toy as his first born. The first day he brought it to work, Blake ordered all employees out to the parking lot. When everyone was gathered around the car, he pushed a button and the hardtop rotated back to rest against the rear deck. He grinned at the expected oohs and aahs and scattered applause. He told them it was his million dollar car.

Frowning, Carly turned away and walked briskly to the entry. Blake Archer chirped his car into lock and trotted over to Carly.

"Hello, Maria Tallchief!" Carly grimaced. How many times did she tell him she did not like the nick-name? And how many times did he tell her it was a compliment to her lovely skin color? And, as usual, Blake swooped down on one knee, blocking her from moving forward, stretched out his arms and began to sing the song from *West Side Story*.

"Oh, Maria, Maria, I just met a girl named Maria."

"Excuse me," she said, trying to move past him. "I must get to work."

"It's okay, Carly." He stood up. "When you're with the boss you can be late." He grinned and tried to take her arm. She brushed past and hurried into the building.

❧

Carly waved to co-workers as she rushed through the data entry room to her cubicle. A new stack of folders sat next to the computer. Each folder bulged with documents about insureds who hoped to sell their life insurance policies. Carly had spent the past two weeks learning a new job at Archer. Now she simply had to speed up productivity. Boring, but a relief after nearly two years at Customer Service—Tracking.

Carly lifted the top folder. The folders were stacked in the order documents were delivered to Archer. This one was labeled Woodruff, Shirley. Carly's first task was to verify that everything Archer needed was in the folder. She ticked off each item on the box on the computer worksheet labeled Viator Checklist.

"Didn't you have a file on Beasley last week?"

Carly looked up. Allison, another of the clerks who entered information into the computer data base, stood there with an open file in her hands.

"I'll have to check. I don't remember the names."

"You asked me what to do about something missing?" Allison prompted.

"Oh, yes, now I remember. I didn't know where to put an incomplete file."

"Sean Beasley?" Allison asked.

"What's the problem?"

"If this is the same Sean Beasley, then he's selling two policies."

"Is there something wrong with that?"

"No. Just that I thought since this file is complete, maybe we can copy the missing document and use it to complete the earlier file."

"I think we should ask Greg," Carly said. Greg was their supervisor.

Allison nodded. "Will do."

"Tell me what he says," Carly shouted as Allison left her work station. "I may need to know this in the future."

Carly withdrew Woodruff, Shirley's application for a viatical or life settlement and began to copy information. When Carly saw the diagnosis, she shut her eyes. She did not want to know. That was the reason she transferred out of Client Services—phone calls with people who were dying from serious illness or from old age. Shirley Woodruff was close to the age Carly's mother would be, had she lived. Same diagnosis. Too much similarity. She did not want to know anything more about Woodruff.

It was too late. There was a hand-written note at the bottom of the last page of the application, a small, graceful script. Shirley Woodruff politely requested the settlement as quickly as possible and as much as possible, because she did not want to lose her rent-controlled apartment before she died. The viatical settlement would keep a roof over her head for the time she had left.

Oh shit, Carly said. She wanted to lock her memory against this. She did not have authority to expedite an application. She could not influence how much Woodruff was paid.

After replacing the application she withdrew the life insurance policy. It was a relief to return to the mundane, to copy information without thinking. Carly was nearly done with the Woodruff file when she heard Aidan Archer as he strolled through the room saying, again and again, "Hello, how are ya?"

The CEO of Archer Life Settlements was in his mid-forties with prematurely white hair around a leathered face, which Aidan described as "sailboat tan." He stopped at Carly's cubicle to ask if she received the missing documents for the Benson case. Carly checked her computer. The Benson file was submitted by a broker who habitually omitted one or more documents.

"Still outstanding," she told him.

Aidan frowned. "That guy's probably with a preferred company."

Carly looked up. He must be really pissed, she thought, to tell me this.

"Interesting," Carly commented. She was tempted to ask what he meant by "a preferred company" but Aidan looked surprised at her comment, as if he did not realize he had spoken aloud.

"Keep up the good work," he said, and walked away. On impulse, she called him back. He turned but did not step toward her cubicle. Carly got up and walked swiftly to him. In a hushed voice she told him about Woodruff's note.

"Is there any way we can rush this?"

"I'll see what I can do," he said, smiled, and turned away.

Carly suspected he would forget as soon as he rounded a corner. She went back to work.

∾

Today was an Ensure day. Stopping for the puppy, back-tracking to Laguna Beach to find a vet, retracing her route to Irvine. Being late to work meant working through lunch, and it was not the first time.

Carly kept two cans of Ensure in the break room fridge, replacing each after it was turned into lunch. She kept two cans in the event she forgot to replace one.

Carly sipped from a straw while working on files. The office phone rang. Ben! she thought with alarm. He would not call unless there was an emergency. Carly had told the receptionist she would not accept any calls while she worked through lunch break, but her brother and Ethan's school were the exceptions.

Sherri, the receptionist, apologized for disturbing her. "No one else is here, and this woman is very upset. I don't know what to tell her and she doesn't want to call back after one."

Carly groaned noisily. She told Sherri to put the woman through.

"You should get a raise for this," Sherri said.

"Tell that to Aidan or Blake," Carly said. "Maybe tell both."

"Ha-ha," Sherri said sarcastically.

When the call was transferred to Carly's line, she answered with her name, omitting that this was the Data Entry Department.

"My name is Emma Candless," the woman began. "My husband, Frank, died last week." Carly expressed sympathy, but the woman continued as if Carly had not spoken.

"He sold the life insurance he owned for fifteen years. A one hundred thousand dollar policy. He was paid nine thousand. Much less than the premiums he paid over those years, but we needed the money." Her voice changed, now hard and angry. "I just found out we could have been paid thirty thousand."

Carly told her she knew nothing about pricing but would look up the policy to see if there was some reason noted in the file. A few clicks, a few more, and Carly began to think either she did know how to access the database for purchased policies or it was not on her computer.

"When did he sell it to Archer?" Carly asked. "I can't find it on my database, but it may be listed somewhere else."

"He didn't sell to Archer. He sold to Buques, but I can't reach them," Mrs. Candless said, obviously crying. "The phone number on Frank's papers no longer works. Directory information has no listing. I saw a newspaper ad for Archer. I thought you might be able to help me find them, since you're also a viatical company."

Carly asked for the spelling of Buques, and checked the computer for a broker with that name. The company was not on her computer. Archer did not do business with Buques. She was relieved Archer had no responsibility. She told this to Mrs. Candless. "I'm sorry I can't help you."

Carly advised the woman to contact her state insurance department. The woman asked if Carly had the phone number. Carly did not ask in what state the woman lived. She had to get her quota of work done. She apologized for not having the information, explaining that this was not her usual work.

The woman hung up without another word. Carly shrugged. It was a lame excuse, but what else could she do? She took the last sip of her Ensure and tossed the can into her wastebasket. Employees began returning. Carly left her desk and headed to the restroom.

As she pushed open the door of the restroom she saw Terri McGuire leaning toward the mirror, examining her eyes. Terri rushed to replace her sunglasses. Sunglasses? Carly wondered about this. Terri nodded at her and mumbled something about checks being distributed as usual, tomorrow.

"That's one thing I never forget," Carly said with a smile.

Terri smiled wanly. Carly nodded and went into the stall. She did not ask if Terri had an eye infection. It would be inappropriate. Terri was management. She was Archer's banker at the local bank for many years before she became an employee and took charge of the accounting department.

Terri was standing at the mirror, staring at herself as if in a trance when Carly went to wash her hands. Carly knew little about Terri. She guessed Terri was in her late forties, which made her at least fifteen years Carly's senior. They were the same height, five foot seven, but Terri was thirty pounds heavier and wore her hair pinned back behind her ears, a nondescript dark color, described by one of the women employees as "cheap, home color job." As Carly tried to find something friendly to say, Terri turned toward the door, said, "Bye," and walked out.

Carly wondered about Terri. She never joked, never joined the women when they lunched at a local eatery, and the one time Carly invited her to join the women for a drink after work, Terri said she had to get home to get dinner for her husband.

Marcia, who worked with Terri in accounting, watched with a wry expression. After Terri left she told Carly, "If I had a husband and I was bringing home bacon, as Terri surely is—much more than when she worked at the bank—I would tell him to make his own dinner."

"Some husbands like to be babied," Carly said, thinking back to her years with Scott. He was not easy to live with, especially after he lost his job. And he never prepared a meal, even if she was late getting home and Ethan was hungry. She hated to be late, to hear as she approached the door, Scott yelling at Ethan and Ethan screaming and throwing things. When she walked in, there would be sudden silence. Her husband and her son would look at her. The one time she had the nerve to ask what caused the blow-up, Scott complained that Ethan's crying gave him a headache. He yelled at the five year old to shut up. And the brat yelled back.

"And he was crying because…?"

"Because you were not here to feed him."

Carly said, "My poor baby." She did not mean Scott, but he took it to mean him. He curled his finger, the come-here sign, and pursed his lips. When she did not move, he made kissing sounds and curled his finger again.

"Carly, a man may want to be babied, but come on!" Marcia said, waving her many-ringed fingers as if to shove away the idea. "Never confuse a large boy for a man. Babies, like shoes, come in a variety of sizes." Marcia giggled. "Also, a variety of styles."

Carly gave her a "thumbs up" sign of agreement. Marcia knew Carly was a widow, but she did not know, because Carly never spoke of it, that her experience with Scott had left her wary. Even if she had time to go bar hopping or join a singles group or online dating, she would not. She did not trust her judgment. And she was determined not to make the same mistake again. Not when she had a real child to consider.

❧

The phone rang again as Carly sat down at her desk. Sherri told her it was Vito Capone, angry because he could not reach Aidan or Blake and insisting on speaking with her. Carly groaned. By way of apology, Sherri went on to tell her, "You also had a call from Norma Gibson, but I told her you no longer worked Client Services. I offered to transfer her to someone else, but I guess she just wanted to chat because she said, 'No thanks,' and hung up."

Carly felt badly about Mrs. Gibson, a lonely old lady, a nice person. But she could not make exceptions for everyone she knew from Client Services. Vito Capone was the total opposite. It could be true that Aidan and Blake were taking a long lunch, but it would not have surprised Carly to learn they avoided Vito. Carly sighed and told Sherri to put through the call from Capone.

❧

Vito Capone waited impatiently to be connected with Carly, staring at the letter from Texas United Life Insurance. He wanted to rip the page. Balling it up was not enough. He wanted to set it afire. That damned insurer, he muttered. Overnight, his $250 thousand death benefit policy, his gold mine, had turned into a cesspool. Archer should be able to fix this. They owed him. Vito made a lot of money for Archer, probably one of their top viators since the early years, the years when the company was called Archer Viatical Settlements. And for the past six years every time he was issued a new life insurance policy, he went directly to Archer, no other company. Vito had counted on this policy. Combined with the other policies he expected would be issued within the month, policies he would sell immediately, he planned to pay cash for the new Caddie. But that would not happen unless Archer took care of the shit the insurer just threw at him.

When he tried the direct phone line for his pal, Aidan Archer, he heard a voice mail message tell him Aidan was out of town. Great.

Probably in New York, wining and dining Wall Street investors. Vito hit zero for the receptionist and asked to be switched to his pal, Blake Archer. Blake was out of town. Probably in Switzerland, talking to bankers. Vito asked to be switched to Client Services. The receptionist asked for a name.

"Carly," he told her. Carly with the sweet, soft voice. He pictured her as a beautiful, leggy blond. The one time he asked if she was blond, she replied in her sweet, soft voice, "I am not at liberty to provide that information."

The receptionist told him that Carly no longer worked in Client Services.

"What is this crap?" he demanded. "Aidan's not there, Blake's not there, and Carly is somewhere else? Put me through to Carly, wherever she is."

When he heard her voice, he was relieved. He told her he had an important letter from Texas United Life. "How can I get a hold of Aidan or Blake? It's a matter of life or death."

Carly laughed. He had pulled the "life or death" routine on her in the past. She offered to take a message. Instead, he told her about bills he had to pay, about the cost for his meds, about being ignored by Archer and how it pissed him. Then he asked when Aidan or Blake was expected to be in the office. She didn't know. Carly suggested he ask their personal assistant.

"Ya mean secretary? Is she as gorgeous as you?"

Carly laughed again. "I'm way older than her. I could be her mother," she said.

"No way, Jose. You're puttin' me on."

"Maybe. Maybe not. But I do have to get back to work, Mr. Capone. So, please excuse me now." And with that, she hung up.

"Pisser," Capone swore when he heard the click. "Blonde bitch."

The Archer brothers had better help him out.

# Chapter Two

DRIVING HOME AND THINKING in rhythm to the bluegrass music on the radio—shop for groceries, prepare dinner, help Ethan with homework—Carly was as relaxed as when she drove PCH. But this was not Pacific Coast Highway. She was inching along in the crawl of rush-hour traffic on the freeway. *The freeway!* Carly smacked the steering wheel. *What the hell is going on?* She never took the freeway to or from work. *Ugh.* It was the fault of that nagging, ever-steadfast conscience. PCH did not go near the vet clinic; the freeway did. And once she exited she would be forced to pass right by the clinic. Which she did not want to do, not at all. *I do not want to face whatshisname again.*

She could imagine what the veterinarian must think of her, seeing a well-dressed woman dump a puppy on the counter and run out without a word. How could she explain? How could she begin to explain her fear of the bill he would present for the puppy's care? If the puppy was injured or sick, the vet bill could be in the hundreds.

So what if she rescued it? The puppy was not her responsibility. That should not make her liable. If she knew of a nearby shelter, she would have brought it there, and that would be the end of that.

Carly did not want the vet to know her name. She did not want to phone, to explain the situation. If he did not know her name or phone number, he could not sue her. She dare not go near the clinic.

But Laguna Beach was a small community. It was likely their paths would cross somewhere, some day. If that happened, she could pretend not to recognize him. Even if he recognized her—she could picture it. He would say, "Aren't you the one who dumped a puppy at my clinic?"

She would say, "No, I never had a dog." If he claimed she looked familiar, she would squint at him, shake her head, tell him it was mistaken identity. She could pull that off, couldn't she?

The exit sign for Laguna Beach appeared and Carly shifted to the right-hand lane, confident she would not have to pretend very much. She would not recognize the vet. After all, she only glimpsed him through the glass door when she drove up. She avoided him completely, completely ignored him, not even a glance his way when she entered the clinic. He was a blurry memory, a clean-shaven man with rimless eyeglasses. It could be anyone.

But it was possible he would recognize her. Carly knew he watched as she took the puppy from her truck, walked into the clinic and dumped the puppy on the counter in front of his assistant. Probably his mouth fell open as she scurried out, without a word. She could imagine his reaction to a woman who looked like an executive assistant or a rising executive doing such a thing. He would never suspect this woman could not pay her bills.

Something in her wanted him to know she was not a piker. Carly considered phoning, using a false name. Once she learned the amount of the bill, she would be able to figure out if paying it was beyond "switching light bulbs." Carly decided she would pay, if it was not too much. But twenty dollars would be too much, when it was a struggle to put aside funds to repair her 2004 Dodge Ram. Without repairs, the truck would not pass emissions inspection.

There were no indulgences to sacrifice, not with a son who had, as the school termed it, "special needs." The cost of meeting those needs, which the school in Parma refused to pay, left her with huge credit card debt. Unless she robbed Wells Fargo Bank, that debt would trail her to the grave.

*Damn, damn,* she said aloud. So many decisions throughout her adulthood, yet she could not deal with this. Ignoring it was not a solution. It would be a theft, the theft of his services.

She dare not use her cell phone to contact the veterinarian—it lacked a number blocking feature. Either she would have to search for a pay phone, Carly realized, or stop at the vet clinic, give a false name, learn the amount of the bill. How would she escape the bill for the puppy's care? The dilemma played in her head like a tape looping round and round. Once the vet knew she lived in Bluebird Canyon, he would expect her to have tons of money. If only she had stayed home today. Or, as Ben liked to say when something untoward happened, "I should have stood in bed."

Carly's truck followed the line of cars along Laguna Canyon Road. The relief she felt to realize she was nearly home flew from her body when her eyes locked on the sign to her left. The sign for the vet clinic. Hell's bells, she said aloud. She signaled for a turn. She would explain. She owed him that much.

As Carly approached the white stucco building, she saw the name on the glass door—Kyle Prenner, D.V.M. The same chubby young girl with pigtails was behind the counter. Carly asked for the doctor, telling the girl, "I'm the one who brought in a puppy this morning, one that had been thrown away."

He must have heard her voice. The doctor came through a door behind and to the side of the counter. Carly had never been to a vet clinic until this morning. She was surprised to see Dr. Prenner in a white coat, like a medical doctor. As he approached, she realized he was the same height as she in her two inch heels, a slim man with a high forehead and dark, curly hair that was receding. His rimless eyeglasses—the one thing she remembered from the morning—were missing. Carly tried to judge his age, something she never was good at, and guessed it was close to her own.

"Kyle Prenner," he said, reaching out to shake her hand.

"Carly Daniels," she said, instantly aware of her mistake. She had just given him her identity.

"The puppy was a throw away? And you rescued it?"

"I thought it was a baby, at first. A human baby."

"That's understandable. The fawn color—from a distance it would appear to be flesh. And the tiny size."

"When I saw how young it was, I knew it could not survive on its own. It was tossed from a car on PCH."

He made a sound like arrgh, as if the image pained him, then asked, "Do you have a dog at home?"

Carly shook her head. "I can't. I live in a rental. My rental agreement does not include pets. Probably goldfish or a bird in a cage could be sneaked in." She tried to smile. Failing that, she looked him directly in the eyes. He had kind eyes and a gentle voice. Embarrassed as their eyes met, Carly looked away. He brought her attention back to him.

"Do you have children?"

"A son. He's ten years old."

"Every dog needs a boy."

This time the smile broke through. It quickly left her face as Carly remembered the vet bill. Before she could respond, Dr. Prenner spoke.

"Well, there's nothing wrong with this puppy, other than losing the tip of an ear, probably bitten by an older, aggressive dog. My guess is a back-yard breeder dumped him because he figured he couldn't sell a damaged dog. But otherwise he's perfect." Turning, he said, "Wait here," and went to the door from which he had emerged. After a few minutes he came back with a small bundle in his arms.

"Can you resist this baby?" Dr. Prenner said, holding out the puppy. Carly reached out a finger. She stroked the tiny head between little floppy ears. The light beige fur was silky, softer than cotton. Dr. Prenner or his assistant had bathed the mud off the puppy. The small round face looked up at her with innocent, trusting eyes.

The girl came out from behind the counter, holding Carly's plastic rain slicker, the one she used to wrap the muddy puppy. "I sponged this off for you."

Carly thanked her. No doubt the sponging of her slicker would be added to the total bill.

"This baby needs a good home," the vet said. This time he pushed the puppy into her arms. "And a boy who'll throw a ball and a Frisbee and keep him busy. He's worth a good few hundred dollars, if you had to buy him. It's a purebred."

"Doctor, it's not mine to sell." She handed the dog back to him. "But perhaps you? To compensate for the expense of caring for him?"

He smiled. "No charge. I do this for the shelter at no charge; why not for your son? Check with your landlord, see if you can add a dog. I like to see them go to caring homes. You cared enough to rescue the pup. That tells me something about you."

She sighed. Again, Carly felt indecisive. And shamed by the praise. If he only knew how close she came to never setting foot here again.

"Doctor, you're a good salesman, good enough to tempt me. But even if Mrs. Pendergast agrees I can't be sure I can afford another mouth to feed."

"Marilyn Pendergast? She's your landlord? Her three dogs are my patients. A dog lover like Marilyn won't say no."

Carly sighed. "Then it's up to me, I guess."

"This might help you decide." Dr. Prenner handed her a computer printout from a stack on the counter. It was a list of "Puppy Needs." "The most expensive part is puppyhood. If you look online you probably can find many used items at low cost. When you're online, try Craigslist. Just don't get a small crate. Puppies grow very fast and you'll need a large one within a couple of months. This puppy will be big."

Carly's eyes danced down the list. The first item was "a loving home." The second was "consistency in training." *Exactly the same as raising a child.* The next items were things she would have to acquire, puppy food, a leash, bowls for food and water. She thanked him, again calling him Dr. Prenner, and he told her to call him Kyle. "Everyone does."

Her car started with a whine, then quit. She tried again and it caught. When the traffic cleared she swung across Laguna Canyon Road and continued her drive home. To her left, at the Sawdust Festival Fairgrounds, workmen were hammering booths for the artists' fair.

She passed the Laguna Playhouse on her right, then the row of little shops that lined both sides of Broadway and heralded the approach to Main Beach. At Main Beach she turned left onto south coast highway, thinking, *A new problem to replace the old.*

No one had to convince her, a puppy would be good for Ethan. He spent most of his free time reading or on the computer. A pet, a dog in particular, was in the literature as good therapy for kids like Ethan. A puppy would force him to play in the yard, get exercise and, possibly, just possibly, help him get friends. But it was nuts to consider at a time like this.

∼

As she drove toward Bluebird Canyon Road Carly remembered the conversation with Patrick Wilson. He did not phone often and she always accepted calls from Patrick. He was one of the viators–one of the insureds–she came to know well from the nearly two years she spent in Client Services-Tracking.

When she first was hired by Archer Life Settlements Carly was given a long, gray file box filled with index cards. Each card had a name, a phone number, and the date she was to contact the insured. These were viators who did not designate a relative or friend as the contact person. Carly was hired because this position required particular people skills, great sensitivity and tact. It was the only customer service position that valued her years as a flight attendant.

When she phoned viators, Carly was instructed to ask when they last had a medical exam and the results. Some of her co-workers joked that the real purpose was to find out if they were dead or alive. If dead, they won't answer the phone.

Carly could not joke about this. Many elderly viators were lonely, living far from family and their friends had pre-deceased them. Too many on her contact list were very sick. Patrick was among the viators diagnosed with a terminal illness. His card came into her box two months after Carly was hired, several years after he sold his policy. He told her he initially designated his parents as contact persons. He changed to himself after his parents complained about the phone calls from Archer, calling them "ghoulish." They resented that Archer was checking on when their son would die.

In the past month, although Patrick knew Carly had moved to Data Entry, he phoned her more often as his health deteriorated. He needed Carly. He had no one else with whom to speak about his failing health. His partner, Brian, could not accept that Patrick may be dying. Carly took a deep breath and turned on her non-business, cheerful voice.

"Am I catching you at a bad time?" Patrick asked.

"Nothing but drudge work," she told him. She knew better than to ask how he was. Patrick began to talk about his viatical settlement. "I wasn't supposed to live this long," he chuckled. "The viatical settlement helped me pay off the car loan and fill the gas tank. With my own car, I could go to doctor appointments and pick up my prescriptions. I didn't have to depend on Brian for everything."

Carly knew Patrick and Brian were registered domestic partners. They had been together ten years. Patrick continued describing how he spent the funds. "I used some of the viatical settlement to go back east to visit my parents."

Trying to make conversation, Carly asked if they visited him here, in California, since his trip back east. "No," Patrick said. "They don't want to see Brian and me living together." His voice sounded so sad that Carly immediately regretted asking a painful question. She decided to ask Patrick about the sale of his life insurance. Other than reading marketing materials, Carly confessed, "I really know nothing, Patrick."

"Well, I knew nothing about viatical settlements until I read about this in the Advocate—that's a gay magazine. This was, maybe, fifteen years ago. The Advocate was filled with ads from settlement companies and viatical brokers. I contacted one of the brokers. He promised to send my application to at least six companies, to see what the offers were. Archer was the highest. They paid fifty-five percent, so I made out pretty well."

Patrick added that he had friends who waited to sell their policies, thinking they would get larger settlements if they waited until they were ailing. But the companies no longer were interested in viaticals, unless the insured was on his death bed. "I was lucky I sold early," he told her.

Then Patrick asked about Carly's son. She told him Ethan was so good at the computer that he spent a lot of time on it. "His latest … project is researching sea urchins." She almost said obsession. Patrick asked Carly to email him a picture of Ethan. She promised to do so, from home, since she absolutely had to get back to work or she would have her supervisor on her back.

As she pulled into the driveway, Carly realized she had forgotten to do grocery shopping. With nothing in the fridge for dinner, Carly decided to take Ethan with her to pick up a pizza and then shop for groceries.

# Chapter Three

TERRI McGUIRE WAS placing coffee mugs and spoons into the dishwasher when her husband walked into the kitchen, wearing his suit and tie, carrying his briefcase.

"We have to talk," he said.

She glanced over her shoulder at him, then looked back at the dishwasher. She closed it, turned the switch, and when she heard the hum she began to walk out of the kitchen. "I've no time to talk. I have to get dressed for work."

He stepped in her way. "You're not going to work today."

Terri looked at him. She felt anger simmering. She knew better than to express it.

"I thought you liked my pay check."

He put his free hand on her shoulder. "You could be in danger. I just got word something is happening in the vicinity of Archer Life Settlements. I just want to keep you safe."

"Something—like a bomb?" Terri pulled a chair out from the table and sat down. This was a double shock. A bomb and Tom acting as if he cared.

"Stay home," he said. He put his hand into his briefcase and pulled out a box. "This is for you."

Terri stared. It was the latest, newest iPhone. What was going on here? This was so unlike Tom.

She thanked him and suddenly realized it was possible Tom had inside information, that her employers and co-workers may not know of the danger.

"I should phone people, let them know to stay away." She got up from the table to look for her cell phone. She had left it on the kitchen counter last night. It was not there. She began to look through her bag, the black leather she always took to work.

"You don't have to call them," Tom said. "They'll know." And he left the house.

The news must be on television, Terri decided. She turned on the small set in the kitchen. She pushed the channel button again and again. Nothing. She tried the radio. Nothing. What if they did not know? What if Tom had inside information, because he was with the government? She had to warn them. Terri began to look for her cell phone. That was odd. It was not in the kitchen. It was not in her purse. Where did she leave it last night, if not in the kitchen or in her purse?

Terri went from room to room, searching. She nearly gave up, frustrated and worried, and nearly did not go into the laundry room. But she did. The bucket and mop that stood in the corner—something was wrong. She never left water in the bucket. But it was half filled with water. At the bottom of the bucket, under the water, was her cell phone.

She could not use the new iPhone to reach anyone from work. All the numbers had drowned in the bucket.

❧

*Today is pay day,* Carly told herself as she turned her truck into the driveway of the office park. When she left work she would have a check to deposit and cash to pay bills, buy food, new shoes for Ethan, and add to the fund for truck repairs. Carly shut off the wipers, the air conditioner, and stilled the motor. She stared ahead, not seeing the drizzle that soundlessly dotted the windshield. An entire week had passed since she was at the vet clinic. She could not decide what to do. Priority was truck repairs.

Carly shut her eyes in anguish, remembering her phone call last night to Kyle Prenner. She wanted to let him know she had not decided. Instead, she told him she had not yet checked with Marilyn, nor told her brother or her son about the puppy because Marilyn might say no.

*Ugh. It probably sounded as if I'm afraid to ask her permission.* She was disgusted with herself. But it was done. Misleading. Imply-ing Marilyn was to blame. *Get moving,* Carly told herself, and reached for the door. She dropped down from the truck, locked the door, and headed at a brisk walk to the Archer building.

Throughout the drive the marine layer cloaked the views of the ocean. Carly had seen the thick, moist fog from her cottage, but she lived near the beach. She did not expect the marine layer to be as dense inland. It made the cars in the parking lot and the huge brass sign of Archer Life Settlements invisible.

Other than these uncommon June days, Carly loved southern California. Every season was spring. No rain after April. Winters were mild, filled with flowers that, in other parts of the nation, were annu-als but bloomed as perennials in her garden. When Carly arrived in southern California in winter, she found it mild enough to go outdoors with nothing more than a light jacket or sweater. Some people—Ben among them— wore shorts throughout the winter. Some men were shirtless when they washed their cars.

Carly was nearly at the building with the invisible Archer Life Set-tlements sign when she heard the familiar growl of Blake Archer's red Ferrari convertible. Hoping to avoid him, Carly hurried to the entry.

"Well, it's no longer June Gloom," said Blake as he trotted over to match her step. His voice was thick with a Slavic accent. Blake claimed he had gone to acting school and switched to business as a smoother, faster road to the Land of Fortune. "Seeing the adorable Carly Dan-iels always brightens my day." Carly shut her eyes quickly at the word "brightens." It sounded like gargling. Blake was not as good with ac-cents as he thought.

"Am I as good as Sid Cesar, or what?" Blake asked, abandoning the accent.

Carly shrugged. She never heard of Sid Cesar.

"You never saw the old re-runs? How about Arnold Schwarzennegger?"

Carly looked at him sharply. *Pompous braggart,* she thought

She opened her mouth to reply but was cut off by the cacophony of multiple sirens growing louder, coming closer, and the screech of tires as cars turned sharply into their driveway. Uniformed men jumped out of Irvine's white and blue police cars. Others, in suits, jumped from black SUVs. Suddenly they were surrounded.

"Don't move," ordered one of the uniforms.

"We work here," Blake told him. A tall, Hispanic woman and a slightly taller, fair-skinned man, both in dark suits, joined them.

"Your names and your IDs," the woman said. Blake took out his wallet. "I'm one of the owners of Archer Life Settlements. What's the problem?"

Carly dug in her purse for her wallet and handed it to the woman. She was told to go to the conference room and wait.

"Is this a raid? Blake said, as uniformed police began to enclose the building in yellow crime scene tape. A news helicopter hovering overhead drowned out his question. Two other men in suits walked over. They shouted above the droning noise that Blake should go with them.

ᖰᕵ

Carly watched as the two men led Blake into the lobby and to the elevator. His eyes jumped around, as if looking for help. *Was he being arrested? Surely not Blake.* Everything she ever heard about him or knew directly told her this was a mistake. Probably his major fault was the exorbitant sums he spent on toys like the Ferrari. Carly knew his brother, Aidan, less well. Unlike Blake, he didn't tease or flirt with female employees. But she was certain he would not be involved in anything nefarious. Aidan adored his beautiful, blond wife and three young children. She had met them a few times when they visited the office.

Once again she was ordered to the conference room. Her heels clicked on the tile floor as she walked briskly through the lobby of Archer Life Settlements, past the restrooms, and turned down the hall. All but the restrooms had glass walls. Carly passed the canteen, also known as the break room. No one there. She passed the physical fitness center. No one there. She passed the screened atrium lined with benches for those who brought lunch or simply needed a respite from drudge work. No one there. The entire opposite side of the hall was the conference room. The entrance was midway.

As she walked to the door Carly could see most of the employees were there, and all were standing with backs to the walls. Standing near the door was a stranger, a man of about fifty years wearing a gray polyester suit and dark gray tie. The center of the room was filled with an oblong, highly polished cherry wood table surrounded by empty leather chairs. Carly stepped in and stood close to Allison, who was near the door. In her last trimester of pregnancy, Allison could not be distant from a bathroom.

The stranger asked Carly if she was the last one. By her curious expression he realized he needed to explain. "Any other employees out there?" She told him she had not seen anyone else.

"Then we'll begin," he said. "You're probably wondering what is going on. Well, as you can see we raided your company. The reason? It's a fraud factory."

The stranger paused long enough for the gasps of shock to subside. "We intend to interview each of you to find out what you know about the fraud. Take your choice: Either here, today, or at your homes. If you go home, we know where you live. We'll visit you at home. That might not sit well with your neighbors. If you stay to be interviewed, you will get your paycheck before you leave."

Marcia raised her hand and fluttered her ringed fingers. "Save your questions," the man snapped.

Ignoring him she asked, "What about my dog?" and pointed to the opening of the large black purse she held against her chest. Marcia was a stout woman who favored stretch tops, short skirts, and dramatic make-up. Everyone looked at Marcia's purse. Sticking out of the bag's opening appeared the tiny head of her "T-cup" Yorkshire Terrier, a red bow between its black and tan ears.

"What about your dog?" the man said, nearly gulping at the word "dog."

"Phoebe needs to be walked. She needs to pee." When the man groaned, Marcia continued. "Phoebe stays in the open desk drawer while I work, but as soon as I stop she expects to go outside to pee." Everyone chuckled, a bit too loudly, eager for an excuse to relieve the tension. The man told her to take her dog out but come right back, or she'll get a home visit.

Carly, emboldened by Marcia's refusal to obey the "save your questions" order, spoke up. "What kind of fraud? Archer buys life insurance policies from people who want to sell them. All of us here," she waved around the room at the others, "what we do boils down to little more than clerical work."

"Save it," he said, and walked out. While the door was open the woman who met Carly and Blake at the entry walked in, pointed to Carly, and motioned for her to follow.

ᔕ

Carly followed the woman to the elevator. Like Carly, the woman wore two inch heels and a business suit. Both were about the same height, slender, and both were dark-skinned but unlike Carly, the woman's face was stern. Carly wanted to ask questions but remained silent. In silence they drifted up to the third floor. Carly followed the woman as they soundlessly marched the thickly carpeted hallway. Nearly at the end, the woman halted at Blake's office. The door was open. She entered. Carly followed her.

Carly had not visited the third floor offices since her interviews, two years earlier. She remembered Blake's as smaller than Aidan's. Both offices were walled in glass and topped with a solar panel. Each had a cherry wood desk in the middle of the room. Blake's chair had faced the hallway and door, but not today. It was on the other side. The agent pointed to the visitor chair. Carly sat down. She faced the hallway wall and door. The agent took the seat opposite.

"I'm Supervising Special Agent Yolanda Ruiz." She placed a business card with a Department of Justice seal on the desk. Her voice was raspy, as if she smoked too much or had been speaking for hours. "My partner is Special Agent Eric Price." Carly glanced up as Price entered, shutting the door. He pulled another visitor chair around the desk, positioned it next to Ruiz, and placed his business card next to Ruiz's.

Yolanda Ruiz looked to be in her forties. Her stern face was accentuated by black hair pulled severely back and knotted. She used nothing more than pale lipstick, as far as Carly could determine. Ruiz began the questioning.

"What is this 'life settlements' business?" she demanded.

"I was told it was like reverse mortgages, only with life insurance. People who are terminally ill or elderly and don't need their life insurance—or they need cash—sell their policies. Except with terminally ill people it's called viatical settlements."

"Did I hear you right? The *insured* sells the policy?" Ruiz looked at Price. He raised his eyebrows. Carly could see this was news to them.

"The insured sells his policy and gets cash. The company used to be Archer Viatical Settlements. Viatical settlements are paid to insureds—policy owners—who are terminally ill. By the time I was hired Archer had switched to buying policies from senior citizens. That's why they changed their name."

"You're saying that life settlements are paid to a senior who sells his own policy? Is that correct?"

"Not necessarily," Carly replied. "As I understand it, sometimes life settlements are called senior settlements. That's when a company only buys policies from seniors. But with life settlements, Archer buys from anyone whose life expectancy is longer than twenty-four months and less than fifteen years. The viator—that's what the insured is called—might not be a senior but has a serious illness."

"So viatical settlements apply to people who are expected to die within twenty-four months," Ruiz concluded, "and life settlements are paid to anyone with more than twenty-four months life expectancy. Is that correct?" Carly nodded.

"And what exactly is your role in these transactions?" This was Price. Carly was surprised to hear his voice. She looked at him. Tall, trim, with a sandy crew cut, he looked to be in his late twenties, maybe early thirties. Carly guessed he was recently discharged from the military.

"Data entry. I process documents. First, I check to be sure we have everything needed. Then I fill in the information on the client data sheet on the computer."

"That's all?" This was Ruiz. Her tone implied Carly was holding something back. Then she said it. "What are you hiding?"

# Chapter Four

CARLY FELT CONFUSED and worried. Why did they think she was hiding something? What could they have in mind?

"Nothing," she told them. "I've only been in Data Entry for a couple of weeks. I transferred from Client Services. I used to phone viators to check up on their health. The new work is just a clerical job. I look through files and when I find the information I enter it into the computer."

"And then?"

"And then go on to the next one."

They asked what documents she reviewed. She told them she followed a check list. She searched the documents she was given to find specific information, which she entered on the client data sheet on the computer. One of the agents pushed a paper in front of her. It was labeled *Viator Checklist*. Yes, that was the guide she used.

Price took over. "So you look at insurance policies, the insureds' applications to Archer, and their medical records. Did you ever see someone diagnosed with a serious illness *before* he or she applied for insurance?"

"I'm not paid to look for that."

"But you enter into the computer the date of diagnosis, isn't that right?"

Carly nodded.

"And you enter the date the insurance policy was issued?" Carly nodded again. She couldn't speak. She was beginning to see where this was going. It frightened her. One of the insureds applied for life insurance but did not tell the insurer the truth about medical history. And that someone sold the newly issued policy—with three inches of medical records to prove he or she was seriously ill.

"Ever heard of 'clean-sheeting'?" Price asked.

Carly shook her head no.

"Are you sure?" Ruiz said, again in a demanding voice.

"Why would I have heard of it?"

"Because it is a money-maker for Archer and other companies. Don't you read newspapers?"

Carly repeated that she never heard of clean-sheeting.

"Clean-sheeting is exactly what Agent Price described." Ruiz said and nodded at Price to continue.

"Clean-sheeting is when a person is diagnosed with a serious illness before he applies for life insurance. The diagnosis is not disclosed on the application. He cleans up his health history in order for the insurer to think he is in excellent health."

Ruiz picked up the description. "If the person doesn't disclose the name of his treating physician, it prevents the insurance company from finding out the truth."

It was Price's turn again. "You admit you look for diagnosis, and for date of issue of the life insurance?"

"That's what's required. I do exactly as I'm instructed. It does mean I have to search through documents for the information. But I don't take time to do anything else. I'm not supposed to because that would affect productivity. And I don't think about what I'm doing. It's automatic. If I took time to think about what I was entering into the computer, I wouldn't get much done. And I usually process twenty or thirty applications a day." Carly realized she was blabbing. She was nervous and speaking too much, saying too much, speaking too fast. She had to calm down.

Ruiz's voice slammed into her. "I believe you were aware. You didn't want to rock any boat. You kept quiet. These documents were sent through the mail. That means we could have you for mail fraud. The payments to the people who clean-sheeted were made by wire. That's wire fraud."

Carly's eyes burned with tears. She pretended to cough and bent her head to search her purse for a tissue. She never had anything to do with mail or with payments. How could she have known about this? How could she be a criminal when she was just an office worker doing a mundane job?

"Tell me," Ruiz said, leaning forward. Carly looked up. She could almost feel the heat of Ruiz's eyes. "Did you ever ask your boss—whoever that is—or one of the Archers why this clean-sheeting was happening?" Carly shook her head. "Did you ever think to ask why your company bought policies from people who committed fraud?" Carly shook her head again. She wanted to say she never was aware of any of this, but she was too frightened to speak.

"You looked the other way," Ruiz said. "And you never reported any of this to any government agency, I take it? That makes you part of the conspiracy. The conspiracy to defraud the United States government, conspiracy to commit mail and wire fraud. Possibly money laundering, as well."

Carly felt her stomach rise to her throat. Her eyes burned. She would not allow herself to cry. Thoughts swirled in her head, confusing her, and she knew if she tried to speak she would choke up. She had never reviewed documents, never connected the dots the way they were doing. All these thoughts tumbled together and her brain froze like when she was a kid and went to school for a math test on a day when she had a heavy cold.

"I needed this job," she said, finally, knowing it came out wrong. She did exactly as instructed, nothing more, not even thinking beyond what she was told to do, her efforts directed toward efficiency and speed. Now she wondered, if she was aware of fraud, what would she have done?

"You needed this job," Ruiz repeated, adding scorn to the words. "You admit you had access to information about fraud. But you needed the job. And that made you willing to break the law."

"I didn't know anything about fraud. I didn't know I was breaking any law." She blinked several times, forcing back tears. "I have a ten year old son. His father died three years ago. I can't go to jail. I used to be a flight attendant; I could have made much more money if I went back to the airline. But my son—he needs me. More so than an ordinary child. He needs special help. I researched how to help him. He's made great progress. But if he lost me...." She choked up completely and began groping blindly in her purse for tissues.

"You admit, then, that you saw these things?" Price asked.

"No. I didn't. That is, maybe my eyes saw it but my brain didn't make the connection. I just did my job mechanically." She blew her nose.

"Willful blindness," Ruiz said.

The questioning continued, Ruiz then Price, then Ruiz, then Price, on and on, repeating the same questions slightly rephrased, as if to trap her into showing she lied with an answer. They did not play "good cop, bad cop." Both were bad cop. "If you don't tell us what you know, we could hold you for obstructing an investigation." "What are you holding back?" "What do you know?" "When did you first see an insured whose policy was issued after he was diagnosed?"

She kept answering, "I didn't," but they refused to believe her. She began to shake, first her hands which she hid in her lap, placing her purse over them, and then it swept through her body and her shoulders shook, visibly. She clenched her teeth but it made no difference. She was filled with terror.

Price had opened his mouth to ask another question but shut it without uttering a word. He motioned to Ruiz to follow him out the door. They were disgusted with her and wanted to give her time to calm down. She stood up. Her legs felt weak. She walked to the far window and looked out. The window faced the rear of the complex, overlooking endless trees. She tried to identify the trees by their leaves;

she looked for birds or ground squirrels, anything to distract her from the terror that consumed her. The marine layer was so low that she could scarcely make out anything but fog.

She took out her cell phone to check the time. It was nearly ten o'clock when they entered this room. Now it was nearly eleven. She wondered if Ruiz and Price had forgotten about her. When she next looked at her cell phone, ten more minutes had passed. She walked around the room, then back to the window. This time she saw a ground squirrel. The door opened. Ruiz and Price came in, closed the door, told Carly to sit and they took their seats.

"Do you know how to do searches on the computer?" Price asked, "and create a list of files with something in common?"

"I've never done that here. I do know how. I'm taking computer courses at Saddleback Valley."

"Your job here is over," Ruiz said. "This company is gone. But we can continue your salary if you're willing to do some computer work for us."

"Does that mean you won't charge me with a crime?"

"That's up to the prosecutor," Ruiz said. "But if he does charge you, helping us will be a plus, something in your favor. If you're convicted, it can mean leniency on your sentence."

Carly shook her head, needing to clear her thoughts. She knew her pulse was racing; she could feel her heart thumping as if it would burst out of her blouse. This panic each time they mentioned charging her with a crime blocked everything else.

"Do I need a lawyer?" she asked in a small voice. If so, she was doomed. There was no way she could afford a lawyer.

"If you're charged and you can't afford a lawyer," Price told her, "the government will provide one. Either a federal public defender or the court will hire a private attorney for you."

Carly nodded. "What computer search do you want me to do?"

"Create lists. First, a list of every person who was diagnosed before they applied for insurance. Make another list of every person who sold a policy right after it was issued. Make another list of every person who sold a policy within the first two years after it was issued, but not right after it was issued. And make a list of every insured whose policy Archer bought, noting whether the person is alive or has died."

"That will take days," Carly told them. "Archer has been buying policies for at least ten years."

"That's fine," Price said. "And be sure to include, along with the insured's name, the contact information. We'll need to talk with some of them."

"Start Monday morning," Ruiz said. "You'll use Aiden's office and his computer. By then our computer guys will have copied the hard drive." Ruiz dismissed her. "You can join your friends in the conference room, get your check, and then go home."

Carly stood up, walked slowly to the door and paused. She knew she was not thinking clearly, but one thought was glued to her mind.

"Are you going to charge me with a crime?" She looked at Ruiz, then at Price. It was Ruiz who answered.

"That's up to the prosecutor. We can make a recommendation for leniency for you, but that's all I can promise."

"Leniency? What does that mean? Why do you think I am guilty of something? If I help you, I'll be doing work I never did before. I may find out things I never knew. How does that make me guilty of a crime?"

"As I said, it's up to the prosecutor. That's how it works."

"That's how the justice system works? Guilty unless proven innocent?"

Ruiz pointed to the open door. "Be here the usual time Monday."

# Chapter Five

THE ELEVATOR GLIDED down to the first floor. Carly stepped out as the doors slid closed behind her. She should have taken the stairs. The elevator was too fast. She stood there, in the ghost-like silence. No ringing phones, no voices, nothing normal. She was in shock. Her outburst—where did it come from? Carly was not a fighter. She never spoke up for herself, never once in her life.

Carly began to walk, slowly, her heels clicking on the tile floor like thunder in the silent building. She hoped everyone was gone. She did not want to see anyone, to have anyone ask about her meeting with the FBI. If her pay check was waiting on the table in the conference room, she would grab it and get the hell away from this place. She wanted to curl up in bed. It would be perfect if Ben and Ethan were not home when she arrived. They would see her truck in the driveway and wonder why she was home so early. She would leave a note on the dining table saying she was sick.

The restroom was empty. A relief. The mirror showed her what she did not want anyone to see—her eyes puffy and red, her face the echo of an earthquake survivor.

Carly splashed cold water on her face, again and again. She splashed more water on her eyes, glad she did not wear mascara today. *That's one good thing.* She grimaced at herself for seeking something good in all this.

The cold water worked. At a quick glance, she appeared unchanged. She ran a comb through her short, black hair. She smoothed her navy jacket, dabbed with a paper towel at droplets of water on her striped blouse. She owned two suits for work, one black and one navy, and a variety of blouses interchangeable with the suits. The cheapest way to dress professionally.

Carly touched up her lipstick. With a finger tip she smeared a little lipstick on her cheeks, washed her hands and tried a smile at the mirror, gave up, and left the restroom. One last stop and then home, to bed. She was exhausted.

Through the glass wall of the conference room Carly saw two people, Marcia and Allison, standing at the far end, chatting. When their eyes met Marcia rushed to the doorway.

"We waited for you. Did they want you to testify against the Archers?"

"No mention of that. Is that what they told you?"

"Let's talk some place else," Marcia said. "Get an early lunch?"

Allison came over, holding out Carly's pay check. This was Terri's usual job.

"Where's Terri?" Carly asked.

"Dunno," Allison said. "Haven't seen her at all today. You joining us at Marie Callender's?"

Carly shrugged. "Might as well."

They walked three abreast to the lobby, passed the guards at the door as if it were an ordinary day, walked under the yellow crime scene tape—Marcia commenting that she did not believe this—and each took her own car. It was a short ride to Culver Drive and Marie Callender's. They were early. The restaurant was nearly empty.

"The back," said Allison with a quick glance at the window, as if she expected they would be followed.

"Stop worrying. We're not criminals," Marcia told her.

"The agents who questioned me said I was." Allison glanced at Carly to see her reaction.

"Me, too. Conspiracy, mail fraud, things like that," Carly said.

Without opening the menu Marcia announced, "I know what I

want." Each ordered something they had eaten in the past, something that did not require thinking, choosing. As soon as the waitress was gone they began talking, all at once, which caused them to giggle at themselves. Carly proposed they talk about something else while they ate. Allison agreed, patting her swollen stomach.

"Is there anything else?" Marcia asked. "The Middle East? The economy? Maybe we can solve a world problem or two."

"Yeah, right," said Allison. "When we don't have a clue about our lives tomorrow."

"Well, look at the light side," Marcia smiled, "aren't they idiots? They emptied all the desk drawers—even took the doggie things. Don't know what kind of evidence they think a dog bowl is, or Carly's picture of Ethan."

"They took Adele's prescription meds," said Allison. "Those are expensive. I don't know how she'll afford to replace them, now that we're unemployed and without insurance. And my baby is due in two months—without insurance. My husband was on my plan, because he's self-employed."

"Did you see what they did to the offices?" Marcia asked Carly. "The FBI broke every file cabinet. They could have used the keys, but they were like animals, like they never saw an office they liked. File drawers, desk drawers—many are bent out of shape. They took every computer. It was madness. Craziness. Totally kooky."

The false cheeriness irked Carly. She did not care what was done to desks or file cabinets. Like Allison and Adele, she needed health insurance—for Ethan. That made finding new employment a huge challenge. The challenge was so much greater than for millions of others who sought work in the worst economy since the Great Depression. When they listed previous employment, it would be a company accused of fraud.

The waitress placed their plates before them and left. Finally, Carly spoke. "They said Archer committed fraud and we're part of it. They asked if I knew anything. I told them I didn't."

"Same here," Marcia said. "There were no records in billing, and

Terri kept the accounts. I was her slave. When she said I should pay a premium on a policy or pay lawyer fees or cut a check to an insured, I followed orders. They should be asking Terri, not me. You think these FBI guys care?" She shook her head. "They said I'll be subpoenaed to testify at the grand jury hearing. About what? I'll find out later."

"When I told them I knew nothing, I was threatened," Allison said. "Were you?"

Carly nodded. They were getting into the heavy stuff she wanted to avoid. She felt close to breaking down.

"They told me that if I don't confess, they could charge me with obstruction of justice," Allison continued. "That could mean a prison sentence of ten years."

All three sat in silence. Carly noticed that Allison and Marcia were eating. She poked at her Chinese chicken salad.

"I wonder what happened to Blake," Marcia said. "I saw you through the window, walking with him when you came to work. Did they arrest him?"

No one knew. Marcia said they should phone him. "Maybe he knows something. Maybe he can help us." She elbowed Carly.

Carly took out her cell phone and hit speed dial. Everyone at work had his number. She heard Blake's brisk, bland, unaccented message. "You reached Blake Archer. Leave a message."

"No answer," she told the others.

"So, leave a message," Marcia said.

"Blake, this is Carly. Please call as soon as possible."

"We need a plan, a way to give those bozos the information they expect," Marcia said. "If we help convict the Archers, we may get off with probation."

"Is that what they told you?" Carly asked. "How is probation good? To be branded criminals but not go to jail?" She looked at her plate, her stomach in turmoil. The restaurant was filling, a table of men who looked like executives at her left, another who looked like salesmen beyond them, a table of women who looked like secretaries. Strangers, people who did not know how their lives could change in the blink of an eye.

Could they tell she was an accused criminal? Carly felt like a criminal. She felt different and apart from all these people. She needed to get away, away from this talk. She needed to be alone, to listen to music, walk on the beach. Carly glanced at her cell phone, pretended she had a text message, called the waitress and asked her to box her meal for takeaway.

"I have to go," she told her friends. "Call you later."

Carly drove around Irvine for a while, unaware of anything but traffic and traffic signals. Finally she headed west and picked up PCH. June Gloom, as thick as in early morning, hid the ocean but it did not matter. Nothing would lift her spirits today. She gripped the wheel tightly, not conscious she was doing this until her fingers began to feel numb.

There was little traffic on Pacific Coast Highway due to the early hour. Main Beach was almost deserted due to June Gloom, which discouraged beach goers. As Carly turned up Bluebird Canyon Road, she sighed, relieved to be near home. She rounded the corner to her street just as a silver Lexus pulled up at the road outside her cottage. She saw the license plate, HOME4U. Her landlady. Not more bad news, Carly thought. Was Marilyn selling the cottage? That would be the last domino in the pile. It would cripple her family, to have to find a new home at a time like this. Carly drove slowly past the Lexus and turned into the driveway.

Marilyn Pendergast, a glamorous trim blond in her sixties or early seventies, waited until Carly was out of the truck before she stepped out of the Lexus. The passenger door opened and Marilyn was joined by the silver-haired Brit, Oliver, a commercial developer she always introduced as "my significant other." They came over as Carly waited on the driveway.

"Kyle Prenner phoned as we were leaving the tennis court," Marilyn said. "I adore that man. How could I refuse? I dashed home for the rental agreement, so we can add a dog."

Carly opened her mouth, about to say she was not certain when Ben and Ethan, hearing car doors slam, came out of the house. Ben was tall, sturdily built, and the complete opposite of Carly, with fair skin, Orphan Annie-auburn curls, drooping mustache and straggly beard. He wore his usual daytime outfit, a tie-dye tee shirt and cut-off jeans. Skinny Ethan was dressed like his uncle.

Ben strode over to Marilyn and Oliver, stuck out his hand, and asked if they had come to see the house. They had met Marilyn at various times and places by chance, but in the two years they lived here Marilyn had not visited the cottage.

"Well, that would be nice. I'd love to see the changes you made, honeybun."

The adults trooped indoors, Ethan lagging at the rear and walking to the back door and out to the fenced yard. Ben stepped back and watched Marilyn's face.

"Oh, my!" Marilyn said, looking up, down, and around the now-large room. When they moved in there was a kitchen that could not accommodate two people at the same time; a wall; a small dining area and a wall; a living room not large enough for a standard sofa and two end tables. Ben had torn down the dividing walls and replaced the two living room windows with a huge bay window that overlooked the front yard. The ceiling and lower part of the walls now had white wood panels. The upper walls were butter cream in color with a sand swirl texture, like stucco.

"You've turned this into the perfect beach house," Marilyn said. She did not comment on the furniture, but may have suspected it was second-hand IKEA. The sofa, end tables, and dining set stood on chrome legs, each small enough to make the room look spacious.

"This is soooo lovely," Marilyn said as she walked around the room, then stopped to stare at the kitchen. "With the singular exception of those ancient, decrepit appliances. To do justice to your handiwork, I will have to replace them." Then, with a wink at Ben she said, "I may decide to double the rent due to your magic. This house is transformed."

"You're not kiddin'. When I first saw it, I told Carly dwarves had built the place."

But it suited them, with three bedrooms and two bathrooms. And the price—most cottages near the beach charged monthly rents of eight thousand and up. Due to its size and condition, this was listed at two thousand. Ben wanted to live in Laguna, close to his friends and work. Carly didn't care, as long as the school provided adequately for Ethan. And so Ben negotiated with Marilyn, who agreed to a lower rental in exchange for improvements Ben would do with his own labor and at his own expense.

"You are really talented, honeybun," Marilyn said. "You should consider this full time, instead of working in a bar." When he shrugged, Marilyn added, "I could refer people to you." He ignored the offer and began to walk away but stopped when he heard Marilyn say, "Now, about the dog."

"Dog?" said Ben. Ethan, standing in the back doorway, echoed the question.

"We *may* get a puppy," Carly told them. "It's a long story. I'll tell you later. I'm not at all certain we should do this."

"Whether now or another time, let's sign the addendum to the rental agreement and we'll be on our way. Kyle said this was a great dog and you would be a great person for it. I would not dare argue with Kyle. He's one of my favorite people."

Carly and Ben added their names to Marilyn's copy and an extra she brought so they would not have to search for their original.

They were about to leave when Marilyn turned back. "One last word. Puppies chew anything and everything. You don't want to let this dog taste all that lovely woodwork or your furniture. Oh, and be sure to go to the off-leash dog park. It's the best way to socialize a dog."

As soon as they were gone, the questions began: What kind of dog? A puppy. A mutt? No, the vet said a purebred. What were you doing at a vet's? She told them the story in brief. What kind of purebred? She didn't know. Why didn't you ask? Because she wasn't sure about getting any dog. Why now? She repeated that now probably was not a good time and so, probably no, they would not take the puppy.

Ben wanted to go to the vet clinic to take a look. Ethan seconded him. Carly said she was too tired. She took the list of puppy needs from her purse and placed it on the table.

"We can go tomorrow or the next day, after work," she promised. She began to prepare a cup of green tea, suddenly realizing that the next two days were not work days. The clinic probably was closed on the weekend. Ethan stood at the table reading the puppy needs list.

"I'm going to look up puppies," Ethan said, turning to the living room where the computer sat on a small second-hand desk in the far corner. None of the bedrooms was large enough for more than a bed and a dresser.

"Imagine Marilyn coming right over," Carly said to Ben. "That was so sweet of her."

"She looks damn good for an old biddy." Ben extracted the sports section from the newspaper. "Can't be due to living in paradise or we'd see more like her. Must be the work of one of those faux youthanizers, probably some hotshot surgeon in LA."

"You are so cynical," Carly said to his back. Ben was headed to the patio to sit under the pergola he built. No doubt he intended to smoke while reading sports news. Carly did not allow smoking in the house, and did not want Ethan to be aware that Ben used pot.

The microwave dinged and Carly withdrew her cup of tea. She sat down to read the newspaper and found herself too tired to read. She flipped pages, glanced at various sales, and suddenly froze. On the obituary page was a name she recognized. Patrick Wilson.

# Chapter Six

PATRICK. THE NEWS STUNNED her. Carly forced herself to remember he was terminally ill. That was the reason he sold his life insurance. For the past two months Patrick's health was declining. Tears filled her eyes. She forgot to send him a picture of Ethan. Last week life seemed filled to the brim with problems. Little did she know how much worse it could be. I am so sorry, she whispered aloud.

They never met, but Patrick was one of the few people with whom she felt close. When she saw Patrick's funeral was in Orange, not far, she searched her purse for the business cards the FBI agents had given her. She opened her cell phone but could not reach either Ruiz or Price. She left messages for both—she would be late to work on Monday due to the death of a dear friend.

Carly called to Ben. Her voice sounded odd and Ben, in the back yard, immediately came. He stood in the door frame, eyebrows raised. Carly told him she would leave home later than usual on Monday, due to Patrick's funeral.

"Why?" she said, not expecting an answer. It was likely Patrick would have died years earlier, if not for the new AIDS "cocktails." Still, she could not get past the question. "Why do bad things happen to good people?"

Ben, of course, knew about Patrick. He knew nearly everything important in Carly's life. "The same meds that kept him alive cause heart problems, diabetes, cancer," Ben said. "It probably was the meds that killed him. They save with one hand, kill with the other."

❧

Sunday, after lunch, Carly stood at the sink scrubbing the pan used to make their grilled cheese sandwiches, and telling herself she should try to nap. She had not slept more than a few hours the past two nights but she needed to do the week's grocery shopping. As she shut off the water, Ben walked in from the back yard to say he was taking the truck to do the grocery shopping.

"Thanks. Please take Ethan. I'm going to nap."

Ben gave her a questioning look but said nothing. Turning toward the living room where Ethan sat at the computer reading about dogs, he told him to get his CD player and ear buds, they were going to the store.

As soon as they were gone Carly buttoned off her phone, climbed upstairs, and stretched out on top of the light blanket. She turned toward the window. All the windows were open. A warm, sea-tinged breeze lifted and fluffed the curtains. Carly tried to fix her mind on the movement of the curtains, tried to picture the ocean, but her brain refused. Other thoughts swirled, tumblers fell, a lock opened, and she lay there, filled with fear. When she heard the truck crawl up the driveway and doors slam, Carly glanced at the clock on the bedside table. An hour had passed. The screen door opened and shut, opened and shut. Footsteps told her Ben and Ethan were carrying grocery bags into the house.

A blast of thunder startled her. In summer? Carly jumped from bed and ran to shut the window. The sky was cloudless, the sun as bright as earlier. Down the street, creeping slowly toward the cottage, was the source of the noise, a red convertible. It paused at each house as the driver checked the numbers. Carly stepped back from the window. The car stopped at the end of their driveway and the motor was shut off. Hiding behind the curtain, Carly listened.

Ben glanced at the car, then at the man who stepped out, a tall, deeply sun-tanned man in sun glasses and a sailor's cap.

"Carly Daniels—is this where she lives?"

Ben and Ethan stared at him. Carly had described the Ferrari. Ben remembered the Maria Tallchief story. He said, "Yeah," and grabbed the last three bags. He handed one to Ethan, and told him to take it inside.

"I'd like to see her."

"That won't happen."

"I'm her boss. Can't you tell her I'm here?"

"Tough shit, man. You're not her boss on the weekend. And she's busy."

"I tried to phone but she's not picking up. Can you at least ask her to come out?"

"No." Ben began walking to the door.

"Why not?"

Ben did not answer. He stepped into the house. The screen door crawled shut as he closed the inside door.

Carly was on the upstairs landing. "Thanks," she said and began walking downstairs. "How did you know I did not want to see him?"

"No way you were sleeping, not with the windows open and that car. If you wanted to see him, you would have come down."

"You know who it is?"

"Who else makes more noise than a school bus?" Ben unpacked a carton of milk as the growl of the Ferrari faded. He placed a carton of eggs in the refrigerator. He glanced at Carly. She looked far away. "What's going on, Carly? You've been outta sorts since Friday."

"Not now." Carly pointed to Ethan, in the corner of the room, on the computer.

"Give me a hand with this stuff and we'll take a walk." When Carly looked about to disagree, he said, "We can leave Ethan for half an hour."

They told Ethan they intended to walk as far as the park and would return shortly.

As they walked down the road Ben said, "I want to hear what's freakin' you out. It's got to be more than Patrick. You hardly knew him. Did you have a problem with Blake?"

Carly did not want to blurt out her fear of prison. It was too much to dump on Ben. He poked her arm.

"Come on. Out with it."

She told him she did not know where to begin.

"Start before the beginning and work your way into it."

She began telling him she soon will be unemployed. When she told him about the raid, the interrogation, what she feared, she stopped walking. "I am frozen with fear."

"What a crazy justice system," Ben said. "First, what they did to you in Parma. Now this."

Carly nodded.

"Why are they after you?"

"I don't know."

"I'll try to find someone who can help. A few guys who come to the Rainbow Club are business owners. They probably know lawyers. There might even be one or two who come to the club who are lawyers."

"One of the agents said if I can't afford a lawyer the court will provide one."

"Government defense attorneys? Not good. Those lawyers are underpaid and over-booked, and they won't have any funds for hiring experts."

"But we can't afford a lawyer."

"Maybe I can trade services with a lawyer, carpentry or other home-fixing services in exchange for his know-how."

She nodded. "I don't want to tell Ethan anything until I have no choice."

Ben agreed. He stopped walking and turned to face her. "Don't let it get you down, Carly. We've been through worse. You know we have. If we can survive that stuff, we can survive this, too."

❧

Patrick's partner, Brian, did not know Carly but he recognized her name, when she introduced herself. He greeted her with a warm hug. He looked ill. Carly knew from Patrick that Brian was not physically ill. He led an active life, a stockbroker who played vigorous racket ball in his free time. She also knew Brian could not accept that Patrick was dying, the reason Patrick phoned her often in the past month. He needed someone who would listen as he mourned his decline.

This was the first funeral of someone Carly knew through Archer. She wandered around, looking at photographs, knowing no one. Brian came over, took her arm and led her to Patrick's parents. Carly did not know what to say. Her eyes burned. Her throat burned. She nodded, shook their hands, and they thanked her for coming.

People entered and mingled. A tape recorder played classical music. Carly remembered Patrick had been a concert cellist. She recognized a concerto by Vivaldi, another by Saint-Saens. Patrick told her he suffered from neuropathy so severe his fingers bled when he touched the bow or used a computer.

Once everyone was seated, Brian stood up. The tape was Patrick, he told the gathering, from one of his concerts. He introduced a slide show prepared by Patrick's family. It began with a chubby toddler, a Little Leaguer, a Boy Scout, a high school valedictorian, a handsome, dark haired, mustached young man.

Carly could not hold back the tears. They flowed harder as memories flashed through her. Patrick asking about her favorite music; she telling him "country." Patrick asking if she listened to classical—ever. She telling him, Yes. Patrick asking if she liked Beethoven, she telling him, Yes. When he asked the name of her favorite classical composer, Carly told him, "Chopin." Patrick said he wished he could play for her.

She did not tell Patrick she had not listened to Chopin for several years. It stirred her too much, and she felt fragile after her father's suicide, her husband's car accident, the death of Mike—Ben's partner—in Iraq, her mother's cancer.

Patrick's music—the background for the slide show—pounded her heart and her head. Patrick was telling her, "I know, Carly." He was the only person who knew the full story of Scott's death.

Too soon after Scott's death her mother was diagnosed with cancer. Four years earlier her father had died. Carly traded her Honda Accord for a used, 2004 double cab RAM pickup. Crammed with their belongings, Carly and Ethan drove to California to care for her mother. Her parents' Ohio house, in which they lived rent-free since Scott became unemployed, sold after they moved into her mother's townhouse. A year later her mother's torture ended.

Carly sobbed harder. She could not stop. She could not control it. She began to have breathing spasms, sounding like an asthmatic. People were glancing at her. She grabbed her purse and rushed out. Walking swiftly with her head down, still clutching tissues to her face, she found her truck and chirped open the door. Then sat, needing to calm herself before she began to drive.

It was more than Patrick, she realized. It was all the deaths she never had time to mourn. Then, too, it was different with Scott, a messy stew of emotions. When she was notified of his death, she was angry—furious—that he was drinking again and lied to her about it. Then relieved. She would not have to deal with a divorce. His death was deserved because he was driving drunk. Luckily he did not injure anyone.

Scott finally agreed to marriage counseling. He came to the house to pick her up. His speech was slurred. He was dizzy and grabbed the door frame to steady himself.

"You're drunk," Carly said, and refused to drive with him. He protested, it was not true, he had stopped drinking a month ago. Shouting, Carly accused him of being a liar, a failure as a husband, totally worthless as a father. He rushed out and drove off, screeching the tires as he raged away from the house and around the corner. "Good riddance," she said aloud.

She heard the crash but never suspected it was him. After the autopsy, Carly learned Scott was an undiagnosed diabetic. The crash was due to a sudden diabetic seizure.

Carly was left with the memory of screaming at Scott. She had driven him to his death as surely as if she had tampered with his brakes.

With a sigh, she forced herself to turn her mind to work. She started the motor. The radio blared Garth Brooks singing, "If Tomorrow Never Comes." She quickly silenced it.

She had not told Patrick the reason she liked country—because it was funny. No matter how much regret was in a song, it was funny.

# Chapter Seven

IRWIN STANLEY LEFT his five year old Beemer with the valet and walked under the arcade and into the Ritz Carlton in Dana Point. He crossed the mezzanine with its wall of windows overlooking the Pacific, and headed for the dining room. The captain led him to the table where Mitchell French waited. French stood to greet him, they shook hands, and Stanley took a seat.

Stanley was glad to be seated. Mitchell French was easily a head taller. With his patrician nose, silver hair, and designer suit he made Irwin Stanley acutely aware of being short and squat. Both men were in their early sixties but Mitchell French was far more successful and far wealthier. Stanley wondered why French wanted to meet with him. He was wise enough to wait for French to begin the serious discussion.

They checked the menu, ordered, exchanged a few pleasantries about the hotel and the weather, and then French began. He asked about Irwin Stanley's wife. Jenny was home now, after a devastating car accident. She had full-time nursing care and daily therapy sessions, but it was not likely she would ever walk again and possibly, due to head injuries, never speak again.

"It must be costing a small fortune," French said. "Or does your insurance cover everything?"

Stanley almost laughed at the idea of insurance covering everything.

"Well, those worries may be over. Here's why I phoned you, Irwin—may I call you Irwin? I have a proposal for you. You do white collar criminal defense—correct? And you've taught some courses in the paralegal program at UCI—correct? I want to hire you to assist with a big fraud case."

Stanley struggled not to choke on a shrimp that was half down his throat. Mitchell French was a senior partner at one of the largest law firms in Dallas. He had dozens of partners and associates. Why would he need Irwin Stanley, who did a smattering of white collar criminal defense mixed with half a dozen other types of law?

French smiled with his lips closed. He had a small mouth and slim lips. They looked as if they rarely smiled.

"This is an Orange County case," he explained. I was brought in from Dallas as lead attorney. It's a corporate fraud thing. I know you have done corporate work, Irwin. We're representing the principals, but some employees will need representation. If they become prosecution witnesses, it would be a conflict of interest for my firm to represent them. Even if one or two are named co-defendants, their interests may be adverse to the principals'."

Stanley nodded. "So you're asking if I'm interested and available."

French smiled again. "There's no question in my mind you'll be interested. And available. There's a ton of money to make sure you are available. The corporation will pay all legal fees and expenses, including for outside lawyers for the employees."

"The corporation doesn't have insurance?"

"Insurance would cover officers and directors, if they had insurance. They do not. But they do have sufficient cash and other assets."

"Tell me more," Stanley said. "Definitely, I am interested."

"Well, you can choose whether to limit your involvement to accompanying an employee to the grand jury hearing—I'm sure there will be one. You would have to hang in for the trial, if that employee testifies. If he or she does testify, be sure to get a good plea deal."

"Yes, no problem. I've done that in the past."

"In the alternative, if an employee is indicted, you can choose to represent the defendant-employee. The firm intends to pay legal expenses for all employees. If there is an indictment it means, of course, more time, more involvement, and more money since you'll have to go to trial."

"To be honest," Stanley began.

"Yes, please do."

"I have little trial experience. Nearly all my cases settle."

"No problem. As lead attorney, I make all the decisions. You can decide, if your client goes to trial, whether to present an opening statement and/or a closing statement. Or not. It will not be necessary, if you are not comfortable doing this. I'll handle everything."

"In that case, certainly I prefer the larger involvement," Stanley said, "but you know I need to do a conflict check. Are you at liberty to disclose the name of the company at this time?"

"Certainly. Archer Life Settlements."

"I read about the raid. I have no conflict, but I'll need to check with my partners. It sounds as if you expect indictments for fraud."

"Yes. And I expect guilty pleas all around, or convictions."

Stanley's eyebrows shot up. "You haven't found grounds for a strong defense?"

Mitchell French stared, unblinking, fixing his eyes on Irwin Stanley's. "First, let's clear up the conflict question. I've done the conflict check. I am not about to waste my time talking with someone who could not take this on. Here's the deal. The defendants either take guilty pleas or they lose at trial. If it goes to trial, your job is to put on the worst defense of your career. That's my job, too."

Irwin Stanley blinked several times. He could not believe what he was hearing. "You expect me to do this?"

"Your retainer will be paid in full once you sign the agreement to represent. If the defendants are convicted, you will receive a bonus equal to the retainer. Send me an invoice for the full amount you expect this to cost to represent one non-principal defendant. You can create an invoice that totals one million, can't you?"

Irwin Stanley was stunned. He could not say one word. Mitchell French's lips moved into a little smile.

"If it turns out there are no other defendants, Irwin, and if you represent an employee-witness, the same financial arrangements apply."

"In other words, my retainer will be sufficient for a worst-case-scenario."

"You got it."

"And why are we going to let these people hang themselves?"

"That's not relevant. Just do your job as outlined. The bonus is contingent on guilty pleas or a conviction."

"Well, I will have to do a conflict check with my colleagues. I can't just take your word for it."

Mitchell French agreed. One cannot be too careful.

❧

Calvin Cutter, the supervising assistant United States attorney for Orange County, called the meeting to order. Prior to the meeting, he met privately with Tom McGuire. Now he introduced Tom to the assembled group.

"The chief prosecuting attorney will be assistant U.S. attorney Tom McGuire."

Tom nodded and Cutter continued. "As you know, the Archer defendants are charged with fraud and violations of all related statutes. The FBI raid turned up numerous documents we can use to show this is an open-and-shut case, and we have a truckload of witnesses."

Going around the table Cutter introduced Wendy Miller, a forfeiture expert from the Department of Justice. Cutter had prepared McGuire with the backgrounds of his Washington colleagues. Miller, he said, was known as "Killer." She would not have taken umbrage, if anyone said it to her face.

Wendy smiled as she looked around the large, oval table in the conference room, "Let's hope some of the insureds die quickly so that we have more funds to distribute."

Joseph Peters, an investigator from the Postal Service, would testify at trial to the elements of mail fraud, and provide evidence from the files of Archer Life Settlements.

Next to Peters was Nancy Masterson, an FBI special agent and accounting expert. Cutter had told McGuire that Masterson was not savvy about insurance, but she did not need to be. Her testimony would be limited to explaining exhibits that showed the flow of funds from Archer bank accounts to viators who clean-sheeted, and link those funds to payments made for fraudulently acquired policies.

Cutter had told McGuire that two individuals at the meeting would be interested observers. One represented a giant insurance company eager to dominate the viatical and life settlements industry. The other man represented an influential congressman.

"Here's the game plan, ladies and gentlemen. Archer defrauded investors of millions of dollars. Archer defrauded insurance companies of tens of millions. We want a speedy resolution. That means squeeze everyone for plea deals. Nothing new about that. If anyone balks, follow the usual procedure. I do not expect we will go to trial, but if we are forced to do so, then all hell breaks loose. Convictions are mandatory. Losing is not an option. A lot of money is riding on this. A lot of promotions are riding on this."

Wendy Miller spoke up. "Are you absolutely certain the judge is on board?"

"Judge Herman Easterly is on board," Cutter said. "If we go to trial, Easterly will grant insignificant defense motions, which will lay the groundwork to deny all their major ones. The backup plan, in case anything goes awry—and I do not have cause to anticipate this will occur—Judge Easterly will have a social visit from the AG."

"In other words," said Miller, "The attorney general is on board. That's good to know."

༖

Mark LaFollette returned to his Scranton office in a daze. His summons to DC, to meet with a high ranking official at the Department of Justice, included strict instructions to keep the meeting secret. He was not to mention the name of the official or even hint about the meeting to anyone—ever.

Mark thought it might have something to do with terrorism or illegal drugs, which was odd. He asked, when he spoke with the DOJ official, who refused to give any other information until they met.

"We may be wasting your time and mine," Mark said. "You may have been given wrong information. I am not a criminal defense attorney. I have no clients who are engaged in nefarious activities."

"Just be here," was all he was told.

It was puzzling. Mark's specialty was business law, split half-and-half between transactional and litigation. The litigation side usually involved new clients. He felt it his mission to keep his transactional clients out of trouble by crafting solid business plans, contracts and agreements. It was such a sane type of law, Mark believed. He would obey the summons, but he was certain he would waste time traveling to and from DC, and waste money, as well. The federal government would not compensate him for his time nor the expenses of the trip.

Mark did tell one person—his wife—and swore her to secrecy. The mystery intrigued her. Together, they tried to figure out what was behind it. Possibly the FBI or the CIA wanted to enlist him for something. Or enlist one of his clients, in which case this meeting was part of a background check.

Another oddity: The meeting was at a D.C. hotel, and not at one of the luxury hotels. Here, again, Mark and his wife hypothesized that the administration wanted to avoid any place frequented by lobbyists or legislators. They wanted to reduce the likelihood someone would recognize the participants.

His telephone invitation was followed by a letter on DOJ stationery, ostensibly to confirm the date and time of the meeting. Mark suspected it also was to assure him this was legitimate, not someone pretending to be with the DOJ.

He signed the hotel register with the name provided by the DOJ official and, following instructions, paid cash for one night. He began to wonder if the meeting was being kept out of official records.

At ten the next morning there was a knock on his door. He used the peephole. By now Mark was nervous. He wondered if he was being set up, if someone outside the administration was behind this. When he looked through the peephole, the man outside held up a badge, holding it long enough for Mark to identify it. Mark opened the door. The man said he was the driver, that "Bud" waited downstairs, in the car. Mark was told to refer to the official as Bud, not to use his actual name.

Mark followed the driver to the lobby and out to a waiting limousine. He recognized Bud from news magazines and television. Mark found it difficult to call him Bud. It was easier to call him nothing.

Mark joined Bud in the back seat and the limousine drove away from the hotel, onto a highway and exited in Virginia countryside. It was pretty outside the window, but Mark could not appreciate the view. Bud told him they would discuss the issue once they were clear of DC. Now, in the countryside, he began. He asked Mark to name all his clients who were in the viatical and life settlements industry. There was only one: Archer.

Bud said, "That's the one we want."

Mark was incredulous. "For what? I read the news reports, and did not believe a word. I have no reason to suspect they did anything illegal."

"We found illegal stuff, Mark. Archer no longer is your client. The company and its principals are going to be indicted for fraud."

Mark disagreed. "Are you referring to the clean-sheeted policies? Sure, I knew about them. I'm the one who set up the trusts. Archer did not commit fraud. The fraud is the work of insurance agents who solicited people to apply for life insurance policies under false pretenses, and the applicants who went along with the scheme. When Archer purchased these purchases, there was no law anywhere to prohibit said purchase."

Bud told him he was wrong. Archer defrauded insurers.

"That's balderdash," Mark said. "If insurers were defrauded, it was their agents and the insureds who did it. That's what I told Aidan and Blake Archer, and that's what I will testify to, if called as a witness."

Bud told him that was the purpose of this meeting: He would not be called and he was not to offer to testify. "Do not contact the defense attorneys."

Mark was astounded. He recovered sufficiently to ask, "And if they contact me?"

"They won't," Bud told him. "However, if there is any slip-up, you say nothing. You know nothing. If necessary, you say that the Archer brothers did not provide full disclosure to you. That will be sufficient to discourage defense attorneys from calling you as a witness."

Mark told him there was a court record in which he testified under oath about this. It was a deposition conducted by the receiver for one of the viatical companies that purchased policies from Archer.

Bud told him the deposition transcript would not be introduced at trial. The receiver will never breathe a word about it. Defense attorneys will not use the transcript nor call him to testify.

"Isn't this selective prosecution?" Mark asked, barely containing his anger. "Most, if not all companies in this industry buy fraudulently acquired policies. Why aren't you going after the ones who do this and also sell to the public?"

Bud told him that was not his concern.

"It is my concern. Unlike Archer, a number of companies resell these policies to the public, and they have been cited by numerous states for violating their Blue Sky Laws."

"Blue Sky Laws are state securities laws. That has nothing to do with a federal indictment."

"I cannot understand this. Archer bought these policies on my advice, and they are not the only companies doing this. If simply buying them is a crime, why is Archer a target? Why are you singling out this one company and allowing far worse offenders to continue business?"

Bud repeated it was not his concern. He did not use a threatening tone, but the threat was implied. "It would be your concern if you were indicted along with the Archers."

"Come on," Mark said, attempting to be jovial. "There are companies out there who are defrauding the public every day, buying fraudulently acquired policies from the insureds and reselling them as better than CDs to retirees who know next to nothing. Archer doesn't do this.

Why aren't you going after the ones who actually harm the public?"

Bud told him the answer to that was on a need-to-know basis, and Mark was not cleared for need-to-know.

Mark was angry. He was fighting mad. But when Bud reminded him that he could be indicted along with the Archer brothers, he said nothing more.

He returned to Scranton deeply troubled. But his hands were tied. If the Department of Justice came after him, he knew they would win. He would be forced to plead guilty to something. He would lose his law license. He was too old to start over again in another occupation, and he had a family that depended on him.

# Chapter Eight

CARLY DROVE SLOWLY away from the funeral parlor. She was unfamiliar with the route along surface streets, but her emotions were brittle and she knew she could not cope with the hectic six-lane freeway. Twice she pulled into gas stations to ask directions, and finally neared the office. When the sign for *Jamba Juice* appeared, Carly turned into the driveway to buy lunch. She was not hungry, but her breakfast was nothing more than a cup of tea. That would not get her through the day. And her cans of Ensure were gone. The FBI had cleaned out everything.

Carly brought a chicken wrap and fruit tea back to the truck, ate in the truck, tossed her garbage into a nearby container, and continued on to the Archer building.

To her surprise, the parking lot was draped in sunshine. She had not noticed the weather in all these hours. Carly stepped from the truck and chirped it closed. She paused to raise her face to the sun. The chill was too deep. The warmth did not penetrate.

As she approached the Archer building, Carly was surprised to see Special Agent Price standing outside the glass door. Was he waiting for her or just grabbing some sun? He made a comment about the nice day, opened the door and held it for her, and they walked to the elevator. Carly entered first, stepped to the right and pressed the button. Agent Price took a position on the left.

"How are you doing?" he said. She looked at him. He had not glanced her way.

"Fine."

"You were at a funeral this morning? A friend?"

"Yes."

"So, are you up to doing work?"

"No problem."

They rode to the third floor in silence. Carly was tempted to thank him for asking, but he was her accuser. He did not really care how she was feeling.

In silence they walked the thick maroon carpet of the hall and stopped at the entrance of Aidan's office. Price unlocked the door. He told her the door would not be locked when she returned on other days. Carly was astonished at the stacks of file boxes—Archer records. They filled every spare area. Price told her this was everything the company purchased from its first year to the present.

"I heard there were some ten thousand policies. It could take more than one week."

He said that was fine, gave her specific instructions, and told her she was free to use the atrium and the break room, or canteen, or whatever you folks call it. Carly thought he blushed slightly, and wondered if he was unsure whether to mention the restroom. She stood staring at him and continued to wonder: Was he not used to working with women? Or women accused of a felony?

"Any questions?

She shook her head. He nodded and left.

Not only was this floor empty but every floor. Empty, silent, filled with ghosts. Carly was tempted to turn on the CD or use the computer to provide music. She decided not to do so, in the event Price or Ruiz came to check up on her.

The boxes were piled four feet high. Carly hoped to find no evidence of fraud. Then this whole horror would go away.

But there must be fraud, if the FBI said there was. Her goal changed. If she found evidence of fraud, perhaps that would get her in the good graces of the FBI. At the least, it might help her understand what was going on and the work would keep her too busy to worry. If it took more than one week, all the better. She needed the pay check.

Carly looked around. She had not been in Aidan's office since the day she was hired. It was obvious why the FBI used this office. No other office had space for all the boxes. Blake's office, down the hall, was slightly smaller. All the glass-enclosed offices had vertical blinds and they were open. She could see straight through to the opposite glass and steel wall.

The cherry wood desk in the middle of the room was huge and elegant. Aidan's computer was newer and probably more sophisticated than the one she used. It was; she saw slots for discs on the sides of the monitor, just above the speaker grills.

Carly did not know Aidan's user name or password, and had not thought to ask. Taking a chance, she tapped the space bar, and the monitor lit up. Then she remembered. The FBI copied the hard drive, and probably tested the computer after replacing it. Or perhaps they did not want to give her the user name and password. Each time she thought about the FBI she felt nervous. She felt nervous to enter these files. She felt nervous about what she was about to learn. Carly stood at the desk, staring at the computer monitor, unable to move.

Suddenly she realized she was humming—a Rodney Atkins song, "If You're Going through Hell."

Rush, hurry, before the devil knows you are there, she told herself. Now to figure out how. Forget everything but finding fraud, Carly told herself. She sat down and began designing spreadsheets. The fourth was "Alive or dead." Why did they need this? To figure out how much of Archer's assets had to be set aside to pay future premiums? Carly opened the file boxes labeled with the earliest date. She was halfway through a second box when a thought halted her. If she spotted possible fraud, would she be accused of having known all along?

When she worked in Client Services, Carly had no access to insured's information, just names and phone numbers. In Data Entry she had access to everything about insureds who might become viators. This was the first time she would see information about policies actually purchased by Archer.

When the first spreadsheet had fifty listings, Carly saw three policies insuring Vito Capone. Could he be the cause of all this? Could one person be the cause? Half an hour later she came across Patrick Wilson's file. He sold his policy in 1995, before the new AIDS drugs were available. It was an employer group term policy issued several years earlier, when Patrick worked full time as a cellist. Carly was surprised to learn Patrick did not live in California at the time.

In the next file box Carly found another familiar name, Ernest O'Toole, a retired dentist and a widower. His children were bitter when he told them he sold his life insurance. They did not approve of his plan to use the funds to travel worldwide, something he always wanted to do. When he returned from his trip he phoned Carly again, this time to invite her to his wedding to a retired nurse he met on the trip. Ernest even offered to pay her airline fare, if she would come. He told Carly she was a virtual matchmaker.

Until now Carly had not realized how much intimacy developed between these people and her. She supposed it was like working at a suicide hot line or a rape crisis hot line; you were bound to get emotionally involved, even though you would never know the person if you stood in the same elevator.

*Smack, smack,* she whispered to herself. *Stop wasting time.* She went back to work. Another half hour and she stood up to stretch. When she sat down again Carly suddenly saw a pattern. Capone was not the only viator listed numerous times. Each of these insureds sold newly issued policies—five here, nine there, twenty for another insured. Each was diagnosed before applying for life insurance. She had found it. Evidence of clean-sheeting. It worried her. *I can't risk someone changing these spread sheets and claiming I falsified information.*

That *someone* was the FBI. Or the prosecutors. Might they use these spread sheets to claim she knew about the fraud? Although she dated every spread sheet, Carly knew dates could be changed or removed. She needed proof. She decided to save the dated spread sheets on a flash drive. That would prove when she first saw these files. Yes, she told herself; *I'll have proof of my innocence, if they try to use this against me.*

Two hours later Carly discovered something else. The Archers' enormous wealth was from fraudulent policies. In the early years most of Archer's "inventory" were legitimate policies, and they often paid fifty percent of the death benefit. When these policies were resold to Wall Street investment companies, Archer was paid eighty percent of the death benefit—a mark up of thirty percent. But when Archer began buying clean-sheeted policies, they usually paid ten percent and resold the policies for fifty percent—a forty percent mark up. The difference between twenty percent and forty percent turned Aidan and Blake Archer into millionaires.

Carly first heard the words "viatical," "life settlements," and "viator" during her employment interview two years ago. She first heard "clean-sheeting" during her interview by Ruiz and Price. What would she have done, if she knew this two years ago? Would she have taken the job? Silly question. She did not know. She never knew until now. How could she be held responsible for fraud that began ten years earlier? Even if the pattern continued to the present, how could she be held responsible?

*Concentrate, Carly,* she whispered. She had to stop worrying. But the question remained, distracting her: Did this pattern continue to the present?

The answer was in other boxes. Carly left the computer, crossed the room, and found the files from recent years. She opened the flaps on a box dated a year ago and a box from two years ago. She leafed through files. There was her answer. Archer no longer paid fifty percent of the death benefit to anyone. The current price for legitimate policies owned by terminally ill people rarely was more than twenty percent of the death benefit.

Carly did a quick calculation. If the death benefit was $100 thousand and the insured was paid fifty percent, that was fifty thousand. Today, if Archer paid twenty percent, the insured lost thirty thousand dollars. The greater profit turned into a jet plane for Archer, a boat, a Ferrari.

No, that was wrong. Carly had seen resale sheets in each file. If a terminally ill viator was paid twenty percent, the policy could be resold to investors for eighty percent. Archer's profit was not thirty thousand. It was sixty thousand.

She thought about Shirley Woodruff, the woman who needed sufficient funds to keep her rent-controlled apartment. She thought about Mrs. Candless, the widow cheated by Buques. *How stupid of me to think Archer was not responsible. Archer was doing the same thing.* She felt such anger that if either of the Archers walked into the office she would scream.

*I feel like Alice falling into the hole and discovering a twisted world in place of the one I knew.* Throughout the two years of her employment at Archer Carly knew nothing more than what she learned from the colorful, shiny brochures given to her when she was hired. In those brochures she read that settlement companies paid more than if insureds cashed out whole life policies with the insurance companies. If they had term insurance, there was nothing to cash out. Insureds who had term insurance had only one choice: Sell the policy. And any amount they were paid was more than zero.

What she did not know until now—what the insureds did not know—was Archer could have paid much more. Maybe smaller profits meant they would not need an entire building, or as many employees. Maybe Carly never would have been hired. But they would have been wealthy, without harming people who trusted them.

People like Shirley Woodruff looked at the cash they hoped to receive within weeks. People like Emma Candless' late husband forgot about the tens of thousands their loved ones lost when the death benefit was paid to investors.

*Enough. Back to work. Like a beaver,* she urged herself, and began working swiftly, going through one file after another, entering information on spreadsheets. Suddenly her cell phone sang out the Looney Tunes melody. The caller ID showed her the name. She groaned but answered.

"Hi, Blake." Solemn tone. She was not ready to confront him.

He began to cry. "I'm not good, Carly. The lawyer wants us to take a plea deal. He says if we try to fight this, we could get twenty years.

Going to trial always is a loser. Prosecutors always win. But we didn't do anything wrong. Why should I say I did something wrong and have to go to jail?"

"Blake, I wish I knew what to say."

"You are a sweetie. I feel better just hearing your voice. That's why I tried to visit you on Sunday. I need to know I still have friends. I feel so alone."

Carly had always felt edgy with Blake, his unpredictable comments, sometimes cruel, sometimes flattering. But the anger that swept through her was gone. She, too, was accused. She, too, was frightened.

"Well," she began. Pushing to the front of her mind was, Why did you come to my home? What did you want of me?

"Hey, Carly, here's an idea to cheer up both of us. Come with me to Rodeo Drive. Get the prettiest dress you see, whatever the price. Then we go to a swanky restaurant to show it off."

Carly tried to laugh but it came out as a scoff. Blake was annoyed. "You prefer those same-old, same-old suits you always wear?"

Same-old Blake, she thought. Today she could not handle it with a flippant rejoinder. "Please, I can't think straight now."

"Start thinking—about letting your hair grow. You would be even more beautiful, if you wore it long. Then I would not only buy you a dress to match your beauty, I'd buy an entire wardrobe."

What an odd conversation for a time like this. Was he in denial? If so, his fears might be greater than hers. Before she had a chance to answer, he spoke again.

"You really need to wear light colors, Carly. Light, bright colors to show off your skin tone. Look up Halle Berry on the internet. Take a cue from how she dresses."

"Blake, I have too much on my mind to even think how to answer that. And I'm not the only one. All of us are worried, all the employees."

"Not to worry. My brother can always start a new company."

"After the trial, you mean?"

"You're too much a worrier. Like my mother."

Again, Carly did not know how to respond.

"It's a compliment, Carly—you remind me of my mother."

"Then thank you." She felt confused.

"Did I ever tell you how I snuck her tiny dog into the hospital when she was dying?"

Carly's thoughts flew in different directions. She had to stifle the impulse to tell him, You may be the most important person in your world, but you are not the most important person in mine. And I know you cheated people who needed help. She tried to change the subject.

"How is your brother? How is Aidan taking this?"

"It's just as bad for him. Worse, maybe, because he has kids. For the first time I'm glad I don't have kids."

"Blake, can I ask you something? Some viators sold policies soon after they were issued. Is that what they mean by fraud?"

"No! If that's fraud, it's the viator's fraud, not ours. Our lawyers told us so before we even began buying those policies."

"What about viators who lied on their insurance applications, then sold the policies?"

"Same thing. It's their fraud. We bought some of those policies from other companies. If buying them makes us guilty of fraud, why are those companies still operating? Huh? Tell me that. Why weren't they raided?"

"How about seniors who sold new policies?"

"Same thing. If there's fraud, it was committed by the insureds and their agents, not us."

"Then why is the government after you?"

"Because someone wants us out of business. There is a conspiracy, Carly—but it's a conspiracy against us." There was hint of anger in his voice. Suddenly he said "Take care," and hung up.

Blake seemed to be feeling better. Not Carly. What good did it do any of them to think there was a conspiracy against Archer?

# Chapter Nine

MILDRED AND HARRY SANTORI were nervous. At any moment they expected an unusual visitor. Why was a California prosecutor traveling all the way to Missouri to speak with them about their investments? Harry had to take a few hours from work, and that upset him. But Thomas McGuire would tell him nothing more by phone.

When they saw the stranger's car pull into the driveway, they knew it had to be the prosecutor. He showed them his identification at the door, and suggested they use the dining room table. Mildred led the way. The prosecutor placed a black leather briefcase on the floor next to his chair, took out a file folder and a yellow pad and placed them on the table.

"Your children are at school?" he asked as they took seats across from him. Harry looked at his watch, signaling he had no patience for small talk.

"Did you want to see our investments?" Mildred asked. "I can get them, if you need to see them."

"No, that's fine. I have copies," McGuire said. He withdrew papers from the folder. "You bought viatical and life settlement investments?"

They told him they did.

"These investments were from Archer Life Settlements," McGuire stated.

"No," Harry said. "We bought them from Star Spangled Life Settlements. They have an office right here, in St. Louis."

McGuire frowned. He had deep grooves at the sides of a narrow mouth. Frown grooves. Frowning was a habit ingrained on his face. His lips moved without disturbing the frown. "The fact is you were victimized by Archer. SSLS bought these policies from Archer, then resold them to you. In effect, you bought them from Archer."

Mildred looked at Harry. He shook his head. "We never heard of that company until now," Mildred said.

"Trust me, that's what happened," McGuire told them. "Archer was the supplier. And, as we sit here today, you no longer have anything. The money you placed in the Archer policies is gone. The policies no longer exist."

Mildred turned white and began to twist her fingers. Harry's face was red with anger.

"You're wrong. It's not possible," he said. "This is a good investment. Warren Buffet invests in life settlements."

"Were you aware you were investing in life insurance policies that were fraudulently acquired?"

"Absolutely not," Harry said, making no attempt to hide his anger.

Mildred's voice was sorrowful. "What do you mean? Did SSLS steal these policies?"

McGuire leaned back in his chair, preparing his speech. "In effect, they were stolen. Archer bought the policies from insureds who stole them from insurance companies. They stole them by lying. Insurers did not know the truth about the health of these insureds. But Archer knew. Archer resold the policies to SSLS. And SSLS knew. Then the policies were resold to you. Because the insureds lied—which is fraud—the insurance companies canceled the policies. There is nothing left of your investment."

"Oh my God!" Mildred exclaimed.

"Are we in trouble?" Harry asked. "Are we responsible for participating in fraud? We didn't have a clue. If we had known, we never would have given that man our money."

McGuire smiled. "I understand. You, and many others, are victims of fraud."

Mildred fanned herself with her hand. "I can't believe this. We lost everything? Our entire life savings? Our IRAs? The children's college fund?"

Harry was too agitated to sit. He shot up from his seat and began to pace the small strip of floor near the table. "Why did you come here to tell us this? I'm sure prosecutors did not go to every investor ripped off by Madoff."

McGuire leaned forward. "Here's the deal." He signaled Harry to sit again. Harry obeyed. "We're going to bring charges for fraud against Archer. Most of the victims are elderly and cannot travel. We have a few witnesses who live locally, but not enough. We want you to testify against them. If you agree, you will get back your entire investment."

"Of course we'll do that," Mildred said. The relief was evident in her voice.

"But we know nothing about Archer," Harry said. "The attorney for Archer could ask about this. Wouldn't that blow our testimony?"

McGuire shook his head. He saw Mildred shake hers along with him. He had her. She was with him all the way. "Archer may not have sold to you directly, but you were the ultimate investors. Archer defrauded you. It's our job, the prosecutors' job, to make this clear to the jury. You can tell the truth. It won't blow your testimony."

"When will the trial occur?" Harry asked. "How much time will it take? I have a business to run, you know."

McGuire stood up. "It will be some months from now, possibly a year. We'll give you enough advance notice to get a babysitter and arrange for your business. Your travel, hotel, and meal expenses for testifying in California will be paid for."

"California?" Mildred said, with some awe.

"Not terribly bad, is it?" Tom McGuire smiled.

✦

Eric Price glanced at the wall clock just outside his cubicle, trying to decide if he should work through lunch. *Shit,* he said aloud. The

Archer case was a migraine-in-the-making. Eric was tasked with weeding through the files, seeking possible evidence, putting whatever he found into new file sleeves with new names—forfeiture, taxes, witnesses, co-conspirators. The new files went onto a rolling file cart, to be delivered to the prosecutors' office. They would make the final decision about which were relevant.

His desk was littered with files. The agents who emptied the Archer building threw everything, pell-mell, into boxes. More boxes crowded the floor. His cubicle was a fire trap.

Eric heard a knock on the acrylic wall. He looked up. It was Nicole Something, one of the secretaries whose desk he passed every time he entered the FBI offices. She introduced herself, reminded him of her position, and apologized for interrupting his work.

"I was told you know about insurance. I need advice. It's personal. Could I treat you to lunch while I pick your brain?"

"I can't give legal advice," Eric told her. "I'm not licensed with the California bar."

She flashed a smile. "I just want an informed opinion."

Eric felt a twinge of caution. He did not want to influence someone's decision. "I can give you my personal opinion. It will be worth exactly what you pay for it."

Nicole said that was fine. "I need to toss around some ideas. I don't know anyone else who might understand."

Eric agreed—on condition he pay for their meal.

"No, no," she said. "I invited you to lunch. It's on me."

"I could argue I'm on a higher pay scale. Or that I don't want you to pay for advice. But the truth is I know so few people here in California, lunch with a colleague must be my treat."

They walked to the restaurant. On the way Nicole told Eric she did not ask what type of food he preferred because the menu was so diverse—hamburgers or chicken prepared dozens of ways, various salads and veggie dishes.

They began walking side-by-side but Eric had to slow his footsteps and shorten the length of his stride. Nicole was tiny. She would be tiny in comparison with his six feet, or in comparison with the women in his family, but Nicole also was slim, so slim he expected she might starve to death if she skipped one meal. Shoulder length dark hair with a fringe of bangs across her forehead, dark eyes, standing no more than five foot two in her one inch heels, he guessed she wore clothes sized zero.

Eric could imagine her tiny, white-haired mother—it was her mother's problem. He asked how her mother became involved in what sounded to Eric like a life insurance scam. Nicole told him her mother attended a church seminar given by a local lawyer and an insurance agent. They urged seniors to apply for life insurance. Seniors were told the agent and the lawyer would arrange for an immediate sale of the policy to an investment company. In exchange, Nicole's mother would get a nice lump of cash. Nicole thought it sounded suspicious, but her mother was eager.

"I'm the youngest of six," Nicole told him as soon as they began to eat. Eric guessed at her age—around thirty, he decided, although she looked like a teen. "My father skipped out when I was a baby, and my mom raised us. She worked part-time as a dog groomer when we were young, then full time, but never had any benefits. Today she has no pension, nothing but half his social security and whatever we kids can toss her way."

"In other words, what the seminar offered was like winning a lottery."

"Exactly. Except I don't want her to do something that could get her in trouble, and I know nothing about insurance. When I asked around the office, I was told you know about insurance."

"I'm not an expert. I never specialized in insurance law." His face was stern. When Eric realized how stiff his jaw was, he made an effort to loosen up. "I was a salesman. I sold insurance, but not life insurance. The stuff I sold insured things—cars, homes, boats. Not people."

He suggested Nicole contact the insurance department.

"I did. When I phoned, the man who answered knew nothing about this. He never heard of such a thing. He said he was surprised to hear that a person with no assets could get five million of life insurance."

Eric's eyebrows rose. That would make her worth more dead than alive, a whole lot more.

"How much are the premiums; do you know?"

"I have no idea. They're probably a bundle. My mom's seventy."

"How would she pay the premiums?"

"She wouldn't. Not a single dollar. They would sell the policy to investors as soon as they knew it was being issued. To make it easy to transfer the policy to investors, they would set up a trust in her name. Initially she would name one of her children as beneficiary."

Eric put down his fork. "This is incredible. It's like someone trying to insure a 1995 Hyundai for a million."

Nicole's mouth fell open. She quickly covered it with her hand, hiding a giggle.

"Sorry. Didn't meant to slight your mother." Nicole continued to giggle and Eric laughed at himself.

He told her he thought she had good reason to be suspicious. "It does sound like fraud, if she has to lie on the application about her assets. But that's just off the top of my head." He promised to look into it as soon as he had some free time.

Carly had worked for two days at the Archer building, seeing no one other than the security guard. When Eric Price came by on the third day, the thick carpeting in the hallway cushioned his footsteps as he walked from the elevator. He rapped three times on the open door, startling Carly. "Sorry," he said, as she jumped.

"What time is it?" Carly asked, turning back to look at the time on the computer.

"Late enough," he said. "You must be tired. Want to go home early?"

"It's not yet five," Carly said, eager to explain the spreadsheets. Price told her he was unsure if Ruiz would join them, even if they waited another day.

"If you really want to stay a bit longer," he began.

"Yes, I do," she said, standing, spread sheets in hand, and crossing to the two small couches that circled a coffee table. She sat down and Agent Price sat on the other couch. Carly took a deep breath. She hoped to sound professional and competent, to dispel the image of a fraud suspect in her own mind as well as his.

"First, may I ask what makes these transactions fraud? Would it be fraud if I sold my life insurance?"

"When did you apply for the policy?"

"When my son was born."

"And did you tell the complete truth on your application?"

"Yes, of course."

"Then there would be no reason to consider it fraud, if you sold it."

"So there is nothing fraudulent about selling it?"

"Not in your case. But it is fraud when someone hides ill health on the application."

"Got it. Now I'm sure I did this correctly." She showed him a spread sheet, turning it around so he could read it. "I found several viators who sold numerous policies. Each of these men applied for life insurance after being diagnosed HIV positive."

Carly pointed to one of the columns. "I added column 'O' for other. That means the date the viator first sold, if it was to another company before it was purchased by Archer. It's more accurate this way." When she asked if these insureds were not the ones who committed fraud, rather than Archer, he stared at the spread sheet but did not touch it.

When he did not reply, she said, "Well, I'm wondering about a few things and, of course, haven't a clue because I don't know the law. Is it fraud if a person who is healthy applies for millions in death benefits? And this person lies about other things on the application?"

"It is fraud if the applicant lies about something important, something that would influence the insurer not to issue the policy, if they knew the truth."

Eric was startled by her question, so soon after meeting with Nicole. He was practiced in hiding his emotions, and he did so now. "Are you referring to insurable interest?"

Carly stared at him for a moment. "Insurable interest?"

"That means the owner and the beneficiary have an interest in the continued life of the insured. It can be a family member, a friend, a business partner. Is that what you mean?"

Carly smiled. "Maybe. Maybe that's what I'm getting at. When these policies are sold to investors, they get new owners and new beneficiaries—people who don't have that interest."

Carly placed a second spread sheet on the table. This was not a requested spread sheet. On it she had listed the ages of the insureds, the dates policies were issued, and the dates of sale.

"It's not complete yet. As you can see, all these insureds are seniors. I know you're interested in viators who were diagnosed with HIV before they applied for life insurance. This may be another kind of fraud—newly issued policies sold as life settlements." Eric nodded.

Carly explained it was not clean-sheeting because the seniors could not hide health problems from the insurers. "Some of these seniors sold the policies immediately, others two or three years after they were issued."

"What's your point?"

"Every senior claimed to need $1 million or more in death benefits. Some gave as the reason estate planning, others named a relative. I think these statements are false."

He raised his eyebrows. Carly took that to be a question. "If they needed $1 million or $5 million or whatever amount, why did they suddenly—and I mean real soon—not need *any* insurance?"

"Need is important. A person who has no assets and no dependents, for example, does not need more than just enough life insurance to pay final expenses."

"Need," Carly repeated. "Then that's key?"

He agreed.

"Well," Carly took a deep breath. "On their applications every one of these seniors claimed to *need* millions for estate planning. One or two people might have had a serious reversal of finances, but every one of these seniors? And some did it several times—applying for several policies and then selling them." Carly felt excited. When he nodded, she wondered if he was simply being polite. She asked, "Does any of this interest you? Does it mean anything?"

"It does interest me. But I don't know if it means anything."

"Well, I think it means they did not need the insurance. They applied under false pretenses—just like those who clean-sheeted. They planned to sell the policy. Just like the people who clean-sheeted. I think they are just as guilty of fraud as those who clean-sheeted."

All he said was, "Okay." It did not interest him. Carly decided to go to a requested spread sheet. On this one she began, but did not yet complete, a list of viators who were alive and those who had died.

"I added a column for date of diagnosis. See this—no diagnosis for this senior and this senior and this senior. If I added another column for other health issues, it might be blank or it might show minor things, like high blood pressure."

"What's your point?" he asked again.

Carly was beginning to feel frustrated. "These are healthy seniors. My guess is you asked for this information so the government will have an idea of how much money to expect from death benefits. Probably to use that cash to pay premiums on the other policies? Well, you need to expect a long wait—years longer than you may think—before these policies mature. These seniors are in excellent health."

She had to translate "mature" for him. "Policies mature when the viator dies." She made a face. "The industry avoids the truth by using the word 'mature.'"

"What problem do you see here?"

"Archer doesn't buy policies from people whose life expectancy is greater than fifteen years. But a healthy seventy-year-old could live another twenty, even thirty years. Like Bob Hope. He died at the age of one hundred. His wife died at age one hundred three."

"And?"

"Well, profit diminishes every year that premiums are paid. *And,*" she emphasized, "premiums for policies that insure seniors for millions are huge."

Now she caught his interest. He lifted the spread sheet, nodding as his eyes moved down the lines. Her heart began to race as she watched him. Although Agent Price tried to keep his face impassive, a muscle twitched in his forehead. Then his eyes focused on the distant wall, as if figuring something. He looked sharply at her.

"Make up another list about these seniors. Put in everything you think is relevant—the insurer, the death benefit, premiums, any health issues, the original named beneficiaries. List the life settlement company to whom they sold the policy, if the initial sale was not to Archer. Oh, and be sure to include the investors who are current beneficiaries. Leave nothing out. Yes, this does interest me. You may have hit on something. Get me the information as fast as you can. Once I check it out, if it turns out to be what I think, I'll take the data upstairs."

*Upstairs?* "Oh, you mean someone higher in the chain of command." Now she had to smile. He was treating her as one of the club. She saluted as she stood up. "Aye, aye, sir."

He grinned, got up, went to the hall and knocked on the open door as he left, as if to say good-bye.

Carly was feeling far better than she had in days. Agent Price liked her work. Was it possible she had found a way out of the swamp of trouble?

She took a bathroom break and smiled genuinely at the mirror. Suddenly she remembered Agent Price's voice as he told her to prepare special data for his use. Interesting, she thought. He seems to have a slight Southern accent. She had not noticed this earlier.

Carly went back to the computer, eager to work on her new assignment. She was deep in concentration when the Looney Tunes ring tone of her cell phone startled her. *Oh, Lordy,* she thought, *it was long past time to change to a sedate ring tone.* When she glanced at the screen, the ID read, "Vet Clinic." She answered and a cheerful male voice greeted her.

"I'm calling on behalf of a puppy who needs a loving home. He asked me to find out what your brother and your son said."

"Hi, Kyle. My brother wants to see the puppy. Ethan is so busy researching puppies on the internet that I can scarcely drag him away for dinner or for bed. So I guess that means both are interested."

"That's good. I'll tell Buster—that's the temporary name we gave him." He asked if she was home now. She told him she was at work and would be working at least one more week. He invited her to bring her family over after work. "I can stay late. I live on the grounds."

Carly hesitated then agreed. "If Ben is not working tonight, we'll come after dinner. Is that good for you?"

"That's great!" he said. "I'll have ice cream waiting. Or does your family prefer frozen yogurt?"

"Please, don't go to any trouble."

"It's my pleasure," he said before hanging up.

Carly sighed. What was she getting into? Who, other than she, could resist a puppy?

On her way home Carly stopped at the nearby Staples for a flash drive. The largest she found held thirty-two gigabytes, and it was expensive, very expensive. But she dare not hesitate. She had no idea how many gigabytes were needed to copy all the files and her spreadsheets. If she bought too many flash drives, she could return the unused one or two. Another thought: If Agent Price continued to treat her with respect, she might give him one of the flash drives with the senior data he requested.

# Chapter Ten

DONALD MACK CONVICTED of fraud?

Eric Price stared at the screen. Wow! After two hours he finally found something for Nicole. Eric glanced out the window. A day that began with June Gloom, a new term added to his vocabulary, had brightened by afternoon. The early evening sky was clear blue, the air bright with sunshine. After all these months in California, he was determined to finally get to the beach. It was late, but there was a bonus. He would be able to watch the sun set over the Pacific.

Donald Mack can wait, he decided. He went to the dresser and pulled from a drawer Bermuda shorts and a polo shirt. As he laced up his sneakers he remembered his neglected, personal "To Do" list. The first, most neglected item, was finding an apartment. Since arriving in California, internet searches turned up nothing reasonably priced other than apartments likely to induce claustrophobia. Never mind, he told himself. He wanted to see the Pacific Ocean.

He checked the map. Newport Beach was not far from the hotel. When he looked up dining at Newport Beach, he found a variety of choices, quick food to fine dining. It would be perfect if he knew someone with whom to share this. Well, that would come. He just needed time to socialize. Eric grabbed his keys, his cell phone, his wallet, and headed out into sunshine.

❧

Newport Beach was exactly as promised. With a good dinner tucked under his belt and his head filled with sea air, Eric dove into Donald Mack's fraud. As he typed he remembered the story of how the secretary's mother was lured to participate in fraud. That was not what the prosecutors were after, but Daniels was right, it was fraud. The prosecutors wanted to pin Archer for buying fraudulent policies from people with HIV. Apparently, they did not care about the seniors who sold fraudulently acquired policies.

Before finding the headline about Donald Mack, Eric found and rejected a number of convictions of viatical companies. All were in Florida state courts, and only one was a conviction of an insured—a man who sold six fraudulently acquired policies and pocketed nearly three hundred thirty thousand dollars. Again, state courts when he found viatical cases in New Jersey and California, and again not relevant to Nicole's mother. Although sales agents were indicted, none of the insureds were. The state of Texas was his first find—convictions of insureds as well as insurance agents. All were charged with felonies for "securing the execution of a document by deception."

Why so few prosecutions? This contradicted what the Archer prosecutors told Yolanda and Eric—that viatical and life settlements fraud was huge, tens of thousands of victims, millions of revenue, billions in death benefits. Where were the prosecutions?

The few he found were in state court. That made sense. Under the McCarran-Ferguson Act of 1945, states had the exclusive right to regulate insurance. This applied to nearly every type of insurance with very few exceptions, most notably employer-provided benefits and Medicare.

The more time Eric searched for answers, the more convinced he became that the Archer case did not belong in federal court. Then, suddenly, the startling press release popped up, claiming to be the first federal conviction specific to viatical settlement fraud: *Mack Convicted of Fraudulently Obtaining Insurance Policies*. The conviction was credited to the combined efforts of the North Carolina Department of Insurance and the Federal Bureau of Investigation. It was in federal court, but there were no other details.

Using the internet he searched the words "Donald Mack" and

"fraud," and there it was. After Mack was diagnosed HIV positive, he obtained two life insurance policies from two different insurance companies. These policies had face values—death benefits—of $150 thousand each. Mack sold them for $18,600 to a Florida viatical company. Once again, the Florida viatical company was not named.

Eric logged on to PACER—Public Access to Court Electronic Records. He found the docket and the documents. The indictment stated that Mack signed the applications in North Carolina but did not fill in answers to health questions. He sent the applications to an insurance agent in Dallas, Texas. That agent completed the forms—providing false answers to health questions. Neither the agent nor the Florida company were named or charged.

Oddly, the indictment described Donald Patrick Mack as *participating* in a scheme to defraud insurance companies. Eric stared at the screen, finding it difficult to believe. How could prosecutors use the word, "participating" and not charge other participants, not a single other one? How could they use the words, "a scheme to defraud insurance companies" and not cite any federal statute? If no federal statute prohibited fraud against insurance companies, then Archer did not violate a federal statute. Then why was this in federal court? Possibly, the prosecutors knew little about insurance fraud. Possibly, they were not aware of McCarran-Ferguson, not aware they lacked federal jurisdiction.

*No,* he told himself, *it could not be simple ignorance.* Eric was frustrated to see that after Mack agreed to plead guilty to one mail fraud charge, prosecutors dropped the other charges. He was sentenced to two years in federal prison and three years probation.

No mention of insurance. Certain he was missing something, Eric returned to the search engine to find every federal law related to life insurance. There was nothing related to private insurance companies.

Using news items Eric drew up more than a dozen names of insureds indicted for fraud in federal courts. When he returned to PACER, he found every one, without exception, mimicked Donald Mack—charges for various types of fraud but no federal law cited about life insurance. Every viator, like Mack, pleaded guilty to one or two counts. Plea deals meant no legal arguments, no appeals.

Who could he get to challenge him with another interpretation? Eric glanced at the clock on the computer. Chuck Wagner, a friend from the FBI Academy, was stationed in Massachusetts. It was three hours later on the east coast, well past Chuck's dinner hour but not near bed time. He dialed. To his relief, Chuck was home and free to talk.

"Okay," said Chuck. "Now that I have an idea what your wheels are spinning, I have a juicy Massachusetts case for you. The defendant was Kevin Blazer. You can look it up—it was in many newspapers. Blazer was diagnosed with AIDS five years before his new 'career' as a professional viator was halted with an indictment. He pocketed $550,000. The cute part is Blazer was indicted for a scheme not only of clean-sheeting but also dirty-sheeting."

"Dirty-sheeting? That's a new one for me."

Chuck explained. "With dirty-sheeting, a healthy person sells his life insurance by giving viatical companies false medical information, nasty stuff to make him appear seriously ill. Blazer was a bit more creative. First, he exhausted clean-sheeting. Since he had AIDS, he clean-sheeted in the usual way—applied for policies in his own name, didn't disclose to the insurers the truth about his health, and was issued nearly $1 million in death benefits. Then he dirty-sheeted."

Chuck paused and Eric could hear him light up a cigarette. "Okay, this is how it went down. He applied for policies in the names of healthy people. He used false identification to pose as these people."

"ID theft?" said Eric.

"Yes, but limited to life insurance. The next step in dirty-sheeting was to use his own medical records when he applied to viatical companies. To use them, he changed the name on the medical records to match those on the life insurance policies."

"So the dirty-sheeting victimized the viatical companies."

"And the investors to whom the policies were sold."

When Eric asked about the conviction, Chuck told him Blazer pled guilty to money laundering and aiding and abetting. Eric shook his head as if to clear his ears of water. Again, a viator not charged with insurance fraud. Again, a viator who did not challenge jurisdiction. Again, a viator who did not go to trial.

He asked Chuck if he knew of any case in which a lawyer who represented a viator challenged the jurisdiction of the federal court. Chuck knew of none. "But, you realize, Eric, I haven't been tracking these cases. The Blazer case was written up in newspapers, which is how I came to know about it."

Eric told him about the McCarran-Ferguson Act, and why he believed the viators could have successfully challenged the jurisdiction of the federal court. "I'm trying to figure out why they chose not to," Eric said. "I would love to read the pleadings that argue this issue. If the viators succeeded, their cases would have been remanded to state court, and probably not picked up. Most states rather allocate their limited resources to violent crimes."

"My guess, Eric—actually it's an either-or. Either their criminal defense lawyers were not aware of the McCarran-Ferguson Act, or the lawyers were aware and deliberately chose not to raise the jurisdictional issue."

"That is a very interesting angle," Eric said, "deliberately not raising jurisdiction." He gave some thought to this and realized Chuck was right. "If the cases were remanded to state court and a state prosecutor picked it up, it would mean state prison. The defendants did not want to take that risk."

"Yep. Here, we're talking about people who are seriously ill. Criminal defense lawyers know few, if any, state prisons provide proper medical care and some close to nothing at all. Add in that most state prisons are dangerous places for non-violent criminals."

Eric thanked him. It did not solve his problem, but he understood these lawyers did the best possible for their clients. He still needed a precedent for indicting Archer in federal court. But that was it for today. Eric was too fatigued to recognize the answer if he found it. He changed to work-out clothes and headed for the hotel's fitness room.

# Chapter Eleven

KYLE PRENNER WATCHED as they came toward the veterinary clinic, one of the most beautiful women he ever met, a kid who obviously was her son, and her brother who was not an obvious relative. All three wore shorts, tee shirts, and sandals. Carly introduced them. Ethan, following Ben, stuck out his hand, said, "How do you do?" and immediately began babbling about puppies.

"Sounds like you learned enough to fill a book," Kyle said when Ethan stopped for a breath.

"That's my Ethan—intense when he's interested in something, and a fantastic memory." Carly patted her son's back.

"So it's not a mutt," Ben said. "What kinda dog is it?"

Kyle saw the challenge on Ben's face. He would have to win him over, or the abandoned pup would not go home with this family. He looked Ben directly in the eyes. "There are no mutts. There are cross-breeds, but no mutts."

"Come on," Ben said. "I've seen dogs that look like they had scrambled genes: a golden retriever head and a dachshund's short, stubby legs, and a whippet's skinny tail."

Kyle laughed. Ben surprised him. The disgruntled expression on his face was only one aspect. The guy had a sense of humor. "This one is a purebred," he assured them. Carly nodded as if to say that was fine with her. Ethan stared past Kyle's shoulder.

Ben shook his head as if to get rid of cobwebs. It was obvious he knew his question had been deflected. And he was stubborn. "So, it's a purebred? What kinda dog?"

"Let me get him first. Then I'll answer your questions." Kyle knew if he told them before they saw the adorable little bundle, they might turn around and leave. He brought Buster into the waiting room and placed him in Ethan's arms.

"I've never held a puppy before," Ethan said. "I never saw one this small." His voice was just above a whisper.

Watching Ethan, hearing what he said, Carly's heart sank. If she did not know earlier, she knew now. The decision no longer was hers.

"I thought you were a good salesman, when we first met," she told Kyle. "I had no idea how good."

He grinned at her.

"Looks sorta like a lab," Ben said, staring at the puppy. "But not quite."

"At this young age, it is difficult to tell. This is a Staffordshire Terrier."

"A pit bull!" Ben snorted. "No way!"

"Let me tell you something about the pit bull," Kyle said, pulling a chair away from the wall and bringing it close to where Ethan stood. Ethan sat. Kyle sat in a nearby chair. Ben looked ready to leave and Carly seemed unsure what to do. She sighed, took a chair, and glanced at Ben. Ben shrugged and, resigned to listening, took another chair.

"Pit bulls are greatly misunderstood." At this Ethan's eyes popped wide and he stared at Kyle. Kyle ignored the reaction and went on. "Unless they are raised by idiots or people who are cruel, they are gentle, loving, and very protective of the people with whom they bond. But most people don't know this. That's why so many people are afraid of them."

Ethan was snuggling the puppy to his cheek while a tiny red tongue licked him. Kyle looked at Ben. Ben looked uncertain. Feeling Kyle's eyes on him, Ben began picking at a loose thread on his shorts. Kyle looked at Carly. He saw her eyes were filled with tears.

Kyle looked back at Ben. "Remember the pit bulls that Michael Vick kept for dog fights, the ones that sent him to prison?" Ben nodded. "Nearly every one found a new home with a family, some with children, and some with other dogs and even with cats. And they are loving and gentle. They didn't want the kind of life Vick subjected them to. Given the right home, even a dog forced to fight for survival will be mellow and trustworthy."

"I'm going to call him DeeOhGee."

"Where'd you get that from?" Ben snapped.

"That's how you spell dog. Dee. Oh. Gee."

"Well," said Carly. She stood up and looked at Ben, then at Kyle. "I guess Ethan has decided for us."

Ethan turned to Kyle. "I know he will need vaccinations for distemper and parvo and rabies. He's too young to start them now, isn't he?"

"You're right. We'll begin at six weeks. My best guess is he's only four weeks old now."

"And then the vaccines don't immediately get the puppy's immune system going. We'll have to wait five to nine days for DeeOhGee's immune system to recognize and respond to the antigens. Until then, we probably shouldn't take him to the dog park. In case other dogs are not vaccinated."

"Right again," said Kyle.

"How will we know if we should wait five, six, seven, eight, or nine days?" Ethan asked.

"You won't. It's better to wait nine days."

"And DeeOhGee might have a reaction to the vaccine. Like depression. Or vomiting. Or diarrhea." Ben gave a low whistle. Carly groaned. She should have hit the internet at night to do some puppy research of her own.

"If any of this occurs, call me. It may not be serious, but since it's your first dog, don't take chances. Call me."

"How do you tell if a dog is depressed?" Ben asked. He looked on the verge of laughing.

Kyle nodded at Ethan. "I bet you looked that up, too."

Ethan nodded. "If you try to pet him or hold him, he may run away. He may howl. He won't play. He won't want to go for a walk. If you take him out, he may not move."

"Well, you've got that down pat. I think this dog is going to the best home in the world."

Ethan started toward the door. "Wait!" Carly called. "We haven't bought puppy things yet. We don't even have puppy food. We can't take him home now." Ethan returned and handed the puppy to the veterinarian.

She turned to Kyle. "What do those vaccinations cost? I need to plan."

"Don't worry about it."

"No, no, I can't let you do that. You've done so much."

"Tell you what, if Ethan agrees, a trade-off. Ethan will come here on Saturday mornings to help walk the dogs that are boarded while their owners are on vacation. He'll help me and while he's doing that he'll learn more about all kinds of dogs."

Ethan tugged at Carly's sleeve, shaking his head yes. She agreed; Ethan could work at the vet clinic on Saturday mornings.

"I can ride my bike here."

"Dude—don't even think of that," Ben said. "PCH and the Canyon Road are too crazy with cars. Your mom or I will drive you."

"So it's settled?" Kyle asked. "When can I expect you to pick up DeeOhGee?"

Carly promised to phone as soon as they had everything they needed. Then she and Ben took her happy ten-year-old home.

"This beats frozen yogurt," he said, "and tide pool critters."

Carly knew Ethan was happy, probably excited, too. His face did not show it, his voice was unchanged, but she knew and she also knew she would have to find ways to prepare him for the experience of being at the vet clinic.

First, the library—there she was certain to find picture books about vet clinics. The internet might be a source of dog barking sounds; she would record these and play them in the house. Carly ran out of ideas. She would have to contact Kyle to find out what sort of things he expected Ethan to do. She would ask him to keep Ethan away from the reception area when it was busy. Carly could tell him Ethan was shy. She did not want to broadcast how vital it was for Ethan to avoid situations that caused sensory overload and might bring on a meltdown. Working at the vet clinic could be a fantastic experience for Ethan, but not if it caused a meltdown. Then everything good would be reversed.

If he wore his ear buds and listened to calming music while at the clinic, that would help. She could ask Kyle to have his teen assistants show Ethan a picture, which she would supply on index cards, to tell him when to do something, such as water in a dog bowl.

The first day, Carly decided, she would wait in her truck for at least half an hour. That way, if Ethan changed his mind about staying, she would be right there. If he found he could handle the new experience, he could come out to the parking lot and tell her to go home.

There was one more thing to consider: Should she tell Kyle to instruct his assistants not to yell at Ethan, if he does something wrong or doesn't do something they ask? Perhaps she could disguise it by reminding Kyle, and asking him to remind the other boys, that Ethan never had a pet and never walked a dog. He had to learn everything from zero up.

She could tell Kyle that Ethan was sensitive and did not take criticism easily. Once she had planned everything as carefully as possible, Carly knew she would cross her fingers and hope for the best.

They were exiting the truck when Carly's phone sang out Looney Tunes. She did not recognize the number.

"This is Carly."

She heard a woman, a young woman. The caller introduced herself as Trish Russell. She paused. When Carly said nothing, she went on, introducing herself as president of Star Spangled Life Settlements.

Very odd, Carly thought. She never met her, never heard of her, and wondered how she acquired Carly's phone number.

"Yes, Ms. Russell, what can I do for you?"

"It's what I can do for you, Carly. I know you are out of a job. I wanted to offer you employment at my company. I understand you are very good at client services and I need another person in that department. Our company is growing and we pay very well."

"It is very kind of you, but I need to find something different. Client services is emotionally draining, and I have too many other things to worry about."

"I understand. Keep my number—in case you change your mind."

Carly agreed, but she knew she would sooner work at a fast food restaurant than client services.

꙳

Vito Capone swaggered into his brother's bar. It was mid-afternoon and the bar was empty. He did not have the Archer money he wanted but he had something else to brag about. He took a stool and told Marco, "the usual." Marco poured scotch into a shot glass and placed it and a bottle of Heineken's on the counter. "You look like the cat who did you-know-what," he told Vito.

"I am a lion or a tiger," Vito grinned. "Know how you're always telling me I'll get arrested?" He waited for Marco to ask. Marco waited for the rest of the information.

Vito swallowed the shot and picked up his beer. "Well, they finally got me. Fraud. A federal grand jury, no less. I guess that puts me in the big league." He waited for his brother's reaction.

Marco leaned on the bar, his face close to Vito's. "You're gonna need a good lawyer. Want me to recommend someone?"

"Nah. I got a good lawyer. A hotshot I heard on NPR. The indictment is no big deal. After I hired Attorney Hotshot, we met with the FBI. *And* a prosecutor from California. Think about that—he came all the way here to meet with me! And I got me a fantas-terrific plea deal."

"Jail time?"

"Nope."

"Nothin'?"

"Not if I help them convict the guys at Archer. I'm important. It took a long time for people to see it, but I'm important."

Marco sniggered. Vito pointed to the shot glass. Marco turned, took the bottle of scotch, and refilled the glass. "Just how important are you?"

"You don't believe me? Don't you remember when the honchos from Archer came here to see me? Well, now a California prosecutor, a federal prosecutor, came all the way to New York, just to see me."

"What makes a two-bit player like you so important?"

Vito stuck his thumbs in his armpits and puffed out his chest, the way he used to do as a kid. He grinned at Marco. He knew this pissed him. "Maybe you don't think so, but I am important. Always was. People now realize it." He swallowed the beer noisily. "So, you remember when the Archer guys came here?"

Marco nodded. "They wanted you to get others to do what you do."

"Right! They wanted me to recruit guys to sell their life insurance. Now, the prosecutors want me to tell a jury all about it."

"You gotta tell a jury you recruited guys to commit fraud?"

Vito frowned. "Don't get hung up on the fraud thing. As it turned out, I never recruited anyone. Archer made up business cards for me and brochures. I left them at bars and clubs for gay men, but never got a call. The prosecutor was okay with that—as long as I tell the jury Archer wanted me to do this."

"And for that you get no jail time?"

"That. And other things." Vito let his voice trail off.

"What other things?"

"I'm gonna say the Archers told me to switch around my social security numbers so it would not show up that I had twenty other policies. Just in case any insurance company checked."

"Veee—toe," he sang out the name. "Veee-toe," he sang again. "You did that years ago, before you ever heard of Archer. I remember the car loan and the mortgage loan. And what else? There was somethin' else."

Vito smirked. "You think the jury's gonna know? No way. They'll know nothin' but what I tell them."

"Prison, Vito. Prison." Marco started to walk away.

"Hey, Marco! You got a Jaguar? A Mercedes? Own rental real estate? Who's the loser here, Marco?"

Marco stepped back and put his face into Vito's once again. "I don't want stolen goods. Every damn thing I own I got the honest way. That's worth somethin'."

"And I'm gettin' a new Caddie. With the works. Jealous, Marco? I could've brung business your way. All you had to do was take a blood test, tell them you were me."

Marco snorted. "Lotta good that did Angelo. You don't pay enough, Vito. Angelo's still falling short every month."

"Angelo's a pussy. If he listened to me…"

"Angelo's a better man than you, Vito."

Vito laughed. "And much poorer."

"What did you give him for his social security number? A lousy hunnerd bucks? That didn't pay his rent for one month. And for taking the blood test for you? A lousy five hunnerd? Still not enough for his rent."

"If Angelo woulda done as I did, he would be doin' okay today."

"Prison, Vito. You're headed to prison. Sooner or later."

"Nah. I'm savvy. I know the system. It's easy. All you gotta do is pay attention. When they ask a question, you can figure out what answer they want. Give them that, you walk."

"What are you talking about?"

"Okay, say the prosecutor guy asks when you stopped beating your wife. You say, yestidday. He asks me about my conversations with the Archers, if the word 'contestable' came up, and if I explained it to them. I see where this is going. I tell him, 'They knew all about it.'"

"Well, you can tell me, Vito. I don't know what you're talking about."

"Contestable?"

Marco nodded.

"Okay, here's the deal. That means a policy can be canceled by in-surers, if they discover fraud. But only if they discover it within two years after they issue the policy. Those are the two years the policy is contestable."

"Why did he want to know about that?"

"To find out if I knew, prob'ly. Then he asks about defrauded investors. Well, the truth is I sold to Archer. I had nothin' to do with investors. But," Vito emphasized the word and repeated it, "But, I read newspapers. I read about people suing these companies, claiming they were defrauded of their life savings. They bought policies like the ones I sold, thinking it was a good investment. Then the insurer canceled the policy."

Vito waited for Marco's reaction. Marco was thinking about what he just heard, trying to put it together.

"What I'm tellin' you, Marco, is the minute the prosecutor says, 'investors,' I know what he wants. And I give it to him."

"How could you tell him somethin'?"

"Because I'm clever, Marco. I tell him I discussed this with Aidan, also with Blake, the concern I had for people who would be investing in these policies, should it go bad, what happens to these people. The prosecutor loved it when I told him Blake said, 'Screw them.' and actually used a different word, which I would not repeat to him. He smiled at that. And when I told Aidan he said, "You just worry about getting the policies to me. The day you send them, the next day, I'll have someone to buy them.'"

"What did the prosecutor say to that?"

Vito laughed. "He said, 'Okay.'"

"So, tell me: Did you really have that conversation with the Archers?"

"Whaddyou think? That's what the prosecutor wanted. I could tell from the questions."

"So they go easy on you for Archer. How about the other companies you did this for? They could turn around and get you for those."

"Marco, I'm trying to tell you—I got immunity. And if they want other big fish, I'll give them that. They don't care if you make it up. They want a headline-making case. What that means is you have to give the finger to a big shot, a top guy. Then you walk."

Marco shook his head. "Gotta admit, so far it's worked for you."

"It's easy, Marco. If ever you get in trouble, ask me what to do. I know how to game insurance companies, and I know how to game the courts."

# Chapter Twelve

WHEN BEN WAS BORN, Carly was six years of age. To this day she had fond memories of his early years. When she went to the mailbox, dreading bills, she thought about Little Ben's idea that the mailman would not leave anything unless they had left something for the mailman. In his young child's mind it was like leaving cookies and milk for Santa. If only this were so.

Bills were nothing compared to finding an envelope from the federal court. Carly carried it into the house by the corner, as if the contents were toxic. With a shaky hand, her letter opener slit open the envelope. Inside was a formal announcement of a grand jury hearing in the case named United States of America versus Carly Daniels. She panicked. She phoned Blake Archer.

"What does this mean? What's going to happen to us?"

Blake did not hear her. "Just a minute," he said. Carly heard music and voices and laughter and silverware clinking. She heard a door shut. Suddenly it was quiet. Blake must have gone to another room. She repeated her questions.

"Don't ask me, Carly. I know nothing about law. That's why we paid hundreds of thousands to lawyers over the years—so this sort of thing wouldn't happen. Well, it's happening anyway and it'll cost a few million. But don't worry, sweet cheeks. I'll call back as soon as I hire an attorney for you."

Carly felt greatly relieved. "Thank you so much, so very much."

For two hours she paced the downstairs of the cottage, holding her cell phone, ready to answer, waiting, waiting. When at last Looney Tunes signaled a call, she knew Blake had kept his word. Irwin Stanley introduced himself as an attorney hired by Archer Life Settlements on her behalf. Bills would be sent to the company, but he was her lawyer. Everything was confidential between them.

Attorney Stanley explained about the grand jury hearing. If Carly wanted to testify on her own behalf, she could—but he would have to wait outside. He would not be allowed to enter the hearing room. If the prosecutor asked anything she was not sure about answering, she would be allowed to scoot into the hall to consult with him.

"How can I decide about testifying? I have no idea what they will ask."

"That's one reason why it could be very risky to testify," Stanley said. "Prosecutors could ask anything—your personal history, your marriage, previous employment, any previous arrests. Not only yours but any family member or friend."

"They won't find anything," Carly told him.

"They'll use this opportunity to question your memory and to observe your reaction to stress. Imagine the stress when prosecutors introduce witnesses, hearsay evidence, even evidence or testimony that might not be admissible at trial."

"I have no idea what you mean."

"Hearsay is like gossip. It's what someone else said about you. A told B and B testifies against you, telling the jury what he heard from A. Say A was an enemy who wanted revenge. A told B that you were a drug addict. Or a stripper. Or a hooker."

Carly stopped him. "You made your point."

"No, I didn't, Carly, unless you are prepared for sneak attacks on your character. The prosecutors want to convince the jury you are not the sort of person they want as a neighbor. Once they don't like you, they'll accept anything they are told. If you never met A or B, never spoke with either of them, it won't matter. You can't introduce evidence or witnesses on your own behalf."

"I can't believe this! It sounds like a Kangaroo Court."

"Not far off, Carly. Prosecutors are permitted to do all this at the grand jury hearing. It's their ball game. The score starts and ends with 'Prosecutors one hundred, Defendants zero.'"

"And I can't have an attorney argue for the truth? Or argue about the unfairness?"

"Nope. No one is allowed to challenge anything the prosecutors say or any evidence they introduce to the grand jury. If you still don't get it, hear this now: The grand jury hearing is the prosecutors' delight. Their success is a given. It's the complete opposite of fairness and justice, and there is absolutely nothing you or I can do about it."

When Carly asked questions based on television programs, Stanley admonished her not to believe what she saw and heard on shows like *Law and Order*. On TV, he told her, when prosecutors are lead characters and seem to struggle to get an indictment, this is pure drama. In the real world they can say anything, introduce any witnesses—even their own grandmother—and any kind of evidence. They can claim these were exactly what the prosecutors want them to be—damaging to the defendant.

He repeated the adage, "A good prosecutor could get a grand jury to indict a ham sandwich."

"But the jury—won't they realize something funny is going on?"

"How would they know? Who's going to tell them?"

"Because I'm not allowed to present anything on my own behalf," Carly repeated in a doomed voice.

"Then there's this, Carly. The grand jury is a bunch of ordinary citizens. They are completely ignorant of the law—except for what prosecutors tell them. They sit without a judge, and they have no investigative powers of their own. And they usually have complete trust in the prosecutor."

"In other words, if I am indicted and go to trial I could end up in prison for ten years, even though I am innocent. And if the viators who actually committed fraud plead guilty, they could get off with six months?"

"You got it," Stanley told her.

"Do I have any other choices?"

"If you have a plea agreement with the prosecutors, you waive the grand jury hearing. In its place, the prosecutors indict you by filing a document called 'Information,' which describes the charges."

"Either way I am indicted?"

"Yes. Shall I set up an appointment with the prosecutors—to discuss a plea?"

"How can I plead guilty, when I knew nothing?"

"Let's do the appointment. Something might turn up that could result in immunity for you."

"I really have no choice, do I?" Stanley confirmed this. Again he urged her to meet with the prosecutors. She told him she would think about this. As soon as she closed her phone, Carly began to plan a meeting of all employees.

❧

Ben stood in the doorway, his helmet dangling from his hand. "Come on, Carly. You need a break. And Ethan wants to go to the beach." Ethan wanted to look for tide pools. He could not go with Ben because Carly did not allow him on the motorcycle.

"Will you be there?"

"For a while. I'm taking the Hog. Probably head out to a club or a friend's house, later."

They agreed to meet somewhere between Main and Bluebird beaches.

Ethan was excited. His tone was, as always, flat and his face gave no hint but he could scarcely catch a breath as he described some of the "sea critters," as Ben called them, sea critters he had read about but not yet found.

"We're not allowed to capture them," Ethan told her as they walked to the end of Bluebird Canyon Road. "We can look, just look. I hope I can find a sea urchin. They hide in rocks. Just once, I saw a red one. They look prickly. Those actually are movable spines. That's why they're called hedgehogs of the sea."

The hassle of crossing South Coast Highway always worsened during tourist season. The four lanes filled with crawling traffic day and night, and the crossing light did not stay green long enough to reach the opposite street at a normal pace. Nearly across three lanes, they ran the remaining distance as cars waiting for the light to change began to creep forward. Carly wondered how anyone old or infirm would safely negotiate this, and scolded herself for being a worrywart.

Once across they walked to the end of Thalia, a short street that led to stone stairs. The number of visible steps changed by the amount of sand that covered the lower steps. Ethan counted as they climbed down and announced, "Fifty-eight, today," just before they jumped over the last two or three.

Carly did not expect to see Ben until they reached Main Beach. She planned to stay a while to watch whatever game he joined, volleyball or basketball. He probably was involved in a game by now. Ben had friends who rented nearby, and he often left his motorcycle in their court yard rather than waste time searching for a parking space.

They climbed over rocks the size of basketballs and continued on, seeing few people, walked around boulders, and continued on, barefoot on the cool sand, with Carly carrying both pair of sandals. She kept watch for rocks he might trip on, with Ethan's head down, intent on finding a sea urchin.

At a level stretch of beach Carly paused to study the ocean. She had forgotten to check the tide table. It could be risky to be on the beach at high tide, when there was little beach to walk and an in-coming tide. Then, vigorous swells swept over the rocks as the ocean rushed inland, stopping only when it crashed against the sea wall. That kind of tide could sweep a small animal out to sea, or cause an adult to lose footing and possibly get carried away in a rip tide. It was a great area for surfers, but neither she nor Ethan knew how to use a body board and they were not strong swimmers.

A figure in the distance came running toward them, shouting and waving. As he drew closer it turned out to be Ben calling, over and over, "Quick! You gotta see this." He beckoned them to follow, and turned back the way he had come. Carly and Ethan hurried toward him, Ethan running as stiffly as a marionette. Carly had tried to teach him to swing his arms; he must have forgotten. The contrast with Ben's grace saddened her.

As they approached they saw Ben had stopped and was talking to a man who wore cut-off jeans. A large, brown dog ran up to the men.

"It's a Labrador Retriever," Ethan told Carly, showing off his new ability to identify a number of breeds. The dog dropped a Frisbee at the feet of the men. As they neared, Ethan told Carly, "It's Doctor Kyle and his dog. I know Java. He brings Java to work."

Kyle introduced them to his dog. Java sniffed them, then plopped his body onto the sand and lay there, mouth open, panting, tongue twice normal size. "Java thinks the beach is for dogs and Frisbees," Kyle told them.

"Why is her tongue so long?" Ethan asked. Java looked as if a dark pink necktie was hanging out of her mouth.

"That's how dogs sweat, through their tongues and their feet. She's already had a pretty good work out, but won't quit until she's nearly totally wiped out." As if she understood him, Java got to her feet.

"Well, come on," Ben said to Ethan. "I'll show you how to throw a Frisbee. You need to know this for DeeOhGee."

Ethan was clumsy. He walked stiffly, never swinging his arms, and had no ability for sports. But he had a patient teacher. Ben sandwiched himself against Ethan's back. After grabbing Ethan's wrist, with the boy's arm resting along his, Ben swung their arms together, as one. Again and again Ben shouted, "Go!" and they swung their arms. After a dozen or more swings he let Ethan try it on his own. Ethan was immediately disappointed. The Frisbee did not travel far nor did it travel in a straight line.

"It's like any sport," Ben told him. "With enough practice, your brain learns what it has to do. In time, it will be like blinking—your brain will just do it, without you thinking about it." He handed the Frisbee to Ethan to try again.

Kyle began to walk inland, toward the sea wall. Carly followed. She was feeling good, peaceful, calm, even playful. The beach and the ocean did this for her. She stopped Kyle with a hand on his arm.

"Thank you for teaching Ethan how to growl."

Kyle looked at her, his face filled with surprise.

"What?" she said. He shrugged. She looked into his eyes, those warm eyes, and told him, "Maybe it's not much to you. But it's a lot for Ethan, how you took him aside to give him pointers. Like when you told him to use a growling voice, the way an older dog talks to a younger dog who is misbehaving."

Kyle was smiling now.

"And you demonstrated growling."

Kyle demonstrated his growl, and both laughed.

"He also told me you had him try a sing-songy voice to show the dogs when their behavior is good, or to call them over."

Kyle blushed. "He's a good kid. Tries hard." He turned away, looked at Ben and Ethan and back at Carly. "It's astonishing how absolutely different you and your brother are. In looks, that is. Is it the same with your personalities?"

Carly knew what he was getting at and it was ridiculous. Personalities are not determined by appearance. Carly's parents knew nothing about her history but, judging from her appearance, she combined Native American genes with genes from a green-eyed someone. She looked at Ethan. There was little trace in him of Scott, his fair-skinned father. That became a problem with her in-laws.

From the start Scott's parents rejected their marriage. When pregnancy tests showed the baby was a boy, Scott's parents were pleased but reserved. Their bitter disappointment was evident when their grandson turned out to resemble Carly. Despite the rush of these memories, Carly tried to sound light-hearted. "We're like most families. Each of us is unique. Don't you find this so with your siblings?"

"I'm an only child. I was curious because I've seen this with dogs, a litter in which some pups are completely different from others. It usually means two fathers."

Carly's mouth fell open. "You mean the same mother and different fathers? Absolutely not! My parents spent years trying and not conceiving. When they decided to adopt, their only requirement was a healthy child. Boy, girl, orange, green—they didn't care. Mom used to say I brought her a double blessing. Six years later Mom went to the hospital fat, I thought. When she came home not fat, she put my new baby brother into my arms. Ben resembles our folks."

Kyle nodded. "Now let me ask about Ethan, if I may." Carly tensed. She knew what was coming. She never knew how to handle this.

"I can tell he is very bright. And he loves to learn. And he doesn't like to make eye contact. And his voice has no inflection. Then, too, your instructions about keeping him away from the reception area when it's busy. Does he have Asperger's?"

"How did you guess?" Anyone could note the signs, but few knew what they indicated.

"In college I had a roomie who had Asperger's. He was majoring in computer technology, very bright guy, poor social skills. My social skills were not much better; I was very shy. We were the undynamic duo." He grinned. "Then one day he told me his story, the difficulties, the challenges. That led me to read up on it. And to have tremendous admiration for him. Today Glenn has a top job at Google, probably earns two or three times what I do."

"That's a lovely story, Kyle. Thank you for telling me."

"Here's another. I know a woman who is raising a grandchild who is autistic. She adopted a mixed breed from the shelter, and came to me with the dog. Over time her grandson, who never before spoke, began to speak. First, to his dog. Then, his gran. Then, me. Later, at school."

"You do know that Asperger's is not autism?" When he opened his mouth to reply, she added, "Well, I know some professionals disagree. They consider it high functioning autism. Regardless, it does qualify the same as autism for special education. That was a huge problem when we lived in Ohio. The Parma schools ... well, that's over now."

"He seems to be doing very well."

"Because we paid to send him to a special school. That's where all our money went, and then some. We finally moved into my parents' house, which they were renting out after they moved here. Eventually we had to use credit cards to finance the $60 grand annual tuition. It was worth it, but lucky us, we don't need to do that any more. Now it would be impossible."

"So, Ethan's no longer in private school. Is he in special ed. classes?"

"Only a few hours each day. The rest of the time he's with the general population. But I have to continue to work with him at home. He still gets upset in crowds, for example. That means we never go to a busy store without Ethan's earbuds and his music."

"He's doing fine at the kennel," Kyle told her. "The barking doesn't seem to bother him—he tried it several times, for short periods, without the earbuds. He gets along with Sam and Tom, my teenage assistants. Of course, they don't say anything to him except, 'Give that dog water,' or 'Walk that dog.'"

Carly smiled. "I'll bet you told them to keep it simple."

Kyle nodded, too embarrassed to return her smile. As he looked away he saw Ben and Ethan coming toward them, Java at their heels. Java plopped down on the sand.

"Tired, girl?" Kyle asked. "Guess it's time to get on home."

Carly asked where he had parked and offered to walk along with him. Ben decided to go to Main Beach and join his friends. When they reached Kyle's SUV, he told them to hop in and he'd drive them home.

# Chapter Thirteen

WHEN MORNING CAME Carly dragged herself out of bed, washed, dressed, woke Ethan, and went down to prepare his breakfast. Every movement felt as if she was sleep-walking. Awake or asleep, she fretted about the grand jury hearing. If her attorney was right, she surely would be indicted. She would become an accused felon. It did not matter that there was no evidence against her. And once she was indicted, her work for the FBI would end. No income. No insurance. No job prospects for an accused felon. Throughout breakfast she tried to be jolly for Ethan's sake. But after the school bus grumbled past the house, she turned from the door, opened a kitchen drawer, took out notepaper, grabbed a pen, and sat down.

Ben stomped down the stairs, jumping the last two. "You still here?" He was ready for volleyball—sneakers, shorts, and tee shirt.

Still trying to be jolly, Carly said, "No. I'm a mirage."

"Me, too," Ben grinned. "Pretend I'm not here. Just do what you were doing."

"I'm trying to figure out a third alternative. A choice I can live with."

"Find one and I'll drink to it."

Carly watched Ben pour his coffee and take a donut from the box on the counter. "I need to know something, Ben. When you went through all those problems, when you had no power over your life, how did you get over it?"

"I didn't." His voice was tight. He did not turn toward her.

"You did. You're light-hearted, fun to be with, have lots of friends. You enjoy life."

"You want the truth?" When she said, "Yes," he left his cup on the counter and walked to the large window in the living room area. He stood there, looking out. "You mean losing Mike?"

Carly lowered her head. When Ben's partner, Mike, was killed in Iraq, she knew it was a great loss but never realized it was a trauma. Carly felt a twinge of envy. Ben had known a relationship far better than any she ever had. Embarrassed, she mumbled, "The time you cut your wrists."

"People handle things differently. For me, that turned into the first step. The second was Mom and Dad and you. The third was a fresh start in California. The fourth was Michael."

"Rebuilding your life," Carly nodded.

"Sort of. Mainly, it just got easier to live with. Easier to forget for entire days. But something that changes you completely… you don't totally recover. You just find ways to go on."

Carly did not know what to say. Her throat was choked with tears. Ben could have gone to college, but chose not to do so. He could have started his own construction company, but chose not to do so. Day after day, year after year, he worked at a bar and played or partied. Carly suddenly was struck with a thought: Ben lived as if he never left his teen years. He had no view of the future, no plans for his future. Carly swallowed the lump in her throat and resolved, one day, to discuss this with him.

She mumbled, "Thanks." Got up, put her cup in the sink, the pad and pen in the drawer, and prepared to go to work.

❧

Carly greeted the security guard, went up in the elevator, turned on the computer—no password was necessary, she now knew—and sat down to work. Half an hour later, as she stood up to stretch while pages printed, Agent Price appeared. He rapped on the open door and, without further ado, instructed Carly to prepare a report with specifics about every senior who sold a policy within three years of issuance.

Carly asked whether her suspicion was correct—that this was fraud. He said, "Just do it" and left. Her face crumbled. Was he displeased with her? With her work? Or did he know she was about to be indicted? The crude dismissal left Carly unsettled for close to an hour.

Her mother would have said, "I beg your pardon!" Her brother would have said, "Having a crappy day?" Marcia would have said, "You need to learn to show more respect." What is the matter with me, Carly thought. Why did she say nothing?

Finally, hurt turned to anger. How dare he treat her this way! Carly was a stranger to anger. She had always believed anger was not helpful. Her blow-up when she thought her husband was drunk was proof of that. But anger sure did beat feeling like a victim. *I will not be a victim,* she told herself. *I am going to find a way out of this.* There was strength in unity, wasn't there? She quickly wrote out a list of employees. During lunch break she would begin a phone chain. She would ask each person to phone three others.

Carly took her sandwich and a bottle of apple juice to a nearby park. She made her three phone calls—Marcia, Allison, Sherri—then tried to relax, watch birds, watch toddlers in a sand box. But she could not stop the thoughts that whirled, the idea of taking Ethan and fleeing the country. She could charge travel expenses to credit cards. If they knew her thoughts, American Express would send letters: *Please leave home without us.* She chuckled. Now she was thinking like Ben.

This was pure fantasy, Carly knew. Ethan needed the special education program. Add the hardship of adjusting to another country, possibly another language, as if Ethan did not have enough challenge adjusting to daily life here. Could they leave Ben? Would he want to join them? Without Ben, the hardship for Ethan—and her, too—would be so much greater. Then there was Ethan's puppy. Doctor Kyle probably would find it a good home. But Ethan was growing more and more attached to his dog. Ethan might grieve, rebel. He might refuse to leave DeeOhGee.

Would the difficulties of fleeing be worse than staying? Carly was not ready to completely discard the idea. It did free her or, at least, relax her, like being in the dentist's chair and imagining herself on a sailboat.

Late in the afternoon Agent Price came by to collect the new spread sheets. He glanced through them, smiling as he flipped pages. Carly was surprised. The fierce look, the intense look—gone. With one smile, Agent Price became a different person. He looked up at her, still smiling.

"Exactly what I wanted. You're good. You probably could get a new job on computers."

"With my reputation?"

"We can't say anything about guilt or innocence, but if a letter of recommendation as to your proficiency will help, contact Agent Ruiz or me. You did, after all, work for us for two weeks."

He reached out to shake her hand, wished her luck, and was gone. Carly was astounded. Confused and astounded. She did not know what to make of Agent Price.

～

On the slow, traffic-snarled drive to his hotel Eric Price played with scenarios that might turn the Archer case into a legitimate federal action. Adding seniors as co-conspirators would be a plus. But without a federal cause to substitute or add to the current indictments, the prosecutors were unlikely to abandon the case, no matter how greatly they violated states' rights.

Two hours after entering his hotel room, Eric had little to show for his efforts. A few federal cases but defendants were charged with securities fraud—for turning viaticated policies into investments and reselling them to the public. Also indicted were doctors who falsified life expectancies and the settlement companies' bought-and-paid for lawyers. None of these cases were relevant. After reviewing most of the Archer files, Eric knew Archer sold policies to other viatical companies, to hedge funds and Wall Street companies, but saw no evidence Archer resold policies to the public. He also found no state securities actions against Archer for sales to the public. That contrasted with companies indicted in federal court after years of administrative actions taken by states under their Blue Sky Laws, the state securities laws.

Eric paced the room, wondering what he had missed. A state insurance statute that provided for referral to the federal government when fraud crossed into another state? He dashed back to the computer, searched state statutes, one state after another, going from insurance statutes to the subcategory of viatical settlements. Nothing.

Fatigued and disheartened, Eric picked up the phone and ordered dinner from the room service menu. He put down the phone and slowly approached the laptop, as if it were about to explode. He began another search. This time the screen filled with something new, something exciting and, possibly, something relevant. Stranger-originated life insurance, known as STOLI.

One state after another recently enacted new statutes to prohibit STOLI. He noted the dates the legislation became effective. He needed to compare these with the spreadsheets. If Archer was involved in STOLI in states with these prohibitions, the company violated state law.

Eric groaned. He did not want state law. He needed a federal statute. His stomach rumbled, reminding Eric of his old habit—becoming obsessed and forgetting food, sleep, just about everything. As a kid, when he was obsessed with reading a book, he chewed his fingernails rather than stop for lunch or dinner. He no longer had a mother or aunt who would drag him to the table. Instead, there was room service.

He remembered the knock at the door—was it ten minutes earlier, or half an hour? He vaguely remembered signing the bill, taking the tray, putting it on top of the bureau, and rushing back to the computer.

Dinner was cold, but it was food and he had eaten worse. He gulped down the hamburger, drank half the contents of a can of Sprite, and saved the French fries for nibbling while he continued research. His next search used the words "agent" and "STOLI." One of the most intriguing news reports, dated April 2010, was headlined, "Fla. Agent Accused of STOLI Fraud." The relief spread through his body. He closed his eyes to savor the moment. He hit "print," and while each page slid out of the printer, finished the can of Sprite.

The Florida agent solicited five seniors as the insureds. Seniors! They acquired $78 million in death benefits, and the agent was paid $1.6 million in commissions. The Florida Department of Financial Services charged the agent with twenty-two violations of state law, including eight counts of insurance fraud and seven of grand theft.

State law again. Eric had no choice but to warn the prosecutors. The way to do so was through his supervisor. And he dreaded trying to convince Yolanda Ruiz the prosecution was wrong. He was nothing in the hierarchy, just a rookie on his first assignment after the Academy. He was haunted by his introduction to Yolanda. The day he arrived at the office she took one look at him and flooded him with a tirade about not under-estimating her because she was a woman and because he thought she was Hispanic. She was not Mexican, Puerto Rican, Guatemalan, or Columbian. Her family came to America centuries ago from Spain. They probably were Americans longer than Eric's family. She joined the FBI straight from law school and worked her way up, with far more hurdles than an Anglo like him knew. Anglo men, Yolanda implied, had life easy simply because they were Anglo men.

Eric began to pace the room. What to do, he kept repeating. Another idea hit him. The mail and wire fraud statutes—they were very broad. They could be applied at the whim of federal prosecutors if there was a legal basis to show the lies on the insureds' applications converted the policies into stolen goods.

How could these policies be stolen goods, if the insurance companies could refuse to issue them? If a thug approached a man on the street, demanded his wallet, and when the man refused the thug walked away, the would-be thief could not be charged with theft. Attempted theft, maybe, but not theft.

Okay, the prosecutors pinned this theory on the claim the insurers were deceived into issuing the policies. But there was a remedy—on the state level. The law in every state allowed insurers two years to discover they were deceived, and then void the policies. Investigate, discover material misrepresentation within two years, rescind the policies: Simple solution.

But that would not bring Archer into the equation, other than as a dealer in stolen goods. Stolen goods? That would not occur if insurers did their job. Eric continued pacing, trying to find a hole in his theory. He kept going back to the insurers. If they could have discovered this and chose not to investigate, were they victims of theft? If you see a burglar break into your home and, watching through a window, see him stuff your valuables into a bag, and you do not call the police, are you a victim? Or a co-conspirator? Isn't that more like watching someone steal your car and taking no action to stop the theft, then reporting it stolen so that you could collect from the insurer?

Insurers had resources to prevent this, Eric knew, which meant these policies were not stolen goods. It was unlike a family who returned from vacation to find their jewelry, art work, and electronics stolen. It did not happen behind the backs of the insurers. Or, it did not have to happen. Eric wondered if some insurers intentionally turned a blind eye, if they allowed this to happen. If so, what was in it for them?

He wanted to consult an insurance professional, someone who taught insurance courses at the college level or at law school. He was missing something. Were prosecutors looking for other types of evidence, something he knew nothing about? If so, why was he not told? Frustrated, Eric punched the bureau where he had placed the dinner tray, causing silverware and dishes to rattle. The investigation would be on sounder footing if prosecutors had on board a consultant who was an insurance professional. But they did not. They were proceeding in a routine way, as if all they need do was poke a finger and the dominoes would fall.

Room service knocked and a timid voice called out to collect his dinner tray. The man probably heard Eric punch the bureau. Feeling sheepish, Eric handed out the tray, shut the door, and told himself this was a signal to take a break.

He threw off his work clothes and quickly dressed in shorts, a tee shirt, and sneakers, grabbed his key and went outside, to jog the hotel grounds. The sunny day had turned into a perfect evening, with cooling air that brought the temperature down ten degrees to seventy.

The panorama of flowers that bordered the walks filled the air with fragrance.

He returned to the hotel room with another idea. He plugged STOLI into Google's search box. There were dozens of news reports of lawsuits, some filed in state courts but most in federal court. These were civil, not criminal lawsuits, but Eric was jubilant. He had stumbled on a gold mine of data. Most were insurers suing to rescind policies. Defendants included the insureds, agents, and trustees—sometimes banks—of the newly-formed life insurance trusts. Now Eric had names.

After saving dozens of these cases, Eric began checking the names. He logged onto the National Crime Information Center database. The NCIC files documented a variety of crimes, identity theft, protection orders, supervised release, wanted persons, national sex offender registry. He found nothing on anyone named in STOLI lawsuits.

Next Eric logged onto N-DEx, law enforcement's national data exchange. This highly secure internet site, located at the Criminal Justice Information Services in West Virginia, was referred to as CJIS at the Academy. Eric ordered himself to refer to it as CJIS, if he spoke to Yolanda about this investigation.

Eric's user account with N-DEx was through the Academy; this was the first time he accessed it since he completed training. "Give me just one person named in the lawsuits," he told the computer. "Just one and I will be joyful."

N-DEx yielded a few arrests for DUI, disorderly conduct, or misdemeanor assault, all too long ago to be significant. Two names popped up as car accident victims, but the incidents were unrelated. Moreover, the car accidents revealed no pattern of linked crimes, such as attempted fraud.

He ran the same search for family members listed as beneficiaries when the policies were issued. Eric found nothing on anyone connected to STOLI.

N-DEx was a great tool, Eric thought, as he switched to a search for *modus operandi*. He entered the search words in the MO box, and they squirted forth too many entries. He narrowed it, and there was nothing closely related. He tried other word combinations. Nothing. Apparently no one had identified the modus operandi he was investigating. Eric entered a subscription to be notified any time someone entered similar information.

Logging off N-DEx, Eric opened the word processor. Despite the failure of this research, he still hoped to turn up something to present to Yolanda. He stared at the empty page on his screen. His brain suddenly shut down. That was it, Eric decided. Enough work for one day. He had earned "down time." Today he would visit the ocean at Laguna Beach.

~

Although the traffic along Laguna Canyon Road crawled—he could have walked faster—it allowed Eric to enjoy the scenery. On the right the canyon rose up close to the road. On the left were various small shops, car repair, massage, and others, and at their back more canyon. As he drove along, slow as a snail, he saw a coyote at the roadside on the right, waiting patiently for a break in traffic that would allow it to dash across the road. To where, he wondered. He looked left and saw a large open space enclosed with a chain link fence and, within, at least two dozen people of varying ages, races, and ethnicities, and dogs as varied in size, color, and breed as their owners. He had never seen a dog park before. The back of the dog park was all canyon and rose up to meet the sky.

When Eric passed a sign for "Prenner Animal Hospital and Boarding," he almost slammed on the brakes. It was not possible to stop, turn, or do anything other than continue in the tight line of cars headed toward the beach. Drumming his fingers on the wheel, he thought he would burst with anticipation. Kyle Prenner. If a fortune teller or an astrology chart told him this would happen, he would not have believed it.

Finally Eric saw a turn lane and was able to reverse direction. He pulled into the clinic parking lot, which was large enough for a half-dozen cars. The clinic was one-story, off-white stone or stucco, he was not sure which, with a glass door. To the left was a six foot tall wood fence, painted white, with a gate. On the fence was a sign showing kennel hours. He got out, slammed the car door, and marched up to the clinic. It no longer was open. The sign on the glass door listed the hours. Wednesdays were the only days the clinic stayed open past six.

He heard dogs barking and realized the boarding kennel had to have someone in attendance. He tried the gate. It was locked. He knocked, then banged, and banged again. Finally a young male voice, probably a teen, called from behind the fence, "It's after hours. You'll have to wait until morning to pick up your dog or cat."

"Wait! Don't go away. I'm not here to pick up a pet. I'm an old friend of Dr. Prenner. Could you get hold of him?"

"Try phoning."

Eric took out his personal cell phone and punched in the numbers on the sign stuck at the side of the road. He heard voice mail or an answering machine pick up—he couldn't be sure which. Should he leave a message? Or just wait for another time to drop by? He decided to leave a message. "Kyle, it's Eric Price. I was driving past, saw your sign, and ...."

The phone picked up. "Wait for me, Eric. I live in back. I'll be right out."

Eric walked back to his rental car and leaned against the door, wondering if Kyle would come through the clinic or the kennel. His heart was beating a tattoo. Suddenly he felt nervous. After two decades, would they have anything in common?

# Chapter Fourteen

U NIMAGINABLE," ERIC TOLD his computer. It was the word that kept recurring from the seconds he drove away from Kyle's clinic. Now, sitting at the computer, he could not remember getting on the freeway. He could not remember the drive back to the hotel. He stared at the computer's welcome screen and saw, instead, Kyle jogging along the path from the side of the clinic, grinning like a Halloween pumpkin. The same grin from two decades ago. For the first time in their lives they hugged. Kyle, the once-shy Kyle, grabbed Eric and Eric, suddenly flooded with feeling, returned the hug.

"What are you doing here?" Kyle asked, as they walked the stone path to the right of the clinic. Kyle was staring at Eric, as if to find the nine-year-old beneath the man. For the same reason Eric wanted to stare at Kyle but he was embarrassed. He kept his eyes on the path as it circled around the back of the clinic. At the far end he saw a gray shingled cottage surrounded by dozens of colorful flowers.

"Your house?"

"My house. But tell me, what are you doing here? How did you find me?"

"Work brought me here," Eric said. "I'm with the FBI now. I figured to take a break and visit the beach. As for finding you, I saw your sign. I thought, How many Kyle Prenners could there be in the U.S.?

And if there are others, probably none that spent his boyhood rescuing stray animals."

Kyle opened the cottage door and they were blocked from entering by an excited, tail-wagging, body-wiggling, large chocolate Labrador Retriever. The dog sniffed Eric's legs, then the hand he extended, approved him and showed her delight by running circles around both men.

"Java. My best girl," Kyle said. He invited Eric to examine his bachelor pad, built to his specifications: two bedrooms and two baths—the guest room intended for his parents' visits—a large living room dominated by Kyle's piano and separated from the kitchen area by a granite-topped bar and two tall stools.

Eric walked to the piano, glanced at the open sheet music, and remembered how Kyle loved playing piano. As a boy he could not be persuaded to leave the piano for a game of softball or hide-and-seek or a Boy Scout outing or a rainy day game of Chutes and Ladders.

"This isn't the same piano you used to have, is it?"

"Are you kidding? That was a baby grand. It wouldn't fit in this room. Actually, it didn't fit in my folk's place, either."

"I remember, now. It filled up the dining room."

"They got rid of the dining room furniture." Kyle chuckled. "And never had dinner guests—other than you—except in summer, when they could barbecue."

Kyle had walked over to the piano. He ran a finger along the keys. When the sound died out, he said, "This is a spinet. It's like the spinet I started on. When my folks thought I showed promise, they replaced it with the baby grand."

"And you were how old then?"

"Five."

Eric leaned over to peer at the pictures mounted on the wall over the piano. Seascapes.

"All local beaches. Taken with a Canon Powershot G2," Kyle told him.

"Photography—a new hobby?"

Kyle nodded, then steered Eric to the wall over his sofa to point out photos taken in various area nature parks. He began naming them. "Cleveland National Forest—a short drive west. That's Majorska Canyon, also a short drive. That's Dana Point Headlands, before they began construction of luxury homes. What's really neat is we can take dogs hiking, off leash. And I've never seen any dog fights."

Due to the piano, Kyle's living room was not spacious enough for seating larger than a love seat and a recliner. Both faced a flat screen television, not large but, as Kyle told him, new. "Twenty-eight inch," Kyle said, clicking it on to show the great resolution. "This replaced the second-hand TV I had for years. I never used to watch anything but news, until I got this."

Eric asked what he usually watched, now that he had a set with great resolution.

"Netflix," Kyle said. "I like science programs, like 'Dogs Decoded.' And anything that transports me to other countries, if it includes scenery, landscapes, cities and towns. I'm a homebody and a virtual traveler."

Eric remembered the plans they exchanged as kids, both wanting to visit other lands, pipe dreams of backpacking together. As adults they continued to have the same dream of travel, but neither had done so.

Beer cans in hand, they moved to Kyle's rear patio, which faced a canyon. Kyle told him it was Laguna Wilderness Park. He pointed out various things he planted near the patio, "The tall ones with orange flowers: Bird of Paradise. The tall ones with purple flowers: Lily of the Nile. That vine is bougainvillea. Over there, a banana tree; and over there, bamboo."

Eric stopped him. He knew nothing about gardening and would never remember the names of things he was seeing for the first time. "Going back to the piano, do your parents still have the baby grand?"

That began a recap of Kyle's history. Kyle told him that after he was rejected by Julliard he knew he did not have what it took to be a great concert pianist. He was good at science, and decided on medicine. And since he was not good with people, Kyle said, nodding at Eric and letting his voice trail off.

"Absolutely not true, and I'm proof—unless you exclude me from the category of people."

Kyle laughed. "In general, it was true, at least from the time I reached teen years. I'm good with four-leggeds, and they're far more tolerant and forgiving. Even box turtles like me," he added with a chuckle. "I really did rescue a box turtle."

Eric shook his head as if finding this incomprehensible. Not knowing what else to say, he told Kyle how startled he was to see his name on a sign as he was en route to Laguna Beach.

Kyle corrected him. "You were headed toward Main Beach. It's one of a dozen or more beaches along the Laguna coast." Java was stretched out on the concrete at Kyle's feet. He leaned over to scratch her stomach. "Actually, it's one long beach separated by rocks and cliffs. Each section has its own name. Diver's Cove, Sleepy Hollow, Thousand Steps—those are a few of the more colorful names."

"Sounds like you really love living here."

"How'd you guess?" Kyle went on to tell Eric it was possible to walk the length of the beach if you had the stamina and were willing to climb rocks. "I'll show you, if you're interested. The entire beach is a nature preserve."

Eric stood up. "I'm game." As they walked back through the house Eric asked about Thousand Steps. Kyle grinned. "That's the one you want to see?"

"Not especially. Just curious."

"To begin, you need to know that most of the beaches are unlike Main Beach, which is at street level. The others are below cliffs. To reach them, you walk stone steps, sixty steps, more or less. But at Thousand Steps there are more than two hundred. Imagine climbing those steps carrying heavy scuba gear. By the time you've climbed two hundred-plus, they feel like a thousand."

No, Kyle told him, he didn't dive but hoped to take lessons one day. "And I'm not a surfer dude, either." He looked hard at Eric. "You look like you could be a surfer dude."

Eric laughed. "Maybe one day."

"When I take diving lessons?" Kyle told him it seemed he never had enough time between his veterinary practice, the boarding kennel, and Java. "Either we're hiking or we go to the beach. Java loves the water and is obsessed with chasing a Frisbee."

The dog had followed them back through the house and was pacing near the front door. Hearing her name she whined, as if to say, Let's go. They piled into Kyle's SUV, with Java standing in back looking out the window, too excited to sit. Just before reaching PCH Kyle turned right and went up to Cliff Drive.

"It's hell to find a parking spot here during tourist season," he said. But it was late June, early evening, and there were several open slots along Cliff Drive. He leashed Java, stuffed quarters into the meter, and they walked a short distance to Heisler Park, a park built above the cliffs. They stopped to watch the sun as it inched lower over the Pacific, shining a golden spotlight on the blue water and streaking the sky with coral. A muted barking traveled across the water. Kyle pointed to reefs in the distance where sea lions made their home.

They walked a macadam path rimmed on the cliff side with a waist-high protective fence of metal tubes. Kyle pointed to a drinking fountain on their left, set into a boulder so that it appeared natural. He talked about the history of the area until Eric changed the subject. Did he have anyone special in his life?

Kyle shook his head. When he asked where Kyle went to meet the opposite sex, Kyle grinned. "I'm waiting for Ms. Right to find me. If it's my karma, it will happen."

Still shy, Eric concluded. Kyle did seem more outgoing than he remembered, but that may be due to the surprise he sprung on him. When Kyle returned the question, Eric told him he never had enough time or money for a serious relationship. From high school on he had juggled school and part-time jobs. "That kind of broke me into the routine of multi-tasking."

"And since then?" Kyle asked.

"After law school I joined a megalaw firm, the lowliest associate on the totem pole. Not fun. Newbies are given twenty hours of work per *day*. We were expected to do it in eight, or ten. So, again, no time for a social life."

"But now you're with the FBI. You should have more time."

"Fingers crossed." Eric was startled as the words left his mouth. He had not used that expression in many years. Kyle seemed not to notice. "Well," Eric continued, "Nine months ago I was in Quantico, now I'm here. Rolling stones don't gather harems." This time Kyle looked startled. "Bad, yeah, I know," Eric said. "I guess I won't appeal to any poets."

They stopped to watch a scuba diver. "How long do you expect to be here?" Kyle asked. "I'd like to take you to some of my favorite places, great seaside restaurants, hiking, whatever gets you going."

"How long will I be here? I really don't know. I'm with the white collar crime unit. We're working a big fraud case just now. When that's done, I'll get another local assignment. There always are white collar crimes to investigate. I could be here two years, maybe three."

"So we can make plans," Kyle said with contentment.

They walked along in silence for a while. Then Kyle asked if he looked different. Eric said, "Yeah, taller."

"But not as tall as you. You sneaked past me." Kyle grinned and Eric was about to do so when Kyle asked about Eric's sisters. He told him both were married now, both had families. No, he didn't see them often. Eric lost touch with them when they were separated, after their parents' death. Each went to live with a different relative; they were miles apart.

There was nothing to say after that but they had reached Main Beach and stopped to watch a lively volleyball match. When they walked on, they came to Java's favorite beach, with few people, all sitting with backs to the cliff wall, watching the surf. Kyle and Eric took turns tossing the Frisbee, which had Java running back and forth and quickly exhausted her. It was dark when they returned to the clinic. They spent another ten minutes in Kyle's SUV, deciding on a date and time to meet again for dinner.

❧

Eric realized he had wasted another half an hour reliving every detail of the past few hours. When did he last feel this energized? This relaxed? Had he ever felt both energized and relaxed? He reminded himself there was work to do.

After clicking open the word processor Eric sat back, trying to gather his thoughts. The fraud investigation was intense. The prosecutors were dead-set to convict the Archers. Were they being myopic? Were they investigating the wrong company? Eric knew he would have to present his findings to Yolanda, but he was reluctant to shift his mood to something stressful. He returned to doing research for Nicole.

∽

Carly set the meeting of employees for noon. Once she knew at least a half dozen people were coming, she left messages for the FBI agents, Price and Ruiz, telling them she would be late returning from lunch due to a dental appointment. She was fearful about being followed.

This fear, bordering on paranoia, led Carly to take extra care with everything. She told her former co-workers to bring bag lunches and drive to a nearby park in Tustin. The park she chose didn't have tennis or basketball courts, nothing more than a playground. That meant parking would be easy and there would be few witnesses to their gathering. Carly felt as if she were setting up a spy network. She had lied to FBI agents. Now she really felt like a criminal.

∽

Eric had no idea where Carly Daniels spent lunch break, and really did not care. Since she would be late returning to the office today, as he entered the FBI offices he stopped at Nicole's cubicle in the secretarial enclave and invited her to lunch.

"You have information for me?

"A bit," he said, holding his thumb and index finger to create a small circle.

"Same place?" she asked.

"Why not?"

Walking to the restaurant Eric had to remind himself to walk slower for this tiny woman. He also reminded Nicole he was not giving legal advice. "So don't ask. What I have is simply the results of research, something anyone could do."

She grinned. "Anyone who knows how to do the research, of course."

They walked quickly, having little else to discuss after exchanging where they lived, Nicole with her mother, Eric in a hotel. Once seated with their sandwiches and iced tea, Eric realized Nicole was so eager to hear what he had learned that she was not eating. He was chewing the chunk he bit from his sandwich and she was watching him, waiting for him to begin. He swallowed quickly and put down his sandwich.

"Bad news-good news," he summarized. "First, it looks to me as if your mother will be a party to fraud, if she goes through with this. That's the bad news. When this type of fraud involved people with AIDS, many were prosecuted and went to prison. The good news is I found no prosecutions of seniors who participate in these schemes."

"Does that mean she's safe? She can take the money?"

"See, Nicole, that is something I cannot do. I will not give you advice. I must limit this to what I learned, nothing more. And with a caveat. It is possible some seniors were prosecuted but there are no accessible records. In other words, maybe it happened but I did not find records of this."

"And maybe it did not happen? What's the likelihood any seniors were prosecuted?"

"My guess, and it's just a guess, probably none."

"So, if she won't be prosecuted and can get money—"

"Here's another caveat. One that might cause you to bank the money, if your mother does this. In other words, don't spend it for several years. I found one case where a private investor, a retiree, sued the insured—also a senior—after the policy was canceled by the insurer."

Nicole was about to take a bite of her sandwich. She put it down on the plate. Her mouth formed the word, "Oh," but she did not speak.

"The insured was eighty," Eric continued, "a survivor of the Holocaust. She was dependent on her brother. When he had bypass surgery and was unable to work, she was lured to participate in the scheme. She knew nothing about insurance."

"Like my mom."

"When she was sued—for the million dollar death benefit—she was shocked."

"I would be shocked. My mom would have conniptions."

"She was doubly shocked to find the investor was told she was dying. This lady was in perfect health. The investor was given false medical reports, to convince him it was a good investment."

Nicole said, "Oh my God."

Eric continued. "The investor used his retirement savings to buy her policy."

"Are you saying if my mom does this she could be ripping off another elderly person?"

"Possibly."

"But she was told the investors were wealthy people in Hong Kong."

"It's likely she was told that to reassure her. These companies don't reveal anything about the investors to the insureds."

"Could they come after me, if my mom names me beneficiary and I have to sign away beneficiary rights?"

Eric shrugged. "Anyone can sue for any reason."

Nicole took another bite of her sandwich. She chewed slowly, thinking. "What happened to that woman? Did she have to pay the investor?"

"There was no way she could have done so. She was paid five thousand for her role in the fraud. The investor paid half a million to buy the $1 million death benefit."

Nicole nodded. She did not expect what came next.

"Her defense could have cost a hundred thousand. She was lucky. The rabbi at the synagogue to which she belonged was friends with a Christian lawyer who agreed to take the case pro bono—for free."

"Did he succeed? Was he able to get her extricated from the lawsuit?"

Eric nodded.

"If that happened to my mom, they probably would come after me to make good on the loss."

"So far I haven't seen evidence of that. But there could be other lawsuits, ones I did not discover. Or lawsuit threats that never reached court, and were settled quietly."

"In other words, many more risks than being nabbed for fraud."

Eric said nothing.

Nicole smiled. "So you are not going to advise me to avoid this or to do it. Right?"

"Right."

"Do you want to know what I decided?" She grinned at him.

"I'm not sure. What I am sure about is I don't want to know if you become a party to fraud. Keep me in the dark." His tone was serious but he smiled.

"Relax, Eric. I definitely will not. Even if we banked the money, I could put my job at risk by participating in fraud. But if my mom goes ahead with it, using one of my brothers or sisters as beneficiary, they have to consider they could be sued one day by an investor. Be prepared for legal fees and a hassle in court."

Eric nodded.

"Good enough, Eric. Thanks for everything. And next time lunch is on me. No 'shop talk.'"

# Chapter Fifteen

CARLY WATCHED WITH EXCITEMENT as the Archer employees drove up, parked, and carrying their lunches, walked to where she sat on a blanket spread on the grass. A few others had brought blankets but it was not enough; some sat on benches. It was an unusually large gathering in the middle of a work day. When Carly worried it might raise suspicion, especially if anyone knew they were plotting against federal prosecutors, Ben said they should start off with their heads bowed and their hands clasped, as if in prayer.

Within fifteen minutes of her arrival everyone was there, everyone except Terri McGuire. She asked who had contacted Terri.

"She was on my list," Sherri said, "but I couldn't reach her on her cell and her home number's not listed."

"You didn't know?" said George. "Her home number's not listed because her husband is Tom McGuire. The AUSA. That means assistant US attorney. The prosecutor."

Carly felt her stomach flip. It was a common name; she never suspected.

"Was she spying at Archer?" Allison asked.

"She would not spy for Tom," Marcia said. "He's a creep. She was talking divorce for the last couple of years, and would have but she worried about supporting her daughter, an adult child with serious health problems. Maybe she didn't tell any of you, but believe me, she was one unhappy camper."

Carly bit her lower lip, feeling acute pain as she realized how much worse life was for Terri, trapped, worried about her child.

"So now she's gone to the other side," Roger said, as if it were a fact.

"If she did, it had to be because she had no choice," Marcia said. "Maybe it was stick with him or she'll be charged, too."

Someone asked if Terri would testify against them. No one knew and they had no idea how to find out.

"What would she say, if she testified against us?" Carly asked.

"She might lie," Sherri said. "That happens in trials." Everyone looked at her, as if she had inside knowledge. Sherri shrugged and gave a small smile. "I read a lot of mysteries."

Carly glanced at her list. Worried she might forget something, she had made up an agenda. "Okay," she said. "Let's plan to ask our lawyers, those of us who have a lawyer. And let's move on. We need to share information and plan how to handle our defense."

Greg said that anyone who needed a lawyer could have one, paid by Archer. Aidan had phoned to tell him this and said to let everyone know.

"That's good to know," said Isabel, a woman in her sixties. "I tried Legal Aid but they don't take on people who have *any* assets. I have a home. What really stinks is I don't qualify for a second loan because I'm not employed."

"My husband didn't want me to take up Aidan's offer," Allison said. "He doesn't want us to owe them anything. We have to think of ourselves first."

Marcia said she accepted the offer after Greg phoned to tell her. Linda said she planned to do so, as well. "I spoke with her—the attorney. She said she has to work for me, in confidence, not Archer, even if they pay her bill. So I'm okay with it."

"I was called to testify at the grand jury hearing," Roger said. This was news to Carly. She remembered discussing it with her attorney. Had she forgotten the date?

A few others chorused Roger.

"I told them I knew about the fraud," said Darla. "I told them I pointed this out to Aidan, and he didn't care. Then I told Blake, and he laughed."

"Did that really happen?" Roger asked. "Or is that what the prosecutors wanted you to say?"

"They agreed not to charge me, if I testify to this."

"Well, I told them what they didn't want to hear," said Roger. "I told them that I didn't like Aidan, and I didn't like Blake. That was the truth. But I wasn't going to smack them in the head or testify against them. I knew nothing about fraud and to this day I have no idea if there was fraud. They subpoenaed me anyway. Maybe they thought that would scare me into saying what they wanted to hear. It didn't."

Carly looked around the group. Other than Roger, no one would meet her eyes.

"What's happening?" she asked. "Something else I don't know about?"

"Didn't you see the papers today? Or watch TV news last night?" Marcia asked.

Carly shook her head. She was afraid to ask. Roger cleared his throat. "The grand jury issued indictments."

"For Archer Life Settlements?"

"Yes."

Every head was lowered, as if they did not want to look at her. In a tiny voice Carly asked, "For Aidan? For Blake?"

Roger answered. "Yes."

Carly swallowed. "For me?"

"Yes."

Carly felt her stomach seize. She stood up, shaky on her legs. "I better go," she said. "I have to phone my attorney."

Carly returned to the Archer building to collect her belongings. The indictment meant her work for the FBI was over. While there, she used her cell phone to leave two messages for Irwin Stanley. She placed a third call from her truck, while sitting in the driveway when she arrived home. As the hours passed, she kept looking at the clock. The phone remained silent. Again and again she checked the battery on the cell phone.

Carly was cleaning up the kitchen after dinner when the doorbell rang. A tall, husky man stood there, facing sideways, looking at her garden. On the sleeves of his navy windbreaker were printed the words, "U.S. Marshal." He turned toward her as Carly approached the screen door. A necklace with a badge rested on his chest, shining up at her as she stared. Heart thumping, worried she was about to be arrested, Carly opened the screen door.

"United States Marshal," he said, and held out a batch of papers. "You've been served."

Carly froze. She stood in the doorway, clutching the papers to her chest, watching the man walk to his car and drive off. When finally her legs began to work, they woodenly brought her to the dining table. She sat. Her heart thumped faster, like an oil derrick, as she read the summons and criminal complaint. *The United States of America versus Carly Nolan Daniels.* She was charged with obstruction of justice. Her head slumped to her chest.

Her cell phone rang. It was attorney Stanley. "Are you alone?" he asked.

"My son is here." Carly glanced at Ethan. He was on the computer. He may be too absorbed to listen to her conversation, but rather than risk it Carly moved to the back yard with her cell phone. The news could not be good, not after being served, not after the way her attorney began the conversation. She told him she was outside now and had privacy.

"You were indicted. You have to appear at court to enter a plea."

Carly sat down hard, gasping for breath, as if she had run a race. She placed a hand on her thumping chest, hoping to still it. "A plea to obstruction of justice?" She told him she had been served with a summons and criminal complaint.

"Yes."

He told her they needed to discuss this prior to the hearing.

"May I phone you tomorrow? My son is still up and about."

He agreed. Carly closed her phone and sat there, trying to think how to handle this, how to handle herself. She went back inside and prepared a cup of valerian tea. For the first time, the tea had no effect. She put on ear phones with soothing, water music. Carly had bought the CD to help Ethan get used to background noise without becoming distracted or upset. The music calmed her enough for the third remedy. She invited Ethan to join her for a walk on the beach.

When they returned, Ethan went to bed. And the panic attack returned.

She spun around quickly, as if motion would stop it, her eyes jumping from wall to wall, as if something in the room or on the walls might help. Nothing. She stood stiffly in the middle of the living room, unable to decide what to do. Liquor could dull the senses, she knew, but it also could make you depressed. She did not need to be more depressed. Her cell phone trilled, startling her because of the late hour. With relief, Carly saw from the caller ID it was Ben.

"I'm comin' home early," he said.

"You saw the TV? The news?"

"Yeah, but that's not the only reason. It's a slow night here. They don't need me, no sense staying." Carly knew what he did not say, "They don't need me and I bet you do." Yes, Ben, I do, she thought.

When Ben arrived, she invited him to the back yard and told him to bring a joint for her. His mouth fell open. "I need to relax," she explained. "Nothing I've tried really works."

He handed her a joint. "Want instructions?" She shook her head. Ben watched as she lit up and took a puff, another, another, as if she needed to force it to work fast.

"I have to call attorney Stanley," she said. She took a several more long, deep puffs, coughed, and began to giggle. Ben grinned. He watched as her eyelids slid down. He poked her. Her eyelids flew open. He took the joint from her.

"Neophyte," he said in a mock scolding voice. "Guess you're done, huh?" She agreed. Falling asleep was not her intent, not this early. "I guess I shouldn't try this alone, when I have trouble sleeping," Carly said. "I might burn the house down."

Together they watched the eleven o'clock news. Carly was aghast at the excitement of reporters. "You'd think they were watching an earthquake. Or a high speed chase," she mumbled.

"They're reading from prosecutors' scripts," Ben told her. "They're human tape recorders. With some doubt about the human part." The more he said, the angrier his voice became. "They're tape recorders," he said again. "They repeat what they're told."

Carly had not looked at newspapers after returning from the employee meeting. She did not want to see news of the indictments in black and white. Now she heard it: The grand jury returned indictments of Aidan Archer, Blake Archer, and Archer Life Settlements— more than forty counts including mail and wire fraud, conspiracy, and money laundering. They faced maximum sentences of twenty years. An employee, Carly Daniels, was charged with obstruction of justice, which carried a maximum sentence of ten years.

"I'm never turning on news when Ethan is around," Carly said. "I don't want him to hear this."

The broadcasters gave a nod to defense attorneys, reporting that each said his client was absolutely and completely innocent, and they would vigorously fight the charges.

"Vigorously," Ben muttered. "Yeah. Right."

The audience, Carly knew, would think what she so often thought. "Lawyer-speak, even when they know their clients are guilty."

Again the next day the indictments were front page news in local newspapers and third page in national newspapers. Reporters attempted to interview the defendants, without success, and they reported the "No comment," from each.

When Carly joined Aidan and Blake Archer at court to hear the charges read aloud and enter a plea, she turned to stone. Before entering the court her attorney again urged her to plead guilty. He was adamant and Carly was equally adamant in her refusal. But everything changed in the court room. Confronted with the formality of the legal system, confronted with the reality of being an accused felon, Carly was unable to speak. She could do no more than nod agreement when the judge addressed her. Judge Easterly insisted she speak. He wanted to be certain she agreed with her attorney's "Not guilty," plea. "Yes," she said in a choking voice.

When Carly and attorney Stanley exited the court house, reporters rushed them, shoving microphones at her face, snapping pictures. The shouts of, "Why'd you do it, Carly?" followed her as she plowed her way through the mob.

The next morning Carly's photograph was on the front page of local newspapers—a broken woman with her head down. She kept hearing, "Why'd you do it, Carly?" And she hid the newspaper so that Ethan would not know.

Thus it began, everything she feared and things she did not know enough to fear.

# Chapter Sixteen

SHORTLY AFTER THE INDICTMENT her attorney received a letter inviting Carly to meet with the prosecutors. Attorney Stanley sent a copy to Carly, attaching a note to phone him to discuss the meeting. Ben said he would go with her. "No way am I going to let you go through this alone. And you know you can't count on much help from a cretin lawyer. They're just out for themselves."

"What can you do?" Carly wrung her hands. "This is not fighting city hall. This is the U.S. government."

"I don't give a rat's ass. You did nothing wrong. I want to make sure they get that. No one screws with you when I'm around. No one's gonna twist your words while I'm sitting there." Carly nodded. She knew she could not get through this alone.

She phoned the lawyer. To save time Irwin Stanley suggested they skip an office visit and get right to it, right then. That was fine with Carly; it would spare having to fill the gas tank.

"The prosecutors will offer you a plea deal," he said. He wanted to know what the prosecutors had on her. He kept asking questions in that vein and she had no answers. "You must have done something or they wouldn't be after you," he insisted.

Her spirit sank lower. That's what most people would think. That was what she used to think, when she read newspaper stories or saw on television that someone was indicted. Now it was her, Carly Daniels, guilty without a trial, without witnesses, without evidence. She took a deep breath, trying to calm herself, trying to think.

"Simply being an employee at Archer seems to be enough," she told him. Carly could hear the fatigue in her voice. She hoped it did not come through to this stranger who was hired to help her. She wondered how much the Archers were paying him. He urged her to think harder.

"If I was involved in fraud, why wasn't I paid more? Why wasn't I involved in any decisions made by the company?"

His reply did not reassure her. "I don't have to believe in your innocence. My job is to make the prosecutors prove their case."

"If I agree to testify against the Archers, I will have to lie."

"Six of one, half a dozen of the other."

Carly had no idea what he meant. "Does a plea deal mean I have to claim I knew things? Will I have to say I am guilty?"

"Exactly. What do you have to offer them? You offer information, you agree to testify against the Archers, and we may get a plea agreement in which you serve no time at all."

Carly shook her head, trying to clear her thoughts. She was glad attorney Stanley could not see her. She was trying to take notes and her hand shook so much she knew she would not be able to read what she had written.

Attorney Stanley told her to call him when she came up with something to offer the prosecutors. "Preferably something sexy."

"Sexy?" She was appalled.

"In legal parlance it means something to excite the prosecutors. Something to help them convict the Archers."

"What can I say, when I knew nothing?"

"If you don't come up with something, the prosecutors will tell you."

"And then I have to testify to this? Which means I have to lie in court? Under oath?"

"I hear you. Keep in mind, Ms. Daniels, hundreds of innocent people do this every year. If it means you don't go to prison, isn't it worth doing?"

Carly told him she would have to think about it.

She imagined saying good-bye to Ethan and going to prison. She imagined seeing Ethan and Ben only when they visited her in prison. She thought about Ethan growing up without her and without the help he needed that only she could provide. Each of these images pushed her to take the plea deal.

Before Ethan returned from school, when they knew they had privacy, Carly discussed it with Ben. Ben did not trust Irwin Stanley. She wondered if her paranoia was infecting Ben. Or was he right? If so, how would she know? She knew so little about the law, about courts, about lawyers. Her television education amounted to storytelling with happy endings. The good guys always won. Nothing to do with real life.

The following day Carly phoned Irwin Stanley. First, she repeated the description of her job duties. Then she told him that prior to her computer searches for the FBI she was completely and totally ignorant of anything approximating fraud at Archer.

"Even now, I am not sure that Archer is responsible for the fraud. But if the company is, none of us peons had anything to do with it."

Attorney Stanley told her not to say that to the prosecutors. "If you're going to play dumb, don't look smart, don't talk smart. Be completely dumb."

Before hanging up he said he would contact the prosecutor, Calvin Cutter, to set up the appointment. He asked Carly to give him dates and times convenient for her; he would try to set an appointment within those parameters.

"Keep in mind, Ms. Daniels, he's expecting a plea deal. Think what you want to get out of this. That should motivate you to find something you can offer in exchange."

After hanging up, Carly could not sit still. She paced the floor. She thought about cleaning the oven or the refrigerator or weeding the garden. But she did not have patience to do any of these things. Exercise would be helpful, but as agitated as she felt, she lacked the energy to ride her bicycle.

She phoned Marcia, then Allison, and a few others. Everyone was being called to the Santa Ana office of the Department of Justice to finalize their plea agreements. Allison had gone the day before.

"I had to do it, Carly. He told me if I didn't cooperate, it wasn't too late to file charges against me for obstruction of justice."

"What does that mean? What does he expect from you?"

"I'm supposed to tell them everything I know. And testify at the trial. Except I don't know anything they want to hear. They told me things they think I know. But I don't. They hinted I could admit to knowing these things, in the event I forgot due to anxiety. Then I could testify to them, and they would not charge me."

"Did you do that?"

"My husband went with me. He said we'll talk it over at home and let them know. I think he wants me to do whatever it takes so that I won't go to jail. We have another appointment next week."

When Carly did not reply, Allison added, "I must think about my baby, Carly. You understand, don't you?" Carly did understand. Too well.

She did not feel better after speaking with any of her former co-workers; all told pretty much the same story. Why was she the only employee who was indicted? Because she refused to lie? Because she balked at committing perjury? But Roger refused to lie. He was not indicted. Was it because she was a single mom? Because she had a special needs child? Did the prosecutors think it would be easy to scare her into doing what they wanted?

She was scared. Carly hated the thought, but much as she fought it, it was real: She was afraid of the US government. That brought her spirits even lower. Afraid of the US government: How could this happen? She knew it happened. Didn't the government treat a star basketball player—or was it a football player—as if he were a terrorist, and then not charge him with anything? He was arrested and imprisoned for two weeks, not because he was a criminal but, the government claimed, to assure he would serve as a witness in a pending trial. But he was never called to testify. When he sued former U.S. Attorney General Ashcroft for violating his constitutional rights, the Supreme Court threw out the suit. Which meant prosecutors could do that to anyone.

Then there were all those innocent people who were sent to jail, sometimes for life, sometimes for death, and exonerated after years and years of being victims of the justice system.

Would she be among the numbers?

Carly felt fear rush through her like fever. Trying to calm herself, she suddenly wondered how long she could hide this from Ethan. If she went to prison, he would have to be prepared. But she was not ready to talk about it. She was too close to tears. Ethan could not read facial clues but if she began to cry, Ethan would know she was frightened. And she would not be able to reassure him.

༄

Irwin Stanley set up the appointment with Calvin Cutter, the assistant United States attorney who supervised the Orange County field office, a division of the Los Angeles Department of Justice. Ben drove the pickup. Carly was visibly shaking. The Orange County field office rented office space in one of the buildings at Civic Center Drive. As their truck neared Civic Center Drive it fell in with a line of cars crawling up and down streets, everyone searching for cheaper, on-street parking or the only alternative, a parking lot not decorated with a "Filled" sign. Finally, Carly spotted a parking structure without the ominous sign. They were required to prepay for an entire day.

"Seven dollars? There goes tonight's pizza," Ben joked.

"An entire day?" It had not occurred to Carly that they might not arrive home on time for Ethan's school bus.

"I know what you're thinking," Ben said. "It's a long shot he would have trouble with bullies on the one day we can't meet the bus. Get that out of your mind."

The parking structure was several blocks from their destination. They walked and walked, passing one tall, concrete, robust building after another. Carly felt like a bug about to be squashed by the giant foot of the government. She could not halt her thoughts. Stupid school girl, she told herself, believing everything she was taught—idealistic slogans and philosophy. All seemed mammoth lies. This was not a government by and for the people, not for ordinary people like her, like Scott, like Ben. They were not important. They had no power.

Her feet pained her. Carly's heeled shoes were not designed for fast, long walks on concrete. Her spirit sank lower as she remembered the last time the government defeated her—her and her Scott—and how devastated her husband was when the Parma school board again refused reimbursement for Ethan's special school.

Today Ethan was in regular school with a few special education classes thrown in, but his progress was a direct result of those years at the special school. They taught Carly how to help Ethan at home, and they made it possible for Ethan to one day lead a normal life, hold a job, relate to people. After Carly and her husband spent every last dollar, they used credit card loans to finance the school, to give Ethan the experience of programs specific to children with autism and Asperger's—programs not available at the public school.

The school board knew their refusal to reimburse tuition violated federal law. They also knew Mr. and Mrs. Daniels could not fight them unless they, like the school board, had limitless funds. Not likely, when the couple paid sixty thousand dollars tuition each year. Not likely, after they refinanced their home to pay tuition. Not likely, after Scott lost his job and remained unemployed. The school board knew it was a slam-dunk, as did Carly and Scott.

Nor were they the only family caught in this trap. Carly remembered Scott's reaction to the newspaper story about the father of an autistic boy. The father, who was not a lawyer, filed suit pro se—for himself—against the school board in Akron, Ohio. He won reimbursement of nearly one hundred sixty thousand dollars, plus many concessions on behalf of his son. It was a tarnished win. The local bar association turned around and sued the father for practicing law without a license. The bar association demanded a fine of ten thousand dollars plus lawyer's fees and "a promise that he would not continue to assist other parents seeking to represent their own children in court."

A similar newspaper story told about a Parma couple who were denied reimbursement for the special school for their autistic son. The father, a nurse, took a second job, the mother, also a nurse, quit her job to learn law and fight the school board in federal court. She lost, filed an appeal, and lost at appeals court. The law firm hired by the school board claimed she could not represent her son because she was not an attorney, and the courts agreed. She petitioned the U.S. Supreme Court. The Supreme Court said, in effect, "Wrong. The parents have the same interest as their son." But when the family returned home, the school board continued to refuse reimbursement. The years passed. The boy grew older. The parents grew poorer. And the school board poured ten times the cost of tuition into the coffers of the law firm.

Carly's husband was obsessed with these news stories. What did they mean to Scott? The system was against them? They did not have a snowball's chance in hell? It did not take long for the pile-up to become too much—losing his job, their credit card loans growing at a phenomenal rate, their home foreclosed. They moved into Carly's parents' home, paying no rent although her parents had collected rent from tenants after moving to California. To pay for food, utilities, and gas for the car, Carly became a clerk at a card shop. They shopped for clothes at consignment stores. And Scott became increasingly withdrawn and depressed.

Now, for the first time, Carly realized the effect on Scott, who spent most of each day in an alcoholic haze, saying little more than he wished he could afford decent bourbon. He refused marriage counseling saying there was nothing wrong with him, the problem was their son. It was their son who was defective.

No, his exact words were, "Your son is the one who is defective. He ruined everything we had."

That was it. She ordered him out of the house. He would not leave. She threatened to get court orders for him to leave.

Carly was marching along with Ben, unaware of where they walked, lost in memories of the pain she associated with Parma, Ohio. Suddenly his voice broke into her memories.

"I don't know if we're close or what," Ben said. "I feel like a rat in a maze."

"Look!" Carly pointed to a map enclosed in glass and attached to a pole, like at shopping malls. They stared at it. The giant letter X was supposed to mark where they were, but they could not figure out how to get to the building. "They might help," Carly said, pointing to people standing alone or in small groups near one of the buildings. Some were talking, others were smoking. Some looked like lawyers, others like people waiting for a case to be heard. A few were so poorly dressed they might be released convicts returning for a parole hearing. The thought shamed Carly. She might, one day, be a convict. These people, like her, might be innocent victims of a system gone awry.

Once they found the correct building, Carly rushed to the first floor restroom. She felt the pressure of too much of everything: morning tea, walking and walking, and nerves. When she checked the mirror, she felt better. Today she wore mascara. That made tears prohibitive, no matter what happened at the meeting. *Ready to serve First Class,* she told herself and smiled.

As Carly walked back to the hall to where Ben waited, she was limping. She looked down to see the heel on her left shoe had broken off. She did not see the piece anywhere, not in the hallway nor in the restroom, when she returned to look for it. Had this happened before they entered the building? And in her anxiety she was unaware of it until now? To hide the broken shoe, Carly walked on her tippy toes.

Ben was pacing the hall. He turned as she approached. "Done making yourself gorgeous?"

"It was a struggle."

Carly saw how at ease Ben seemed in his one suit and tie. He looked as if he wore this outfit frequently, yet the last time was a friend's wedding and the time before was their mother's funeral.

They entered the office. A receptionist sat behind a glass partition, as in the dental office. Carly told her she had an appointment with Prosecutor Calvin Cutter. They were asked to take a seat. Ben whispered, "When did that lawyer whatshisface say he would be here?"

"Attorney Stanley. Irwin Stanley. Supposedly now."

Ten minutes later the door opened and a short, chubby, balding man in a brown polyester suit hustled in, carrying a hefty leather brief-case the size of a small suitcase. Carly recognized him from the hearing and stood up. He walked over and greeted her as Ms. Davidson.

"Daniels," she said and reached down to shake his hand. Carly, in her heels, was a few inches taller than Irwin Stanley. Ben stood up, towering over Irwin Stanley. Despite the suit, Ben looked like a bruiser next to the squat lawyer.

"So you're Stan-the-man," Ben said. "Car trouble make you late?" Carly gave him a sharp glance, a reminder to "cool it." He cooled it slightly. When she introduced her brother and Irwin Stanley to each other, Ben ignored the lawyer's out-stretched hand. Attorney Stanley rushing in at the last moment did not endear him to her brother.

The phone rang, the receptionist answered and told them to follow her. When they entered his office the supervising assistant US attorney—AUSA—was standing but did not step away from his desk. Carly was surprised at how young he was. Calvin Cutter appeared to be no more than forty, tall with movie star features, and dark hair. He wore a navy suit with a striped tie, and a flag pin in the button hole. Another man stood near the window, leafing through a file he held open in his hands. He glanced at them, then returned his gaze to the file. He looked to be in his late fifties, paunchy, with thinning gray hair in an obvious comb-over.

Attorney Stanley introduced himself and his client, adding that Ms. Daniels' brother, Benjamin Nolan, would sit in, if they did not mind. Cutter introduced the man at the window—Tom McGuire. "Mr. McGuire is the lead prosecutor for U.S. versus Archer, et al." Cutter invited everyone to the conference table. When they were seated, he asked Carly if she had brought a proffer.

"I don't know what that is. Was I supposed to have one?" She looked at Irwin Stanley. He told McGuire they did not bring one.

"Okay, then," McGuire said. "We can begin. Start with when you first came to work at Archer Life Settlements."

And so it went for an hour, Cutter sitting back and listening and McGuire asking questions about her life, her work, if she took drugs—

prescription or otherwise—if she drank alcohol, asking details, going back to ask again, as if she had forgotten something or, perhaps, intentionally omitted something. He asked about the fraud, he asked specifics about the fraud. She told him that she was not aware the company bought policies from people who lied on their insurance applications. The third time he asked, Carly said she learned this recently, when she did research for the FBI investigators.

Damn, she thought. Her attorney told her not to say this. She could not even look at Irwin Stanley now.

McGuire looked at her with disbelief etched all over his face, then began to ask again, rephrasing the questions. "You knew, Ms. Daniels. We have evidence you knew about this for nearly two years. We have witnesses who will testify against you. It's time to come clean."

Two hours into the meeting, McGuire grew impatient with Carly's denials. He warned her she faced obstruction of justice charges for withholding information. If she persisted in her stubbornness, they would consider filing a superseding indictment.

"A revised complaint," her attorney explained.

McGuire went on. "We'll add other charges, conspiracy, mail fraud, wire fraud, money laundering. You have a choice, young lady. Confess now or face multiple charges."

"Why are you doing this to me?" Carly asked. She felt humiliated by the whiney voice. All this time, throughout all the questioning, she appeared calm, sitting with her hands folded on the table. Her jaw was stiff. She felt as if she had been biting back this question for the past two hours, fearful that asking might cause greater anger toward her.

"We're not doing anything to you," McGuire said. "You did this to yourself. It's all on you, Ms. Daniels."

Carly stared at him. He really believes this, she realized. He believes he is right and I did wrong. She bit her lower lip. She did not know what to say.

Finally her attorney broke the silence. "What do you think she is withholding?"

Cutter decided to add his two cents. "Admit she knew about the fraud. Admit she had access to the life insurance policies and the medical records. Admit she participated, directly or indirectly, in the conspiracy. We'll offer her immunity, if she testifies."

Irwin Stanley turned to Carly. "Immunity means you won't be prosecuted for any wrong-doing." Carly looked at Ben, silently asking his advice.

"This is shit! This system is f***ed up," Ben said, bolting from his chair. "You'll offer immunity if she lies? Come on, Carly, we're outta here."

Carly did not know what to do. She looked at attorney Stanley. He shrugged. Then he turned to the prosecutors. "In what way was Ms. Daniels a participant?"

"*She* knows," McGuire said, pointing his finger and glaring at Carly as if he could hypnotize her into saying what he wanted to hear. "She should tell you all about it, counselor. And you—you need to advise your client to plead guilty. Remind her that if she insists on going to trial, she can forget about the single charge of obstruction of justice. We'll pile on additional charges. She'll face twenty years."

"No," Carly said in a choked voice.

"Blackmail!" Ben growled. He had not taken his seat during this exchange.

"You mean extortion," attorney Stanley said, turning to Ben.

"Thanks." Ben said. "You're a big help." Fire seemed to leap from his eyes as they shifted from Cutter to McGuire and back again. "This is justice? Blackmail her into lying so you can win your case? Tell her it's the only way to save her skin? That's a lot of bullshit. You're the ones guilty of obstruction of justice."

Cutter smiled. Like a cat outside a mouse hole, Carly thought. "It's perfectly legal," he said, nodding at Carly. "Ask your lawyer. He'll confirm this. *Bordenkircher v. Hayes.* In 1978 the Supreme Court held there was absolutely nothing wrong with threatening additional charges that would increase the potential sentence, if a defendant refused to plead guilty. In other words, if we carry out the threat it will not violate due process—as long as the choice is made clear during plea negotiations.

We've made it clear. You have a choice, Ms. Daniels. You really need to think of your young child. I understand you're a single parent."

"Some choice," Ben said. "Like the choice of death by guillotine or death by firing squad." He grabbed Carly's hand and tugged. She let him lead her out of the office. Irwin Stanley followed them to the elevator.

"We need to discuss this further," he told Carly. "You could testify to what they want. Take a plea, get immunity. If you wait and later decide to take a plea, it won't be as good. You might get probation or a sentence of six months."

"F*** you," said Ben. "What sewer did you climb out of? The same as those guys?"

The elevator doors slid open, they filed in, and stood in silence, Ben and Carly near the right wall, Irwin Stanley near the left wall. At street level Ben grabbed her hand again and pulled her away from Stanley.

"I'm sorry," he said when they were a yard ahead of Stanley. "I hope I didn't make things tougher for you."

"It's okay. You can't make things worse. I wish I could show anger the way you do."

Ben stopped walking. He looked down at her foot. "Are you limping?"

She showed him her shoe.

"Here's a choice. Get the shoe fixed or go out for a nice lunch."

Carly wanted to smile. She did not manage it. "Pick a place, Ben-O."

# Chapter Seventeen

PRISON WAS A CERTAINTY. The prosecutors gave Carly three weeks to change her mind and plead guilty. One week passed. A second week passed. She could not get out of her head that a conviction for obstruction of justice could mean ten years in prison. Since the federal prison system had no parole, Ethan would be an adult before she was released. Exactly three weeks later, prosecutors filed the superseding indictment, stacking the charges. The basketful of felonies meant she now faced twenty years in prison. There was no hope. The feds held all the cards. Carly forced herself to find a way to deal with the reality, the reality of prison.

Were there prisons in or near Orange County? Carly hoped so. She wanted to spare Ben and Ethan a trip that took hours or worse—an airplane trip—when they came to visit.

Carly phoned attorney Stanley to ask if he could arrange for a prison near home. "The good news," Stanley told her, "is you would go to a federal prison. State prisons are torture chambers. Federal prisons are much better."

Cheery news, she thought.

"There are no federal prisons in California that are exclusively female," he continued. "The nearest that house women inmates are in Los Angeles and San Diego."

"Women inmates," she repeated, solemnly.

Stanley told her to use the internet—the Bureau of Prisons had a web site—to learn more about federal prisons. The internet also listed organizations that provided legal assistance to prisoners with children. Once again he warned Carly that the longer she waited to plead guilty, the worse it would be. The prosecutors would not offer such great leniency, if she changed her mind months down the road.

After the phone call, Carly again considered perjury and admitting to guilt. Would it be worse than abandoning Ethan? How would she explain it to him? But each time she pictured herself swearing on a Bible and then lying, she wondered how would she live with herself—for the rest of her life? One day she would have to explain her lies to Ethan, explain why she swore to tell the truth and then lied, why she did not go to prison but was a felon.

If she pleaded guilty and was labeled a felon, would she ever get a decent job? Would she find herself unable to get a decent rental? It was happening again, back and forth for days, fear festering like an infected wound. Her intestines were as troubled as her head. Whatever she tried to eat or drink tasted like cardboard or dishwater. Whatever she swallowed erupted inside her.

Carly's clothes began to sag. She did not need to step on a scale. Thin from the start, the mirror showed her a scarecrow. Only two months and she looked like this. She would have to find a way to keep down food, and stuff herself until she put the weight back on. Sleep was another problem. In sleep, monsters set traps for her, monsters caught her, tortured her, monsters chased Ethan and Carly, locked in a cage, was unable to help him.

She was haunted by the memory of the prosecutor, his impassive face, his voice—so arrogant—telling her he had the backing of the Supreme Court. Surely there was something she could do. Her attorney had no idea. Ben had no idea. The only idea was something Kyle suggested—a web site. That would not stop the trial. That would not prevent a conviction. It might be an emotional release, but she could not escape the total loss of control over her life.

With the trial months away, Carly kept telling herself she must find a way to stop feeling so helpless, some way to hold herself together. She wept while mopping floors, pulling weeds, showering. She sat for long periods, staring at nothing. *No, I will not be a victim. I am strong.* Needing to convince herself, Carly made up a list of difficulties she had faced throughout her life, beginning with childhood. Each topic was a roman numeral. Capital A beneath the topic were the details. Capital B was how she handled the problem.

Her earliest ugly memory was nasty kids who asked about her skin color, pointedly reminding Carly that her parents were fair-skinned, her red-haired mother especially so. When Carly came home sobbing, her parents told her she was chosen and more wanted than surprise babies that came from a mother's body.

As she looked through her list, Carly realized that she had never really dealt with anything, not even the problems with Scott. Did she lack courage? Intelligence? Stamina? As she squeezed out problems from her life, Carly realized she had a habit of denying them, of pretending the next day would better. "I'll think about it tomorrow." *My Scarlett O'Hara syndrome,* she chided herself.

Carly had never faced the horror Ben knew. When he was fourteen, then fifteen, he signaled his suffering and suffered alone, in silence. The signals were subtle—plunging grades at school, gloominess, quickness to anger, refusal to go to church. The family attributed it to teen years. Not until he was hospitalized for slashing his wrists did they learn he was a victim of sexual abuse.

When the phone call from her mother reached Carly, she had just landed in Paris. Carly remembered her panic when she heard, "He lost a considerable amount of blood. He's just hanging on."

Ben, her baby brother, a tortured teen, in such great pain he chose death. Carly traded schedules with another flight attendant and took the next plane back to New York, then paid for the first flight to Ohio. Neither she nor Ben ever saw themselves as anything but siblings, although Ben was a birth child and Carly adopted. Yes, it was Ben's problem but it was her parents' and it was hers. They were family.

Surrounded by love, Ben told them his other secret. So young, he saw the abuse as punishment for being gay. He could not return home. He was too ashamed to go to school, to leave the house, to go anywhere. Their father sent Ben and their mom to California to start their new life. He followed after he sold his hardware store and listed their home with a rental agent.

Family—that was the source of her strength. Deal with it directly, Carly told herself, or change course, but do not hide. Carly resolved to use her parents' example. It was the only way to regain control of her life.

How? How could she regain control of her life? The image of the prosecutor boasting about the Supreme Court in his hip pocket—was it possible he said this just to scare her? It worked. But maybe he was not telling the truth.

Carly phoned attorney Stanley, this time to ask the name of the Supreme Court case Cutter mentioned. Stanley told her Cutter was right. Carly asked again for the name and the spelling. She had to see for herself. What if short, squat, disheveled Irwin Stanley, like her, took Cutter's word for it? What if both were deceived?

Half an hour after Ethan went to bed, when she was certain he was asleep, she turned on the computer. Dread flowed through her. If Ethan called to her or came out of bed, she would not be able to hide her feelings. She wanted to keep Ethan innocent for as long as possible.

She typed the case name in the search engine and hit enter. The monitor filled with a list that continued for pages. There were legal treatises and law blogs from lawyers and law school professors. Cutter was right. As terrible as it seemed, the Supreme Court ruled the way Cutter said. Every lawyer and law professor strongly criticized the ruling in *Bordenkircher v. Hayes*. Most alarming was what happened to Hayes, the defendant. It did apply to her.

Carly stared at the computer screen, stunned. She opened her cell phone. She punched in Ben's number. She rarely phoned him at work. He would know something was up. Ben said, No, he was not too busy to talk but he wanted to go out back; it was more private.

"The Hayes case," she told him. "He forged a check for eighty-eight dollars. The prosecutor offered him a sentence of five years for a guilty plea. Hayes refused. The prosecutor threatened to stack charges, if he went to trial. And that's exactly what happened. Hayes was found guilty and sentenced to life in prison."

"Five years if he pled guilty and life in prison for refusing the prosecutor? What a whacked-up system this is."

"When it reached the Supreme Court, they said it was okay because the prosecutors told him this would happen during plea negotiations."

"I guess it means you can't count on fairness. Not from judges, for sure."

"I don't know what to do. When I told attorney Stanley I wanted to look up this case, he warned me again about going to trial, that the odds were a jury would find me guilty."

Carly remembered her voice as plaintive, when she told Irwin Stanley, "I do not want to believe the best choice for an innocent person is to plead guilty."

Stanley tried to be reassuring. "Lots of innocent people plead guilty. It's just good sense. If you place your life in the hands of a jury, don't blame them at sentencing. The jury will not know you faced ten to twenty years in prison."

"Ben, the Hayes ruling was in 1978. More than thirty years ago!"

"I don't know what to tell you, Carly. I'll try to get home early to give you a hand with research. Maybe we can find something helpful."

Over and over Carly read heated criticism of the Supreme Court's ruling. She learned nothing useful, other than the acronym, SCOTUS—the Supreme Court Of The United States. Again and again the Hayes ruling was criticized as infringing on a criminal defendant's Constitutional rights. One lawyer wrote that the opposite should have occurred: SCOTUS should have used this opportunity to develop rules to "prohibit using the prosecutor's charging power for tactical advantage."

Carly came across a paper by a Harvard Law School professor, William J. Stuntz, who called this "vindictive prosecution." Stuntz said the

Hayes case was tailor-made to halt the threat of capital punishment by prosecutors. If SCOTUS had done this, Stuntz wrote, it "would have spared many thousands of defendants guilty pleas produced by what amounts to legalized extortion."

Ben was right, without the fancy language.

She wished Ben were home. Ben liked to sound like a street thug, but it was pretense. He was an outstanding student until his sophomore year in high school. *Oh Ben,* she thought. *You're so much smarter than me. I'll bet you can find something in this stuff that escapes me.*

Carly felt faint, wavering between anger and despair. Not even a Harvard Law professor and others with similar pedigrees were powerful enough nor influential enough to make a difference. Did they do more than write? Carly lacked the stamina to continue. Her heart was thumping like an oil derrick. The nightmares of sleep were waking nightmares.

She stopped to microwave and drink a cup of tea, hoping it would calm her.

When she went back to the computer, she found a law scholar who detailed how prosecutors threatened friends or family of criminal defendants, unless the defendant pled guilty. What might they do to Ben?

Ethan was indirectly threatened, and the prosecutors knew that. But Ben, a bartender—would they accuse him of selling drinks to minors? That would involve his bosses, the owners. Ben worked at Rainbow Club since he was old enough to serve drinks. The owners would be able to hire a good attorney. No, prosecutors would not challenge the owners, but they might go after Ben for something else. Drugs, perhaps. They could set him up and threaten others into testifying against him.

Was she becoming paranoid? The pot Ben sometimes smoked could lead to a drug conviction. Although California state law allowed the sale and use of medical marijuana, both were crimes under federal law. Oh, yes, they had her here. If they threatened Ben, she could not let him suffer because she refused to cave.

Ben was right—this was blackmail, or, as Professor Stuntz wrote, legalized extortion. And Cutter was right—the Supreme Court permitted him to do this.

Harvard Law professor Stuntz wrote if the Court had used this opportunity to limit the power of prosecutors, "it probably would have spared some innocent defendants criminal convictions."

He means me, Carly thought, as tears flooded her eyes. Law professor Stuntz understood. His words were powerful. A Harvard law professor. But if he were her lawyer, she would be in the same pickle as now.

Carly felt crushed to discover those ultra-wise judges of the Supreme Court condoned a prosecutor who extorted someone to lie in court. How could they permit forcing someone to commit perjury? Cutter offered her immunity if she lied. According to the Supreme Court, this was permissible—as long as everything was on the table at plea negotiations.

Ben was right—the prosecutors were guilty of obstruction of justice. A lot of good it did to know this. But how could a conviction based on lies be justice? How could anyone believe such a conviction was fair and just?

The answer came immediately. It was happening—now—before any trial. The media's stories, with barely concealed excitement, portrayed everyone who was indicted as guilty. Reporters threw in the word "alleged," but that was nothing more than CYA. And the public believed in their guilt.

It would be far worse after a conviction. The media—newspapers, television, and talk radio—would convince the public the prosecutors had made the public safer.

Carly shut down the computer. She had learned more than she wanted to know. Knowledge was not power. She felt as weak and helpless as a baby. She wanted to fight this, but it was impossible. Awake, she feared what might happen tomorrow. Or next week. Or where she may be next year. How much worse to be haunted with these fears in sleep.

She rifled through the CD collection. She found Rodney Atkins,

"If You're Going Through Hell." She put the CD in the player, put the ear phones in her ears, and set the player for the song to repeat over and over. Yeah, she murmured; if you're scared, don't show it.

～

"You're goin' to get a crick in your neck."

Carly jumped. Ben was standing over her, shaking her shoulder.

"What time is it?" Carly was not sure she was awake. It felt as if Ben were in her dream, telling her to stop scaring herself.

"I quit at closing—two o'clock. So it's about ten after now. Why are you sleeping here? Bed bugs?" He chuckled.

"I wish," Carly said, and gave him a quick summary of what was worse than bed bugs.

He held up a finger, went to the refrigerator, took out a beer, and brought it to the computer. While it booted, Ben told her they would research together. "We'll look for someone who stood up to these prosecutors. Maybe a judge that overturned a conviction. Or a jury that acquitted defendants."

"Start with the search terms I found," Carly said. She stayed on the sofa. She told Ben to call her over, if he found anything good.

Ben typed in "prosecutorial misconduct" and hundreds of responses filled the computer screen, everything from legal treatises to news stories. He tried "vindictive prosecution," and had the same result. "Wrong search words," he said.

"Hey!" he called out. "This might be something. *Federal Prosecutors Likely to Keep Jobs after Case Collapse.*'"

A case that collapsed? Curious, Carly went over to the computer, leaned over Ben's shoulder and read. The article was from the December 2010 issue of *USA Today.* To the left of the title was the picture of an adorable baby girl, identified as five-months-old Sabrina Paige Aisenberg.

Carly remembered the story from television. She told Ben she could not stand to read further. She went back to the sofa. Ben read the details silently.

Baby Sabrina was kidnapped from her Florida home in November

1997. After searching the neighborhood, the parents called the police. Instead of searching for the baby, investigators focused on the parents as prime suspects. Less than two years later federal prosecutors in Tampa, Florida charged them with conspiracy and false statements. The prosecutors claimed as evidence wire taps they had placed on the Aisenberg's phones.

Ben turned to tell Carly about the phone taps. He had just read that prosecutors told a Grand Jury and a magistrate judge that Marlene Aisenberg could be heard telling her husband the baby was dead and buried, and that he did it.

Carly said she heard the phone tapes when the television show played them. She remembered it was impossible to understand the words on the tapes. No one at the TV show could understand them.

When Ben breathed something that sounded to Carly like, "Thank God," she asked what happened. He had just read about a federal judge who listened to the tapes and said he could not hear incriminating statements. Neither could another prosecutor. As a result, the federal judge ruled the tapes inadmissible.

"And, get this," Ben said with glee. "The judge accused the detectives of lying about the case. Then the judge ordered them to throw out all evidence from the phone taps. And it gets better. After that, the Justice Department withdrew the case against the parents. Case dismissed—in 2001. Four years after the baby disappeared."

"Do they say anything about the baby? Was she ever found?"

"Gotta check the search engine for that," Ben said. All he found was news about the Aisenbergs suing the prosecutors for malicious prosecution, and their lawsuit thrown out by a federal judge because prosecutors cannot be sued.

"So, bottom line," Carly concluded, "prosecutors can do anything to you, your family, your friends, not only with permission from the Supreme Court but they cannot be sued."

Ben did not answer. He was reading. When he said, "Uh oh," Carly said, "Tell me," but she was not sure she wanted to know.

"In 2008 those prosecutors went after the parents again. They claimed to have a new lead—a tip from a man they described as a 'credible' jail informant."

Carly went to the computer and leaned over Ben's shoulder. Prosecutors claimed the jailed informant told them the Aisenbergs agreed to sell him their boat if he disposed of Sabrina's body at sea. The informant never was named, and no charges were filed as a result of this "credible" lead.

The *USA Today* report said that a Justice Department inquiry found the lead prosecutor, Stephen Kunz, recklessly broke the rules when he charged the parents with lying about the baby's disappearance. At that point the government finally and completely closed its case against the parents, and paid their defense lawyers nearly $1.5 million.

Prosecutor Stephen Kunz did not suffer for his misdeeds, nor did he lose the power to persecute innocent people. He did lose his position as supervisor for the U.S. Attorney's office in Tampa, but was reassigned to the civil division. And in 2003 Kunz was reassigned, once again prosecuting criminal cases, this time in Tallahassee, Florida—a stone's throw from his previous den of iniquity.

Carly returned to the sofa and fell back onto the cushions. She worried about the prosecutors who were intent on sending her to prison. Did they have a history like that of Stephen Kunz? If so, how could she find out? And if she knew, what could she do about it, other than be emotionally prepared—if possible—for the worst?

Ben kept reading and summarizing aloud, unaware that Carly was past caring, unable to pay attention. "According to *USA Today*, Kunz was not a maverick. What he did to the Aisenbergs was not an isolated case. It's a lengthy report with numerous instances of prosecutors around the nation who wrongly persecuted people or withheld evidence or, in other ways, seriously violated the Constitutional rights of the people they victimized."

Ben stood up and stretched. "Geez," he said. "What a racket. Every one of these prosecutors kept their jobs. Some, like Kunz, simply went to another office. I could lose my job for any of a number of little things. But not them. They destroy people, and keep getting paid with taxpayer dollars."

"Before all this began," Carly told Ben, "I was a dope. A fool. I was naive and trusting." She went into the kitchen for a glass of water, talking all the while. "I thought research would help me understand. I learned facts don't matter. Truth doesn't matter. The law means nothing to prosecutors, since they can use their power to do anything to anyone. I just don't understand why this is allowed."

Ben was doing knee bends. He stretched his back and it crackled. "I'm goin' to keep looking," He sat down at the computer again. "There must be at least a few cases where lawyers turned the tables on prosecutors."

"Ted Stevens," Carly suggested.

"Sure, but did that happen with ordinary people? That's the question." Ben kept typing and reading. Now and then he gave Carly a quick summary. When prosecutorial misconduct was blatant and defendants had really sharp attorneys, some judges threw out the case. Two reversed a jury conviction. More often the judges found excuses to support the prosecutors—usually labeling it "harmless error." In effect, they were saying the defendants were so guilty that the wrong acts of prosecutors were inconsequential.

Carly realized that if the jury found her guilty, there would be no second chance. No one would say it was wrong. There was no DNA to prove a wrongful conviction.

Her breathing was shallow and rapid, her stomach in spasm. She recognized the panic attack. Carly had stocked up on valerian tea. Slowly drinking the hot tea was part of the process of calming herself. Just now she felt too tired to get up from the couch to microwave a cup.

"Ben, see if you can find anything about viatical companies that were indicted—what happened to their employees. I meant to look, and forgot."

Ben started a new search. "Nothing like Archer. These are companies convicted of Ponzi schemes. They didn't actually have life insurance policies to sell. They tricked investors with computer-generated documents and collected millions." He kept looking. Finally, Ben concluded there was no mention of employees.

He shut off the computer, stretched, told Carly, "That's it for me." Then he noticed her on the couch, slumped over as if she had stomach pains, tears running down her face.

"Hey! You can't give up, Carly. You have to fight."

"With what? How?"

"You'll find a way. How about Kyle's idea—a web site? You know that old saying, 'a lie can go halfway around the world while the truth is putting its boots on'? Start getting your boots on. Do a web site."

Carly poohed the idea. "We're talking about court, and judges and juries. How will a web site make a difference?"

"Maybe you have to try. At least do something. It's better than taking it on the chin. Hell, I went through a pretty rough few years, nothing like this, but I was just a kid so it was just as bad. I thought the world had ended, there was no reason to live. And Mom came at me with her favorite story. Remember it?"

Carly lifted her head. Nodded. And Ben started the story.

"A good man arrives at the gates of Heaven and asks to be let in. St. Peter asks to see his scars. The man says, 'I have no scars. And—.'"

He waited for Carly to join him in the last line: "St. Peter says, 'What a pity. Was there nothing worth fighting for?'"

# Chapter Eighteen

*PRESENTATION DAY*, ERIC MUMBLED as he exited the parking structure and crossed the pedestrian bridge. He walked briskly, needing to spike his adrenalin. He felt like an old car in need of a tune-up. His briefcase was stuffed with folders. He knew it would take all his skill, all his power of persuasion, all the files he had accumulated. He entered the building and headed for the elevator. The FBI's Orange County satellite office was within walking distance of the federal court house, in a four-story, mid-rise, pink and gray building shared with the Federal Public Defender, the District Attorney, and others. The building was said to contain fifty thousand square feet. The FBI rented half the space.

Eric's cubicle was smaller than his hotel bathroom. It was outfitted with a desk, a phone, a computer, a file cabinet, shelves for books, and a rolling file cart. Every surface was piled with files. File boxes were stacked on the floor. Eric ignored them as he sat, reviewing his notes for what seemed to be the hundredth time. Two hours later he continued to sit there, reviewing his presentation. He worried about confronting Yolanda with a theory she was certain to reject, unless he managed the most effective presentation of his adult life.

He glanced in the direction of her office. Yolanda Ruiz, as supervising special agent, had a private office with actual walls and windows on two sides. Eric could not hear anything from this distance, nor could he see if her door was open unless he left the safety of his cubicle.

Two hours of procrastination. Eric decided if he waited any longer he would have to admit to cowardice. He glanced at his watch, compared it to the wall clock outside his cubicle, gathered his file folders and began the long walk to Yolanda's office. The door was closed. He knocked once, opened the door, and poked in his head. She looked up from the computer.

"I hope this is important. You caught me in the middle of something."

"It is important but I can come back later."

Yolanda told him to sit and spill the beans. He began with his doubts about the fraud case, about the McCarran-Ferguson Act and why, if there was fraud at Archer, prosecution belonged to the state insurance departments, not the feds.

"You're wrong, Eric. There is plenty of case law permitting RICO actions, as one example of a federal action. The key question is: Does the federal law advance a state's interest in combating insurance fraud?"

"The prosecutors bulldozed their way in. McCarran-Ferguson prohibits federal law from overriding state insurance regulation, unless it does so explicitly. The indictment does not cite a single federal law that explicitly regulates insurance or overrides McCarran-Ferguson."

"Didn't you hear me? Federal law does not override state regulation, if it advances the state's interest in combating fraud."

"Then why is the indictment silent about state insurance law?"

"Why does it matter?"

"The indictments do not refer to any federal statute that explicitly overrides state regulation. That's important. The McCarran Ferguson Act exempts the business of insurance from federal regulation to the extent it is regulated by the states. Viaticals are regulated by the states."

"You're wasting my time, Eric," she snapped." It does not matter as long as federal law does not frustrate an articulated state policy or disturb the state's administrative regime."

Eric fell silent. He knew the prosecutors were wrong. How could he convince Yolanda? And if he did convince her, what then? He had not thought this through.

"Forget it, Eric. Federal prosecutors are convinced it's a good case. They're convinced they'll convict. No one but you is concerned about states' rights and that old Congressional act."

"And if a defense attorney raises the issue of lack of federal juris-diction? Won't the case be thrown out?"

"Trust me, none of the defense attorneys will raise this issue."

"You can't be certain."

"I am certain, Eric. From the prosecutors' mouths."

"Are you saying what I think you're saying?"

"I'm saying this case is much bigger than you can imagine. Leave it alone, Eric."

Eric stared at her. "I took an oath—'to support and defend the Constitution of the United States against all enemies, foreign and do-mestic.' How do I 'faithfully discharge the duties of the office' if this is a wrongful prosecution and I say nothing?"

Yolanda frowned. "Don't be a baby. Every agent takes that oath. I thought you were a smart cookie. Haven't you learned yet that you work for a bureaucracy? It's like working for IBM or the gas company. You take your marching orders. I take my marching orders. We do as we are told. Even if what we're told benefits no one other than people far above us."

"Someone wants the Archers destroyed?" Eric shook his head as if to clear it. "Someone 'upstairs'? How far upstairs?"

"All the way," Yolanda said. "All the way to Congress."

"You mean there's another Duke Cunningham?"

They locked eyes. Yolanda's were fuming. Clearly, she did not want to remember Randy "Duke" Cunningham, one of the most powerful Republicans in the House of Representatives. He represented voters in San Diego, California for eight terms, until an investigative journal-ist exposed Cunningham for taking millions in bribes from defense contractors. Until that exposé, Cunningham had free rein to plunder the defense budget. He did so year after year, while simultaneously attacking anyone who wanted the defense budget cut. In 2006 Duke Cunningham was sentenced to more than eight years in federal prison.

Yolanda continued to stare. Eric met the challenge. "Another Scott Bloch?" he asked. Yolanda shook her head as if to say, Wrong answer.

She had to know the Bloch case. This time the FBI did its job—until it was undermined by head honchos at the Department of Justice. Scott Bloch was a Bush official who headed the Office of Special Counsel. He also was counsel to the Department of Justice's Task Force for Faith-based and Community Initiatives. The FBI investigation exposed Bloch as a bigot who violated his oath of office.

Bloch's task as head of the OSC was to uphold anti-discrimination laws and whistle blower protections for federal employees. Instead, he did everything possible to undermine the OSC. Bloch was accused of deleting hundreds of files related to whistle blower disclosures, complaints of retaliation, and reprisal; rolling back protections for federal employees against discrimination based on sexual orientation; staffing key OSC positions with cronies who shared his bigotry; retaliation against OSC staffers who opposed his wrongdoing; assigning interns to issue closure letters in hundreds of whistle blower complaints—without investigation; intimidating OSC employees from cooperating with government investigators; misusing his prosecutorial power for political purposes, and of reassigning his perceived critics within the OSC to field offices across the country, with ten days to accept or be fired.

After an FBI raid of his home and other efforts by the FBI to investigate the allegations, they found Bloch hired a Geek Squad to "scrub" his computer in an effort to halt the inquiry into whether he violated the Hatch Act—mixing political activity with his official job. *Destruction of evidence*, Eric wanted to say. *Obstruction of justice.* He met Yolanda's stare and said nothing.

The FBI did its job but when the case reached the hands of Department of Justice prosecutors, instead of charging Bloch with perjury, obstruction of justice, and destruction of evidence, prosecutors worked closely with Bloch's defense team.

The intent of the collaboration was to ensure Bloch's penalty was nothing greater than probation. Bloch left OSC while the investigation was on-going, was issued a law license and, Eric remembered with some bitterness, was immediately hired by a D.C. law firm, Tarone & McLaughlin.

In 2010, Bloch pled guilty to one count of criminal contempt of Congress, a misdemeanor. The following year a magistrate judge sentenced him to one month in prison and one year of supervised release. One month in prison? Advocates for his victims were furious. Bloch was furious: He expected probation. His lawyers appealed. And Bloch, a lawyer, claimed he "didn't understand" his guilty plea carried a minimum sentence.

Unlike similar cases, prosecutors did not oppose Bloch's motion to withdraw his guilty plea. Bloch remained free to practice law pending the appeal. On August 3, 2011, a federal court judge reversed the ruling, thereby allowing Bloch to withdraw his guilty plea.

Yolanda lowered her head, pulled a paper from a pile on her desk, and appeared to be reading. Eric suspected it was a ruse.

"The judge controls the court," Eric said. "He could raise the jurisdictional issue *sua sponte*."

Yolanda did not look up. "You know that expression, 'Be afraid; be very afraid'?"

Eric opened his mouth to reply but Yolanda looked up and glared. "You have a lot of learning ahead of you, Eric Price. Wait. Watch. If the prosecutors flounder; if the defense doesn't follow its marching orders; if the majority of the judge's rulings don't favor the prosecution, His Honor will be paid a social visit by His Eminence the attorney general."

Eric wanted to curse. "And we're supposed to help prosecute people who may be innocent of the charged crimes?"

She frowned. "Don't get your briefs in a bunch, Eric. One: They're not innocent. They're not even 'not guilty' until a jury says so. Two: You need to be a team player. That should be uppermost in your mind. You're a rookie. You want a career in the FBI? Be a team player. Now, that's all the mothering I'm capable of in one day." She pointed to the door and hit the space bar of her computer, bringing it back to life.

"I'm not done, Yolanda. There's another issue. Senior fraud. The case is much, much bigger."

She looked up. She leaned back in her chair. "You mean elder abuse? Seniors being defrauded?"

"I mean seniors as co-conspirators. And insurers as co-conspirators. And some jumbo banks. And—"

"Seriously?" Yolanda smiled. "Sounds like fun. Is this going to take long? Should I get myself a Pepsi?" He told her, "Let's go. I'll get one, too."

Once they were seated again he began with a story. "You know of Larry King?"

"The very old and much-married TV guy?"

"That's him. In 2007, when he was seventy-three, he filed suit in state court in California. It was removed to federal court; that's where I found the documents." Eric withdrew the complaint from his folder and placed it on Yolanda's desk.

"Thirty-one pages," she noted.

"King claimed an unscrupulous insurance brokerage swindled him by persuading him to participate in a series of 'highly complex life insurance transactions.' Essentially, he applied for and was issued policies with death benefits that totaled $15 million. The second part of the scheme was to flip these policies—to sell them. Immediately. He also sold an older five million policy. He claimed the deals did not benefit him but disproportionately benefitted the insurance broker, who collected large commissions, bonuses, and override payments."

"Explain what is wrong with this. I handle many kinds of white collar crime, Eric. I can't begin to know every angle."

"First, King fraudulently acquired the policies. He intended to resell them. And he did. He was pissed when another insurance broker told him he could have been paid more. That's the real reason behind the lawsuit."

"You're saying he deceived the insurers into issuing policies. He led the insurers to believe he needed this insurance, when his intent was to sell it to investors. As a result, the investor-owners and beneficiaries had no insurable interest." When Eric nodded agreement, she asked "Isn't that a problem for the insurers to tackle, not us?"

"One of the companies that bought these multimillion dollar policies was charged by New York State with bid-rigging and fraud in connection with life settlements."

"And?"

"I'll come back to that. First, I want to tell you about the Nevada man who applied for ten million death benefits. The policy was issued on his claim of a net worth of ten-point-four million, income of two hundred twenty thousand, and a declaration that he never filed bankruptcy. The insurer sued to void the policy after learning of the insured's bankruptcy a year earlier—with net worth of minus."

Eric withdrew from his folder several pages printed from his word processor. The pages listed dozens of lawsuits filed across the nation, STOLI lawsuits. He explained about STOLI.

"Some writers call it IOLI—Investor Owned Life Insurance. Others call it SPINLife. Regardless of the name, the intent of the insureds, the seniors, is to acquire policies for resale. And that violates public policy as well as insurable interest law."

Yolanda was examining the page from Eric's word processor. "I see some big players, American General, Principal, Phoenix Life, Penn Mutual, Sun Life. You have Jefferson Pilot hyphenated with Lincoln National. What's that about?"

"Lincoln National bought Jeff Pilot, then had to file suit or defend itself in lawsuits related to policies issued by Jeff Pilot. That's in addition to their own STOLI lawsuits. Double whammy for Lincoln."

"And how does this relate to Archer?"

"Archer was involved in buying STOLI policies from seniors." He showed her the Archer spreadsheets. She looked at the pages, saying nothing.

"The point is, Archer is just one of many companies doing this. There also are premium finance companies—they pay the premiums for the first two years, until the policy is past the contestable period."

"Charging interest, no doubt?"

"At usurious rates."

"There also are banks who serve as trustees, and insurance brokers all over the country soliciting seniors. My guess is several thousand people, other than the insureds, are making money on these deals. Chief among investors are Wall Street firms and hedge funds, and investment companies abroad, all of whom might be leading us toward another economic meltdown. This industry has always been rife with fraud, but now there are new dimensions."

"All very interesting. But where do you see a violation of federal law?"

Eric took another sip of his Pepsi, to give him time to formulate the answer.

"First, I think this has to stop. Second, I've been trying to find a way to exercise federal control over this fraud, without running afoul of McCarran-Ferguson. The answer may be an antitrust action."

"I need to think about that. Leave those papers with me, Eric. I'm not sure an antitrust action is appropriate, but let me look over what you've got, and we'll meet again."

"Should I continue researching this?"

"No, work on the Archer case. You'll probably be called to testify."

"Me? Why not you? You're senior. With all your years at the FBI, you would be far more impressive."

"Ah, but your baby face will win over jurors. Many men, women, too, don't like a tough female."

Great, Eric thought. My first time testifying and I have to use my authority to help convict people who may not be guilty. Hope I can sleep at night.

As if she read his mind, Yolanda added, "Remember: It's an important career move to show you're a team player."

# Chapter Nineteen

WHEN HER PHONE trilled Carly looked at the caller ID. She had learned to screen calls. It was the only way to avoid nasty messages from strangers. When she saw the caller was Vet Clinic, she pressed the answer button.

"I wondered if you and Ethan would join me for dinner—a back yard barbecue and a great movie about penguins," he said.

Carly sighed. "The trial begins today. I really can't think past that."

"I know it's the first day of trial. I thought this might give you something to look forward to. A nice ending to the day, whatever happens."

"Not today. Thanks, Kyle."

It was thoughtful and considerate, but she was not up to dinner. Carly wondered how she could she eat dinner with Kyle when her stomach was such a mess. What if she tried to brave her way through dinner and became sick? She looked outside at Ethan. She was surprised to realize how much he had grown in the past year and a half. He looked like a reed, so tall and thin. Ethan had just turned twelve, and was as tall as some boys who were two or three years older. A sharp pain cut through her stomach. His teen years were on the horizon. Any kid's teen years were difficult. How would Ethan handle the challenges, if she went to prison? How much worse for him, knowing she was in prison. Not quite dead but cut off from every minute of his life. Day after day, knowing his mother was a felon. An inmate.

Carly glanced at the wall clock. Ten minutes before the school bus was due. Two hours before she was due at court. Doomsday had arrived. Carly had no more bridges to cross. She was trapped.

Carly took her cup of tea from the microwave and brought it to the table. She placed the cup down and flipped through the newspaper. There was nothing worth reading. Everywhere in the world horrible things were happening.

Ben galloped down the stairs, strode to the counter, poured a cup of coffee, and took a Danish from the box. "One of the guys who comes to the bar is a lawyer." Suddenly he realized what he said. "Hee-hee. The bar—get it? He goes to one bar or another."

Carly frowned. She was in no mood for humor.

"I get it. No jokes, not even corny ones." Ben continued, "Anyway, here's the story. I asked him about the superseding indictment. He said Stan-the-man should challenge the prosecutors, fight it all the way to the Supreme Court, if necessary. Maybe the Supremes need the opportunity to overturn the Hayes ruling. They might actually be waiting for the chance."

"I did ask Irwin Stanley if there was anything that he could do. He said no."

Ben took a small paper from his shirt pocket. Since he would accompany Carly to court, he wore a dress shirt tucked into jeans, and motorcycle boots. "Apprendi versus New Jersey. That's the case. This guy is not a criminal defense attorney but my questions interested him. He decided to look it up. He said Apprendi and a slew of cases." Ben glanced at the paper in his hand. "Booker, Blakely—those are the ones to tell Stan-the-man. They cite Apprendi and, to my pal, at least, they point the way the Supremes might go, if given the chance."

"Isn't it too late to raise new issues?"

"I asked Joel. He said it's too late only if it never comes up at trial. Which means, to me, that Stan-the-man needs to raise the issue *now*. The issue is: you were threatened, a threat that would deny you due process by punishing you for going to trial. That's the way I understood Joel's explanation, and it makes sense to me. If it's raised now, it can be pursued on appeal."

"Maybe a different lawyer, Ben, but I don't think Stanley is sharp enough. Or he's too busy with other cases. Or something."

Ben looked at his sister. She had on the navy suit she interchanged with a black suit when she worked at Archer, and a light blue blouse. A silver dolphin pin—a birthday gift from Ethan and him—was on her lapel. Her hair was twisted into a French knot, and she wore their mother's pearl earrings. There were dark circles under her eyes.

"No gardening today, huh?"

Ben watched the corners of her lips lift slightly, as Carly tried to smile. For at least the tenth time since this craziness began, Ben wished he had gone to college and law school. If he had the learning, he was certain he would be able to help her. A lawyer like the ones who represented Senator Stevens was far beyond their imaginations, probably charging a thousand an hour.

"No bike riding today?"

"You know it."

"No web site?"

"I'll work on it tonight."

"Did you return the library books?"

"Ben, why are you trying to make idle conversation?"

"Forgetaboutit." He stomped across the room and went out back, pulling a pack of cigarettes from a pocket as he went. Regular cigarettes, Carly saw. He did not want to go to court with the odor of marijuana on his clothes.

Carly did return all the books she borrowed from the library. At first she read about trials and law, but none of what she learned was helpful. Fiction was helpful. Fiction was the road away from the reality that threatened her. In fiction, the good guys and gals won.

The most positive thing she did for herself during these months was her web site. She began with a pad, a pen, and a list—what to include on the web site and how to market it. Needing to learn about marketing and, specifically, internet marketing, she borrowed books from the community college library and consulted her instructors. After experimenting with various web site designs, she prepared press releases. When she was ready to upload a few pages she sent press releases to newspapers and to every web site that offered free press release distribution. Ethan and she walked the neighborhood, placing flyers under door mats. Ben tacked up copies around town, asked shopkeepers to put them in windows, and told all who came into the bar about her web site. Carly hoped the web site would help with her mission: to prove her innocence to the public, if not the courts.

She began the web site as a diary. People were nosy. They liked to read other's letters and if they found a diary or journal, most would read it. She would let the public peek into her life.

"Dear Diary," she wrote on the first day. I am an accused felon. Prosecutors want everyone to believe I am a felon. There is no proof because I did nothing but clerical work. I expect most people will believe the prosecutors, simply because they are prosecutors. I used to believe prosecutors. Now I know better. It's true, I worked at Archer. But I am no guiltier than the cleaning crew. If the jury believes the prosecutors, I will carry the scar of being a felon for my entire life. If I am a felon, I am an accidental felon."

She had three hundred hits on her web site the first week.

The second week she added, "The prosecutors want me to testify against Archer Life Settlements. Since I knew nothing about fraud, I have nothing to say. They do not like that. They hinted they could tell me what to say, if I agree to testify. Other employees told me they had the same experience, when they met with the prosecutors."

She added legal documents to the web site: the search warrant for the raid, the first indictment and the superseding indictment. She planned to add more, if attorney Stanley gave her other documents.

Four weeks after her web site went online, she had six hundred visitors. Then she added a different category, also a letter: "Dear Prosecutors." That gave her the opportunity to tell the prosecutors why she thought they were wrong.

When her attorney heard about the web site he was furious. He did not visit it but he heard about it. The prosecutors informed him. They were angry. Irwin Stanley warned Carly she was making enemies of the prosecutors. If she did not shut down her web site, she could expect them to go after her as if she were a rabid dog.

"What more could they do to me?" she asked. Her tone was challenging.

"If you're found guilty," attorney Stanley said in a stern voice, "they could recommend leniency at sentencing, or they could recommend the maximum. Which do you prefer?"

Carly told him she would think about it, but as soon as she closed her cell phone she decided not to think about it. She needed to tell her story. She wanted neighbors, shopkeepers, parents of Ethan's school mates, future employers—everyone who presumed guilt based on media reports, everyone who thought the way she used to think when someone was indicted—to know the truth.

Her web site really took off when she wrote about her family. Carly told of her father's "Last Love Letter," which is how she titled it. It was written to her mother, just before he took his life two years before Carly moved to California. The family knew he had Alzheimer's. They did not know, her father wrote, the disease was progressing quickly. He would leave his beloved one way or the other, he said. He'd rather leave her with good memories. He rather spare her having to care for a shell when the person who loved her was gone. "Remember I loved you dearly, above all else," he said in closing.

Carly added at the bottom that today her family consisted of her brother, Ben, and her son, Ethan, and they were committed to survive the ordeal of the trial and whatever the outcome would be.

Suddenly there were fewer nasty emails. Carly was astonished to find hundreds of support messages in her email box. She replied to each, "Thank you. Your support means so much."

When the volume of hits to her web site reached more than one thousand, Ben told her, "You're not the only writer in this family, Carly. DeeOhGee also wrote a book. He used a pseudonym. Look it up on Amazon, 'The Yellow Spot,' by I. P. Daily."

She could not laugh. To show she appreciated his effort, Carly punched his arm.

Carly finished her tea and washed the cup. The one bright spot in her life, her son, Ethan, was in the back yard, yelling, "Good!" each time DeeOhGee caught a Frisbee or a ball. Carly raised her eyes heavenward.

*Thank you for keeping him innocent and happy,* she whispered.

Carly was about to call Ethan to come indoors when her cell phone trilled. She was unused to the sedate sound. After changing from Looney Tunes, she had few calls, as if she had a contagious disease, as if people wanted to avoid her. When she went grocery shopping, she worried that people recognized her from newspaper photos and concluded she was guilty. Her computer course at the community college was down to one night a week due to cost. When she walked the halls she was sure people stared and looked away quickly. If not for the stares, she would think she was invisible.

The caller ID said, "Vet Clinic." Kyle, again?

"I know you're going to court soon. Would you like company? Moral support?"

"That is terribly kind. But no, you have a busy practice. I don't want you to make sacrifices for me."

"Isn't that what friends are for?"

"What if a dog is hit by a car or bitten by a rattler and rushed to your clinic? You have more important things to do. Besides, you wouldn't be allowed to sit with me. I have to sit at the defense table."

"How about when you testify? Would you want some moral support then?"

"I won't testify. My attorney warned me not to. The prosecutors will do everything they can to undermine my credibility. They could use accusing glares, smirks, a pointed finger, anything they can think of to make my testimony sound suspect."

"Well, if you change your mind, I can make arrangements for someone to cover for me at the clinic."

After shutting her cell phone she went to the back door and called Ethan, reminding him to crate DeeOhGee. No one would be home for hours; the puppy had to be crated. DeeOhGee was getting spoiled. When Ben was home during the day he let the pup stay with him when he worked in the garage—his construction site—or the yard.

Ethan came in, the puppy at his heels. Carly reminded Ethan to brush his hair. She looked at DeeOhGee, surprised to notice how big and boxy he had become in such a short time. Now too large and too heavy to pick up, his pearls of baby teeth—milk teeth, Ethan told her—were gone, replaced with large, beautifully white teeth. These teeth seemed to pop into place overnight and complete, unlike children whose second teeth erupted gradually and grew to full size slowly.

"He must be crated, Ethan," she urged, as the puppy played "catch me if you can" and Ethan chased him around the room. Carly rushed to close the back door, to prevent DeeOhGee from escaping into the fenced yard.

"I know," Ethan said breathlessly. "Those big teeth can eat more than just a windowsill. He could eat a whole window."

Doctor Kyle had told him that eye contact was important in training dogs. They want to see your eyes, which is why some dogs jump up on people—to look at their eyes. That was why Doctor Kyle often bent down to introduce himself to a dog. But only after letting the dog sniff you, standing back and acting as if the dog was shy, letting the dog make the first move, letting it lick your hand so that you know the dog is friendly and won't bite. He didn't want the boy trusting every dog unquestioningly.

Ethan was learning to have eye contact, at least with dogs.

"I like when Ben brings DeeOhGee to meet me at the bus," Ethan said as he locked the crate. "The other kids call him Super Dog." Carly had filled the crate bowl with water and tossed a cow hoof stuffed with canned meat into the crate, an enticement for the pup to enter the crate. He also had a couple of squeaky toys and a formerly stuffed toy squirrel, whose stuffing was quickly pulled out by DeeOhGee's teeth.

Ben stepped out of the first floor lavatory, hair brush stroking his scraggily beard. "I have to go to Santa Ana, Ethan. But I'll be back in time for the school bus."

"You'll be gone all day? When will you sleep?"

Ben grinned. "What I'm doing today probably will put me to sleep."

Ethan asked, "What's that, what you're doing?" Before Ben could answer they heard the school bus plowing up the road. Ethan grabbed his backpack and bolted from the house. Carly ran to the door to watch as Ethan boarded. She always worried about other children mistreating him.

Ben stepped up beside her. "What's today going to be about?"

"Mr. Stanley told me they first choose a jury, then lawyers make opening statements. Opening statements are when they tell the jury a story of what the trial is about, each from their own point of view."

They walked back inside. Carly placed her cell phone in her purse. "Did you tell him about Terri?"

"He said he would have to confer with French, the lead attorney. The one who's representing Aidan and Blake. I've tried to reach Blake to find out if he knows. I left two messages. He hasn't called back."

"Call him now."

"There's not much time. We have to get going."

"Call him. Make it quick, then we'll go."

Carly did. This time he answered the phone. His tone was solemn. "Yes, Carly. Nervous?"

"Of course. Aren't you?"

"Of course."

"Did you tell your lawyer about Terri McGuire being the wife of the prosecutor?"

"I did. And he said to forget about it. If we bring this up, it will make the prosecutors mad. Gotta go now. See you in an hour. Chin up."

Carly told Ben what she had learned.

"And that means?"

Carly shrugged. It worried her. Why didn't they want to use this information? Terri had to know if there was fraud, since she was in charge of the bank accounts. Carly needed her to testify, to tell the jury that Carly never had access to the files.

"I'll tell you what it means, Carly. The lawyers are afraid of the prosecutors. And they won't put on a strong defense. They're probably already thinking of their next case."

"Why would they be afraid of the prosecutors?"

"No clue. But it's strange. Why should it matter? What would the prosecutors do, if they were angry, that they're not doing now?"

"Don't look at me," Carly said. "I don't understand anything about this."

# Chapter Twenty

KYLE PACED FROM THE doorway of the clinic to the end of the drive-way and back, impatient for Eric to arrive. He remembered the last time they dined together, after playing basketball in the Prenner driveway, the hoop attached above the garage door. It was a Saturday. Eric's parents had gone to an early dinner and movie. The boys had dinner with Kyle's parents, after which all four watched television. As the hours ticked by, Kyle's mother began to fret. She was a congenital worrier but Kyle's father agreed, this was unusual for Eric's parents. If they knew they were going to be late, they would phone.

Kyle's parents invited Eric to sleep over. Kyle had a bunk bed in his room, and Eric often slept over. He phoned to notify his teenage sisters, and the boys went upstairs to change to pajamas. Their pillow fight was interrupted by the ringing of the doorbell. Expecting Eric's parents, the boys ran downstairs.

Two police officers stood there. Kyle's parents shooed the boys back upstairs and took the police officers into the living room. When they called the boys down, they told Eric to get dressed, his sisters were waiting for him. Kyle went back up with Eric. Eric was upset. "I told them I was sleeping over. Why'd they call the cops? And these aren't even guys I know."

Those were Eric's last words before he was rushed out the door by the police officers. They were his last words to Kyle until the day he showed up at the clinic, twenty years later.

After the police officers left with Eric, Kyle learned that Eric's parents were killed in a car accident. The following day Eric and his sisters were gone. Some time after, a moving van emptied the house. It remained vacant for months, until it was sold to a new family. Because Kyle kept asking about Eric, his parents finally told him: each of the Price children was sent to live with a different relative. They did not know where any of them lived.

Kyle remembered how painful it was to lose his best friend. As a boy he imagined it to be similar to how Eric felt, losing his parents. It was years before he realized how much greater the loss was for Eric.

He wanted to ask, but knew he would not, why Eric never phoned, why he never visited, why he never sent a post card. The reasons probably were worse than anything Kyle could imagine, and he did not want to spoil their reunion.

Eric waved as his rental car pulled into the driveway. He parked, shut off the motor and they boarded Kyle's SUV.

"I'm taking you to one of the greatest views along the coast. Good food, too," Kyle said as they drove along Laguna Canyon Road, nearly to the ocean, and turned left onto South Coast Highway. Kyle pointed out art shops, crafts shops, tattoo parlors, Asian food, health food shops, antique dealers, and artists' studios. The shops lined the streets, filling the lower parts of two-story buildings. People strolled the sidewalks, casually dressed and walking as leisurely as the bumper-to-bumper traffic. With the weather again perfect, the ordinary weekday evening looked like a holiday at the beach.

Kyle turned onto Street of the Green Lantern. They followed the flow of the road as it curved and climbed a cliff, and pulled into the lot at Canon's restaurant.

"Lots of good restaurants on the water here," Kyle told him. "Equally good ones practically sitting on the beach in Laguna but where we're going is special, as you'll see in a few minutes. It has the most spectacular view—the marina below and the ocean."

Kyle had made reservations, to be certain they would get seats on the terrace, which overlooked the marina. They were led to their table. After ordering drinks they stood at the rail, admiring the view. A rosy sun streaked the darkening sky. The marina was filled with boats of all sizes and shapes. Kyle pointed to one he called a sportfisherman, another he called a catamaran, another he called a sailboat.

"That one I could figure out for myself," Eric said, grinning.

"Well, I didn't know how much of a landlubber you were."

"Not in spirit. I like the water."

"I'm glad you'll be here in winter. You would enjoy the whale watching cruise. Summer speaks for itself, but winter is something else. Summer tourists have no idea."

As they took their seats, Kyle told him about the Festival of Boats, another winter special with a boat parade. Eric began to look at the menu. He made a decision, looked up, and noticed Kyle wearing eyeglasses.

"When did that start?" Eric asked.

"It's nothing. A bit of near-sightedness, since I was thirteen. It's the dim light that forces me to wear these." It was dark now, except for the lights on boats and along the boardwalk, and the tiny candles that glowed in jars at the center of the table.

The waiter brought their drinks, gin and tonic for each. Something they had in common—neither liked strong drinks nor drank alcohol with any frequency. They ordered dinner and told the waiter to take his time. As Kyle put away his eyeglasses he saw Eric push back his chair, stretch out his legs, lean back and breath deeply, filling his lungs with the cooling air of dusk, fragrant with salty sea.

"Relaxing, isn't it?" Kyle said. He felt pleased he had chosen this restaurant for their first shared meal in many years.

"Exactly what I need. It's been a grind, being new and tackling a heavy duty fraud case plus a few other investigations."

Kyle was practiced in reading body language since his patients could not describe symptoms. He did not need that skill just now. Watching Eric begin to relax, he could see the boy behind the man's face. It was as if the years were swept away. He reminded himself that much had happened in the past two decades; he could not expect the closeness they once shared. Each had experiences unknown to the other, that made them strangers today. He knew the affection he felt for Eric was that of an eleven-year-old toward an admiring younger boy, an almost-brother. He had to keep telling himself he really did not know the man who sat across the table from him. And yet, something in him wanted to try to recapture the closeness.

"You used to talk about being an airplane pilot. Did you ever pursue it?"

Eric sat up, laughing. "No, but I can't believe you remember!"

"Well, you know why I chose veterinary medicine. Now it's you're your turn. Tell me why you decided to go into law."

Eric paused long enough to gulp his drink. "You remember my dad was a cop?" Kyle nodded. "You probably don't know he took college courses for a criminal justice degree. His eventual goal was to become a lawyer. As young as I was, he talked to me about it. Probably to explain why he was always busy with books, when he was home."

"I remember he brought a book with him, when he came to your Little League games."

"What he saw as a cop pissed him royally: People who should not have been charged with a crime but were sent to jail because they didn't know the law, or they couldn't afford a good lawyer, or simply because they were the wrong color."

"And you decided to be a criminal defense lawyer?"

Eric took another swipe at his drink. "Criminal defense was his thing, not mine."

"But your Dad's example meant something to you, obviously."

"Yep. He was the first person in the family to go to college, and he went to law school part time, at night. The lesson I got from that was ordinary folks like us could become lawyers. It also meant it was possible, even if you don't have the money to pay for it. That turned out to be my situation."

He leaned forward, lowered his voice, and his expression turned serious. "Did you know, did your folks ever tell you, why I moved away?" Kyle nodded and lowered his head. He no longer could meet

Eric's eyes. His own were moist. Eric lost his family, moved far away, and both of them lost years as best friends.

Eric went on. "You may have heard my folks were killed." Kyle nodded. He tried to meet Eric's eyes. He knew this was important to Eric. He nodded again, telling Eric to continue.

"Maybe you were not told the whole story. Probably not. My sisters and I were orphaned by a drunk driver. It wasn't a car accident. They were crossing the street from the restaurant to where they parked the car. He came speeding down the street and plowed them down."

Eric took a large swill of his drink. "I looked it up. After I became a lawyer, I was able to access the details." He stared at his half empty glass. "Their killer pled out and got five years. We got a life sentence; he got five years. I've no sympathy for the truly guilty. That's why it never interested me to become a defense lawyer."

They were silent for what seemed an inordinate amount of time. Kyle tried to think of something to say to lighten things a bit, or change the topic.

"My next guess," he tried, "is you decided to become a prosecutor."

Eric shook his head. "Nope. Not me. It was the prosecutor that let my parents' killer get off with five years. Another of the things that angered my Dad—prosecutors who make plea deals with people who are guilty as hell." His glass was nearly empty. He took a small sip and sat back, a thoughtful look on his face.

"I wasn't sure what area of law would interest me. I figured a varied experience would help me decide. Right out of law school I was hired by a high profile law firm, one of those megalaw firms. Offices in cities around this country and other countries, and enough secretaries and paralegals floating around to crush the thick carpeting."

Kyle gave a low whistle. Eric grinned at him. "Yes, it could have been a ticket to wealth. Most newly minted lawyers would think I hit it lucky. I did, at first. But before long I hated it. I could not stomach what I learned. What I was supposed to do."

Eric took another sip of his drink, emptying the glass, and continued. "You probably have no idea what I'm talking about. The people disgusted me. For them, the practice of law was a money machine. Ethics? Morality? Justice? Archaic words. As useless to them as an appendix. The altar of money was everything."

Kyle watched Eric's expression change from anger to disgust to something else, something he could not identify. "You decided to leave? To look for another law firm?"

"Not at first. I needed the money. I had a major tab for student loans. As Satre said, 'Only the guy who isn't rowing has time to rock the boat.'"

Kyle chuckled. "When did you start reading Satre?"

"College. I liked him."

Kyle told him he did, too. "'We are our choices'—one of my favorite quotes."

Eric nodded. "To go on with my tale of woe, weeks passed, and then months, then a year. I was a bundle of nerves, getting heartburn, certain if I stayed I would end up with blood pressure problems or worse." He forced a laugh at himself. "Dramatic, huh? I was getting good at 'pity party.'"

Kyle rubbed his chin. "That sounds like a perfect description of being caught between a rock and hard place."

"What finally pushed me to a decision was something I copied from a book by Carlos Castenada. He's another of my favorites. This one I pinned to the wall near my desk in my apartment. I read it, again and again."

Kyle's eyebrows raised, asking the question.

"You're going to laugh at this," Eric said. "But I read it so often during those two years it became my Jiminy Cricket."

"Pinocchio. I remember. 'Let your conscience be your guide.'"

Eric grinned. "Exactly. It became embedded in my brain. I could quote it then, can quote it now, and I'll probably remember it when I'm ninety." Eric looked up at the now dark sky over the marina, as if seeing the quote in the stars. "Before you embark on any path ask the question: Does this path have a heart? If the answer is no, you will know it, and then you must choose another path."

"I can see how that would affect you."

"Castenada goes on to say, '"When a man finally realizes that he has taken a path without a heart, the path is ready to kill him. At that point very few men can stop to deliberate, and leave the path.'"

"You realized you were on a path without a heart."

"And it was ready to kill me."

"And so you left a lucrative career."

"For the FBI. Here, I can feel good about what I'm doing."

"I think I have an idea what you're getting at. A few years ago I dated a woman who became a criminal defense lawyer after her sister was raped. The rapist served one year. She—my date, the lawyer sister—vowed never to let that happen to anyone else."

"Are you saying she took on defendants in order to punish them? Intentionally betraying their trust? She would have fit in at Big Law, where I was."

"I could not convince her how wrong this was. Or that she should become a prosecutor, instead. Needless to say, it was a first and last date."

Eric told him of some of his dates that went awry, and they had a few laughs over the stories. Then Kyle asked if the "big fraud case," as Eric described it, the one that brought him to southern California, was Archer Life Settlements. Eric nodded. Kyle told him he read about it in the newspaper. He saw that Carly Daniels was indicted. Eric frowned. He told Kyle he could not talk about it. It was absolutely forbidden to discuss ongoing cases with outsiders.

"I know her, Eric. I know her brother. I know her son. I know their dog. Something is wrong here."

"She spoke to you about this?"

"She doesn't volunteer much. But I know she would not do anything illegal or immoral or unethical. What's going to happen to her?"

"You know her really well? Is she somebody special?"

Kyle realized he had created a false impression. He felt embarrassed to admit he knew little about Carly. He had no idea how she lived her life; he knew little about her past. She could be a closet alcoholic, or moonlighting as a lap dancer. No. He knew enough to be certain there was nothing sordid about her. Was she special? He could agree to that because he believed every person was special, every person was unique, just as every dog or cat or bird was unique.

"Well, is she?" Eric prodded. "Special?"

"I think she's a special person. As to special in my life, if that's what you're asking, it's too early to know. But I do care about her and her family."

Eric raised his water glass. "Here's to your karma."

Kyle grinned and raised his water glass. Then he remembered his question. "Help me here. What's going to happen to her? Do you have any idea?"

"I can't answer these questions, Kyle. I can give you general information, but nothing specific to this case."

Kyle nodded. "Agreed. Whatever you tell me is more than I know right now."

"In most cases, defendants are urged to accept a plea agreement. That means admitting their guilt. If a defendant doesn't accept a plea, they go to trial."

"I think it's unlikely Carly will plead guilty. When I last spoke with her, she said she knew she didn't do anything wrong."

"Whether a defendant did or did not do something wrong does not enter into the equation. Prosecutors want a guilty plea."

"And if she refuses?"

"As I said before, if a defendant refuses a plea agreement, they go to trial."

"Some time ago I read in the New York Times about a lawyer in Florida, Denis deVlaming. When he meets with a new client, he pulls out a calculator. The client thinks he's calculating the fee. What he's doing is tallying all the additional punishments the prosecutor can add to figure the likely sentence, if the client is convicted at trial."

"That's reality, Kyle."

"So the reality is if Carly refuses a plea, even though she's innocent she could get sent away for years?"

"Some prosecutors are vengeful. They don't want to go to trial. You know that expression, 'throw the book at them'? That's the weapon prosecutors use when they are vengeful."

"Why do prosecutors do this? Why target innocent people?"

Eric shrugged. "They enjoy their power. And there's no accountability. No penalty whatsoever. Even when an appeals court faults a prosecutor, they rarely name the person."

"Carly told me she thinks the prosecutors are out to get her."

"She may be paranoid. On the other hand, it could be true, if she's stubborn and refuses a plea deal."

"A single mother with a special needs child—they would send her to prison?"

"The jury decides guilty or not guilty. If the jury finds a defendant guilty, the judge decides the sentence. In theory. In reality, most judges follow the sentencing recommendation of the prosecutors."

"Which means if the prosecutors don't like her, she's had it."

"Kyle, you're trying to worm information out of me about this particular case. I can't do it." Eric looked at his empty glass, waved to the waiter and pointed to his glass. Neither of them spoke until the waiter replaced the empty glass with another gin and tonic

"People of color usually have it worse, don't they?" Kyle asked.

"You could get that from reading Newsweek," Eric said."

Kyle ignored the sarcasm. "Even if they are women, Eric? Even if they have children?"

"It's part of American history, Kyle. We even execute parents and leave their children as orphans. That's what happened in 1953—the U.S. government executed the mother and father of very young children, Ethel and Julius Rosenberg. They were executed for spying. They had two young sons."

Kyle stared at Eric. His face no longer resembled the boy he once knew. Eric was an embittered child turned into an angry adult. Ethel and Julius Rosenberg were executed by the government; Eric's parents were executed by a drunk driver. The justice system had no concern for the children left behind.

Kyle remembered Eric saying, when they ordered drinks, he wanted something mild since he rarely drank liquor. Kyle looked at his own, nearly untouched drink. He took another sip. He should not worry; two drinks would not hurt Eric. They had yet to eat dinner. Eric probably needed something to help him relax. The view and the salty air had lost their magic.

The waiter placed their dinners before them and departed.

"I'm sorry about bringing this up now. Bringing it up here," said Kyle. "It kind of spoiled what should have been a nice escape for both of us."

Eric nodded. He picked up his fork.

"Sorry, Eric, but I can't get it out of my mind. Is there anything I can do to help Carly? Or can't you say?"

"If you're asking me for legal advice, I can't do that. Even if I knew—and I don't know criminal defense—I can't get into specifics about an ongoing case. So tell me about the box turtle you rescued."

# Chapter Twenty-One

It was the first day of trial. Carly drove the truck, gripping the steering wheel until her fingers felt numb, biting her lip until it was sore. Ben rode his motorcycle so that he would be able to return home in time for Ethan's school bus. Ethan could stay alone for a while, but they worried about bullies at the bus stop. There had been too many incidents in the past.

Shortly before they reached Civic Center Drive Carly signaled to Ben to pull into the driveway of an office building. She stepped out from her truck, telling him she wanted to remind him there was no parking near the court house.

"Let's try to find parking spaces along the street. If only one of us has to pay for parking, it will be less expensive."

"Yeah," he said. "Don't wanna give some parking magnate my pizza fund."

Carly nodded, as if he had not told her this before, as if they had not planned the trip in advance, as if they had not studied the map and discussed the route again and again. Ben patted her back. He understood why Carly had to go over the details again.

They circled Civic Center Drive and surrounding streets several times. There were no vacancies. Traffic was building, forcing them to inch along between other vehicles looking for parking. They began to look for paid parking and found many "lot filled" signs. Finally, several blocks from the court house, they found a parking lot, drove in, paid the fee, parked, and began walking.

Ben thought they were early enough to stop at the court house cafeteria for coffee. But the federal building they entered was not the court house. It was the site of a melee of federal agencies—Homeland Security, Immigration, HUD, and others. They headed out to the plaza again, Carly moaning that she could not keep up with him. Walking fast in heels on hard pavement was like walking barefoot on rocks. Several times they stopped to examine glass-enclosed maps hung on poles but, again, found them confusing.

"We should have made a dry run," Carly moaned, as they looked around the many office buildings at Civic Center. Now they could identify the Orange County court house, the Welfare Department, City Hall, and the County Law Library. There were far too many other buildings.

"You were here last year, with your lawyer. How did you find it?"

"I met him at a Burger King and we drove together. I was in such a daze, I didn't see a thing."

"I'm sure the court is still here," Ben said, "Probably hiding in plain sight."

They asked a man in a suit, hoping he was a government employee or a lawyer who could direct them.

"You can't miss it," he said, pointing past their shoulders and skyward. "It's the second highest building in Orange County." Turning, they saw an eleven story, light pink building. It clearly stood out. Carly felt foolish for missing it.

"If we came by helicopter," Ben grinned, "we woulda seen it right away."

Near the entrance Carly looked up at the pink concrete, surprised at its wavy appearance. "I expected something formidable, like in the movies. This doesn't look like a court house. If not for those gold letters way up there, who would guess?"

The gold letters spelled, "Ronald Reagan Federal Building and

United States Court House." Fearing they would be late, they rushed
to the entrance, oblivious of the bronze sculptures on travertine bases
that adorned each side of the glass entrance.

"Hurry up and wait time," Ben mumbled as they watched the line
ahead of them present government-issued ID and remove shoes, belts,
and anything metallic from their pockets before walking through
the metal detector. Apparently there were no exceptions to the rules.
People with juror badges had to follow the procedure, as did the media
and lawyers.

They had just passed through and were collecting their belongings
when a lawyer loudly protested to a guard that he had done this every
day for the past two weeks; didn't the guard recognize him by now?
When Ben opened his mouth to make a comment, Carly stopped him
by touching his arm. It distressed her to realize Ben was so nervous
that he was ready to wisecrack about mundane events. They walked
through the marble lobby to the elevator.

"Real marble?" Ben grumbled. "Nice use of our tax dollars."

Behind them a guard with a booming voice directed a reporter to
the media room on the first floor.

The elevator deposited them on the sixth floor and they walked
through the public gallery, looking for the court room assigned to their
case. The public gallery was sheathed in glass, offering views of the
city and a microscopic, distant view of the ocean. For the first time in
her life, a peek at the ocean had no effect on Carly.

Carly's attorney was not waiting outside the courtroom, as promised. They entered the court room. Like the exterior of the building, it
was unlike anything in movies with a twenty foot domed ceiling and
blond wood furniture. Carly's attorney was near the front, standing
at a table, chatting with another attorney. When he spotted her, he
waved and pointed to a seat at the defense table.

Ben walked with her to the defense table. Irwin Stanley started
to say something to him. Ben knew he was not allowed past the gate.
He abandoned his plan to tell Stanley to do his damned best for Carly.
Instead he said, "You don't have to tell me. I'll be in the audience."

"Gallery," corrected Stanley. Ben gave him one of his famous dirty looks. He moved back through the gate to a seat in the first row, directly behind the defense table. The woman next to him was doused in expensive perfume. Ben wrinkled his nose in an effort not to sneeze. The woman turned to him to ask if he was with Carly. When he replied, she introduced herself as Aidan's wife.

The bailiff announced the case, announced Judge Herman Easterly, and called, "All rise." Everyone stood to watch the judge emerge from a door behind the clerk's corral. He walked slowly, a man whose black robe bulged away from his body, creating an A-frame from his head. He was in his late sixties, clean-shaven, with two chins that hung over the collar of his robe. He climbed the steps to his seat. Judge Easterly's first words, addressed to everyone in the room, were orders to turn off cell phones. He ordered no tape recorders and no photographs, still or video, to be taken while court was in session.

And the day began. And the hours passed, questioning and accepting or rejecting jurors. Each attorney rejected some potential jurors for reasons unknown to Carly.

At the end of the day, as they left the court house, attorney Stanley took Carly aside to tell her not to wear heels. She was too tall, he said. Without heels, Carly was five foot seven.

"You should look fragile and vulnerable," he explained.

And not taller than him, she thought.

He gave her another bit of advice: Don't wear a suit. Wear a blouse and skirt or a simple dress. "You look like a lawyer," he said, eying her up and down. "You don't want to give the jury the impression you're a successful professional."

Carly bit her lip to keep from answering.

Jury selection was continued to the following day and so boring Carly did not need Ben's support. She told him not to come. There would be worse days, she was certain, such as the day the jury returned a verdict.

Ben said, "I'll agree to a degree." He told her he would come late morning, roughly around the time they took a recess, and go home after lunch. When she opened her mouth to protest, he added, "Not every day."

Carly could not argue. She saw worry on his face. Ben hid it well, continuing everything he had done before they fell into the sinkhole. Now it was little improvements on the house, nothing major. He cracked jokes, some corny, some clever. He played volleyball and basketball, but not as often and not for as many hours.

Carly knew he was worried. She saw it when he bit his fingernails, which Ben had not done in years. And he headed to the back yard to smoke more often that he used to do. Whether he worried about the outcome of the trial or the effect it had on her, she did not know.

It was nearly a week before they had a jury plus two alternates, in the event a juror became sick or for other reasons was dismissed. They were ready to start the actual trial.

∽

As she watched the gallery fill with spectators, Carly pretended it was television. It became real when a few former co-workers came through the door, caught her eye, and waved. Roger was among them. They were not testifying. Anyone scheduled to testify was not allowed to watch. It was sobering to realize these employees were here because they had not found new employment.

The guards closed the doors, barring those who could not get seats. *Who are all these people?* Carly knew a section of the gallery was reserved for reporters. They were obvious, with electronic or old-fashioned note pads or sketch pads.

Judge Easterly was announced and everyone stood until he climbed the steps—Carly thought there were three—spread his cloak, and took his seat, high above all the lesser mortals, a legal throne. Judge Easterly stared until everyone resumed seats and fell silent. The judge turned to the jury and gave a little speech warning them not to mistake what lawyers said as evidence. He turned to the prosecution table and invited them to give their opening statement to the jury. Prosecutor Calvin Cutter stood and walked to the jury box. A tall man with a bland face, deep set eyes, a bit of gray along his sideburns, he wore a navy suit with a white shirt and red tie. The red, white, and blue of his clothing matched the flag pin in his button hole, leaving no doubt Cutter represented the United States government. And he began with those words: He was here on behalf of the United States.

Carly tried to focus her thoughts elsewhere. She did not want to hear words that portrayed her as an enemy of her country. She examined the paneling on the walls, scarcely hearing Cutter enumerate the charges. Carly Daniels ... money laundering, wire fraud.... She could not turn her mind to the ocean, to Ethan—that filled her with sorrow. She thought about her mother and father, and was grateful they did not know about this.

How mightily it affected them to learn about the two years in which young, still small Ben suffered in silence. Carly was as much affected as her parents. Now she knew first-hand about trust violated. Each word uttered by Cutter was a saber that pierced deeply into her. The man was of no consequence; she could ignore him. But not Cutter, the voice of the United States of America.

"This is a fraud case," Cutter told the jury, "and it's about lies, and it's about a second set of lies told to cover up the first set." The jury and the packed gallery listened, rapt. Cutter explained about viatical settlements, how they helped terminally ill people, then how it became perverse, an instrument of fraud. He told them some people lied to insurance companies in order to acquire life insurance policies and sold these policies to Archer. Archer resold these policies to investors.

Cutter claimed that when terminally ill people did this, it was because Archer put them up to it. Archer had a far greater profit when the policies were resold to investors. The fraudulent policies were purchased for much smaller amounts than legitimate policies, which meant an instant and greater profit for Archer.

*Yes, I know that now,* Carly thought. He wanted the jury to believe she knew this all along.

"I told you this was about lies," Cutter continued. "The first lie was made by the terminally ill man, usually someone with AIDS or who was HIV-positive. He couldn't go to the insurance company and say,

'I'm going to die soon. Would you sell me a policy?' Since the insurance company would not issue them a policy, these people answered 'No' to every question on the application that asked if they had an illness, if they visited a doctor in the last five years, if they were hospitalized."

Cutter spoke quietly, walking slowly back and forth parallel to the jury box, making eye contact with each juror. "And you will see," he said, "they did this not one time, not two times, not three times, sometimes as many as twenty or thirty times. These people acquired many policies through their fraud. And Archer knew about the fraud. Archer knew the answers on the insurance applications were false. Knowing this, Archer bought the policies, numerous policies issued to the same people. And that is basically the scheme to defraud charged in this case."

Then Cutter again named the defendants, Archer the corporation; Aidan Archer, the president of the company and chief architect of the fraud; and Blake Archer, the vice president and co-decision maker. "There are some individuals who aided and abetted this scheme to defraud, who made it possible, and they had full knowledge of what they were doing. The key person who aided and abetted is Carly Daniels. We are charging Carly Daniels with participation in the conspiracy to defraud. These were the folks in control."

When he spoke her name, Cutter looked at her. *He expects me to put down my head in shame.* She hoped Ben would restrain himself. The thought of Ben made her bold. She glared at Cutter, sending him hate with a stiff face and fixed eyes.

Cutter blithely continued to describe other charges in the indictment and how they applied. "The charges all relate to this scheme to defraud. The first type of charge is mail fraud. That means they used a commercial carrier like Federal Express or Airborne to deliver overnight packages as part of the scheme to defraud. Wire fraud is one of the charges because they used bank wire transfers of money as part of this scheme to defraud. You're going to see that money laundering is one of the charges because the scheme involved buying and selling things Archer knew were obtained illegally. But Archer bought and sold them anyway. And you're going to see the defendants, Aidan Archer, Blake Archer, and Carly Daniels, are charged with conspiracy to do these things. That's an agreement to get these things accomplished."

Cutter went on and on, describing details to support the charges, then told the jury they would bring as witnesses employees of the company, some investors who were defrauded, and some of the insurance companies who were defrauded. Other witnesses would include federal agents who would testify about their investigation. And the jury would hear from some of the viators who lied on their insurance applications, then sold the policies to Archer.

"Some of them are downright disreputable. You will see for yourselves, they are just plain old disreputable. They are the people who conspired with the defendants. They are the people who the defendants chose to do business with. They have direct knowledge of the conspiracy and how it operated."

He warned the jury they would see a large number of documents, further evidence of the conspiracy to defraud. Finally, he concluded saying, "And, folks, when you have seen all the witnesses, when you have looked at the documents which we introduce, the United States will prove to you that these defendants are guilty of each and every charge in the indictment handed down by the federal grand jury."

The judge called a recess before inviting defense attorneys to present their opening statement. Carly wanted to rush out. But she took her time moving through the small gate and into the courtroom, then linked her arm with Ben's and let him guide her through the crowd.

"Whatdaya think of Judge Jowls?" he asked. She shook her head. She was way beyond anything light-hearted. Her emotions were frozen. They followed the crowd into the hall and moved toward the restrooms, Carly going into one, Ben into the other.

Sherri, the Archer receptionist, stood at the sink, facing the door. Her face brightened as soon as she saw Carly. Sherri looked around, saw no one else in the restroom, and began talking in a hushed voice.

"Carly, my sister-in-law is a paralegal. I told her about your internet search. About prosecutors?" Carly nodded. "Well, she looked up information about Cutter and McGuire, stuff you probably could not find. She said Cutter is a political hack. He has little trial experience. He worked for a congressman out of D.C. for years, then got the position as U.S. attorney as a reward for whatever dirt he carried neatly."

"And McGuire?"

"From what she told me, he's just an old fogey who never had a headline-making case in his life. Just another hack."

"So what does that mean? How can I use this?"

"I don't know. Maybe your lawyer can figure it out. Peggy said it's likely Cutter is pushing for a bigger plum. Since he has little trial experience, this could be his career-maker. Also, Peggy said if your lawyer pushes you to settle it's because he'll be paid whether he wins or loses. So, lawyers rather settle and get paid for doing less work."

"Settle? There is no settlement in a criminal case. I would have to plead guilty." Now Carly realized why her attorney urged her to take a plea deal. The slender hope she clung to all these months drained out of her. She hoped Irwin Stanley did not take her refusal to take a plea deal as a personal affront.

If Carly needed proof of no hook on which to hang hope, it came after she returned to the courtroom and took her seat at the defense table. Judge Easterly invited the defense attorneys to give their opening statements. Each defense lawyer was permitted to give a separate opening and closing statement, since they represented different defendants. Carly had read about it online and Sherri told her the same thing. The opening statement was the way the lawyer told the jury, "This is the story we are going to prove."

The prosecutors had told their story. The defense attorneys declined. They announced to the court they would not make opening statements at this time. The jury was left with one story: the prosecutor's.

On to the next step—the prosecutors proving the allegations.

# Chapter Twenty-Two

Terri's husband, Tom McGuire, called his first witness: Vito Capone. Carly's eyes opened wide. This was the man who phoned her too often when she was in Client Services. Now she knew she would have crossed the street if she saw him approaching. He looked like a thug.

Vito Capone wore a black suit with a black shirt and a silver tie. He flashed a fancy watch and smiled repeatedly, showing tobacco-stained teeth, as he admitted to fraud. He excused it as necessary because he was sick and needed the money—his medications cost twelve thousand a month, he said. He said he spoke with the Archer brothers numerous times. They instructed him how to apply for these policies and agreed to buy every one that was issued.

Capone stated he had spoken to Carly numerous times. Carly knew that was true. But when he said she reminded him to contact Sean Beasley about blood swapping—using a healthy person's blood when Capone needed a blood sample for a policy with large death benefits— Carly gasped. That never happened. She never knew anyone did that. She scribbled a quick note to her attorney and poked his arm, pointing to the note she wanted him to read. He nodded.

Capone said either Aidan or Blake told him to scramble his Social Security number, but he was not sure what to do. He phoned Carly

Daniels. She educated him about ways to do this.

How do I hate thee, let me count the lies, Carly thought, and made strokes on her pad, crossing every four with a fifth before beginning again. On the opposite side of the page she did the same for possible lies, ones she suspected but did not know for certain.

Capone described his first conversation with Blake, how Blake urged him to get as many policies as he could. When McGuire asked if he had others, in addition to the one he told Blake about during their first conversation, Capone said, "Well, he asked that, too—if I had other policies. And I said I did but they were, you know, new policies and I didn't think they were, you know, able to be sold."

McGuire asked, "How new, Mr. Capone?"

Capone said, "I'm talking months, maybe two months, three months old."

McGuire tried to clarify: "Two or three months old from the time you acquired the policies to this conversation?"

Capone agreed. Carly nodded thoughtfully. Capone had these policies before he ever spoke to Aidan or Blake. Capone was involved in fraud before he ever did business with the Archers. She thought this should let the Archer brothers off the hook. If the Archers were off the hook, so was she.

Capone seemed to realize this. He quickly added, "And he pushed me to send him the policies, very reassuring they could be sold, it's not illegal, we have buyers, we have investors who will buy it and wait out, you know, the two year period, and basically it was a bunch of tales I was told. But anyway I went along with it. I was in a position where I needed to raise money, and I sent the policies to him. And I—in the interim, I asked him again, I said, 'Is this legal?' And I said, 'And what happens to these people who buy these policies and lay out this money and something within that two-year frame happens? And basically, he told me, Well, then they're—he used a foul word—he said they're—I don't know if I can say the word. But they're screwed; we'll go with that word."

McGuire let that go and switched topics, asking Capone if he knew or one of the Archer brothers discussed the MIB—the Medical Information Bureau—during their conversations. Carly hoped the defense lawyers would go back to the testimony about other policies. She had seen a few that insured Capone, policies Archer purchased from other companies.

Capone said he understand the MIB to be the insurance investigation bureau. "I told Aidan Archer, I said, you have to justify when you buy insurance why you would need the amount. If your income doesn't match the amount of insurance in such excess that you're purchasing, this all gets reported to the MIB or IAB, I thought it was called Insurance Investigation Bureau."

He looked at McGuire and got the nod and one word, "Okay." Capone went on. "And I was concerned, because I said I don't think I'll be able to get any more policies. And he told me there are ways that we can, you know, get around that."

McGuire asked if Capone was concerned that by doing this something possibly could go wrong. When Capone said, Yes, McGuire asked what Aidan Archer told him.

Capone said, "He was very reassuring. Everything, you know, everything would be okay, it was on the up-and-up, it would be okay. And I knew it was illegal but I went along with it—in the hopes that nothing would go wrong. But then it did."

Capone admitted he had applied for several policies with large death benefits. McGuire had him repeat that these policies required a medical exam and blood testing. It was the Archer's idea, he said, for him to get an imposter to take the exam. As for the blood sample, he never followed up with Beasley.

The Archers' attorney, Mitchell French, stood to cross examine Capone. French was tall but Carly thought he looked like a weasel, despite a patrician nose and gray hair. He had a small mustache, a long, narrow face, and tiny, bullet eyes. Irwin Stanley whispered, "Giorgio Armani." When Carly shrugged, he said, "The suit." It was a two-button black striped suit, obviously expensive but Carly did not know the name Armani. When Mitchell French pointed to a chart he brought for use with Capone, his watch gleamed in the ceiling lights. Attorney Stanley informed Carly the watch was a Rolex.

"You claim that Aidan Archer and Blake Archer taught you to mix up your social security numbers on the insurance applications, is that correct? And your first contact with them was when?"

French's chart showed that Capone had done this for many years and with insurance policies he sold to other companies—before he ever heard of Archer. He also switched social security numbers when he applied for a car loan, a credit card application, and a mortgage. Capone claimed on an insurance application several years prior to his first contact with Archer that his net worth was $6 million.

Capone laughed. "I wish!"

"So you were a liar long before you ever spoke to either of the Archer brothers or Ms. Daniels?"

Carly felt reassured. French was making mincemeat of Capone and his lies.

Then French asked Capone how he had come to the court that morning. He said he took a cab. From where, French asked. The Hyatt. Did you travel alone in the cab? No, he shared it with Sean Beasley and another viator who was scheduled to testify against the Archers.

Then French asked about his plea agreement with the prosecutors.

"You pled guilty in this courtroom in front of Judge Easterly, right?"

"Correct."

"But you still haven't been sentenced, right?"

"That's correct."

"And the crime that you pled guilty to, you pled guilty to ... what was that again?"

"I believe it's mail fraud and wire fraud."

"And you came into this court and admitted to doing that; correct?"

French led him through each step, getting "Correct" as the answer to each question, then asked "And you're hoping to avoid prison; correct?"

"I hope."

"In fact, you're hoping that very strongly; correct?"

French then established that McGuire had signed the plea agree-ment. And that plea agreement said if Capone cooperated fully with the prosecution, they could move for a downward departure, ask the court to give him a lighter sentence than he otherwise would receive. French put the plea agreement on the screen to allow the jury to see the actual document. And he read aloud:

"If the defendant provides substantial assistance in the investiga-tion or prosecution of other persons who have committed an offense, the United States will file a motion for downward departure." Capone agreed.

"And then the last sentence," French went on, "'The decision to file a motion is solely within the discretion of the United States.' If Mr. McGuire decides he doesn't want to file that motion, there is nothing you can do about it, correct?" Capone agreed. "And I take it you want Mr. McGuire to be happy with you, correct? You're doing your best to make him happy with you, aren't you?"

Capone agreed with everything. Then French reminded him that he told many lies in order to get money, and was testifying today as part of his cooperation agreement with the government—in hope of avoiding prison. So now there is more than money at stake. His free-dom was at stake. Capone agreed. French left it at that.

But then the prosecutor had another go at him. This allowed Capone to repeat the many ways in which he was corrupted by the Archers and Carly. Hammering it home, and Carly feared this would be what the jury remembered. McGuire then tried to dispel the im-plications of testifying viators staying at the same hotel and traveling in the same taxi. McGuire asked if the men had discussed the case.

"Absolutely not."

Carly uttered a small sound, hrrmph; she did not believe this for a minute. But the prosecutor, satisfied, nodded and this witness was dismissed. The court took a brief recess, during which time Irwin Stanley told Carly not to gasp, not to make any noise, not to nod her head—the jury could misconstrue her reactions. Just be impassive. "Pretend to be a statue."

When court resumed, McGuire called his next witness, Sean Beasley. Beasley wore a short sleeved shirt that showed his brawny arms. His arms were covered with a labyrinth of tattoos, like black lace. He, too, had spoken with Carly. "She would call to find out if I was dead yet."

He said it was a joke between them because Carly had told him she was going to change the numbers on his medical information, to make it seem he was sicker than he actually was.

Carly shut her eyes. It was difficult to hold back the gasp that leaped to her throat, the urge to scream, "Liar!" She had never seen his medical records, not until she did research for Ruiz and Price.

Attorney French looked shaken by this statement. During cross examination he questioned Beasley: Did you tell this to the prosecutors? He said he told the grand jury. French repeated the question. Beasley said he did, but could not remember if it was at the first or second meeting. French asked with whom. Beasley said the meeting was with McGuire and a federal agent. French asked if they took notes. Beasley said he was sure McGuire did.

French tried to pin him down on the date, whether it was before or after the grand jury hearing, before or after he entered a guilty plea before the judge, this judge, Herman Easterly.

"I honestly don't remember. I honestly don't."

French then asked if McGuire had shown Beasley his medical records and asked him to point out where Ms. Daniels made changes. Beasley said no.

"They just took your word for it?" French asked. Beasley said he assumed so. French asked to approach the bench. All the lawyers gathered before the judge's bench, out of hearing of the jury and the audience. The bench hearing took so much time that French was not able to continue with Beasley. The judge asked the lawyers if they would agree to take a lunch break now; they agreed.

As soon as the break was called Carly asked her lawyer about the bench conference. "Not here," he said. "This has to be private. Confidential."

He refused to go with her to an empty room or sit in the car to tell her what happened. He wanted his lunch and he wanted to eat without disturbance or complications. That worried Carly. Why did he expect she would disturb him, or cause complications?

Ben joined her for lunch—they had packed a picnic basket in order to save money. They rushed to the parking garage, rushed back to the court house, carrying the picnic basket, and took their lunch to one of the benches in the plaza that united the buildings at the Civic Center. Court was due to begin again at two; Ben did not stay for the afternoon session. He wanted to arrive home before Ethan's school bus.

The afternoon was similar to the morning, establishing that prosecutors put Beasley at the Hyatt, took the same cab as Capone and others, was urged by the Archers to find anyone like him who would apply for life insurance to sell to Archer. He said Carly sent him notes—but he didn't save them. He had a plea agreement signed by McGuire in which, if he provided substantial assistance he might not go to prison.

French then handed Beasley a copy of his plea agreement. "I want to look at some of the benefits that you get under this plea agreement. Now, the first benefit is that the government can't use against you any of the testimony that you're giving here today; correct?"

Beasley agreed.

"And that means that no matter what you admit to on that witness stand today the government can't use what you've said to bring new charges against you; correct?"

Which meant, Carly realized, if they exposed his perjury he could not be charged with perjury or obstruction of justice. Beasley collected tens of thousands of dollars which, in earlier testimony, he admitted he did not declare as income on a tax return. Now he would walk free, simply for telling a good story about her and Aidan and Blake.

That was the pattern with each of these men.

Carly faced dozens of charges, the evidence against her their testimony but these liars who actually committed fraud faced a maximum of five years. When the prosecutor had his chance to redeem Beasley's testimony, and McGuire mentioned Carly's name, she saw a few jurors look at her. She wished she could read their expressions, what it meant, what they thought about her.

Shortly after four thirty the judge called a halt to the first day of trial. The jury left, the audience snaked out, the lawyers gathered their files and stuffed them into wide briefcases. Carly waited for the last spectators to leave. She saw the prosecutors clap each other on the back and watched as they walked from the courtroom with broad smiles.

Carly waited until Irwin Stanley was about to leave, and walked with him to the elevator. They rode down silently but as they exited the court house Carly told him she had some questions. He brushed her off, saying he had to rush back to the office to prepare for tomorrow, and waddled hurriedly to his car.

# Chapter Twenty-Three

WHEN SHE SAW THE RAIN, Carly rushed to leave extra time for the drive to court. In winter, when it rained, the clouds dumped three seasons' of water. Everything flooded—roadways, highways, surface streets, and highways were especially treacherous, slick from months of oil now combined with rain water. Drivers unused to this weather did not slow, splashing through deep puddles that soaked their brakes, and throwing off spray that blinded other drivers.

Carly took her time driving to Santa Ana and arrived with ten minutes to spare. Sheltered by a large, black umbrella, her head under a lime green hooded rain slicker, her feet protected with black rubber boots that rose mid-calf, she walked to the court house. As she approached, Carly stopped at one of the bronze sculptures she scarcely noticed on previous days, as she rushed past. A glance into the glass entry showed a short line at the metal detector. Who would brave this weather, other than lawyers and their clients?

Carly had read about the sculptures on the internet. There was one on each side of the entry, one to represent the Wisdom and the other to represent the Power of the law. She stopped at "Wisdom," a woman, sitting, long hair draped over her left shoulder, a huge book open in her lap. One hand rested on the book.

Was wisdom the book? It appeared to be slipping from her lap.

And the woman appeared to have no interest in the book. She looked to her right, as if wisdom was not in the huge, heavy book. Her head was tilted away and slightly down, ignoring not only the book but the owl at her feet, on the other side of her body. Was the owl wisdom? If so, why did she look the other way?

Carly wondered if this sculpture represented the mystery, rather than the wisdom, of the law. Or was the message that wisdom was not found in books? Since the owl was not helping, perhaps it meant there was no help. The woman's face was passive, as if she had neither energy nor interest in seeking wisdom. Perhaps she did not expect to find it, or had given up her quest.

Carly walked around the glass entry to the other side and stopped to stare at the bronze statue that represented "Power." A man in a loincloth with a physique suited to a body builder, a man on steroids. Carly was startled by the huge pecs. She went back to the woman sculpture. The sculptor had minimized the woman's breasts; she was nearly flat-chested. Carly returned to the man, Power.

Mister Power's right hand was raised to his jaw and tightly fisted. His left hand casually held a weapon. It looked like a bow, an old-fashioned type of bow. At his feet were an eagle and a snake. The eagle was power that could soar. The snake was power that could kill. No, Carly corrected herself. Eagles also kill. They are birds of prey. Killing by land or by sky, that was what the eagle and the snake represented.

Carly looked again at the snake. What was the meaning? She remembered Genesis 3:1, "And the snake is more subtle then any beast of the field which the Lord God had made." Why did the sculptor include the snake? Either she did not understand the meaning, or the sculptor wanted to warn those who enter court: subtle and dangerous things result from the power of the law.

The man's face did not look threatening but it did look stern, like the judge who sat on his throne high above the court. The judge did not have to look threatening to wield power. He had power. The law was power. But wisdom was doubtful. Carly nodded and began to walk to the glass entrance.

She agreed with the message. The woman, lacking power, was in search of wisdom. The wisdom to understand, perhaps? The wisdom to acknowledge the reality that she had no power? Did that mean the law had power but no wisdom? Were these sculptures showing all who entered that the law was weak on wisdom and strong on power?

∾

Once past check-in, Carly rushed to the restroom to change from boots to shoes. She gathered her umbrella, her boots, her slicker, her purse, and headed for the elevator. The hallway was empty as she approached the court room. Carly took a deep breath, pushed open the door, and walked through the empty court. The rhythmic tapping of her heels was a lonely sound. No one else was in the court room. Carly suddenly was overcome with loneliness. She passed through the gate that separated spectators from participants, and took her seat. She thought about Ethan in school, about Ben, today waiting tables for the lunch crowd at a seaside restaurant. Carly had to awaken him to give him the message. It was good he had another gig. Paying the rent on time was their first priority.

Ben no longer came to court. After he let it be known he was available to wait tables or tend bar at lunch time, he had frequent last minute calls from area restaurants. That meant he had to be home to receive the call, rush to dress, and get to the restaurant on time.

Carly was glad Ben stopped coming. He stopped after three days, and missed the next seven days when Carly told him there was nothing going on, just more viators, one after another, the same story about their tax free dollars from fraud, passing the blame to the Archer brothers and, when asked about Carly, mumbling, "Yeah, I spoke to her. She told me Aidan or Blake was in a hurry for my policy." Repetitious. Boring. And each one chipped away any hope Carly would be acquitted.

Most of the viators who testified were strangers to Carly. She was certain she never spoke with them. If she did, it was brief and inconsequential, so much so that she had no memory of it. The problem was too many of these witnesses. Taken together, they demonstrated exactly what Cutter told them on the first day. Archer did business with "disreputables." That was the type of company it was.

Yesterday, during recess, she asked Irwin Stanley about the witnesses on the defense list. Once again he deferred to Mitchell French, the lead defense counsel. She asked him why, wasn't he supposed to represent her, no one else? He said French was the lead counsel; he made decisions that would affect all the defendants.

This bothered Carly throughout her ride home and through dinner. She no longer discussed the trial with Ben. Her version differed greatly from that of reporters. But yesterday, when he asked, she told him of her frustration with attorney Stanley.

"Maybe he's being paid to be incompetent," Ben said. "You know it happens. Maybe the prosecutors have something on him and promised not to act on it, if he played their game."

Then Ben left for his bartending job. A few hours later Ethan went to bed. Alone, Carly could not stop thinking about Ben's suspicion. When she could not sleep, she decided to phone Irwin Stanley, knowing she would have to leave a message. She begged him to call defense witnesses who were decent people, people who sold legitimate policies, people whose lives improved due to the settlement. She could supply some names. And if he decided not to do this, would he please explain the reason? She wanted to say, Since I'm calling at night that should give you time to— What? Find an excuse?

As the court room began to fill, Carly sighed, glad it was Friday, grateful for the two day respite. Each day of trial drained her. Each day she returned home exhausted. Irwin Stanley joined her at the table, placed his suitcase-sized briefcase on the floor and began unloading file binders. Carly asked if he got her message. He said, "No time to discuss this now."

The morning was consumed with more testimony from insureds whose fraud gave them more money than Carly ever had in her life— and tax free, to boot. They seemed proud of their accomplishment. Carly suspected they were competing for headlines. She could imagine them rushing each morning to grab a newspaper, eager to see their names in print, to read how they were described. She tried to tune out their testimony. When she could not tune out, she wanted to scream. To calm herself, she drew doodles on the pad Irwin Stanley gave her. She had pages and pages of boxes, squares, rectangles, boxes within boxes. She called this her "intolerance page."

These pages were at the back of her pad, beneath the pages on which she wrote notes to attorney Stanley. One of her most frequent notes was, "Not true." Each time she wrote this, Carly poked attorney Stanley, silently bidding him to look at the pad. After so many days, she wrote a headline at the top page of her pad, "Not True."

Once again during recess attorney Stanley reminded Carly there was no way to prove these stories untrue unless she testified, and if she did testify that would leave the jury with he said-she said. When she asked about her message, he said, "Trying to explain trial strategy to you would be like trying to explain chess to an aborigine."

"Try me," Carly said, knowing he would not. He frowned and began to leaf through one of the file binders.

After lunch break, the prosecutors called their next witness, Patricia Russell. Carly's attorney whispered, "She's a key witness for us as well as for the prosecutors."

Carly watched an attractive brunette in her mid-forties stride confidently down the aisle, as confident as a model on a runway, three inch heels clicking on the marble floor. She passed through the gate, mounted the witness stand and turned to face the court. Patricia Russell wore a baby blue business suit, large pearl and sapphire earrings, and a matching pin on the jacket lapel. She was sworn in and took her seat. She nodded a greeting to the prosecutors.

Tom McGuire rose from his seat and stepped forward, nodded at his witness, and asked her to describe her background, her family, her education, her employment.

She said she was the mother of four; she had attended college but did not graduate. Her history was ordinary and Carly began to lose interest. She continued to wonder why such an ordinary woman was a witness until, at the end of her recitation of work history, she informed the court, "Most recently, I was CEO of a viatical and life settlements company called Star Spangled Life Settlements."

Carly felt as if a bolt of lightning had hit her. This was Trish Russell, the woman who phoned to offer Carly employment after Archer was raided.

McGuire asked Trish Russell where she currently resided.

"At Danbury Correctional Camp for Women in Danbury, Connecticut."

Prison? Carly stared at Trish Russell. She came here from prison? How could she be so composed? So confident?

Now Carly knew they had little in common. Both had limited formal education, both were working mothers with families, but it stopped there. Carly was engulfed in shame when she walked around a grocery store. Wherever she went, she felt as if her forehead was branded with the symbol of an accused felon. But Trish Russell, a convicted felon, someone who already had experienced prison, acted and perhaps felt no guilt. Odd, Carly mused; Trish Russell seemed to enjoy being the center of attention, regardless of the reason.

I could never enjoy this, Carly thought, but I can learn from her. This witness had earned her full attention.

# Chapter Twenty-Four

McGUIRE ASKED Ms. RUSSELL what caused her to reside at Danbury Correctional Center. "Some difficulty with the law, Ms. Russell?"

"As a result of a federal investigation into the viatical and life settlement industry. I entered a plea of guilty to one charge of mail fraud and one charge of money laundering."

"Were you represented by an attorney?"

"Yes, I was."

Twice more McGuire asked about her guilty plea. Finally, Trish Russell lost patience. "This is not my favorite thing to say for the fourth time. One charge of mail fraud and one charge of money laundering. The underlying—"

"What were—"

"Shall I continue?"

"Yes."

"The underlying conduct that resulted in my guilty plea to those charges is as follows: I ran a viatical and life settlement company, a funding company. What that means is my company located investors to put up money to buy life insurance policies for sale by people who had terminal or life-threatening illnesses, or elderly people who had a very abbreviated life expectancy. We matched up those policies with people who had money to spend for those policies."

McGuire began to ask another question. "Is that—"

Trish Russell cut him off. "That's a perfect legitimate business. I was convicted because a number of those policies were obtained fraudulently. By the insured. The original application for insurance contained what was known as a material misrepresentation. That is, the insured lied outright or had materially omitted important information that the insurance company needed to make their own determination about whether or not to issue the life insurance policy."

Again McGuire opened his mouth, made a noise, and was cut short. Trish Russell was not done. "And further, because my company was aware of the fraud and the policies were taken into our portfolio and matched up anyway, that constituted the problem. So that was the mail fraud, in that we used the mails, of course, to circulate documents and so forth. The money laundering was because we had a bank account at Chase Manhattan Bank."

Carly knew that if those same circumstances applied to the Archers, they would be convicted. She knew there was no proof she was aware of the fraud. She never had access to the records until she began working for the FBI. But would that make a difference? Or might the jury decide, "A plague on all your houses."

McGuire asked a few questions about the bank account, then asked Trish to tell about the sentence she received.

"I received a sentence of thirty-four months."

Carly wrote that on her pad. Circled the number. Wondered why Trish, who was directly involved with fraud was sentenced to no more than thirty-four months, while Carly was threatened with ten years for obstruction of justice.

McGuire asked Russell about her contacts with investigators.

"Originally, when I retained counsel, it was the recommendation of my lawyer that I put together a document which he called a proffer, and basically the proffer said what I knew about the viatical industry and where I believed other individuals may have committed acts or engaged in conduct similar or related to the same conduct that I was currently in trouble for."

"Are you telling us that you cooperated?"

"I certainly tried my best."

"Tell the jury if you have had contact with this U.S. attorney's office."

"Yes I have."

"On how many occasions?"

"I believe now about three or four."

"Have you had contacts with other United States Attorneys' Offices?"

"Yes, I have. In five other cities."

"As you met with those various United States Attorneys, what was your position with them? What did you do when you met with them?"

"I basically told my story and answered questions as completely as I could."

"Okay. Now, do you know what the term '5K1' or 'downward departure at sentencing' means?"

"I certainly do."

"What does it mean to you?"

"It saved me about half the time I would have had to have in prison. It's the motion that the government makes to the Court asking that an individual receive a reduction in their sentence based on their cooperation with the United States government."

"Did you testify before the grand jury here in Santa Ana?"

Trish said she did. When McGuire asked if she testified at other grand juries in other cities and if she testified at trials in other cities, her answer was yes to both questions. Carly was astonished that Trish testified at so many trials. Maybe that's why she is so composed, Carly decided. Lots of practice. Plus, each time she traveled to another trial, she got to leave prison and she got to wear her glamour clothes.

When McGuire asked specifics about her business Trish said, "Star Spangled Life Settlements, in the course of its business, purchased over, oh, it has to be over two hundred fifty million dollars worth of policies. Of that amount, I believe that close to sixty-eight million dollars of face value—face value is the amount of the policy—were fraudulently obtained."

And that thought led Carly to wonder how Trish, who had no formal experience running a company and no college degree, qualified for the huge loans she needed to purchase policies. Or did she sell policies she had not yet purchased, and used investors' money to acquire policies? Carly wrote a note to ask attorney Stanley to find out, if the prosecutor did not ask.

"Now, you indicated that your real role was as a funding company; is that a fair descrip—"

"Correct."

"Okay. Tell us who your clients were; who your funders were, please."

"Most of SSLS's investors or funders were individuals of moderate means."

"Could you give us an idea of the average individual investor?"

"Sure. Sure."

"Could you do that, please?"

"The individual investors were primarily very conservative investors. For the most part, these were individuals who did not want to risk money in the stock market. They weren't willing to tolerate that kind of uncertainty. They expressed almost uniformly a very high comfort level with the fact that a viatical settlement, when it works out properly, will eventually pay out, and it doesn't matter if the stock market crashes or the economy falls. As long as the insurance premiums are paid and the insured eventually passes away, they will receive their money."

"I want to jump ahead with you just a moment. Did you have occasion to do business with the Archer company?"

"Yes, I did."

"With Mr. Aidan Archer?"

"Yes, I did. Both Aidan and Blake Archer."

"With Ms. Daniels?" McGuire turned to stare at Carly.

"I spoke with her one time."

Carly gasped. Irwin Stanley tapped her arm to remind her to be still. She quickly wrote a note about that single phone call—the offer of employment—and tapped his arm to show him the note. He ignored her. His eyes were fixed on Patricia Russell. Perhaps he did not want to miss a word. Perhaps it was because she was attractive and charismatic.

McGuire glanced at the yellow pad in his hands and looked up. "I think you indicated that overall you sold some two hundred fifty million dollars' worth of policies, sixty-eight million of which were fraudulent on the applications. Can you give us some idea of the approximate numbers of investors you found for policies you purchased from Archer?

"I believe eventually we signed contracts on ninety-two policies from Archer."

"Can you tell this jury the value of the ninety-two policies?"

"No, I couldn't really say. But the average face value of the policy was, generally speaking, fifty thousand or above."

Carly felt faint. She could not get past Trish Russell's statement that they had spoken one time. Trish Russell had implicated her. Carly worried what this would mean to the jury.

McGuire veered off to ask Trish to give the jury some idea what led up to her first meeting with the Archers brothers. "Sure," she replied. "I had been trying to organize some way of doing business with Archer for a while. My company had raised an awful lot of investor money, and finding sufficient numbers of policies was always a challenge. So I was aware that Archer was an important broker and I was anxious to open business channels with them."

Carly was half-listening when she heard the words that answered her question. She quickly wrote, "money from investors first, then policies."

"All right. And what did Archer bring to that, and what did Star Spangled bring to that?"

"Well, SSLS brought a ton of money. Archer represented that they had vast numbers of viaticated life insurance policies."

"Okay. Did you have any discussions about a contract?"

"Yes."

"Tell the jury about that, please."

Trish turned to face the jury. She smiled. They were her friends.

"The Archers were very anxious for an exclusive dealing agreement with SSLS." Still smiling, she turned back to McGuire.

"What was your understanding of what an exclusive agreement or contract would contain?"

"Well, we actually did execute one. The agreement basically said that SSLS had an obligation to review and purchase from Archer as many policies as we possibly could. We had a right of refusal, of course, on any individual policy, and SSLS also retained the right to go to other sourcing brokers if Archer at any point was unable to fulfill our demand for numbers of policies."

"What kind of insurance contracts were contemplated in this agreement?"

"Contestable life insurance contracts."

Carly stifled a gasp. Contestable? This was the focus? Policies that were recently issued, that could be contested and voided by the insurer, if they discovered fraud? Trish wanted these? Archer was ready to supply them? *It's over,* Carly thought. Trish had just confirmed Archer's knowing involvement in fraudulently acquired policies, Aidan's and Blake's involvement and, by association, Carly's.

"That first day that you met, did you have that contract all prepared and ready?"

"No, we were in agreement on most of the major points. I finished sort of finessing the agreement with Mr. Mark LaFollette, who was counsel to Archer at the time."

"Did you discuss your sources of money?"

"We discussed how much money SSLS would continuously be able to bring to the table and where it would be coming from. In the beginning of our business, we marketed directly to individuals. Very shortly after we began advertising for more agents and teaching them what our company offered, how to present that information, marketing to their own clients, their own base of business. All those agents had individual clients who, in turn, would do business with our company. The only difference is that the insurance agent also received a commission from the insurers."

"Are you saying, Ms. Russell, these insurance agents received commissions from the insurers when they submitted applications for new policies?"

"Once the policies were issued, the insurance company paid them commissions."

"And they received another commission when your company bought the policy?"

"Correct."

"Earlier I asked you about trade association meetings and discussions about fraud. Did you and either of the Archer brothers discuss this?"

"The issue of fraud, it was just part of the flavor of the water in the well. The discussions were related to issues regarding the setting up of trusts and how paperwork would be handled and how policies would be generated."

"Did you have any discussions with either of the Archers, or did they make any comments about steps to prevent an insurance company from knowing that a viatical settlement company was involved?"

"Sure."

"Tell us about them."

"Well, again, it was primarily within the context of discussions about trusts and how they would be handled. At the time before we did business with Archer, we didn't use trusts. Do I need to talk about what trusts are?"

"We're going to come to that in a little bit. I'm really asking you, did either of the Archers ever indicate anything about steps to take to keep the insurance companies from knowing Archer was involved?"

"Well, that's why they insisted on a trust. The trust obscured the fact that a viatication was in process. Archer took steps to keep the insurance companies from knowing, because as soon as they saw the name of a viatical company it would be 'a red flag.'"

"In other words, then the insurer would investigate."

"Yes—if it was a new policy. People who sold policies they owned for years did not trigger 'a red flag.' As to steps taken, I remember

distinctly we were walking through Archer's offices and we were talking about paperwork. Aidan Archer made it a point to tell me there
were employees who had contacts inside the insurance companies, that
paperwork was handled very carefully, that people were rewarded for
pushing paperwork through and were very careful not to do anything
that would—and these are his words—'raise a red flag' with the investigative unit at the insurance companies."

"Okay. Did either of them ever tell you whether they took steps—
other than the trusts—to prevent the insurance companies from knowing a viatical settlement company was involved?"

"I inferred that by Mr. Archer's repetition of the fact that only *certain people in his company* processed information and dealt only with
specific customer service people at the various insurance companies."

"Was Carly Daniels, the defendant, mentioned as one of those
'certain people'?"

"No names were mentioned."

Carly felt a rush of gratitude that Trish did not lie about her. She
continued to stare at Trish Russell while, from the corner of her eye,
she saw Tom McGuire stride to his table, lift a paper, and step toward
the judge's bench. "Your Honor, I want to display now Government's
Exhibit 1.5."

The judge said, "All right." McGuire pointed at the court clerk to
turn on the screen, and asked the witness if she was able to view it.
When she said she could, he clicked to another screen. "I want to show
you the letter that comes with that, please. And let's look up at the top
and see if it's dated."

The monitor faced the jury. Trish Russell twisted sideways and
leaned forward, trying to view the monitor. "Yes, it is dated," she said.

McGuire approached the marshal. "Mr. Marshal, I've got a copy
of this exhibit if you would hand her this copy, I think we can maybe
go a little quicker." The marshal stepped over to him, took the copy,
and delivered it to Russell. Trish read the letter. When she looked up,
McGuire said, "Okay. Let's go to the letter itself. What's going on in
this letter?"

"I asked for a written assessment of how much contestable life insurance volume Archer could supply."

Carly wrote on her pad, "Trish wanted contestable policies. Only contestable."

"Would you please read the contents of the letter?"

"The letters states, 'Dear Ms. Russell: Thank you for your recent inquiry regarding the volume of contestable life insurance policies that could be supplied to your firm. Archer, Incorporated, is the largest viatical brokerage in the United States. In the past year Archer placed 100 million in contestable viatical contracts. Assuming that our firm would bid for our policies competitively, it would not be unreasonable to assume that Archer could provide an aggregate face value of several hundred million dollars of contestable policies annually. If I can be of further assistance, please call. Very truly yours, Blake Archer."

Carly was so upset she had difficulty writing about this. Now she knew it was true. Archer was a fraud factory. Now the jury knew. According to the prosecutors, she, Carly Daniels, knew this all along. Carly wondered how much of this Terri McGuire knew. She had a sudden thought: If Terri knew, that might be why her husband, the prosecutor Tom McGuire, believed Carly also knew.

"Now, then, your discussions with the Archers and others about an exclusive dealing agreement. Mr. Marshal, if you would hand the witness what is marked as Government's Exhibit 1.81, and, again, that was on the list, Your Honor." The marshal carried it from McGuire to the witness. McGuire asked, "This copy of the agreement was faxed to you. Do you recall from whom it was faxed?"

"This is a fully executed copy. So I believe would have come from Archer."

"I don't want to go through this contract with you page by page—"

"Good." Trish Russell smiled broadly at McGuire. She had interrupted him again. He looked at her sharply, frowned, and continued as if she had not done so. "But I want to ask you just to tell us what your understanding of this contract is, please."

"Well, it's much as I stated before; that SSLS would first utilize Archer policies to meet the needs of its investors, and Archer would offer its policies to us first. We had a right of first refusal. I didn't have to accept anything that Archer offered. And if Archer was, at any in time, not able to supply the number of that SSLS needed, I could go to other sourcing brokers for those policies."

"How many different ones did you deal with?"

"I would say probably twenty or more, some not as large as Archer but substantial businesses, and others quite small."

Judge Forester asked Tom McGuire if this was a good place to stop for recess. McGuire agreed, and the court recessed for half an hour.

# Chapter Twenty-Five

CARLY FOLLOWED HER ATTORNEY into the hall. "How is Ms. Russell's testimony going to help us?"

He said he needed to use the restroom. He did not return before the marshal announced that court was about to resume. Carly returned to her seat at the defense table.

McGuire began by asking his witness, "Comparatively speaking, how did you find Aidan and Blake Archer and Archer Life Settlements to deal with?"

"Difficult personalities."

"What about secretiveness?"

"Yeah, I would say fairly secretive as well."

"Tell us what you mean by that, please."

"With virtually every other company I knew exactly how much money was going to the insured person. With Archer, all I was permitted to know was a gross bid; that is, I would pay twenty-five percent, nineteen percent—whatever it came out to be. But I never knew nor could I find out how much Archer kept and how much the insured actually got paid."

Carly wrote, "Russell paid Archer *19%, 25%.*" That meant Archer paid much less to the insureds. It also meant Russell could have resold them for double and made a good profit. Did she resell for more than double? Carly hoped one of the attorneys would ask about this.

"Would you receive a packet of information before you funded the policies?"

"No. This is how it worked and this was, you know, part of why the business process was a little more cumbersome with Archer. Archer would fax over to SSLS a data summary sheet that had certain vital statistics—the insured, how old the insured was, what the illness was, what state they were from."

"Would it indicate the date of the diagnosis of the illness?"

"No, I don't believe so."

Carly made a note of this. She wondered how Trish could be certain she was buying a fraudulently acquired policy, if she did not know the date of diagnosis. Or was Trish lying? McGuire asked details about the information Archer provided.

"Was it important to you to have medical information?"

"It was critical."

"Why?"

"Because I was concerned about fraud in the viatical industry, but—"

"I can't hear you."

Carly had not heard the reply. She wondered why Trish Russell's voice suddenly dropped so low. Was she about to say something that would further injure the Archers?

Trish smiled, took a deep breath, and began again. "I was concerned about fraud, but it was the wrong kind of fraud I was looking at. My concern was viators—insureds—who dummied up their medical records to appear sicker than they really were. So I was really very, very focused on that aspect. I had seen a few instances of it and it worried me. Additionally, it was necessary to get a statement of life expectancy from a third-party medical reviewer, either a private physician or a company that specialized in generating those reports."

"So, you're talking about viaticals here. Insureds with short life expectancies."

"Yes. That was the bulk of our business."

"Well, once you got all the documents, with regard to what was on the medicals and the time that the application was made, was there anything there that was clear to you about the health of the insured?"

"Yes, it was clear that on many cases the insured had a terminal illness that predated the application of their life insurance policy."

Carly felt confused. Didn't Russell say earlier that she did not get this information? Or did she mean she did not get it from Archer, but other companies provided it?

"You've indicated that occasionally you kicked back or wouldn't seek to fund a policy. Is that right?" Russell agreed. McGuire asked, "For what reason?"

"Usually because there was an error in the data sheet or, you know, I felt there was some type of impediment to the viatication of the policy."

Carly noted this and added, *What kind of impediment?*

"Did you ever kick one back because of fraud on the application?"

"No."

Carly noted this: *Fraud was not an impediment.*

"Okay. Can you tell us, from your knowledge at your end of the business, did any of those ninety-two policies you received from Archer—well, of course, people invested in those; correct?"

"Yes."

"Did any of those investors, at some time or other, lose their investment?"

"Yes."

"How did that happen?"

"The policies were investigated by the insurance companies, and cancelled."

"These were from the ninety-two policies that Archer furnished to your company?"

"Yes."

"Can you give us some idea of the dollar value of the loss to those investors of the ninety-two policies?"

"It was certainly in the millions of dollars."

Carly hoped McGuire would ask how much SSLS charged investors. She wondered how many investors were involved.

"Do you know, as of today, if any of those investors have been made whole?"

"Well, because, well, the—no, they have not."

"Does the term 'multiple policies' mean anything to you?"

"Within the context of my industry, it means several policies, more than one policy, on the same individual."

"Okay. And when one individual obtained more than one—we're talking about the insured, now, aren't we?"

"Correct."

"And when an insured got more than one policy, would all of them be from the same insurance company?"

"No."

"What would it be?"

"It would be spread out over a number of insurance carriers."

Carly wrote that down. Her spread sheets showed several insureds who were issued multiple policies by the same insurer. Now she was certain Russell was lying. Why?

"Okay. Tell us, if you know, what happens when a policy that is contestable is rescinded by an insurance company."

"The policy becomes null and void. It becomes worthless."

"Okay. What about premiums paid in?"

"Insurers return them to the owner of the policy. Those funds would come back to Star Spangled Life Settlements since we were the owner. Investors were the beneficiaries."

McGuire turned to the judge. "Your Honor, I don't think I have any further questions, and it is late in the day."

That was odd, Carly thought. Why didn't he ask if she returned the premiums to the investors whose policies were rescinded? Did she keep them?

Judge Easterly agreed to end at that point for the day and the week. He reminded the witness to be at court Monday morning, and reminded the jury not to speak about the case with anyone, not to read newspaper reports or watch or listen to any other media reports about the trial.

Carly stood up. Her joints felt arthritic. The moment she realized who Patricia Russell was, her body had stiffened and she remained tense throughout the hours of testimony, trying to determine what might be helpful to her defense. She hurried after Irwin Stanley, following him from the court house, eager to ask, again, how this testimony would help her. He rushed ahead to his car. Just as she approached, he started the motor. Carly called out, raising her hand in a stop sign. He waved and drove off.

Carly walked slowly to her truck, wondering about Patricia Russell, how she became so confident.

# Chapter Twenty-Six

ERIC, SHE WAS A CLERK. A clerk! She didn't earn enough to buy her own home—anywhere."

Eric had glanced at the caller ID when his phone rang as he approached his hotel room. He ignored it. An hour in the hotel's fitness center and fifteen minutes in the outdoor pool did not invigorate him. He was too worn out to talk to anyone, and definitely not sociable. The needle-sharp, hot shower helped, but when he was toweling off the phone rang again. He saw the ID: Kyle again. He answered. Now he knew he should have let it to go voice message.

"Eric, listen to me. Carly is a good person. What's being done to her is wrong, terribly wrong. I phoned her, to check how she was doing. She was a wreck. She told me a bunch of creeps—they even look like creeps—lied about her. She said there was no evidence to support what they said. But that doesn't matter, does it, if the jury believes them?"

"That's correct."

"Reporters on television just repeat the testimony against Carly. They don't question anything. And it's absolutely false."

Eric was tempted to shut the phone without another word. There was no way to stop Kyle. Eric felt his nerve endings tighten, but managed to speak in a calm voice. "You know I can't discuss the case with you."

Kyle matched the calm tone. "Well, someone has to do something to help her. Tell me what I can do. You must know. Or who I should call to get her help. I'm talking about me, not you."

Eric walked back into the bathroom to hang up his towel. "Maybe you're wrong about her. Maybe Daniels is a good liar and fooled you."

"No!" Kyle shouted. "I know she is a good person. I know she is not guilty."

"Daniels is that important to you?"

"Yes. No. I mean, I care, of course, as anyone would when someone is falsely charged with a crime."

Eric suppressed a groan. He did not want Kyle to hear his frustration, his impatience. He did not want to pursue this topic but he did not know how to shut Kyle up. He sat down on the bed, pushing pillows up behind him.

"You're telling me you think the testimony against her is false? You know her that well? Well enough to be convinced? You know the type of work she did?"

"Yes, yes, yes—and to make matters worse, reporters believe the lies. Which means public opinion will be against her."

"I'll tell you, because you can't hear me shrug—I'm shrugging." Eric tried to laugh aloud. It did not come out a good sound. "There's nothing I can do about reporters, Kyle. Nothing anyone can do."

"I can't see any way for the truth to come out. Carly was advised not to testify. The lawyer warned her if she testified the prosecutor could rip her apart, make her seem unbalanced."

"Kyle, please. Let me off the hook. I can't talk about this case. In general, a plea deal is the way to go."

Eric could hear Kyle's footsteps nearly stomping his wood floor as he paced. Kyle? Always calm Kyle—agitated? Eric could think of nothing to say. He was beginning to feel angry that Kyle put him on the spot, and angry at the Daniels woman for putting Eric and Kyle at odds with each other. He tried to dampen down the anger and remain calm. Kyle was not calm. He was nearly shouting.

"The whole thing takes such a toll! It's such an ordeal. Why are they doing this to her?"

"Again, speaking generally, for some prosecutors it's all about winning, not truth. It's possible your friend looked vulnerable to them, a single mother, a special needs child. They may have expected her to cooperate, easily, quickly. Instead, she resisted. They know they have the power to break her, and they probably tried. But she was stubborn, and that made them angry."

"And that's our justice system?"

"Unfortunately."

"You mean they would punish her with a jail sentence just because she is stubborn?"

"Many prosecutors are like that. It's what motivated my father to study law."

"Her lawyer keeps telling her to take a plea deal."

"We're back to that again," Eric said, and was impressed with how well he controlled his impatience, his anger. He took a deep breath. "Let me tell you about a case that may explain this better. It came before the Supreme Court in October 2011. A guy named Cooper shot a fleeing woman four times–in the legs and buttocks. He was offered a plea deal of four to seven years. His lawyer advised Cooper to go to trial. His reason–because the bullets were below the waist he could not be convicted of assault with intent to murder. So, Cooper rejected the plea, went to trial, was charged with assault with intent to murder, and the jury found him guilty. He was sentenced to fifteen to thirty years."

"I don't understand. Why was he offered four to seven years for such a horrible crime?"

"It saved the state time and money not to go to trial."

"He deserved thirty years. Why was this before the Supreme Court? I thought they accept very few cases."

"The issues were ineffective representation and plea bargaining. Cooper claimed he went to trial on his lawyer's advice, and it was bad advice. Ineffective representation."

"What does this mean in terms of Carly?"

"Nothing, because I can't discuss her case. All I'm saying is, sometimes it's wiser to accept a plea deal."

"Even if it means perjury? That's what it means to Carly. She would have to swear to tell the truth and then lie. Not only lie about her own guilt, but lie in court about her employers, when she knew nothing."

"This is getting too close to the taboo area, Kyle. I really cannot discuss her with you."

Eric heard what sounded like an involuntary groan from Kyle. He wanted to cut off the conversation. He tried to figure out how to do this tactfully. When he heard Kyle say, "So Carly is doomed?" he decided to launch another story.

"Here's an example of prosecutors going wild. It's not first-hand. A few years ago Louisiana federal prosecutors gave pictures and other information to inmates so they could testify against an innocent couple who were charged with selling drugs. In exchange for their testimony, the inmates were promised a reduction in their own sentences. Based on the testimony of the inmates, who pointed to the couple at court, they were convicted."

"Geez," said Kyle. "I never knew these kinds of things happened."

Eric said, "If it was a routine drug bust and conviction, it would not have been written up. What happened is an inmate who wanted to testify paid twenty-five hundred to get the pictures and information. But the inmate who was paid never delivered. He was transferred to another prison, and did not return the twenty-five hundred."

"So the inmate who paid the money was defrauded."

"Hold on a minute," Eric said. "I'm reaching the good part, but first I want to get a coke." Eric put the phone down and went to the small refrigerator, withdrew a can, opened it, and took a drink. When he picked up the phone again and heard silence, he said, "You there?" He heard the phone pick up at the other end.

"I decided to get myself a coke, too."

Eric could hear the smile in Kyle's voice. "Now, the reason the story was written up. This was one of the rare times when the plot was exposed."

"All ears at this end."

"The inmate who was defrauded–you can imagine how pissed he

was. So pissed, he wrote a letter to another federal prosecutor–not one involved in the case. His letter described all this. It was turned over to the judge by the uninvolved prosecutor. The judge was irate. And, of course, reversed the conviction."

"Okay, happy ending. Now I want to know what the judge did about those corrupt prosecutors."

"Nothing, Kyle. There's not much a judge can do. Prosecutors have immunity. There is no accountability. None. Zippo"

"That's enough to motivate anyone who is corrupt."

"I know of only two federal judges out of the entire system who brought these actions to the attention of the Department of Justice. The judges were pretty much ignored."

"So innocent people get set up, and the guilty go free. Carly told me the guys who are testifying against her may not serve a day–their reward for helping get convictions. And yet they're the ones who actually committed fraud."

"What can I tell you, Kyle? This is not why I went to law school."

"It's kind of sick, don't you think?"

"What can I say? I told you before, Kyle–it's all up to the prosecutors. There is nothing I could do, even if I was in a position to help. The only way an innocent person can beat them is to have a good attorney. Actually, a terrific attorney."

"I don't know how good her attorney is. He keeps pressuring her to take a plea deal."

"Shit!" Eric said, completely disgusted and unable to hold back. He took a deep breath and continued in a calm voice. "I'll tell you one more thing, and then we end this conversation. In a 2011 article, The New York Times reported that ninety-seven percent of convictions in federal courts the previous year were the result of guilty pleas, and the numbers were similar in previous years."

"Because prosecutors squeeze people, even if they're innocent?"

"Prosecutorial misconduct is a disease without a cure."

"What do you mean?"

"It's like malaria. You can't tell which mosquitoes carry it, there's no prevention and there's no cure."

"That's not exactly true—about malaria, I mean."

"Visit one of the Innocence Projects web sites, and you'll see what I mean. You'll find dozens of stories of innocent people who were intimidated into guilty pleas and exonerated after many years in prison. They're just a sampling—the tip of the iceberg, so to speak."

Kyle groaned. "I don't think I want to know more than I do right now."

Eric yawned noisily. "It's late. I'm beat. Gotta hit the sack so that I can earn my taxpayer salary mañana."

Tired as he was, after hanging up the phone, shutting the light, and stretching out in bed, Eric could not sleep. He kicked the covers off, pulled them back on, kicked them off again. His anger at Kyle was full blown now, but not as great as the anger he felt at the Daniels woman for driving a wedge in their friendship. He did not want to be angry with Kyle. He tried to redirect all the anger at Daniels.

Kyle knew nothing about Eric's life after his parents' death, and Eric had no intention of telling him but now. On the verge of losing Kyle, he again felt the loneliness of those years. Finding Kyle was like finding a lost piece of himself. Kyle's parents—he called them Auntie and Uncle. He was at their house more than his own. He and Kyle were like brothers, not just pals. Brothers. Being with Kyle again brought Eric back to who he was, the person he had hidden away when everyday life became too painful to care about anyone. For the first time in years Eric was tempted to lower his defenses. "Rejoin the human race," he told himself with a cynical chuckle.

The more he thought about it, the more he decided it was cruel, insensitive, and uncaring for Kyle to keep after him on this. Eric had explained to Kyle that he could put his career at risk to violate the rules. He simply could not discuss an active case with an outsider. But Kyle did not care about Eric's career.

It wasn't as if Kyle had a serious relationship with Daniels. They were casual acquaintances—through her dog, forgodsake. Daniels did not need Kyle; she had a family. So why was Kyle obsessing? It was his easy life. Kyle could afford to be obsessed with someone in trouble, the same as he became obsessed with saving a dog, a cat, a turtle.

Turning on his side, Eric concluded the Bureau was where he wanted to be. After he was there a while, after he made friends and had colleagues who trusted him, they would be like family. And it was honorable work. This was his future. Eric flipped to his other side. As he buried his head in the pillow he decided he would not jeopardize his career for Kyle, and certainly not for Daniels.

He knew he needed more in his life. This would not disturb him so greatly, rob him of sleep, if he had more than work in his life. Eric turned onto his back, thinking he would get a dog once he finished rotation and could live in one place, travel only on assignments. He needed a dog. Until he was nine years of age, he had a beagle. Until his parents were killed and the family divided. Eric never learned what happened to Chip, after he and his sisters were separated. As a kid he never had the courage to ask.

He spent the next twenty minutes thinking back to when he was eight years old, the last full year of childhood before disaster tore the family apart, the last full year of being an innocent kid playing with his dog Chip. With images of Chip, sleep came.

༄

Carly was determined to use the weekend to relax. On Saturday she and Ethan took his pup to Dana Point Harbor. After lunching at an outdoor café they strolled the plank boardwalk, peering into the windows of shops, stopping to look at boats. On the ocean side of the boardwalk the marina was filled with motor and sail boats of varying sizes and designs, many with quirky names printed on the hull. On the land side boutiques sold souvenirs, candles, clothing, and shops offered boat rental and scuba gear rental. As they rounded a bend Ethan pointed to brown pelicans, one on each post of the dock. DeeOhGee lunged at them and the pelicans took off, filling the sky above the harbor.

Sunday they tried the dog park for the first time on a weekend. The off-leash park along the Canyon Road had no parking area, and the street was filled. They parked several blocks away, in a city lot that required quarters for the meter, then walked back. As they approached the gate, DeeOhGee strained at the leash, eager to get inside, but Ethan's footsteps slowed. Carly resolved the tug-o-war by taking the leash.

"What's wrong?"

"Too many people," he mumbled.

They had never seen the park packed with people and dogs and, it seemed, more people than dogs. Carly looked inside the chain link fence as they walked by and saw what appeared to be families. No wonder there seemed to be more people than dogs. She wondered if it would be dangerous for a pack of dogs to run, dangerous for the dogs as well as the people they might crash into.

Ethan's nervous fingers had difficulty unlocking the leash from DeeOhGee's harness. They had learned to unleash DeeOhGee while standing between the double gates, which allowed their dog to be as free as the others once they entered. Ethan finally had the leash off. They pushed open the second gate and entered the park.

Carly was adjusting the locking hinge on the gate when they were surrounded by a pack of dogs, so many that they pushed her up against the gate. Dogs of all sizes, all colors, breeds and mixed-breeds, at least ten. They were trapped.

DeeOhGee's always-wagging tail went down and stayed there, curled under his body for protection. The other dogs pushed and snapped at each other, fighting to be the first to get to the newcomer, all eager to sniff his privates or to mount him. Three dogs won the competition to mount, forming a conga line, the first on DeeOhGee, the others on the backs of the dog in front, each humping a dog. DeeOh-Gee cowered and whined.

Carly yelled, Ethan yelled, and when the dogs ignored them Ethan astonished her by jumping up and down as he shouted, "Go! Go! Go!"

It tugged at her heart and brought tears to her eyes to realize how brave Ethan was, trying to protect his dog. He did not succeed. They ignored him. Carly did not know what to do. She knew less about dogs than Ethan.

They were stuck at the gate, unable to move due to the pack of dogs, and DeeOhGee was whining, unable to get away. If anyone wanted to enter or leave, they would be blocked. Finally, a man and a woman, strangers, came over and chased off the pack. The woman told Carly that weekends could be a problem because of people who brought un-socialized dogs. Sometimes the people were problems, too, not cleaning up after their dogs. Carly decided to leave. When she asked Ethan, he gave her a "thumbs up" sign.

As they walked back to the truck, Carly asked whether he wanted to go to the beach to watch Ben's volleyball game, or go home and toss a Frisbee in the back yard. "Both," he said.

Carly smiled. "You're the boss today."

It reminded Carly of when they lived in Ohio and had to catch good weather when they had it. Now it was happiness they had to catch on the fly. If she was convicted ... no, she would not let herself think that way, not on the weekend.

# Chapter Twenty-Seven

IRWIN STANLEY GREETED HER AS they entered the courtroom. "Today is our turn for cross-examination." It was the first time Carly had seen him smile.

Judge Easterly took his seat, nodded at Mitchell French, Archer's attorney, and French stood up, a yellow legal pad in his hands. Each question he directed to Trish Russell was followed with a glance at the yellow pad. Each question repeated statements from her earlier testimony appended with the word, correct, and of course Russell agreed to each. Carly was puzzled. What was the purpose? He challenged nothing. It was boring. Then French asked a different question.

"And at that time, you had no legal background or training; correct?

"I still have no legal background or training."

"You wondered whether there might be legal issues in purchasing policies from viators who may have obtained them by fraud?"

"Yes."

"And at the same time, you felt there were a number of insurance companies that didn't want to go to the expense of checking out the information on insurance policies."

"I assumed they didn't want to, but I had no direct knowledge."

"Because you wondered about legal issues, the owner of the viatical company that employed you prior to when you founded SSLS directed you to a prominent Park Avenue lawyer, Alvin Burns."

Once again French was repeating Friday's testimony. "You visited Burns; you explained the nature of the viatical business; you did so fully and did not withhold anything, correct?" Again, each statement was a turned into a question and Russell replied, "Correct."

French continued, "He told you that, in his exact words—"

McGuire stood up. "Your Honor," he said, speaking over French. French ignored the interruption, finishing his sentence in a louder voice, "that you were on the side of the angels."

Judge Easterly held up a hand to French and eyeballed him. "Just a minute." He turned to the prosecutor and nodded.

McGuire said, "I am going to object as to what some person—"

"Sustained."

Mitchell French frowned. He looked down. He raised his gaze to Judge Easterly. "Judge, could I have a side bar on this, please?"

When Irwin Stanley did not join the side bar, Carly whispered to him. "What is going on?" He shrugged. She whispered again, "Why aren't you going up there?"

He whispered back. "French can handle it." Carly tried again. "Is this related to how Trish will help the defense?" Stanley held up one finger. He was intent on his computer screen. He had the transcript of the trial on the screen, sent to his computer as soon as testimony was recorded.

The judge had the jury removed from the court while the attorneys continued to argue. Carly was so frustrated she could not sit still. She asked her attorney, "Am I permitted to leave court for ten minutes?" When he did not answer, she said, "Ladies' Room."

"Good idea." He rose and followed her. As they stepped into hallway Carly put a hand on his arm to detain him. "Please explain what is going on. The reason for the side bar?"

"Ms. Russell is listed as a co-conspirator."

"I understand that. She's a prosecution witness. But French wanted to tell the court she was on the side of the angels. Why is that important?"

"The gist is: Russell believed her conduct was legal. French wants to emphasize that she sought legal advice. He will argue this is critical to her state of mind. Since the Archers also sought legal advice, it's relevant to them, as well."

"In what way?"

"Well, the court should take into consideration something called 'scienter.' That means intent, knowledge of wrong-doing. Through Russell, we want to show that the Archers and you, not just Russell, had no knowledge of wrong-doing because all of you acted on legal advice."

"So far it looks to me that the Archers are guilty," Carly said.

"It doesn't matter, if they followed legal advice. Russell's dealings with the Archers were after she consulted with lawyers. Lawyers told her what she was doing was legal. If this excuses Russell, it excuses the Archers. That's why we think Russell is our most important witness."

"Are you saying even if it was wrong to buy fraudulent policies and resell them, because a lawyer told them it was not illegal, they cannot be found guilty?"

"Exactly."

"Then why is McGuire opposed to this?"

"No doubt he is challenging it as hearsay. Russell was about to quote a third party—someone not called to testify—and that's hearsay."

"Why not call the lawyer who advised her? And the lawyer who advised the Archers?"

Irwin Stanley shrugged. "That's up to French, as lead attorney."

"If I tell you to call the Archers' lawyers, aren't you supposed to do whatever I request as long as it is legitimate?"

"Ms. Daniels, you have no understanding of trial strategy. Attorney French decided on the strategy, and we follow his lead."

Carly stood there, watching, as Irwin Stanley disappeared into the Men's Room. She was sinking into a morass of helplessness. How was this good strategy? Suddenly realizing the trial was on-going, she rushed to the Ladies' Room and rushed back to the court room in time to hear Judge Easterly announce, "I'm going to sustain the objection, but I'm going to let her tell her belief, and I think I would allow you," he nodded at McGuire, "to ask her on what she bases that. She says on legal advice, but I don't want to go any further with it."

French walked half-way to the witness box. "After talking with this lawyer in New York, did you have the belief that what you were doing was legal?"

"Yes, I did."

"Did you also speak to the former director of insurance for the State of New York?"

"Yes, I did."

"And did that further confirm that what you thought you were doing was legal?"

"Yes, it did."

"And you knew, at the time, that Mr. Burns was a New York lawyer for twenty-five years?" He asked about Burns, his college and law schools, the pictures on his office walls of famous people, on and on. The questions seemed meaningless to Carly.

"Now, let me ask you a little bit about contestable policies. As I understand it, SSLS largely dealt in contestable policies?"

"Yes, almost exclusively. Toward the latter half of our business life, it was almost exclusively senior or elder settlements."

"I think your calculation was that, in total, SSLS bought approximately two hundred fifty million dollars' worth of face value insurance policies?"

Aha! Carly thought. At last someone is going to put the numbers into perspective.

"A little more than that, yes."

French asked details about the numbers, finally reaching the point he wanted to make. "And so the sixty-eight million, if my math is half-way decent, was about twenty-seven percent of the total SSLS portfolio. Would that be about right?"

Russell agreed.

"Okay. So, of the two hundred fifty million you did, Archer policies would have been about three to four percent in terms of face value?"

"It may have been, but this is very hypothetical, Mr. French."

Carly was scribbling away, trying to make sense of the changing numbers. It seemed French wanted to show Archer policies were a very small percentage of Russell's business. But Russell changed her original numbers. Why? To cast blame on Archer for what she and her company did to investors? Or did she have a deal with the prosecutors to dirty-up Archer? "Okay," French continued and again repeated her prior testimony, sentence after sentence, with a pause for Russell to agree. Carly began to think French wanted to emphasize certain statements but before she figured out his purpose, he changed tack. "You've not been charged with anything here in California, right?"

"Correct."

"And, at the time you operated SSLS, you believed the insurance companies were empowered by the insured in their contracts to do full investigations and that they could obtain medical records and interviews with people and associates and bank records and so forth?"

"Well, that's not a belief; that's a fact."

"Then why did you plead guilty?"

Oh. My. Gosh, Carly thought. If she is not guilty, then the Archers are not guilty.

He waited for the answer. Trish Russell sighed. She took a deep breath. Her voice no longer was soft. It was angry. "The FBI agent who investigated my company threatened to prosecute my husband, and told me I could be prosecuted in every district in the United States."

"How would you describe the pressure by the government on you to plead guilty?"

"It was beyond anything that I could ever have imagined."

Mitchell French tilted his head toward her, said, "Thank you very much," and walked back to the defense table.

Judge Easterly looked at the defense table. "Mr. Stanley."

"No questions." Carly looked questioningly at Irwin Stanley. He was playing with his laptop computer.

The judge glanced at the clock, saw that it was approaching the noon hour, and recessed court.

"What is the agenda for the afternoon?" Carly asked attorney Stanley as they left the court room.

"McGuire gets another shot at Russell. Then we get another shot."

As they approached the elevator Carly asked, "In what way did Russell help us? I can't figure it out."

"It's too complex to explain to a non-lawyer."

Carly felt like shaking him. She stepped to the back of the elevator. She would be among the last to leave—the main floor. Stanley was going to the third floor cafeteria. As she left the court house, Carly took her peanut butter and jelly sandwich out of her bag, then the bottle of juice, and went to find a bench in the sun. She spent the lunch break trying to figure out how Patricia Russell helped the defense, and what type of strategy French had in mind. Failing to find any answers, she decided she would, again, try to get Irwin Stanley to explain it to her.

# Chapter Twenty-Eight

ONCE AGAIN RUSSELL WORE a designer suit, jewelry, heels, and smiled a greeting at the jury after she mounted to the witness box.

For the first half hour of his redirect prosecutor Tom McGuire asked questions about every lawyer who represented Russell in various states where she had FBI interviews or appeared at trials. He asked about their co-counsel, their ages, their specialties. All the lawyers were former federal prosecutors who now specialized in criminal defense. Carly could not imagine the expense of hiring all these attorneys and that was a wake-up call. She and Russell were not in the same league, not at all.

As McGuire droned on about the lawyers, inching toward a full hour of this, Carly tried to find meaning for the Archers, for her, for the trial in general. Then Mitchell French stood up. "Judge, I'm going to object."

Judge Forester glanced at him then, to Tom McGuire, "Well, don't lead."

Carly wrote, "Lead?" to attorney Stanley. He scribbled back, again without any capital letters, "A question that suggests the answer."

French spoke again. "It was relevance, Judge."

Judge Forester frowned. "Oh, well. Overruled."

McGuire continued as if he had not been interrupted. "Now, about the second lawyer."

Relevance, Carly thought. French is right; none of this is related to anything. And the judge is willing to allow him to waste everyone's time and patience. Or is this how McGuire wags his power at the defense lawyers? That was too scary. She quickly dismissed the idea.

Another half hour of the same boring question-and-answer and French stood again. "Objection. This is irrelevant."

"Overruled."

McGuire continued. "And you also had a lady by the name—"

Carly was so bored she began counting the number of sentences in which McGuire mentioned one of Russell's lawyers. Suddenly she remembered the television shows, the ones attorney Stanley scoffed at for teaching her nothing. In the shows, when a lawyer objected on the basis of relevance, the judges asked the challenged attorney to explain where he was going with that line of questioning. Not Judge Easterly. Why not? Had he stopped paying attention?

McGuire seemed on the verge of concluding this line of questioning when he said, "And all in all, you had five attorneys. Is that correct?"

"It feels like more than five."

"Well, have I left anybody out?"

"Well, yes, as a matter of fact, but that's okay."

Carly nearly groaned aloud. But finally it was over. McGuire clicked the remote in his hand and the monitor came alive, displaying a document. He asked Russell if she recognized it.

"I sure do."

"What is it?"

"This is the bill of information that was filed in the criminal case."

"Okay."

The screen was positioned for the jury; Carly could not see the full screen. Irwin Stanley stood up and stepped toward the jury box to get a better view. When he returned to the defense table, she looked up at him, hoping he would explain. He said nothing as Trish Russell spoke.

"My criminal case," Russell explained.

"Is that another way of saying this is the charge that was brought against you?"

"These are the charges I pled guilty to."

Carly wondered what this had to do with the Archers. If Trish Russell's testimony or her responses to cross examination had value for the defense, then McGuire wanted the jury to know she was a bad egg. It was frustrating not to know what Russell had said that was helpful to the defense.

"Do you see where it says 'The fraud.' Do you see that?"

"Yes."

"Would you please read the first paragraph to the jury?"

Trish Russell leaned forward and twisted her body. "This is in bold caps. It says, 'The fraud, No. 1. It was part of the scheme to defraud that individuals would and did obtain—'" She turned to McGuire. "I'm having a hard time reading this. I'm sorry."

"Let me help you then, okay?"

When Russell agreed, McGuire slowly continued from where she left off. "'...life insurance policies by falsely representing to the insurance company that they were not HIV positive.'" He looked up at Russell. "Did you know that to be the case really from the very beginning, long before the FBI agents ever came to you; and that is, this industry and your business is founded on the initial act that the insured lied on his insurance application?"

"The viatical industry is not founded on fraud. The contestable policy niche that developed certainly was. My business was in the contestable policy niche. We wanted contestable policies, only contestable policies. There are companies that do not deal in contestables."

"Did you know, then, from the very beginning that with regard to contestable policies that a great many of the insureds lied on their applications?"

"Yes, I was aware of that."

"Are most of the contestable policies obtained via fraud?"

"Yes, that would be true."

"And you knew that?"

"Yes, I did."

"And that was a fact that was known essentially as the seminal act, that's the beginning act of one of these fraudulent contestable policies?"

"Yes."

"You don't deny that you knew that from the beginning?"

"I knew that before I ever started Star Spangled Life Settlements."

"And do I understand that your testimony essentially on direct and on cross is the industry knew this?"

"The industry knew it."

Attorney Stanley poked Carly and pointed to his pad. He had written, "Yes!"

"Okay. Now let's look at the second paragraph. 'It was further part of the scheme to defraud that individuals, after having fraudulently obtained insurance policies, would and did seek to viaticate those policies through Star Spangled Life Settlements.'"

"Among other companies, yes."

"Okay. I want to drop down to No. 4. 'It was further a part of the scheme to defraud that Star Spangled Life Settlements would and did seek to conceal from insurance companies that their policies were being viaticated.' Now, by that act of concealing, what are some of the things that you did?"

"Everything possible to conceal the fact that a viatication was in process."

"Would you, for instance, have your employees conceal from insurance companies that you were a viatical funding company?"

"It was the counsel of one of those lawyers to change our letterhead and to rotate our phone numbers."

"A lawyer told you to do that?" His voice rose.

"Yes, Mr. McGuire."

"The lawyer told you to conceal from the insurance company that you were doing this?" McGuire seemed genuinely shocked. When Trish replied, "Yes," McGuire said, "Wow!"

Irwin Stanley, sitting next to Carly, echoed, "Wow," almost inaudibly. Carly wrote a note to him: *What does that mean?*

"Later," he whispered. Judge Easterly said something to McGuire. McGuire looked up at the judge.

"What did he say?" Carly asked Irwin Stanley.

"He asked if that was a question," Stanley whispered.

"No, sir," McGuire told the judge. "It was an exclamation."

The spectators chuckled, no doubt grateful for relief from the tension. Carly felt more and more lost. What did any of this mean for her?

"Did the lawyer tell you to hide from the insurers that these fraudulent policies were being viaticated?"

"Yes. But it wasn't couched in that language. I want to be clear about this, because it's important. It was in this kind of language: 'Because you're dealing with HIV and AIDS individuals, you have a tremendous liability to protect confidentiality. You could suffer all kinds of civil aggravation if something was done, even unintentionally, that puts someone's health status and condition out on Front Street."

"If I follow what you're saying, the advice of counsel was to protect the identity or the medical of condition of the insured?"

"Not to protect their medical records, which we had to do under all circumstances anyway—those were very sensitive documents. But because we were dealing with other parties, primarily insurance companies, SSLS could not be the agent of any third party discovering the health status of an individual."

"You were protecting yourself from civil liability for disclosure to third persons?"

"That's a much better way of saying it, yes."

"Okay. You weren't asking, then—or were you? I don't know. Were you asking, look, in the meantime, let me ask you—"

Mitchell French stood and addressed Judge Easterly. "Judge, I assume I can go into this area, to which they objected before. I mean, it seems like the door has been opened."

"Well, I don't know what's left to escape," Judge Easterly replied. "I'm inclined to agree with you, Mr. French."

Stanley wrote her a note: "good for us." McGuire went to his next question.

"Were you asking the lawyers in terms of, am I committing a crime here?"

"I absolutely said that, Mr. McGuire. And for me it was when I was with the former company, as an employee. So it was to the CEO there, I said specifically, 'There's fraud in these policies, there's a lot of fraud in the industry. Is that a problem?'"

Trish Russell stared into gallery, turned toward the jury, seemed to be gauging their opinion of her. When her gaze shifted back to McGuire, she said, "I remember discussing this with you before and you said, 'Well, you're just a fence then.'"

"Well, you know what? I got to ask you one more question. What in the world did you plead guilty for?"

Carly closed her eyes. There it was, the same statement French made. Even though earlier the prosecutor called her a fence, now he questioned her guilt. Will this end the case? Carly felt so hopeful she knew, if it did not end now, she would be crushed with disappointment.

Trish tried to explain her guilty plea. "I tortured myself about this. I asked my lawyer, 'Can I withdraw that?' And he said, 'Look, in the law we intend the natural consequences of our conduct, and knowing that there was fraud in those policies you knew that there would be a fraud perpetrated on those insurance companies, and you were right in that line."

"Well, were you?"

"I was in that line. I mean, that's a fact beyond dispute. And that's why I pled guilty. I believe in being accountable."

Uh oh, Carly thought. Now she's admitting fraud on the insurance companies. That means guilt for the Archers, too. And me.

"Let me ask you this, Ms. Russell. After all is said and done, are you guilty of what is alleged in this information?"

"I committed that conduct. I did."

Well, I did not, Carly thought. She wished she could scream it to the court.

"I have no further questions, Your Honor."

Judge Easterly called for lunch recess. Carly grabbed Irwin Stanley's arm. Something happened; she hoped he would explain it to her. "I need to speak with you."

He said, "Okay," and waited for her to walk out of the court. As soon as they were in the hall, she asked, "What was the 'wow' about?"

"The prosecutors objected to us introducing testimony that Archer relied on advice of counsel. If a defendant relies on advice of counsel, the defendant is not guilty of doing wrong. But we don't plan to call the attorneys to testify. The prosecutors argued that without the attorneys' testimony, it was hearsay. Remember what I told you about hearsay?"

"Yes—it's like gossip. A testifies that B said such-and-such."

"Correct," Stanley said. "The prosecutors argued it was hearsay and hearsay is inadmissible. The judge agreed. But then we have Russell telling the court she proceeded on advice of counsel. So, McGuire opened that door. Once it's open, we are allowed to use the testimony the prosecutors wanted to keep out."

"Then that's good for us? And McGuire—he was surprised a lawyer told Trish Russell it was okay?"

"Yup. That was when he said, 'Wow.'"

"He seemed surprised she pleaded guilty. As if he thought she was not guilty. What was that about?"

"If she proceeded on advice of counsel, then she is not guilty."

"That's good for us, isn't it?" Carly heard the hope in her voice. "I mean, if it's good for the Archers, it's got to be good for me, too. Am I right?"

"If it's good for the Archers, it's good for you, yes."

"Is it good for them?"

"Well, that may be another story."

"I thought there was testimony the Archers paid lots of attorneys."

"It depends on what they told those lawyers. Did they tell them everything? Or did they hide things from them?"

Carly shook her head. "I wish I knew. That's my problem. I never knew anything. That's why I could not—"

"I know," Stanley said. He seemed annoyed to hear this again. "One more thing for you to keep in mind, Ms. Daniels. McGuire deliberately asked Russell about blood swapping and soliciting viators to get more insurance. He asked again and again, to make a point. The point is, that's among the charges the prosecutors brought against Archer.

Russell denied she did this. The prosecutors' witnesses testified Archer did this. So, don't get your hopes up."

He excused himself and disappeared into the men's room. Carly pushed into the ladies' room, wondering how Stanley's last remark fit with the description of Russell as a good witness for the Archers. She continued pondering this when she went downstairs, sat on a bench in the sun, and took her sandwich out of her purse. When she returned to court, Trish Russell again mounted to the witness box, was reminded by the judge that she was sworn to tell the truth, and she sat primly, waiting for French to begin his re-cross. French stood in front of the defense table, took a sideways step, and blocked Carly's view.

"Ms. Russell, when you met with the Park Avenue lawyer in New York, and he told you, after hearing the details, what you were doing was legal and you were on the side of the angels?"

"He said if there was a fraud, it was down there, it was not our company's. It wasn't our fraud, okay? And there was a line we couldn't cross over. That line involved what Mr. McGuire just asked me, 'Did you ever go out and ask somebody to do this.' But he did say, 'No, what you're doing, you're good. In fact, you're on the side of the angels.'"

"Even though you knew the insureds lied or may have lied on their applications?"

"Yes."

"You knew that Mr. Archer was consulting regularly with attorney Mark LaFollette; right?"

"I presumed that he was."

"Well, you were on the line with Mr. LaFollette."

"Frequently."

"Talking about contestable policies and trusts?"

"I can't say that we ever discussed contestable policies, but we certainly discussed trusts."

"Okay. And the trusts were largely for contestable policies; right?"

"Yes."

Powerful, Carly thought. Mitchell French just established that

Archer's attorney was aware of the contestable policies. This should help, but would it? Not if Trish Russell prevailed. She was making great effort to hide the fact about discussing contestable policies with the Archer's attorney. French nearly forced it out of her—by getting her to admit the trusts were largely for contestable policies. Carly wished he would emphasize this, do what McGuire did—ask the same question again and again, each time slightly different. Instead, French said, "Thank you very much," and returned to his chair.

Tom McGuire stood up. Irwin Stanley scribbled a note on Carly's pad. "He wants to undo the help she gave us."

*"What help,"* Carly wrote but Stanley was focused on McGuire.

Tom McGuire remained behind the prosecution table and glanced down at his pad.

"Ms. Russell, you said in response to Mr. French's questions just now, you had some conversations with the Park Avenue lawyer in New York. And if I got it down correct, he said something about the fraud that was 'down there.' What were you referring to?"

"I'm sorry, that was unclear. When I described the fact that policies were based on misrepresentation, he said, 'Clearly there's a fraud. Sometimes it might involve a life insurance agent and sometimes it doesn't, but the fraud is with those individuals.' And he sort of striated the thing. On one level you have the insured, on another level you have the insurance agent, one up from that is the licensed viatical broker, and then up from that is your company."

"And then you said in response to Mr. French that this lawyer said something to the effect there was a line that you shouldn't cross."

"Yes, that's correct."

"And what did that mean?"

"Well, he really hammered that point. What he meant was that—at least what I took this to mean—was the funding company could have no involvement at all in generating life insurance policies; that, you know, we couldn't hook up a sick individual with an insurance agent, that I couldn't introduce two people who were sick and just tell them to go have a conversation around the corner. I mean, nothing like that.

It had to be arm's length. He recommended that we use only licensed viatical brokers."

"Did he indicate what the problem would be if you became involved in the process and went out and, to use your words, 'hooked up with individuals' to get policies?"

"Well, sure. He said then you're actively committing a fraud, you're actively engaged in committing the fraud. You're part of the origination of the fraud."

"Thank you."

Judge Forester looked at the defense table. "Anything else?"

Mitchell French said, "No, Judge."

The judge looked at Tom McGuire. "May Ms. Russell be finally excused?"

McGuire said, "Yes, Your Honor." French said, "Yes, sir."

Judge Easterly told Patricia Russell, "Thank you, ma'am. You'll finally be excused." And, to Tom McGuire, "Call your next witness."

Russell had clinched it for the prosecutors. Carly was dispirited. But when McGuire called Marcia, the first of the employees to testify, Carly became alert.

# Chapter Twenty-Nine

MARCIA TRIED TO POUR WATER into a plastic cup she removed from the stack on the table in front of the witness chair, but her hand was shaking and she spilled the water. She laughed too loudly as she said, "I'm a klutz," and abandoned her effort.

In response to McGuire's questions Marcia described her job, through all the years she was employed at Archer, as limited to writing and mailing checks—to viators, to lawyers, to viatical brokers. There was a computer list of names, addresses, dates the checks were due, and the amount. She never saw a single life insurance policy. She did know there was fraud because she sat in at some management meetings as secretary. On one such occasion Aidan Archer announced they no longer would buy these policies. They also hired a computer specialist to design a program to red-flag brokers who had brought these policies to Archer. Marcia was not exact about the dates. She thought it was after Florida's legislature passed a new statute directly addressing this as fraud.

"I remember they were upset. Florida was the first state to pass this kind of law. The Archers decided it was too risky to continue; other states were likely to pass the same law. So they decided to change."

As evidence, the prosecutors introduced copies of Marcia's management meeting notes.

On cross examination Marcia repeated that after that meeting Archer planned to screen policies carefully. "They wanted to red-flag brokers who had brought these policies to Archer, to be sure they did not continue."

Mitchell French said to Marcia, "So, if Archer was involved in clean-sheeting in the past, they stopped as soon as one state passed a law against it."

"As far as I know."

McGuire's rebuttal had Marcia repeat, in order to drive home, that Archer did knowingly and willingly buy fraudulently acquired policies. He also established that Marcia did not know if Archer actually stopped buying fraudulently acquired policies.

Other employees were called. Each person supported the case against Aidan and Blake and, by implication, Carly. Judge Easterly must have been as weary as Carly; he called an early end to the day.

Carly had a huge headache. The strain was getting to her. And she felt tired enough to sleep in the truck, right there in the parking lot. She stopped at the cafeteria to buy coffee and took the cup with her, eager to be out of the court house. Marcia caught up with her as she was opening the door of the truck.

"I want you to know why I was not in touch these last few weeks. I was instructed not to talk to you until after I testify."

"That's okay. Call me. I have to get home to Ethan."

ﮩ

Kyle was surprised to see the caller ID on his phone. He had just closed the clinic and was changing his clothes, planning to take Java to the beach. He knew immediately something was wrong. Carly rarely phoned. He tried to hide the worry with a nonchalant question, "What's up?"

"I called to thank you, Kyle." She paused. He could hear her take a deep breath. "From the bottom of my heart. Something happened—Ben was called to work the lunch crowd at Sun and Surf. He didn't get back in time for Ethan's school bus."

What they always feared happened again. As the bus pulled away, four or five boys attacked Ethan, shouting obscenities, calling him zombie, freak, and worse, knocked him down and began kicking him. Suddenly DeeOhGee appeared, racing down the road.

"He rarely barks, Kyle. I never heard him growl. But Ethan said he came tearing down the road barking, as if to yell, 'Here I come!' As he neared, he growled. He sounded ferocious—even to Ethan. The boys farthest from Ethan heard and yelled to the others." She took another deep breath. "Any dog, I suppose, would have scared them, running at them and growling, but a pit bull? The bad rep they have worked for Ethan."

Carly paused again. "Oh my gosh," she said. "I'm still breathless over this."

"Take your time," Kyle said. "I want to hear the whole story."

"I want to tell you the whole story. The gang realized they were about to be attacked and started running in the other direction. DeeOhGee kept going, full speed ahead."

Kyle chuckled. He could imagine how Ethan must have felt. He had been the target of bullies when he was a boy, simply because he was a loner and at the head of the class scholastically.

"Ethan called him," Carly continued, "and DeeOhGee stopped and ran to Ethan. Just then Ben came roaring up the street on his motorcycle. He found Ethan on the ground, dirty and bloody and hugging DeeOhGee."

Kyle asked if Ethan was injured, if he needed a doctor or to go to the hospital.

"Nothing serious, Kyle."

Kyle was relieved to hear this. If Ethan needed a doctor or to go to the hospital, how would Ben have gotten him there? Surely not on the motorcycle. He had no idea if Ben had friends nearby who owned a car. He wanted to tell Carly to have Ben call him for a ride, if ever such a thing happened again. But he said nothing, just waited for Carly to continue.

"Scrapes, bruises. He's sitting with ice on his face as we speak. It doesn't seem as if anything is broken."

"If Ben wasn't home, how did DeeOhGee get out?"

"Ben had to leave suddenly, on short notice. The lucky thing is he couldn't get DeeOhGee into the crate. He had to take a chance things in the house would not be chewed."

"Did he do any damage?"

"Only a window screen. That's how he broke out—barreling through the screen at the side window. Ben said DeeOhGee waits at the side window for the bus, when it's close to time. He must have radar to have heard Ethan scream."

"Ethan didn't have to scream very loud for DeeOhGee to know there was trouble. Dogs' hearing is nine times that of humans."

"I'm sure glad of that." Carly began to sob. Kyle wanted to go to her, but he was hesitant to even suggest it.

"Please…," he began.

She apologized. She said she was crying for happiness. She was so relieved that Ethan was not hurt.

"It's time something good happened in your life," he told her. "Did you call the police?"

"No. They won't help. This was not the first time, Kyle. When we reported an attack on Ethan, the police officer said, 'What did he do to provoke them? He must have done something.'"

"Maybe one of the boys is his relative. I know a couple on the force who can be trusted. Want me to get hold of them?"

"I don't think that's necessary now," Carly said. "Those bullies learned they can't attack Ethan and get away with it. For the first time in his life Ethan truly is protected."

Carly said she was so very, very grateful Kyle talked them into getting this dog. Kyle chanced asking, again, if she wanted him to be at court for her. She said it was too boring to sit through. Upsetting or boring. She told Ben not to bother coming and would not want to burden anyone else with it.

He told her it would not be a burden to pretend he was DeeOhGee and be ready to break a window screen or two. That made her laugh. A small laugh, but it made him feel good that he could make her laugh.

After the phone call Kyle felt too jittery for the beach. He decided on a hike, which meant jeans and hiking boots instead of shorts and sandals. Java whined with excitement as they drove up and around the winding roads of Laguna Canyon to Top of the World. It was a residential street lined with luxury houses, each with an amazing view of the canyon dropping away and the Pacific Ocean beyond it. Kyle parked on the curl of the dead-end street. He leashed Java and they walked past a small playground and cut onto a trail that led down into the canyon. Once they were well away from people and houses, he removed the lead and gave Java the go-ahead to chase rabbits.

This was what he loved about winter in southern California. The temperature was mild, but too cold for rattlesnakes. On those rare occasions when he saw a rattler in winter, it was stretched out across a trail, sunbathing. He had to look for the markings to be sure it was not a twig from a tree. A stretched-out rattler was like a twig. It had to be coiled to strike. Sunbathing rattlers did not attract Java since they were cold-blooded and had no smell. Not moving and no smell, Java just ran past or jumped over it, as did Kyle the first time he saw a relaxed rattler.

He whistled and Java came running back. He opened the thermos jug and gave Java water. Java slurped and ran off again. Kyle did not worry about coyotes—they hunted by night—but he worried about other wild animals that lived in the canyon. Although Java was much bigger than a lynx or a bobcat, Kyle knew bobcats could bring down game, like deer, that were ten times its size. Java was too domesticated for him to feel confident she could hold her own, if trapped in battle with a wild animal. Java had lived in a house her entire life, slept on a pillow, even watched television with him. Java was more human than wild animal. That was why he kept her running back to him, to be sure she was not too far away, or hurt and unable to return to him.

They hiked often but today Kyle kept whistling for Java to return. He realized he was fretting about Java's safety as if she were Carly. It was Carly, not Java, who was in danger. And there was absolutely nothing Carly, or her brother, or anyone could do. Carly's future depended on the judge and her attorney. Eric did not flat-out state this, but Kyle understood.

He wanted to help her, to do something, but what? Kyle phoned a few criminal defense attorneys. He began with lawyers listed in the phone book as specialists in criminal defense. The first three said they did not handle this type of case. The fourth, explaining that he handled drunk driving, hit-and-run, petty theft, advised Kyle to look for an attorney who specialized in white collar crime defense. When Kyle did, the list included Irwin Stanley, Carly's attorney.

The man seemed to have a decent background, suitable education and experience, as far as Kyle could tell. He phoned two others. The receptionist in each office transferred him to a paralegal, a man at one office, a woman at the other. Each insisted he give them information which they would transmit to the lawyer. No, he could not speak directly with the lawyer. If the lawyer was interested, Kyle would get a call-back for an appointment. If the lawyer did not believe the case fit his or her practice, Kyle would get a letter declining his request and reminding him about the statute of limitations.

It was worse when he told the paralegals he was inquiring on behalf of a friend. Some seemed not to believe him. Others said he should have the friend contact the law office directly. The last one he tried, after listening to him for ten minutes, informed Kyle it was not possible to change lawyers in mid-trial simply because the client believes he is not doing a good job.

Unless he was busy with an animal, Kyle found himself thinking and worrying about Carly—all the time these last few weeks. He told himself the reason was as simple as John Donne's poem, "No man is an island." Two lines of that poem rang like clarions in Kyle's memory: "Each man's death diminishes me, For I am involved in mankind." If Carly were convicted, it would be like death. It would change the lives of her young son, her brother—everyone who cared about her.

Now, as he struggled up a steep, sand-packed hill, Kyle asked himself, Was it more than that? Would he be as consumed if the person was another pet owner? He remembered when Eric asked if Carly was special. Kyle realized he was evasive with Eric. No more evasive than with himself. It was time to be honest with himself. Possibly there was a future for their relationship, but only if she was not convicted. In that fantasy of a future, Kyle wanted to believe they would get to know each other better, socialize, be more than casual friends.

Possibly that would happen, once this burden was lifted, when Carly resumed a normal life. What was Carly's normal life? He really did not know. She was a very private person. She did not share much of herself. Kyle had to admit he did not know Carly well. The little he knew were things he picked up here and there. He did not even know what type of work she did before she was employed at Archer. He knew they had lived in Ohio. He knew she was devoted to her son. One day, while the boy was helping at the clinic, Kyle asked if his grandparents still lived in Ohio. Ethan said, "They moved to California. Now they're in heaven."

Kyle knew about Carly's computer courses from the time he invited Carly and Ethan for a barbecue on a Tuesday. She begged off, saying that was a school night. She explained that two nights a week she took computer courses at Saddleback Valley Community College.

He knew that much about her.

The computer course was a good excuse, but Kyle never worked up the nerve to repeat his invitation until the day the trial began. Bad timing.

After he phoned lawyers, he realized he could not help Carly but she might be able to help herself. When he asked if she knew how to design a web site and she said, "Yes," looking at him as if he might be thinking to employ her, he suggested she set up a web site for herself, to tell her story to the world. He offered to pay the expenses. He did have a web site for his veterinary practice. Kyle knew it was not expensive to register a domain name, and the cost for web host service had dropped greatly in recent years.

Carly refused to allow him to pay the costs. He offered a loan, repayable once she was employed. He had to make the offer twice—the second time asking if she had given it thought—and it was a couple of weeks before she agreed, but only if he let her work it off.

"Perhaps by doing grocery shopping for you? Or helping with your garden? I'd offer to clean house but I hate to do my own."

Kyle chuckled. "You would be such a high-class helper," he told her, "I would have to budget fifty dollars an hour."

Her frown made Kyle realize this was a serious issue for Carly. The word *charity* came to mind, as if he was reading her mind. She would not accept charity. But there was something of value she could do for him, something he wanted and had neglected for too long.

Kyle asked Carly to design pamphlets or brochures for the veterinary clinic. Instead of a bunch of papers stapled together to advise new dog or cat owners—the bundle he had given her at the first visit—he could offer something colorful, with pictures. She could add her information as designer to the last page.

Carly clapped her hands. "Perfect!"

Kyle felt a bit sneaky. If they worked together on this, they would meet now and then. He would see her more often. They might get to know each other better.

They did meet a few times at the clinic, twice for what Carly described as "a working lunch," but he learned little more about her than he knew before. Carly never spoke about herself, her life now or before they met, or what she hoped for the future. Kyle wondered if memories and thoughts of the future were too painful. He knew she had lost her husband and her parents within a short span of years. That must have darkened whatever good memories she from that time.

When Carly agreed to the web site, Kyle felt great relief. It was a form of empowerment. It would give her a voice. A good part of Carly's burden, he believed, was being silenced, stifled, unable to get the truth out. Her web site could be an arrow to the future. If the jury found her not guilty, everyone who had seen it would rejoice. If she was found guilty, everyone who had seen her web site would know there was something seriously wrong with the justice system.

That was months ago. Now, when Kyle thought of Carly being convicted and possibly sent to prison, he choked up. He was walking along a canyon trail, a variety of birds chirping at him, the scent of sage clinging to his jeans, the sense of being alone in a wilderness that was centuries old. Today, the restorative effect of the canyon failed. Today he was choked up. If Carly was convicted, Ben and Ethan would need him to be a very good friend.

# Chapter Thirty

ERIC FOLLOWED THE RENTAL AGENT to the second apartment. This was the first time he took a personal day and only because Yolanda announced she had a family emergency. When he heard this Eric suppressed a laugh—he pictured a spare bedroom in which she kept a family of reptiles.

Each apartment was at the top of a long flight of outdoor steps. Eric wondered about a resident with a sprained ankle or back, or a heavy parcel to carry upstairs—in rain. Although rain was rare, when he arrived in February, he drove from the airport in a blinding downpour and flooded streets.

He was nearly at the landing when The Lone Ranger music alerted him to a call on his personal cell phone. Without thinking, he pulled it from his pocket, glanced at the caller ID, and put it away. Kyle no longer left messages. He knew not to expect Eric to return a message. It had reached the point that Eric had to avoid Kyle. Gone were their plans to hike in Cleveland National Forest, take in a show at Laguna Playhouse, sail to Catalina. Any get-together with Kyle carried the risk of discussing the Archer trial.

Again the phone summoned him. Eric shut it down. *Kyle was a pain in the butt.* He quickly corrected himself. *That was Kyle being Kyle, eager to rescue another stray.* Kyle was a burden he did not need on top of problems with Yolanda, who insisted he bury his suspicions of wrongful prosecution.

But Eric's curiosity about the Archer trial finally got the better of him. Days earlier, he sought out the court reporter to ask for copies of the trial dailies. Since Eric was an investigator, she did not question his interest. He was surprised when she warmly welcomed him to her cubicle, her smile constant throughout their conversation.

"No problem," she said, pushing her hair behind her ears, promising to send, via computer, the unedited daily copy—and she would make it her personal priority.

A bolt of lightning shot through him. Day after day Eric was filled with tension, so much so he did not really see her until that moment. Suddenly he did: Cheryl Salzman, young, attractive, with no rings on any fingers nor any other visible place on her body.

He apologized for giving her additional work.

"No, no," she protested, "don't think about it. It's nothing more than keying in your email address and attaching the file."

When he asked about cost, she said, "No charge. Yours is a copy of what the lawyers get. Just remember this is unedited. I do a really terrific job for the finished copy."

Throughout their brief conversation she locked eyes with him until after he thanked her and turned away. As soon as he was out of her presence Eric decided he would invite her to dinner to show his appreciation. But not until later, after the trial. He could not risk complications.

Cheryl would be Step Two of restarting his life. Step One was finding a rental. The rental agent unlocked the door to the apartment. Eric approached the door just as his business phone buzzed. His breath caught. A text message from Cheryl. He told the rental agent he had an emergency, and rushed back to the hotel.

He calmed his conscience by telling himself he was looking for more evidence to support an investigation into senior fraud. Since this was not yet an official investigation, he had given Cheryl his yahoo account. Once he logged on and opened the envelope, he scrolled through the transcript, looking for viator testimony.

Eric had not seen daily logs since leaving Big Law. He knew this was raw material, the basis for official transcripts. If he had asked Cheryl to weed out and send only the viator testimony, it would have meant more work for her. As a result, he now had the full transcript.

As Eric scrolled an odd phrase caught his eye. He backed up to the beginning of that section. It was a bench hearing before the judge and outside the presence of the jury. He began to read.

The prosecutors wanted to call as witnesses seventeen defrauded investors. They referred to them as "ultimate investors," claiming Archer was responsible because Archer knew the policies would be resold. Defense lawyers argued against this testimony saying the investors had no connection to Archer. Archer resold policies to sophisticated investors and other viatical companies, and did so with full disclosure. Other viatical companies were responsible for defrauding these people. If allowed, their testimony would be prejudicial, evoking the jury's sympathy for their loss.

Defense attorneys put forth a robust argument, Eric thought, but what caught his eye was the phrase, perhaps accidentally uttered by a defense attorney: *"I'm not even sure what their names are."*

Eric was stunned. How could the defense not know the names of the investors? They were entitled to the names and their statements as well as proof of their investments, as part of discovery. Prosecutors were required to turn over anything that might be exculpatory— evidence indicating doubt about guilt. As in the Duke Lacrosse case, many did not do so unless pressed, repeatedly, by defense counsel. If the prosecutors held back, the Archer attorneys had time to compel the documents. After a judge issued an order to compel, the prosecutors' noncompliance could be grounds for a mistrial. That was a key issue in overturning the Ted Stevens conviction.

Eric went to PACER to check the Archer docket. He saw no motions to compel. Did they file the motion but it was not entered on the electronic docket? If so, why was it not referred to during the bench hearing?

Eric's head was spinning. *Is this what Yolanda meant about the defense's marching orders? Is this why defense attorneys waited until the eleventh hour to revisit the issue—but never filed a motion to compel?*

The judge ruled for the prosecution: "The Court believes all this is part of the alleged conspiracy … the testimony is relevant … the probative value outweighs the prejudicial effect and the Court sees no violation of due process here."

Disgusted, Eric ended this inquiry and resumed his search for viator testimony. While he was searching, he remembered something he had read in the management meetings. Now he had to see Yolanda again.

∾

Carly sent Ethan to a nearby park, telling him to give DeeOhGee practice walking on a leash. She was not ready to tell Ethan anything, and her attorney would be phoning with news, probably not good news. He never had good news. Carly hoped their conversation would be brief, ending before Ethan returned home so that she would have time to compose herself. Each day of trial it became increasingly difficult for Carly to hide from Ethan that she was under great stress. She struggled not to snap at him for little things, not to shout at the dog for grabbing a book from the shelves, not to break into tears when she dropped a dish while setting the table.

Had Ethan been able to pick up clues from facial expression or voice tone, Carly would not have been able to keep him innocent. She knew she would have time to prepare him, if she were convicted. Attorney Stanley assured her—courts allowed a couple of months for convicted defendants to arrange their affairs before they were required to appear for imprisonment. Irwin Stanley knew of one case in which the court allowed a man to have additional time to attend his child's graduation.

"That must have been a joyous occasion," Carly commented.

Attorney Stanley did not like her tone of voice. "No need to be snide, Ms. Daniels."

His call was fifteen minutes late. Carly paced the living room, wondering if he forgot, debating whether to phone him. If she did, she might tie up her phone at the exact time her lawyer tried to reach her. Another five minutes passed. She gave up and turned on the television. That was a mistake.

The newscaster, one of the Hollywood hopefuls, stood outside the court house and, in a voice delirious with excitement, informed the public that testimony showed the Archers instructed insureds how to commit fraud. "The Archers and Carly Daniels," he repeated, his face as animated as his voice. And, he continued, lowering his voice to an ominous tone, one man who was employed by insurance companies to do paramedic exams took extra blood from healthy applicants and used that for his own insurance applications, and also sold blood to others.

The viewing audience was informed about another of Archer Life Settlements "disreputables," as the prosecutors labeled them, a man who had his brother take the exam in his stead. Imposter fraud. The reporter mentioned this was not the first case of imposter fraud related to the viatical and life industry. The first reached the California appellate court more than ten years earlier.

The phone trilled, startling Carly. She answered, shutting off the television while answering and forgetting to check the ID screen.

"It's Kyle. I saw the news on television. Bad day?"

"Yes, but I can't talk now. I'm waiting for my attorney to call. The lawyers had an argument with the judge."

Kyle told her to call him later, any time. He would wait up for her call. "I know you'd rather not talk about this when Ethan is around." She thanked him and pressed the button to disconnect. Her phone instantly trilled again. This time it was attorney Stanley.

"First," he said, "I tried to find out why you, a lowly clerk, became a target. I asked Cutter directly. He said they were at the building the day of the raid. They saw you with Blake Archer. They figured you were coming to work together because you had something going between you, that maybe you knew things, from 'pillow talk.'"

"That's ridiculous. And disgusting."

"They may know differently now, but they're not about to back down. Prosecutors don't admit mistakes, even when a defendant is exonerated with DNA."

Carly was impatient. She did not want to hear more bad news, but if she had no choice she rather hear news that affected her life.

"You were going to tell me about the bench argument."

"Oh, yes. About the FBI agents. We wanted the notes taken by the agents and the prosecutor, notes from when Capone and his pals were interviewed. The notes are supposed to be turned over to us. It's a cardinal rule of court, to prevent trial by ambush. McGuire said he *thinks* he took scratch notes. Before French—the Archer's attorney—had a chance to say he wanted them, the judge said he didn't think they would be helpful since French did a good job impeaching Capone and the others."

"I saw the news reports. The reporter isn't convinced they were impeached."

"Reporters! They'll make a deadly car accident exciting."

"But if reporters think the testimony is credible, won't the public think we're guilty? And if reporters believe it, what's to prevent the jury from doing so?"

"Nothing we can do about that, since the judge didn't agree. Here's what he said. I have the transcript in front of me. 'I don't know how you can impeach them more than you've already done. You've made liars out of them ten thousand times. What else do you want to do?'"

Stanley coughed, asked her to wait while he fetched a glass of water. When he picked up the phone again, he said, "French told the judge he wanted the agent's notes because Capone said he told the FBI agent about you, Carly. And he told the FBI about Blake telling him to switch his blood with his brother for a blood test. He said he told the FBI agent that Blake was going to have you keep on his back until he did this."

"If this were true, it directly implicates me, doesn't it?"

Stanley excused himself to take another drink of water. "I had Chinese, Szeuchan, really hot stuff, for dinner. As to your question, yes, you and the Archer brothers. That's why, as French told the court, he wanted those notes—so he could get the agent to testify that Capone never said those things. He wanted the notes to prove Capone made up the stories for trial. Cutter argued that if the agent admits Capone never said these things, the notes are superfluous. In other words, he doesn't want us to have notes taken by the agent or by McGuire."

"What does this mean?

"If French could show Capone is lying, it will cast doubt on the testimony of all the viators. For the prosecutor, it could be mere posturing—arguing for the sake of arguing. Or arguing, thinking if he loses this one he'll be entitled to win a more important battle."

"What does it mean for me?"

"Don't worry about it. We have everything under control."

Carly did not think so. The judge denied this request. If it was as important as Stanley indicated, this was not good news.

"May I ask a silly question?"

Stanley told her to go ahead.

"Why does the judge think the notes are not important? Maybe he's convinced Capone is a liar, Beasley is a liar, the others are liars, but he can't know what the jury thinks."

"Good question, Carly. I don't know."

"Is the judge on the side of the prosecutors?"

"Judges are supposed to be impartial."

"I know that. But I've been doing some reading. I knew nothing about trials, courts, nothing about anything. I came across stories about judges who almost always rule for prosecutors."

"That does happen."

"If he refuses to allow you to see these notes, the jury won't get this information, either. It doesn't seem right for the judge to refuse to give you information that might make a difference."

"He doesn't think so. And it's too late. The judge already decided on this."

"What if the jury thinks prosecutors are never wrong? I've been reading stories about juries. The minute a prosecutor tells them he represents the People or the United States of America, the jury believes everything he says."

"That's one of the major reasons not to go to trial, Carly."

"I read everything I could find about the Aisenberg's kidnapped baby. It was heart-breaking, Mr. Stanley. When the truth finally came out, people still did not believe they were innocent. People posted comments online claiming the parents are guilty of killing their baby. Even after the judge threw out the case because prosecutors lied, and the Justice Department found the prosecutors did wrong."

"Once again, Carly, that's the risk you chose to take. Even if you're acquitted, some people will always believe the prosecutors charged you because you were guilty."

"Thanks," she said, and hung up abruptly.

Now it would be a challenge to lift her spirits. Carly looked through the CD collection but could not stop thinking, Even when prosecutors lose, they win. She searched for the musical, "The King and I," needing to hear the lyrics from "I whistle a happy tune." Once she found it, she played it again, and again, and again. Because she was alone, she played the music loud, filling the cottage with music as she rushed around, dusting every piece of furniture in frenzy. When she was done and went into the back yard to look at her garden, the music followed her.

Ethan and DeeOhGee returned to a house filled with music, but it was too much noise for Ethan. Carly shut off the CD player.

Stanley's message continued to upset her long after Ethan was in bed. Carly stayed in the living room, listening to music with earplugs, waiting for Ben to return from work. When he did, Carly asked him to join her in the back yard, to be absolutely certain Ethan heard nothing. Then she told him about her conversation with Irwin Stanley. They sat at their small, round plastic table, Carly with a cup of tea, Ben with a bottle of beer.

"I keep trying to find you a better lawyer," Ben said. "It seems white collar criminal defense is an elite specialty and no one knows anyone to recommend. I did speak with one of the regulars who is a criminal defense attorney—he likes murder trials." Ben grinned. Carly stared at him. She saw no humor in this. "Anyway, this guy asked me why your attorney did not sever your case from the Archers. That means separate them, have two trials. That way you wouldn't have been taint-ed with accusations of things they did."

"Attorney Stanley explained this early on, Ben. He said judges don't like to do that because it's more expensive for the court. If he filed a motion to sever, his motion would be denied and the judge might be pissed at him for asking."

"Well, Carly, the only sage advice I can give is a famous quote. 'It's not how hard you're hit but how hard you keep getting hit and still keep moving.' Rocky Balboa."

They clinked cup and bottle, a toast to Rocky Balboa.

# Chapter Thirty-One

W HEN COURT RESUMED the next day, Allison was called to testify. Allison agreed with McGuire that she and Carly did the
same work, that their cubicles were next to each other, that Allison
had access to complete files and did, indeed, look at files beyond her
work description. As a result, she was aware of fraud. Throughout her
testimony, Allison did not look at Carly.

When asked if Ms. Daniels accessed these files, Allison said she did
not know since they never discussed it. When asked could Ms. Daniels
have accessed the files, Allison agreed it was possible.

Irwin Stanley conducted the cross-examination. He asked when
Allison began working at Archer, when Carly began working in the
data entry department, and whether Carly had access to a computer
prior to working in data entry. He established that Carly began work
in the data entry department two weeks prior to the raid. Three other
employees testified about bringing the fraud to the attention of Aidan
or Blake, and were told not to worry. When asked about Carly Daniels,
they said they had no knowledge of her involvement.

The next group of witnesses were insurance companies' representatives. Each claimed they would not have issued policies to the applicants, if they knew the truth about their health. Archer hid from
them the fact these policies were viaticated by taking ownership in

the form of life insurance trusts. That also made it easy to transfer the death benefits to new beneficiaries—investors—without alerting the insurance companies.

When questioned by defense attorneys, they admitted they did no investigation. Yes, they could have checked with the Medical Information Bureau and learned about the health of the viators and the existence of multiple policies, but chose not to do so. Prosecutors bounced back for re-direct, reemphasizing the harm done to insurers by Archer.

On Thursday the prosecutors called Barton Cox, a pudgy man with the face of a frog. As he walked past Carly's table, she caught a whiff of sweat and cigar smoke. Carly knew Ben would have fun if he saw this man. The defense attorneys were irate. As soon as Cox was sworn, they asked the judge for a hearing. The jury was escorted out of court. This time Carly knew the crux of the controversy. Early that morning her attorney had told her they wanted to keep the receiver from testifying.

"What is a receiver?"

"All federally appointed receivers are lawyers. They collect assets and make distributions to defrauded investors. The defense plans to argue against allowing his testimony."

"Why? What's the harm?"

"He wants to blame Archer for investors' losses. But Archer did not sell to these investors. Archer actually terminated their agreement with SSLS when they learned the policies were being resold to the public."

The judge ruled against the defense. Cox pulled the microphone near his mouth and introduced himself as the court-appointed receiver for Star Spangled Life Settlements, "which I shall hereafter refer to as 'SSLS'."

He testified that he represented the interests of seniors who were victims of Archer's fraud. Prosecutors asked about the number of SSLS investors whose policies originated with Archer, and the amount of their losses. Cox presented a chart to show sixty SSLS investors who owned contestable policies Archer resold to SSLS. There were columns to show the amounts invested by each and the face amount of the policies. Each of these policies no longer was in force. All were rescinded by insurers, wiping out every dollar investors paid to purchase them.

Defense attorneys attempted to get Cox to admit Archer was not the direct cause of their victimization. Cox was adamant: Archer sold those policies to SSLS who, in turn, sold the fraudulent policies to hundreds of seniors. They lost their life savings, due to Archer's fraud.

Defense attorneys tried another avenue: They asked how many policies were active, not rescinded, and how much these would pay when the insureds died. Cox was not prepared to present those numbers. Loss was all.

What was there for the prosecutors to challenge, Carly wondered as McGuire rose to take his second shot. He had Cox repeat that Archer was responsible for losses to retirees.

Carly no longer had any good feelings about the Archer brothers, but her future was tied to theirs. She felt like screaming or sobbing as it became increasingly apparent the defense attorneys were doing little to defend Archer Life Settlements from Cox's accusations.

During lunch, she asked attorney Stanley why they did not find a way to bring up that Archer terminated their agreement with SSLS, after learning the policies were resold to the public?

He was startled by the question. "How did you know that?"

"You told me this morning."

"Oh, right. Well, we can't introduce the termination letter without someone testifying to it—either of the Archers or the attorney who drafted it. And that would be very risky, to have any of them testify."

Following Cox, the prosecutors intended to call seventeen of the SSLS investors whose policies were rescinded due to fraud. Again, the defense objected. The judge ruled against them but limited testimony to three investors.

All testified they were led to believe this was a safe, conservative investment like CDs, but with much higher yields. When prosecutors asked, they testified they never would have invested if they knew the policies were fraudulently acquired.

Archer's attorney, French, asked the investors if they ever heard the name Archer before the prosecutors contacted them. Not one did. He told them to look at Aidan, look at Blake; had they ever seen them before? Uniformly, the answer was no.

Carly knew Archer had investors, but believed these were wealthy, sophisticated people or Wall Street investment companies. She knew from Marcia that Aidan and Blake often traveled in their private jet. Marcia also told her about credit card charges from wining and dining hedge fund managers—an amount that would have paid her mortgage for several months.

When she arrived home, Carly refused to answer Ben's questions about what happened. She could not talk about it. She did not want to think about it.

But after Ethan was in bed, Carly went on the computer. She wanted to find over-turned convictions. She found a news story about the Seventh Circuit Court of Appeals and a woman like her.

The appeal was filed by a woman who had been in prison for four months. Right at the hearing, the appeals court not only reversed the federal conviction but ordered her immediate release. They ruled that Georgia Thompson had not violated any federal statute.

Thompson later said that the U.S. attorney, a George W. Bush appointee, offered her leniency if she cooperated in a case against the governor, a Democrat in a tight re-election campaign. She had not violated any federal statute, but ended up in prison. Carly felt the walls closing in on her.

# Chapter Thirty-Two

I FOUND ADDITIONAL information that could be significant," Eric announced as he entered Yolanda's office. He shut the door and headed directly for the chair opposite her desk. Both visitor chairs were plain, hard wood, no doubt to prevent drop-in visitors from staying too long. For long meetings, Yolanda invited visitors to the conference table, which had cushioned chairs. Eric held out the file.

"What are we talking about now?"

Eric apologized. He had forgotten Yolanda's thoughts were not centered on viatical and life settlement fraud.

"To start, insurance companies as tacit co-conspirators in fraud."

"Ah, yes, now I recall. AIG and other biggies suing to rescind fraudulent policies and keep the premiums."

"First, a little background. Before issuing a life insurance policy, insurers require the existence of an 'insurable interest'—a relationship between the insured and the beneficiary based on familial or 'blood,' a relationship through marriage, or a financial relationship. The purpose is to prevent a named beneficiary from having the incentive to cause the insured's death. With that in mind, I have two cases that clearly evidence the negligence of insurers."

Eric withdrew a few pages from the file he brought with him. "This one was named by the media, 'The Ghastly Grannies.'" He summarized the news articles. "Two elderly women—ages seventy-five and seventy-three at the time of their arrest—approached homeless men and offered them an apartment, rent and utilities free. In exchange, they were required to sign an application for life insurance in which the women were named as beneficiaries. Once the men signed, the women used those signatures to forge signatures on additional applications. Two years after the policies were issued, the women killed these men, apparently drugging them and then causing hit-and-run 'accidents.' Over several years they collected nearly three million in death benefits, and had applications for other homeless men waiting to be sent to insurers."

"Are you saying the insurers never checked to find out these men were unemployed, had no assets, and only recently began living in apartments?"

"Exactly. With one of the homeless men, they applied for more than a dozen different life insurance policies. They wrote on the applications that he was a real estate investor, earned sixty-five thousand a year and, in one application, they stated he was involved in business that brought in half a million each year. The year he died, the Social Security Administration reported his taxable income as forty-two dollars."

"And how do you see the insurers as co-conspirators?"

"Intentional negligence. They have investigative units. Garden State Life investigated and refused to pay. Empire General issued a policy for half a million and paid. There were other insurers, as well. They have the resources to learn about multiple policies on each man; that the insureds did not work; that one of the deceased usually was drunk. At the least, the negligence of the life insurers violated their fiduciary duty to their stockholders."

"What are the implications for us?"

"Wait. I have another case that dovetails with this. U.S. Bank was sued by the Phoenix companies. USB was the investor—it bought the policy. Phoenix wanted to rescind the policy and keep the premiums. They filed suit two years after issuing five million in death benefits to a seventy-years-old woman. Her application for insurance stated she had a net worth of nine point one million and an annual income of four hundred ten thousand. The truth, which Phoenix learned too late: the woman spoke little English and lived on social security. She was paid six thousand and got a free medical exam, in exchange for signing the papers that created this STOLI."

"Once more I ask, what are the implications for us?"

"There are many similar lawsuits. Phoenix was denied the right to rescind because they filed too late and, under Minnesota state insurance law, fraud does not supersede the contestable clause. In New Jersey it would, and the policy would be void. But not in Minnesota."

"I still don't get your point, Eric."

"These cases support the argument that Archer cannot be held liable for deceiving insurance companies."

Yolanda smacked her desk. She stood up abruptly, her face filled with anger. "Are you going to bring that up again? That wrongful prosecution garbage?"

Eric realized his mistake. "Forget it. I wanted to find a solid federal cause of action for Archer and I found it. Here, take a look at these notes. They are from management meetings found on Aidan's and Blake's computers."

Yolanda ignored the file. She turned away with disgust, walked to the far end of her office, paused, then turned to face him. "Eric, Eric, what am I going to do with you?" She shook her head. "The trial began a few weeks ago. It's a done deal."

Eric took a breath to calm himself, and started again.

"The big picture is that Archer's schemes are not unique to Archer. Other companies are engaged in the same things, undeterred by any regulators. This is similar to the mortgage scams that brought down the economy. This also involves Wall Street—some of the giants and hedge funds—and it's international because policies issued here are sold to investors all over the world."

"Although I can't speak for prosecutors, I have no doubt they would love to target Wall Street conglomerates. But not now and not with this. Possibly in the future. Save it."

Eric paused to rethink how he might better present this. "What if doing nothing had a direct effect on Social Security, Medicare, Medicaid, food stamps—just about every government benefit?"

"Now you're talking federal budget and the economy. That might be an issue for politicians or for Congress, not us."

"Okay, try this. A man in his forties, married, a father, a homeowner, suffers a disabling illness. It's terminal but not before every cent—college funds, retirement funds—everything is gone. He sells his life insurance policy to prevent foreclosure on the family home."

"Where are you going with this, Eric? Are you trying to tell me you believe in this godforsaken industry?"

Eric gripped the folder, struggling with frustration.

"I understand why people sell their policies. When they are financially desperate and can't get cash anywhere else, this is the only solution. But they are being ripped off by many of the companies. Here's an example. Say this man, we'll call him Joe Blow, has a death benefit of five hundred thousand. He goes to sell it. The broker gets one offer—from Archer. It's for thirty percent of the death benefit. That's gross. The broker's deal with Archer lets him name his commission. He takes half. The broker and Joe each get seventy-five thousand."

"What is the problem? No one forced Joe to sell."

"Necessity forced Joe to sell. And no one told him he did not have to sell the entire policy. He did not know he could have asked the insurer to reissue it as two policies, each with two hundred fifty thou death benefit, same issue date as the original. He could have kept one for the family and sold the other."

"You expect these companies to educate the consumer? How idealistic are you, Eric?"

"Forget educating them. What's wrong is Joe gets no other offers. Just Archer's. He does not know if other companies would have offered more. Archer has a menu of schemes to keep prices low and keep insureds from getting other offers."

"So they're unethical. Unless you have something illegal, something that violates a federal statute, it's a waste of time to pursue this, Eric."

"What's wrong is this. When Joe Blow dies, his family does not get any death benefits. By the time Joe dies the settlement is gone. Now the family can't pay real estate taxes, can't pay for medical care, can't sell the home for a decent price in today's market. They lose their home. Now they're homeless. Now they need every government benefit. Multiply that by hundreds, by thousands. It will have a huge impact on the federal budget."

Yolanda looked down at her computer screen. "Unless you can tell me exactly what is illegal about this—*exactly*—our meeting is over."

"How about violation of antitrust law? Will that do?"

"The purpose of the Sherman Act is to protect the public from conduct which unfairly tends to destroy competition. How does this apply?"

"The Archers' schemes—and they're not the only ones doing this." Eric stood up and began to pace as he thought out the steps. "One scheme lowers the price paid to the insured. Since the price is based primarily on life expectancy, Archer—and a few others—assign artificially longer life expectancies. Longer life expectancies mean the policy is cheaper to buy. Archer's life expectancies are false. The insured always dies early—by Archer figures."

"What you're telling me is the insured—the consumer—is harmed. That's a problem for state insurance regulators. Your pet, McCarran-Ferguson." Yolanda smiled. "So far, you have not shown me anything about violations of antitrust law."

Eric sat down again. "That's the second scheme, the one clearly directed to cutting out competition. Archer offered brokers a bonus to prevent them from shopping policies to competitors who might pay more. They even paid a bonus to competitors who were interested in bidding, so they would back off, not bid, and allow Archer to buy for the lower price."

"If other companies worked with Archer on this, where is the antitrust violation?"

"It does not matter that we stopped Archer, not when a dozen others are doing the same thing. That's why an antitrust action is the answer—to stop the dirty dozen. When these schemes shut out competitors, they also harm consumers."

"You're saying a dozen other companies have similar anti-competition schemes?"

Eric grinned. "Archer called it a 'right of first refusal.' I call it 'a kill fee.' Insureds had only one choice: sell to Archer or don't sell."

"There you go—no competition. Resulting in harm to consumers."

"It works with McCarran-Ferguson, too. State regulation exempts from antitrust laws only insurer activity that has an impact within that state. Regulation by one state does not provide an exemption for activity beyond its borders. Here's the cute part. The Archer brothers knew this was prohibited by some states—two, to be exact. New York and Florida challenged another company that did the exact same thing."

"They were challenged under state insurance law?"

"Yep. And that's why it failed—only two states held their feet to the fire. Not one other state, not even so-called progressive California. As a result, Archer knew every other state was ripe for the pickings."

Yolanda sat back in her chair. "Wow!" she said. "This does, indeed, look like Sherman Act." She swivelled in her chair and pulled from the book shelves behind her a fat volume bound in black leather. She began reading aloud, "The federal reach of the Sherman Act, the Clayton Act, and the Federal Trade Commission Act is applicable to the business of insurance only to the extent where: (1) such business is not regulated by state law," Yolanda looked up, meeting his eye, before continuing, "or (2) there are insurer acts of, boycott, coercion, or intimidation.'"

"Yes!" Eric thought to himself. "She gets it." He told her, "Price-fixing and restraint of trade are Sherman Act violations. Unless they are sanctioned by state law, these acts are subject to federal antitrust prosecution. And that's exactly what is happening."

"And you say only two states took action?"

"The others could but don't. That's why applying the Sherman Act to this would not invalidate, impair or supersede state insurance law. Federal and state regulatory schemes would work in tandem. Viatical and life settlement companies are not insurance companies, but they are regulated under state insurance statutes. Initially the intent of viatical statutes was to protect the insureds. But the industry has become so complex states can't keep up with the violations. Bottom line: other than New York and Florida, these companies can do just about anything, unimpeded by state regulation."

"An antitrust suit would have to come from the DOJ. How do you propose getting them interested in this unusual industry?"

"My guess is this came to the attention of the New York attorney general via complaints from competitors. Then Florida picked it up. It might be possible to encourage more complaints by competitors of Archer and the company New York charged. We could start with their competitors."

"See what you can find, Eric. And come up with a few ideas for how to motivate action."

Yolanda was about to dismiss him, but Eric had more to say. "There is a model—the Microsoft litigation. In 1990 the FTC began investigating and the Justice Department took over the probe in 1993. Then, in 1997, Texas opened a probe of Microsoft; the following year twenty states joined the antitrust lawsuit against Microsoft—alongside the Justice Department. It was the states that forced real action and, finally, resolution."

"Three years between the FTC and the DOJ investigation, eight years before there was action. Let that be a warning: You'll have to be patient, Eric. These settlement companies have megabucks. They'll fight all the way. That means long, drawn-out, expensive litigation. The government is not in a good position to tackle expensive litigation."

"Well, now there's Google. It's considered the new Microsoft and Texas is looking into whether Google's business practices thwart competition. And, the Senate anti-trust committee plans to hold hearings about Google's alleged anti-competitive practices. So, they are not backing away."

"Yes," Yolanda said, smiling. "This definitely is the way to go, with one caveat."

Eric looked startled. What the heck was she going to tell him now?

"We need numerous complaints before any agency takes notice. It's not likely the insureds filed complaints."

Eric agreed. "Most don't know they were defrauded. If they do realize it, it's rare when a seriously ill insured can afford to hire an attorney."

"That is pivotal, Eric. Without complaints, it's unlikely other states will pursue this. Without state attorneys general on board, it's unlikely any federal agency will touch it. But let's assume all the ducks are in a row. We line up twenty states and a federal agency. It will take years. Years, Eric."

"We could start with Archer's competitors."

"Forget Archer. It's over for them. But you're on the right track to consider other companies, and anti-trust is the remedy. Now run numbers. See if we can't create awareness, get some state attorneys general on board, then try to interest the DOJ."

"I also have an idea to kick off the investigation. A few seniors who live locally participated in STOLI—Archer's insureds. We could visit with them, learn what is happening in our back yard. Then maybe the California A.G. will be interested."

"Okay, make a few phone calls. Just say we would like their help with an investigation, absolutely no liability for them. You don't want to scare off anyone with information."

"Right. I'll get on it today."

"This really gets you going, huh?"

"Well," Eric looked down, embarrassed. "Duke Cunningham was exposed by an investigative journalist, not the FBI. I don't want to see anything similar, which could imply we are shirking our responsibility to protect the public." Yolanda smiled at him.

# Chapter Thirty-Three

THE NEW WEEK BEGAN with more prosecution witnesses from the Department of Justice. First up was an FBI accountant who described how she traced funds from Archer's bank accounts to the bank accounts of testifying viators. Another agent testified to the use of Federal Express or Airborne, to support the mail fraud charge. Carly thought the defense attorneys cross-examined each of these witnesses simply because it was expected, but they gained no ground, or there was no ground to gain. Despite this, the prosecutors felt obliged to return to their witnesses to run through a recap of their previous testimony.

The trial dragged. The testimony and the meaningless back and forth bored her. To keep herself awake, Carly filled her pad with doodles. There was nothing of interest for her to capture, as she did when Russell testified. At one point she was nodding off during an FBI agent's testimony when attorney Stanley poked her with his elbow.

And then, suddenly, she remembered Terri McGuire. She scribbled a note to Irwin Stanley. "Banks accounts: shouldn't McGuire's wife testify?"

"No can do," he scribbled beneath her note, once again without any capital letters.

At the end of the day attorney Stanley showed her the witness list for the defense. He told her their turn to present their side probably would not occur until the following week. The defense planned to call as their witnesses the maintenance man for the Archer building and a new in-house attorney. None of the Gucci or Armani wealthy investors, none of the viators who sold legitimate policies. Was this how the lawyers intended to convince a jury that Archer was not a fraud factory?

Carly stayed in her chair in the empty courtroom, unable to shake the numbness that followed in the wake of shock. Their convictions were assured. She had to start thinking about how to prepare Ethan. She would have to prepare Ben. Without her salary, Ben could not afford a two bedroom anything in Laguna Beach. Carly decided she would have to spend the weekend checking want ads, trying to find low cost rentals in a safe neighborhood, one within a school district that had an adequate special education program.

What a mess, Carly thought.

The bailiff came over, bent toward her, and gently asked if she needed help. "Just tired," she said. Thanking him for his concern, she gathered her purse and her pad with doodles and ridiculous notes scribbled to her lawyer, and left the court room.

⌒

After dinner Carly had a surprise visitor—Marcia. "Now that I'm done testifying, we're allowed to be friends again," she said, handing Carly a lemon meringue pie in a box from Marie Callender's. "I baked it myself," Marcia said with a wink. "Marie let me into the kitchen, on condition I teach her my recipe."

Carly quickly placed the box on the table, squinting to hold back tears. When she turned back she hugged Marcia.

"This for a pie? What would you do if I brought a casserole? Give me a massage?"

"How did you find where I live?"

"Stopped at the Rainbow Bar and asked your brother. It wasn't the first time I was in a gay bar. Years ago, my second husband and I went to one that everyone said had great entertainment and a terrific band."

"Your second husband? You never mentioned being married." Carly glanced at Marcia's left hand. Rings on every finger, but none looked like a wedding band.

"My first was at the age of nineteen, divorced at twenty when I refused to participate in his physical fitness regime, which meant I was a punching bag. My second was a talented hair dresser. That's what brought us to California—he had several Hollywood-ees who loved him almost as much as I did. And, let me tell you, Carly, I looked fantastic all those years. One morning I woke up and he did not. It was a shock. After that, I moved to Orange County. He was in superb health—ran five miles four times a week, never sick. But his heart gave out."

"I am so sorry to hear that."

"Well, skipping right along, I met Ben at the trial. When I saw that hunk sitting next to Aidan's wife, I just had to meet him. I actually grabbed his arm—he was leaving. I think he purposely told me where he worked, when he realized I was flirting."

"Ben rarely comes now, and only for a short time. He works nights and he has to be back in time for Ethan's school bus. I told him not to come at all." Carly shrugged, as if to say, What more could I do to stop him?

"Is that your son out back?" Marcia was looking through the screen door that led to the back yard.

"Yes, Ethan and his puppy."

"*That's* a puppy?"

Carly laughed. The puppy was huge, but still a puppy.

"I have some stuff to tell you," Marcia said, turning serious. "I thought you might like to know some things I know about Archer. I was recruited a few times to play secretary at management meetings, when they couldn't get their 'personal assistant,'" she used a snide tone, "or Terri to take notes."

"Do I need to hear this?" It did not sound good, and Carly was filled to the brim with toxic information.

"First, I have to know, do you still have good feelings about Blake?" Marcia asked.

Carly shrugged. "I don't know if I ever had good feelings about him. Looking back, it seems I tolerated him. Because he was the boss. I excused him when he was clueless or insensitive. Again, I guess, because he was the boss."

"Did he ever ask you out?"

"No!" Carly was shocked at the idea. She thought about it briefly and said, "If ever he was inclined to, I doubt he would. He's too careful. It could lead to sexual harassment charges, since I never gave him reason to think I was interested in him."

"Just had to know. How about Aidan?"

"I don't think any of us had much contact with Aidan. The one time I tried to speak with him, to ask a favor for an insured who was dying, I got the feeling he didn't give a damn."

"Good. I needed to know because I'm going to tell you things not too nice about them."

"Great, just what I need." Carly got up from the table. "Let me put up some coffee—you drink coffee, right? Regular or decaf?" She began to prepare coffee for Marcia and tea for herself. "Let me get Ethan started for bed. Then we can talk."

Carly called Ethan in. He came, DeeOhGee at his heels. Carly introduced him to Marcia, telling Ethan Marcia was a friend from work. Ethan looked past her shoulder and mumbled, "Hello." Marcia asked the name of his dog.

"Come again?" Marcia said, leaning forward to hear Ethan's whisper.

"Interesting name," she said. "Different. My dog is Phoebe. Also different."

DeeOhGee was sniffing Phoebe who, as usual, had her head sticking out of a large bag. Carly decided not to tell Marcia the type of dog that was sniffing her tiny one.

Carly pointed to the pie, telling Ethan he could have a slice if he was quick getting into his PJs. He ran upstairs. Carly sat down again, waiting for the coffee.

"Ethan's shy, huh? I get shy. Would you believe I was shy, when I was his age?"

Carly did not correct her. She answered the second question. "If you were shy, I was a giraffe. Now tell me, why should I hear things I really don't need to know?"

"Two reasons. If you are protecting them, don't. Don't put yourself at risk for them. They don't deserve it."

"And the other reason?"

"Selfish. I want to tell someone. I was sworn to secrecy by The Brothers, but what could they do to me, now—fire me?" Marcia laughed sardonically. "I tried to tell prosecutors, but they were not interested since it's mostly about ethics and morals."

Ethan returned. While he ate his pie and drank milk, Carly took Marcia into the back yard, to show her the vegetable garden she planted.

"Very nice, but I'm really busting to tell you about this," Marcia said. "Blake had these 'great ideas,'" she made finger quotes in the air, "to bring in more business. One would allow brokers to decide how much of Archer's purchase offer to keep for themselves. They could keep ninety percent, if they wanted, and give what was left to the insured."

Carly stared at Marcia. "Tell me they didn't actually do this." She thought about people she knew who sold policies to Archer. She thought about Shirley Woodruff, who almost sold her policy in order to keep her rent-controlled apartment.

"Why were the prosecutors not interested in this?"

"Maybe it's not legally wrong. Don't forget, Archer had several attorneys advising them."

Ethan was at the screen door, waving. And the gnats were out. Carly ushered Marcia back indoors, kissed Ethan good-night, and he went upstairs to bed.

"Now it's our turn for pie," Carly said. "You cut while I pour. And let's enjoy our little repast before you tell me more gory details."

Marcia was a fast eater. She was done quickly and began her story again. "Here's another 'brainstorm' of Blake's: assign long life expectancies to the insureds, longer than actual estimates."

"What does that mean? I really know so little about this industry."

"You probably know the purchase price is based primarily on life expectancy and the amount of premiums they expect to pay for those years?" Carly nodded. "If life expectancy companies decide Mr. Jones has two years to live, Archer tells the insured it's ten years, and they pay Jones much less."

"This makes me really angry," Carly said. "People who are terminally ill are cheated every which way."

"I had to share this with someone."

"Want another piece of pie?"

"Don't mind if I do. Now you know why Aidan said, at the Christmas party, that revenues had tripled."

Another thought occurred to Carly. "Do you know if it's true, what Archer says in their marketing brochure? Do they actually pay more than insurance companies?"

"They must. Otherwise, insureds would go to the insurance company, wouldn't they?"

"They lose either way, don't they? If they can't afford the premiums, but still need some insurance."

"I used to do phone appointments for insurance salesmen. One of the slogans was, 'The only important premium to pay is the one just before you die.'"

Carly began gathering their dishes.

"I guess you want me to leave, huh? Another big day tomorrow?"

Carly thanked her for the visit and for understanding she needed an early night in order to hold up at court the next day.

# Chapter Thirty-Four

A NOTHER DAY BEGAN with lawyers arguing. Again, they introduced themselves to the judge, stated the names of their clients, and the judge greeted each as if they had not been there day after day for weeks. Carly kept yawning. She had no idea what the argument was about. After a while she took out a fiction book she brought for times when she lunched alone.

A second hour passed while the lawyers haggled. Carly wondered about the jurors who wrestled their way to court in morning rush-hour traffic only to be stuck in the jury room. They were obligated to be on time and were paid forty dollars a day plus ten dollars for parking fees.

Today the result of the hearing was a bit different. Either the two sides reached agreement or there was a ruling, possibly both if there was more than one issue. When they were done, each side introduced bundles of documents. When Irwin Stanley returned to the defense table, she asked what was going on. He told her not to worry; it was routine trial preparation.

The jury returned and the trial resumed. The prosecutors called one of the FBI agents who had interrogated Aidan. That took a few hours, both before and after lunch, with testimony frequently interrupted by defense objections, which led to more arguments at the bench. When the defense took its turn to cross-examine, testimony was again interrupted, this time by the prosecutor's objections and more bench conferences. Before the day was out, the prosecutor had his second chance to drive home the points he wanted the jury to remember.

The following day the same ping-pong match was played in regard to the FBI agent who interviewed Blake. Carly wondered if the agents were telling the truth. Since neither Aidan nor Blake would be testifying, the agents could say they were told all sorts of things.

On the third day the target was Carly. Prosecutors called as their witness FBI special agent Eric Price. Carly gasped when she heard his name. She watched as Agent Price was sworn in and took his seat. She stared at him with increasing anger. She was certain he avoided looking at her. Was he setting her up the whole time she worked for him and Ruiz? Would they use the research they ordered as evidence against her? Carly had not thought to bring her flash drive to court. She picked up the pen and began to draw boxes on the pad her lawyer gave her. Boxes within boxes. Square boxes. Rectangle boxes. The voices of McGuire and Price were background noise, as if a television played in another room.

It hurt to remember she had begun to think Agent Price was a nice person. Carly wrote on her pad, "phony, traitor, two-faced Janus," as McGuire ran Price through his background. McGuire established that Price was new to the FBI. He spent considerable time getting on record Price's great qualifications as a former attorney with a large, prestigious law firm, and someone with a background in insurance. McGuire smiled at the defense table. He seemed to say, Gotcha.

McGuire began questioning Price about his investigation into the operations of Archer Life Settlements. First, general questions about the company, the numbers of employees, the numbers of offices, how many file boxes Price reviewed. When he shifted to the interrogation of Carly Daniels, McGuire asked rapid-fire questions, statements turned into questions by ending each with the word, "correct?" McGuire obviously expected quick yes answers. He was eager to get to the meat of the testimony.

"When you and Agent Ruiz interrogated Carly Daniels, she told you she knew nothing about fraud; correct?" Price agreed.

"And in claiming ignorance of the fraud, you concluded she lied; correct?"

Price said, "No."

Carly's eyes flew open. She saw McGuire frown. She saw him rub his chin. His gaze was fixed on his witness. "Allow me to rephrase. Daniels lied to federal agents when she claimed no knowledge of fraud. She may be better looking," he turned to stare at Carly, then turned to the jury, "but she's as disreputable as those who sat in the witness chair at the start of this trial."

Defense attorneys shouted objections. McGuire withdrew his comment and repeated his question: "In claiming ignorance of the fraud, you concluded that she lied; correct?"

Price hesitated. He looked down. Then he looked up at McGuire. "I have no reason to believe she knew about any fraud as of the last day she was employed at Archer. In other words, I do not believe she had knowledge of the fraud at the time we interrogated her. And by the way, we did not warn her of her Miranda rights. It was not a formal interrogation."

McGuire's face stiffened and quickly changed to a slight smile. "What did she say or do to lead you to think she was telling the truth?"

"Her denials, of course, coupled with a description of her work duties which, of course, we verified."

"She *acted* surprised? And you believed her?" McGuire's tone implied Price was young and being new to the FBI, naive. He wanted the jury to believe Price was deceived.

Price said both he and agent Ruiz believed Ms. Daniels. They believed her to the extent they hired her to do research for them.

"Are these the results of her computer searches?" McGuire handed Price a sheaf of pages. Price flipped through the pages. He agreed they appeared to be the same, as far as he could tell from a quick look.

"Do you see a date on them?" he asked Price. The papers rustled as Price looked through them. He did not find any that were dated.

"Would you continue to believe she told you the truth, Agent Price, if you learned these pages were printed from Daniels' work station computer?"

Price looked surprised. He glanced at Carly but her head was down. The gallery was abuzz with people reacting to this disclosure.

Carly pretended to be writing, but she was in shock. With her head lowered, no one would see the tears that swelled her eyes. There it was—her paranoia confirmed. The spread sheets would be used to convict her. She scribbled a note to attorney Stanley. "These are not from my work computer."

He scribbled back to her in his usual way, without capital letters. She converted them in her head: "Wrong. We have a copy."

She scribbled another note. "I dated them."

He wrote back, "You dated those from Aidan's computer. The undated ones are from your work station."

She hastily scribbled another note. "I have a flash drive as proof."

He waved her off. "Pay attention," he scribbled a few minutes later.

Price said, "These appear to be the pages from Aidan Archer's computer. I doubt they are from her work station computer."

"What makes you uncertain, Agent Price?"

"For one, when she found evidence of fraud in the files, she was surprised."

McGuire nodded dramatically, as if this was expected. "Ms. Daniels *acted* surprised. Did it occur to you, Agent Price, that Ms. Daniels acted surprised in order to influence you? Isn't that possible Agent Price?"

"Yes, it is possible," Eric said, and tried to say more. McGuire stopped him, demanding a simple answer to a simple question. "A yes or no answer is sufficient."

McGuire then fired a series of questions at Price, demanding yes or no answers. "Her position was data entry; correct? And that is a simple clerical position; correct? Which means Ms. Daniels would not, under normal circumstances, access these records; correct? But she could have done so at any time; correct? Others did this, why not Carly

Daniels?" When the defense objected, he withdrew the last question. But it was there, for the jury to hear.

"Tell me, Agent Price, is it possible Ms. Daniels not only accessed these files but made use of them because she was part of the conspiracy?"

Price agreed it was possible. "But," he added, "Not likely."

"Agent Price, I realize you are new to this game. It seems I need to remind you: a simple yes or no answer is all that is required."

"I understand, but I have sound reasons to believe it unlikely Ms. Daniels ever saw those files prior to when she worked for us."

Carly looked up, surprised, and saw McGuire's face redden as he strained to control his temper. "Are you saying you believe her computer was hacked?"

"No."

"Do you have reason to believe someone other than Daniels accessed these files using Daniels' computer? With or without hacking?"

"No," Eric said quietly. "I believe there is evidence her computer was not hacked. Just as there is evidence Ms. Daniels' computer was never used to access these files prior to the raid."

McGuire glared at him. "How could you possibly know that?"

"May I explain?" Eric asked the judge, directly. The judge agreed.

McGuire's face was a deep red. He looked about to explode. He turned to the judge. "Permission to treat Agent Price as a hostile witness."

The courtroom erupted with excitement. Reporters were scribbling about the key witness against Daniels turning. The judge silenced the court with his gavel and granted the request.

McGuire's eyes locked on Price, daring him to continue. He backed up slowly toward the jury box. He stood next to it, blocking one of the jurors from his view of Price. The juror tapped him on the shoulder. McGuire returned to the prosecution table and sat down.

Eric took a deep breath and turned to face the jury. "You probably heard about software you can install on your computer to monitor your kids? To be sure they're not playing games or sending email instead of doing homework?" He paused, waiting until he saw a few jurors nod. "Or chatting with a pedophile? Well, many employers monitor their employees' computers for similar reasons. They want to be sure their employees are not accessing inappropriate websites, like *Facebook*, or playing games. If employees spent considerable time on inappropriate websites, this would affect productivity. And some employers monitor their employees' computers because of concerns about confidentiality. They use the same kind of software. Or spyware. That's what Archer did."

He glanced at McGuire and quickly shifted his gaze to the gallery. Every seat was filled. Every eye was on Eric Price. The court room was quiet enough to hear the clock tick.

"Archer did this—used spyware. It's likely they did this out of concerns for sensitive personal information about the insureds, and confidential information about policies and pricing." He turned back to McGuire. "The Archer brothers used spyware to monitor every single computer used by every employee. Ms. Daniels' computer was monitored, along with all the others." He nodded at McGuire. McGuire did nothing.

Eric returned to the jury, the educator instructing a class. "This is how it works. It's stealth technology. That means the software is completely invisible for monitored users. Employees are not aware they are being monitored. This gives employers like Archer total control over the networked computers. They can actually stop and start remote computers. They can copy files from remote computers. This is true spyware, and it's legitimate."

He paused to pull a cup from the stack on the witness stand, poured water from the pitcher, and took a drink. He turned back to the gallery.

"Some companies inform their employees they are doing this, along with warning them about penalties for violating company policy. Archer did not inform their employees. Archer's employees did not know that *every key stroke was recorded* by spyware. They did not know their every key stroke was sent back to the computers of Aidan and Blake Archer."

Eric paused. He shifted in his seat. He took another sip of water.

"Because of this spyware, the Archer brothers would have known if and when Allison Walker peered at files that were prohibited to her. They would have known if she printed them, or copied them to a disk, or forwarded anything to someone else, in or out of the network. They would have known if she sent email to her husband." He paused and looked at the jury again. He looked directly at McGuire, who clearly was fuming. Eric looked away, not wanting to be distracted. He turned again to the jury. "It's important to understand that this type of monitoring system works without anyone knowing their computer is being monitored. The administrator—Aidan or Blake—has full control. They can access their employees' computers in real time without it interfering with their own work. Because it's saved on the administrator's computer, this monitoring can be done even if the employer is thousands of miles away."

He looked at the reporters who were scribbling away, trying to keep up with the essence of what he was saying, since they could not get every word.

"You may wonder how we know this," Eric continued. "We found the spyware when we examined the hard drives of every computer at Archer Life Settlements. By 'we' I don't mean I had anything to do with it." He smiled at the jury. "I mean the FBI's computer forensic lab. We have one right here in Orange County. The Regional Computer Forensics Laboratory—RCFL—opened in Santa Ana in 2011. RCFL has all the gadgets to trace cybercrime, from pedophiles to internet fraud to hackers. And it has over thirty FBI-trained and certified forensic examiners working collaboratively. Copying the hard drives of Archer's computers was one of the simplest tasks asked of them."

He turned back to the gallery. "Our lab copied every hard drive, including those on the executives' computers—Aidan's and Blake's. When Ms. Daniels began doing computer searches for us, it was after Aidan Archer's computer was returned. What she did not know is we did not return the computer with the original hard drive. We did not return the original hard drive because we were going to allow her access to all the files. All except one."

Again a hubbub of noise from the gallery. The judge tapped his gavel for silence.

Eric continued. "Ms. Daniels worked on Aidan Archer's computer using a hard drive that was exactly the same as the original except for the Central Logs Database. That's where the monitoring information was stored, along with the list of user names and the collection of recordings. We saw these files. Ms. Daniels did not."

As Eric's gaze moved back to McGuire, he was startled to see Yolanda Ruiz sitting at the prosecution table, next to Cutter, the U.S. attorney. He had not seen her enter. He concluded, "And that's how we know Ms. Daniels had no knowledge of the fraud."

McGuire jumped to his feet. "Can you be certain she did not hack her own computer after hours, from a home computer?"

"I have no idea of the extent of her computer skills," Eric said. "Possibly she is competent to hack into a computer. Or knows someone who could do this for her."

McGuire nodded his head and began to grin. Now he had her.

"But," Eric continued, and McGuire turned to look at him sharply. "regardless of her computer skills, I am certain neither Ms. Daniels nor anyone else hacked into the corporation's computers."

"You keep saying 'certain.' How can you be certain?" McGuire asked, lacing his question with a tinge of scorn. Nothing about Agent Price's background indicated he was a computer geek.

Eric looked directly at McGuire. "Like you, I wondered about a hacker. After learning about the spyware, I asked the technicians at the lab. They did not know the answers to all my questions. I then contacted several companies that market this type of spyware. I learned the spyware does not make computers hacker-proof. The company needs to use anti-virus software. They can install this as well, but they need to program it to allow an exception for the spyware they want."

He took another drink from the water glass. "At most of the spyware companies I checked—I checked a few but not all who market this type of software—the answer was: They do not have a feature that would reveal hacking."

McGuire began to grin. This was what he hoped to hear.

"So, Agent Price, can we conclude the spyware could not prevent hacking?"

Eric, of course agreed. He added, "As far as I can tell, there is no program that prevents hacking."

"Therefore, Agent Price, are you willing to conclude the possibility that Ms. Daniels, or a co-conspirator of hers, hacked into her work computer?"

Eric agreed to the possibility, adding, "The spyware used by Archer could not prevent hacking." McGuire was grinning, expecting more information to help him nail Carly Daniels.

Eric continued. "But." He paused and repeated the word, "But it would reveal *if* a computer was hacked. None at Archer were hacked."

"Absolutely none?" McGuire had begun to walk back to the prosecutors' table. He whirled around to demand an answer. "How can you be certain?"

"I asked the FBI techs to recheck every computer and compare with the monitor files. I wanted to know if a computer was used at a time when nobody was supposed to be at work. The company that provided Archer's spyware told me that if someone logged on—say a hacker cracked the user name and password of an employee and logged on remotely— the monitoring software would show they did this. It would reveal this and also show the commands they ran, the programs they ran, and it would record a screen shot of every action on the hacked computer."

McGuire nodded, then asked if it were possible that Ms. Daniels or someone who conspired with her sent her computer a viral email that, when opened, set up a program to allow an outsider to access the computer.

Eric agreed it was possible but, again, not undetectable. "The software—the spyware—installed on Archer computers would have recorded such an event. The email would show up in the administrator files on Aidan Archer's or Blake Archer's computer."

"Let me ask you about these administrator files. What is the time frame for how long they were saved?"

"The company began using this spyware approximately seventeen months before the raid shut them down. They did not delete any administrator files. As to Ms. Daniels, she did not have access to computers until two weeks before the company was shut down. That's when she was transferred to the data entry department."

McGuire stared at Eric. He turned toward his desk, walking slowly as if in thought. Eric suddenly added, "To be absolutely clear, the administrator logs have all records of Ms. Daniels' computer activity."

McGuire turned back to Eric. His voice boomed through the court room. "One last question, Agent Price. Why didn't you give me this information earlier?"

Again the court room erupted. Judge Easterly banged his gavel repeatedly before he gained control.

"Do you want an honest answer?"

"You took an oath to tell the truth, didn't you?"

Yolanda stared hard at Eric.

Eric looked at his lap, then at the jug of water. He poured new water into the plastic cup. He took a sip. "Okay. Here it is. Absolute truth. You were given a memo with this information."

"Well, excuse me. I probably overlooked it when I was busy preparing for trial."

"I handed the memo to you when I was in your office, after I told you about this. The memo is a summary of what I told you."

"This witness is dismissed," McGuire said angrily, turning his back on Eric and walking to the prosecution table.

The noise that followed McGuire's dismissal could only be calmed by the judge banging his gavel. "Agent Price," Judge Easterly said, "Stay right there. You are not dismissed."

Irwin Stanley was on his feet. He had objected to McGuire's taut dismissal, reminding the judge that it was defense counsel's turn for cross-examination of Agent Price. He addressed Price from the defense table. "Did the FBI techs who examined the administrator files find any employee computer used during non-work hours?"

Eric said they had not.

When Stanley asked if the FBI techs found any employee who used the computer for a longer time than necessary for assigned duties, such as typically spending ten minutes on a file and suddenly spending half an hour, Eric said no. Then he added, "With one qualification. The administrator logs were not set up to record and save the activity of either Aidan Archer or Blake Archer. So we do not have complete information on their computer use."

"Did you review all the Archer files? Irwin Stanley asked.

"Not all."

"What did you skip?"

"Anything that appeared not relevant to the charges."

"Can you give us an example?"

"Employee applications for group health insurance."

Stanley nodded. "Okay. That makes sense. Did you review employee salaries?"

Eric said he did.

"Was the salary paid to Carly Daniels far in excess of the salaries paid to other clerks?"

Eric said, "It was exactly the same."

Stanley concluded by asking Price if, on the basis of this, he believed Carly Daniels was innocent of all charges; that she never was party to a conspiracy; that she had no knowledge of fraud at Archer Life Settlements until she did research on the "doctored" computer in Aidan's office. Price answered affirmatively to each question.

"Based on these facts, Agent Price, do you believe Carly Daniels obstructed the investigation?"

"I believe she did not."

The prosecution had an opportunity to undo the damage through re-cross. McGuire asked Eric, "Is it possible for the administrator logs to be changed to hide activity?"

Eric said he did not know since it did not occur to him to ask the software developer this question. "But," he added, and saw McGuire cringe at the word, "since the logs were exactly the same on Aidan Archer's computer and on Blake Archer's computer, I think it's reasonable to assume nothing was changed."

McGuire then reminded Eric about the memo he claimed—emphasizing the word "claimed"—to have given him about the spyware. He asked Eric to describe it. Eric reached into a pocket and drew out a copy.

McGuire looked at it, taking time to study every word, as if he had never seen it before. Then he asked, "When, exactly, Agent Price, did you deliver this? What day? What time?"

Eric replied, "To be absolutely certain, Mr. McGuire, I would rather ask your secretary to provide your appointment book."

At that point McGuire dismissed Eric as a witness.

The reporters rushed from the courtroom to get the story in print, on the air and published to their online web sites.

# Chapter Thirty-Five

HER CELL PHONE trilled as she neared Bluebird Canyon. It was Kyle. He sounded excited. "What happened today?"

"What do you mean?"

"All they said on the news is, 'Shock and awe at Archer trial. Complete coverage at six.'"

Carly had forgotten about the reporters. She drove home in a state of confusion, disbelief and a smidgen of hope. *My rainbow day,* she kept thinking. *There may be a chance.* Her attorney said it was a good day for her, but they could not count on anything. Juries were not predictable. The verdict could go either way. Carly warned Kyle not to trust what reporters were saying.

As she pulled into the driveway Ben stepped out the door, carrying his helmet. He was on his way to his bartending job at the Rainbow Club.

"Talk to Ethan," Ben shouted as he jumped on his motorcycle. "Meltdown."

Carly told Kyle she would call back later; she had just arrived home and had to tend to Ethan. "Call any time," he told her.

She walked inside and saw Ethan staring at the computer. Maybe Ben meant "meltdown pending," she thought.

When she said, "Hello," Ethan did not respond. It was as if she had not spoken. Carly went to him. "What's wrong, Ethan?"

He stared at the computer. Carly bent and looked at the screen. It was filled with the web site of the local newspaper. Huge block letters screamed, "Was Daniels Set Up?"

Carly had forgotten Ethan could access the news on the computer. He could have done this at any time in the past year and a half. Thankfully, he had not, until now.

Carly put a hand on his shoulder. "Come sit and talk with me."

He did not move.

"We need to talk," she told Ethan. "It's important. I know you're upset."

When he did not respond, she lifted his hand from his knee and took it in hers. He did not move. She took two steps away, pulling him gently. "Come," she repeated. "Please."

He rose slowly, his hand limp in hers, his head down. Dragging his feet, he followed her to the sofa. He stood there until Carly sat. She patted the cushion. He obeyed but seated himself at the opposite end. He looked straight ahead.

"Tell me. What upsets you, Ethan?"

"Are you going to jail?"

Carly opened her mouth. Uncertain how to answer, she shut it again. How could she explain to a twelve year old what she did not understand herself?

Before she could decide Ethan, looking straight ahead, said, "Kids at school told me. They said you're going to jail. They said it was in all the newspapers. They said I was really dumb not to know."

"I'll tell you all about it, Ethan, everything, whatever you want to know. I'll answer every question as best as I can."

"Are you are going to jail?"

"I don't know for sure."

"Why?" He was in profile. Carly could see him swallow. Tears slowly ran down his cheeks. She slid along the cushion to sit close to him, and took his hand in hers. When he did not respond, she folded his hand in both of hers.

Still looking ahead, Ethan said, "I want to know why. Why you are going to jail. You don't do anything wrong. You always stop at stop signs and red lights. You don't steal things."

Carly took a deep breath. "It's hard to explain, Ethan. It's hard for me … to understand. The prosecutors—the government lawyers— made a mistake. They thought I did something wrong. I told them I didn't, but they didn't believe me."

"Why didn't they believe you? You don't lie."

"Some prosecutors think the worst of everyone."

"What's going to happen to me? Will I go to jail, too?"

"Ethan, you will always have a home with Uncle Ben. You know he loves you."

Ethan's pulled his hand away from hers and clenched his fists. His jaw tightened.

"You feel like throwing something, Ethan?" He did not answer. "Well, I feel like throwing something." That startled him. He turned his head part way towards her. He did not look at her. Carly realized he was focused at the corner of the room, at the computer.

"Is Ted Stevens one of the good guys or one of the bad guys?"

Carly looked at the computer. There was a smaller headline, beneath the one asking if Daniels was set up. She read, "Ted Stevens Redux?"

"Ted Stevens was a very important man, a grandfather, a senator in Congress for many, many years. Some government lawyers lied about Ted Stevens. They said he did bad things. But Ted Stevens had very good lawyers. They found it was the government lawyers who did bad things. It was the government lawyers who lied. Now everyone knows the truth."

"Is that what happened to you? Government lawyers lied about you?"

She nodded. "Until today."

"On the computer it says you were set up."

"I was—until today. Maybe. Today a different government lawyer told the court the truth. That's why the newspaper wrote I was set up. Maybe now it will go away."

He repeated the word, "Maybe."

Carly put her arm around Ethan and pulled him close. "Do you have any other questions?" He shook his head. "I am so sorry you had to find out like this. I didn't tell you before for a good reason. I didn't want you to worry."

Ethan swallowed.

"Ethan, if you have more questions, it doesn't have to be now, any time—ask me. I will tell you the truth. Even if it makes you sad. Even if it makes you angry. I promise."

Carly held him and began to hum. It was part of Rodney Atkins' song about going through hell. For the first time she hummed the part about angels holding out a hand to pull you back up on your feet.

⌒

Eric was on his way to Yolanda's office when his cell phone sang out The Lone Ranger. He opened it automatically, unaware which phone it was. He told Kyle he was about to start an important meeting and would get back to him. The excuse Eric used many times to avoid Kyle was real. It could very well be the end of his career with the Bureau. No wonder his stomach was in knots. After one of the worst nights of his life, his head was dull from lack of sleep. He had no thought other than the labels Yolanda could apply to him, polite labels like "rogue," but he could well imagine the ones she would not say.

Eric's sense of doom began as he walked out of the courtroom yesterday. It continued through the night and into the early hours of today. He finally slept, but when he awakened, it began again, worrying the sore he had created for himself.

*Did I screw up everything? What alternative did I have? If I get booted out, where do I go? What will I do? How good will I feel about myself? And yet, how could I do otherwise?*

His head was on a pillow but felt as if it rested on a rock. Eric tried every trick he knew to reassure himself he did the right thing, and to hell with consequences. Instead of counting sheep he tried to count people in history who went against prevailing winds, despite knowing it imperiled them and, sometimes, their families.

The one most prominent in his memory was Albion Tourgée, a North Carolina lawyer who challenged the Supreme Court's support of slavery. The Justices shot him down. But Tourgée did not relent. He continued his efforts—one of the most courageous white abolitionists before, during, and after the Civil War.

*He defied the Supreme Court. Did that make him a traitor? Or a courageous idealist?*

Eric did not believe he was like Tourgée. Yes, he was an idealist; he would admit to that. But he lacked the courage and strength of spirit.

Sleep eluded him, his brain a whirlwind of thoughts and emotions. If he got up and walked the hotel grounds, it would make no difference. Things were what they were. He had to live with the consequences of his actions.

When he shifted from thinking about Tourgée, Eric thought about having his own place, his own kitchen. He would heat milk and mix it with honey, his mother's remedy for sleeplessness. He turned on his side.

He remembered his father telling him he wanted to become a lawyer because innocent people went to jail while the guilty walked free. When Eric asked what he would do about that, his father tapped the law book he was reading. "I'm learning."

He turned on his other side. His father told young Eric that sometimes one person can do terrible things to many people, and sometimes one person can do good things for many people. He told Eric, "Maybe I'll help one person at a time, and not many in total. But each life touches other lives."

Eric flipped onto his back, and other thoughts crowded out the memories. Who was behind the persecution of Archer Life Settlements? *Persecution?* It was prosecution. He needed sleep or he was likely to make the same slip when he met with Yolanda. He got out of bed and began to do sit-ups. Not smart, he knew, to rev his body when it should slow down, but exercise often was an antidote to anxiety. His brain was on over-drive.

Back in bed, he began scrolling through names of people in

Congress who might have commandeered the prosecution. Who would benefit from taking out Archer? People in Congress had more power and influence than a president, more than almost anyone in the nation. Who had more power and influence? Enough power to influence those in Congress?

The answer was people with very deep pockets. Their money could motivate people in Congress far more than any ideal, far beyond any need of their constituents. Who in Congress, he wondered, might be on the receiving end of buckets of money from the company that replaced Archer Life Settlements? Not necessarily money already received, but the promise of future payments. Or both. He had no answer.

Why target Archer? There were larger companies. But among licensed companies, Archer was the largest. Is that what made Archer a target? Is that the reason? A competitor wanted Archer destroyed? Who would benefit most from taking out Archer?

After a few hours sleep he awakened with the knowledge it was futile to try to uncover who was behind this. If he succeeded, there was nothing he could do with the information. It would do him no good. It would do no good for anyone.

When he entered the FBI's office and passed the secretaries' enclave, he was handed a message from Yolanda: "My office ten o'clock." At half past nine Nicole Somebody, the secretary—he could not remember her last name—stepped into Eric's cubicle and held out a package.

"This just came for you."

Eric thanked her. When he saw the bookstore label on the box, he ripped it open. It was "Betrayal," the memoir of a former assistant supervising agent at the FBI's Boston office. Eric ordered the book after reading reviews that suggested the experiences of Robert Fitzpatrick paralleled his own fears about his future. Fitzpatrick's decades of outstanding achievement counted little when he tried to bring down a murderer and organized crime kingpin. Whitey Bulgar was protected by the FBI and by politicians, and they ganged up on Fitzpatrick. Twenty years after being booted out he told his story, everything, including the one unwritten but well known code he actually violated, "Don't embarrass the Bureau."

Eric opened the book. This happened to Fitzpatrick after decades of leading high profile investigations. What hope was there for a rookie? Eric could almost hear Yolanda, "Be afraid. Be very afraid."

As if on cue, Yolanda's head appeared at the opening to his cubicle.

"I'll be with you in five," she said. Her eyes fell on the book Eric was holding. She froze. Nodding, she turned away and walked in the opposite direction from her office.

Eric began to read. His heart was thumping. Eric wondered if it was wise to read this. He felt pretty far near the edge. He kept reading.

Yolanda rapped on the acrylic wall as she passed en route to her office, waving for Eric to follow. He did, answering Kyle's phone call as he approached her office. Yolanda walked straight to her desk, signaled him to shut the door, picked up a file and took it to the conference table at the other end of the room. Eric trailed her. Yolanda sat down and folded her hands on top of the file. She did not invite him to sit. She stared at him. He stood there, like a recalcitrant school boy before a principal.

"So. Mr. Hostile Witness. I have one question. Why did you research spyware?"

"Curiosity." He shrugged. "The techs told me what they found. I was curious to learn more. And I wondered about hackers."

"You were not authorized for that investigation. Had you not done so, you would not have undermined McGuire."

Eric was tempted to say "McGuire should not have asked those questions. He violated the cardinal rule of trial—Never ask a question you don't know the answer to." He clenched his jaw to keep from saying anything that would make the situation worse. Suddenly he heard his voice: "Did I embarrass the Bureau?"

Yolanda looked startled. She composed herself quickly. "Let me be very clear, Eric Price. You made a huge mistake yesterday. You flagrantly demonstrated that you are not a team player. You not only jeopardized the Archer case, you made enemies of Cutter, McGuire, and everyone in the queue above them. These are powerful people, Eric, far more powerful than you know or even imagine, or ever will be."

Eric pulled out a chair, expecting Yolanda to order him to stay where he was. Instead, she paused. Once he was seated, she continued berating him.

"This is not something you can shrug and brush off. You must know your longevity within the Bureau is at risk." She paused suddenly, as if reminded of something, then went on. "If nothing else, consider self-preservation. You now are at a crossroads. If you remain with the Bureau, unless you shape up fast, you are likely to be reassigned to the boondocks to investigate leaves and grass."

Eric swallowed hard.

"If you don't like the boondocks and choose to leave, you will face the economics of the real world. Just in case you thought you could return to a law firm, they're like every other business—laying off people. Add to that your reputation of not being a team player, which the media has made very public, it's doubtful you would get as far as an interview."

Eric wavered between acting humble and regretful versus rebellious, even antagonistic. Finally, he said, "I understand. That's why I ordered Robert Fitzpatrick's book. It happened to him. It could happen to me, far more readily. But from what I know, I admire him."

Yolanda tapped the file, then opened it. Surprised, Eric took out his pen and a yellow pad. It seemed they were done with the topic of his testimony. Betrayal. He wondered how much Yolanda knew of Fitzpatrick's story, or of the many laudatory reviews of his memoir. He wondered about the effect the book and its reviews had on the bureaucracy that was the FBI.

Yolanda lifted a pink message slip from her file. "One of the seniors you contacted. You left a message, and she returned your call. I set up an appointment for us with Marilyn Pendergast."

"Us?"

"I like to visit a house beautiful. You can stay here and do paperwork, if you prefer. Or you can join me at two o'clock for a ride to one of the luxury enclaves in Irvine."

# Chapter Thirty-Six

THE PROSECUTION RESTED. It was time for the defense to present their case. Judge Easterly gave the nod to Mitchell French, the lead defense attorney. He rose from his chair, stepped briskly to the jury box, and eyed each juror with a nod and a smile. He did look like the host at a gala with perfectly tailored hair, perfectly tailored suit and high gloss shoes.

"Hugo Boss," Irwin Stanley whispered to Carly. She looked at him questioningly. "Designer suit," he explained.

This was the opening statement French elected not to give at the start of trial. He began with a scathing review of each viator, padded with additional information he learned about them since they testified. Each time he concluded his summary of a witness French paused, walked up and down before the jury box, and eye-balled each juror as if he expected them to agree.

"Let me move to Vito Capone," French said. "One of a kind. Says he's all out of money, he had to hock his jewelry. I think he still had some of it with him here. He wants to walk out of this court room in those black suede booties and go back to Manhattan so he can drive the Lincoln Continental or Jaguar or whatever else car he's buying. Do you remember that? Give me a break."

Mitchell French smirked, then nodded his head. *So what if they agree the man was sleaze?* Carly thought. *What difference does that make?*

French continued. "Sean Beasley. He comes to court in a cab with Vito Capone. He's supposed to have his story down, he's met with the government over and over, and he sure knows how the 'stay out of jail card' works. On cross, he can't remember who was supposed to be involved. You know—'It's been some time. I can't remember.' But does he remember the cab ride over from Camp Hyatt? Or does he remember the lunch at the elegant Mediterranean restaurant with Capone? He doesn't say 'Vito Capone,' like he's just met him. He says, 'Vito.'"

Carly closed her eyes. This was a disaster. He was entering the room backwards. Instead of arguing innocence, he was proving the prosecutors' point that Archer dealt with disreputables.

By the time French was done with every viator who testified and began to address the law, Carly's head felt stuffed with cotton batting. If she could not pay attention, how could she expect the jury to do so? She had no idea whether French actually said anything of value. And then he called his first witness.

Harry Jenkins, the maintenance man at the Archer building, was nearly six feet tall and built like an athlete. He wore a blue oxford shirt, sleeves rolled up. Casual for California, Carly thought. She remembered the OJ trial on television. It, too, was a California court and the witnesses were casual, so much so some brought their own water bottles to the stand.

French asked Jenkins to spell his name for the court reporter, asked where he was from, where he was raised, and how old he was. Jenkins said he was forty-seven years of age and a native of California. When French asked if he was familiar with Archer Life Settlements, Jenkins replied, "I worked there."

"What did you do for Archer?"

"I maintained their building."

"How long have you worked for Archer?"

"About three years."

"Before you worked for Archer, what did you do for a living?"

"I was in drywall construction, interior drywall construction."

"Where was that?"

"Basically all over the United States, in different parts of the country."

Then French drew his attention to the June day of the raid. "Did you go to work that day?" Jenkins said he did. French asked at what time, and what did he typically do when he arrived at work. "I usually go in the building, take the elevator to the top floor, get me a cup of coffee and, you know, kind of check out things as I go. And then I usually go outside and smoke me a cigarette while I'm drinking my coffee."

French asked if he went for a smoke that morning. His next question was, "What happened when you came down the elevator and the doors opened into the lobby?"

"I saw a whole big bunch of people in the lobby that had no reason being there."

"And do you remember what you said, the first thing you said?"

"Well, the first thing I said is, I asked them was we making a movie."

He was told no, he said, and they told him nothing else. But they were trying to get the elevators to go up. He asked about this, and they asked who he was. When he told them he was "the guy that runs the building," they said he was the guy they needed to see.

"At that point, you know, I guess they wanted me to take them up in the building, and I told them I wasn't going to take them up. And then they told me they had a search warrant and showed it to me, and they told me who they was at that point."

French continued to ask what happened next and next and next. Jenkins offered them his keys. An agent in the lobby told him, "If I was you, I would be looking for a new job."

French asked about other employees. Jenkins said, "They were all in a state of panic. You know, they didn't know what to do."

In response to more questions about the raid Jenkins confirmed that law enforcement officials removed truckloads of documents, "working all day long. I saw them take out box after box."

When McGuire got up to cross-examine Jenkins, he asked if Jenkins recognized any of the FBI agents sitting at the prosecution table. Carly looked as well, wondering if Ruiz or Price were there. The agents at the prosecution table were the men who had interrogated the Archers.

"Are they wearing clothes similar to what they wore the day of the raid?" Jenkins agreed. McGuire then asked, "And were other agents there, too? And a whole lot of them had on suits, too, didn't they?"

Jenkins replied, "Yes sir."

"Okay. I don't have anything more. Thank you very much, sir." And with that, Jenkins was dismissed.

How does it help to tell the jury the employees were bullied and intimidated? How did that help us, Carly wondered. What did this have to do with innocence?

Carly looked at the adjoining defense table. Blake and Aidan sat next to Mitchell French's empty chair, staring straight ahead, their faces impassive. Carly wondered if they were in a trance. Were they also stymied to understand this ridiculous defense?

Her eyes felt gritty, as if filled with sand as Carly fought back tears. She could fight tears but not thoughts. It kept circling in her brain: For the life of me I cannot figure out what Harry contributed to undermining the charges. Was this Mitchell French's way to tell the jury there was no defense? When Carly again looked at Aidan and Blake, she wondered how they could sit passively, how they could allow this. Maybe they did not know this would happen. But they should have known. They were paying the bills. Their freedom was at stake, as much as hers. And they were far more educated, far more savvy than she was. How could they let this happen?

Carly kept glancing at Aidan and Blake, wishing to see them confer with each other, needing to see a sign of discomfort about French's handling of their defense.

Mitchell French called his second witness. Andrew Harkin, a thin, fragile-appearing man in his late forties, was sworn in. Harkin was Archer's newly hired, in-house attorney. He admitted this was his first time testifying in any court. He spoke in a low voice and had to be reminded, repeatedly, to draw the microphone nearer to him, to speak louder. Harkin's sole contribution was the statement that at the time Archer purchased fraudulently acquired policies no law prohibited these transactions. Archer stopped buying these policies as soon as the first state, Florida, enacted a law prohibiting this.

When McGuire cross-examined Harkin, he hammered him about criminal fraud statutes, wire fraud, providing false information in an insurance application, stolen property. Harkin knew nothing about criminal law. McGuire had found his gotcha witness. He demanded of Harkin, "When you identified one hundred twenty policies that were clean-sheeted, did you bring this to the attention of any law enforcement agency?"

"No. There was no duty to do so."

"Were you aware that Archer purchased one thousand seventy policies where the diagnosis date of the terminal illness preceded the date of the insurance application?"

"No."

Mitchell French, on re-cross, tried to redeem Harkin. "You stated that you were not familiar with criminal statutes. But I take it that it's no surprise to you that there might be criminal statutes that apply when a viator, or an insured, lies on an application."

"Yes."

"That would apply to the insured, right?"

"The insured and, possibly, the agent."

This Carly understood. It confirmed what she told Agent Price, that the insured and the agent were the ones who committed fraud.

The prosecution was given another shot at Harkin. McGuire asked if he was aware that Archer continued to pay premiums on fraudulent policies after the company was raided. Harkin answered, "Yes." Carly wondered what was terrible about that? She scribbled a note to Irwin Stanley. He read it and shrugged.

With no other witnesses to call, the defense rested. Testimony was over. Before the judge could move to the next step—closing arguments—Mitchell French asked Judge Easterly for a side bar. He granted it.

The hands on the wall clock clicked from one minute to the next and again and again, while the attorneys argued at the bench.

Judge Easterly decided to excuse the jury. Carly took out the book she brought with her—about training dogs—and began to read.

When the lawyers finally returned to their seats, Carly wrote a note to her lawyer asking what that was about. "Jury instructions," he wrote back in his usual, no-capital letters style.

After the jury took their seats, prosecutor Cutter stood to present his closing statement. He greeted the judge and then the jury and began by reminding the jury that Archer was a fraud factory, operating all over the country, soliciting policies from people with AIDS, trying to hide this, then reselling to investors, and they did this with the help of people like Carly Daniels.

Standing before the jury box, Cutter said, "I told you in my opening statement that we would prove the defendants in this case, Aidan Archer, Blake Archer, and Carly Daniels were dealing in fraudulently obtained life insurance policies and that they knew it, that they encouraged it, and that they had schemes to conceal their lies. And that's what we have proven to you."

He went on to say he would summarize the evidence that showed they proved all these points. And so he did. Carly tuned out.

Mitchell French nearly leaped from his seat to present his closing statement. He walked briskly toward the jury box, talking as he walked. "Ladies and gentlemen, I told you this was about two young men who had a dream. Aidan Archer and Blake Archer started a company in a new industry, without clear legal guidance, an industry that had no history and no regulations."

*Young men with a dream?* What nonsense, Carly thought. Aidan and Blake were not Steve Jobs and Steve Wozniak, working out of the family's garage to create a computer. Did Mitchell French think the jury was stupid enough to believe the Archer brothers were backwoods dolts who stumbled on a gold mine? The jury knew this business turned two ordinary people into millionaires. They were far wealthier than all the members of the jury, combined, and probably most who sat in the gallery.

French segued to the day of the raid, naming many employees—

including some who did not testify—and describing how they were bullied and threatened, describing the anguish this caused them. Carly was astounded. If the company was a fraud factory, what difference did it make if employees were scared?

French went on to describe other people who did not testify but whose testimony might have helped the defense. He acted as if what he was telling the jury was a recap of actual testimony. Carly felt like fleeing the court room. She remembered the judge cautioning the jury at the start of the trial that anything lawyers told them was to be ignored unless supported by testimony or other evidence. Surely some on the jury would remember.

Carly felt herself sink lower and lower. What kind of defense was this, to tell the jury Archer employees were "brow-beaten" by investigators, and threatened, and warned they would go to prison and their spouses would leave them, their mothers would cry, their children would grow up without them? When Mitchell French shifted to the viators, telling the jury how federal agents "worked and worked and worked on viators" to get them to testify against Archer, Carly was so weighted with sorrow she would have been unable to flee if there was a fire in the court room.

*How was any of this supposed to help? What did this have to do with innocence? Where were the witnesses who might have helped?*

Mitchell French finally switched to trial testimony, reminding the jury of viators who declared on their tax returns no more than ten thousand in income, but owned a home, four cars including a Mercedes and a Jaguar, and pocketed $400 thousand from the sale of policies. Each time he began a description of another of the loathsome viators he told the jury, "Now let me tell you about another piece of work." Carly groaned inwardly with every repetition of the phrase.

French continued attacking the viators. "Why does the United States permit Vito Capone and the other con men who actually committed fraud to stay in the same hotel, to eat together alone in fancy restaurants across the street all alone? What do you expect? What do you really think you can expect when you leave con artists, people of the streets, alone during the course of the trial? When you close your eyes and ears to witnesses like that, and leave them under the same roof alone, those men are motivated, they're not stupid. Avoiding jail motivates con men like nothing else."

Once again Carly thought this did nothing more than support the prosecutors' characterization of Archer as in cahoots with low-life people. It seemed indecent for this characterization to come from a man in a custom suit and expensive jewelry, a man who looked down his patrician nose and referred to the viators as street people. Then he switched, again dismaying Carly as he reminded the jury about Harry Jenkins being told he would be out of a job.

Carly knew Mitchell French was highly educated, taught at a law school, and had tons of experience. It did not seem possible that a lawyer with that resume considered the testimony of the custodian to be relevant. Was this an imposter pretending to be Mitchell French? Carly almost giggled at the thought.

"Now when you get to the Archer employees," French said, staring into the gallery at those who had testified and now sat watching, nodding to each one he recognized. "You just yell at them, tell them they work for crooks, pound your fists, call them liars, and threaten them with indictments." French reminded the jury about the prosecution's futile cross-examination of Harry Jenkins, asking the maintenance man, "Were the investigators wearing business suits that morning?" With a smirk, French asked the jury, "What has that question got to do with anything?"

Incredibly, French continued to belabor that point. He challenged the jury: "Who do you believe, an agent who testifies she did not tell Harry Jenkins he would be out of a job, or that working man who was damn worried when he was threatened he would be out of a job? Who do you believe? People remember when they are treated like dogs."

Was he trying to convince the jury not to believe the federal agents? Apparently so, since he repeated his main point: The jury must find them not guilty because they meant well and were harassed by government officials.

"My time with you is almost over," French told the jury. Carly imagined they were as grateful to be done with him as she felt. But he was not telling the truth. He was not yet done.

"If I have upset you with a question or taken too long with a witness, or not been prepared, please do not hold that against my clients." Carly froze. *He admits he was not prepared? Why apologize to the jury? Why not to Aidan, Blake, and me?*

Carly had to force herself to listen. French again strutted before the jury, showing off his designer suit, his expensive cuff links as she shot his cuffs, stepping carefully in his high gloss shoes, appealing to the jury to like him, seeming to expect if the jury liked him they would excuse his incompetence. He continued to cajole the jury.

"I tried very hard to minimize the inconvenience to you, but this is a very important matter to my clients. Also, I don't get a chance to reply to the government's rebuttal, okay? Those are the rules, and I accept them. And the reason is, the government has the enormous burden in a criminal case. It's beyond a reasonable doubt. And that's why they get a second chance. But if something comes up in rebuttal, I ask you to consider what I've said and what I might have said if I were given a chance."

Then French went back to lambasting the lying viators. "I ask you to return a verdict of not guilty on every count in the indictment, and let those broken, beaten men go home."

Carly's attorney was restless. He kept flicking his ball point pen open and close. She knew from previous days he did not want to take his turn near lunch time or near the end of the day. French did that once, a cross-examination of a prosecution witness, and was interrupted for lunch recess. He finished after lunch, when everyone was sleepy from lunch and few remembered what went before the recess.

Judge Easterly called a recess for lunch. Irwin Stanley, Carly Daniel's attorney, would give his closing argument in the afternoon, followed by the prosecution's rebuttal.

Carly headed to her truck where she had an energy drink in an insulated bag. It was all her stomach could manage without erupting in turmoil. Irwin Stanley had told her there was no parole in the federal system. If she were sentenced to ten years or more, good behavior would not shorten the time. Carly finished her energy drink and took a brisk walk around the parking area. She ignored reporters who called out to her. It no longer mattered if they did not like her. They no longer could influence the trial.

When everyone was again seated in the court room, Irwin Stanley asked permission to approach the bench. He was joined by Cutter, McGuire, and French. It was a brief exchange and when the attorneys returned to their tables Judge Easterly made an unexpected announcement. Irwin Stanley's closing argument would be postponed to the following morning.

"Tomorrow will be the last day of trial," he told the jury. "Mr. Stanley will present his closing argument, then the prosecutors have an opportunity to rebut the closing arguments of the defense. Then I give you jury instructions. That will take up most of the day. Then you retire to deliberate on the verdicts. Court is adjourned."

Stanley rushed to throw his files into his briefcase.

"I don't understand," Carly said to her attorney. "What happened? Why are you postponing this?"

"Family emergency. Plus, the judge realized that we still need many hours to wrap up closing and further discussion about jury instructions."

Carly walked out in a daze. She thought this would be the last day of trial. The jurors probably were disappointed for the same reason. Everyone's ordeal would be prolonged.

# Chapter Thirty-Seven

MARILYN PENDERGAST'S HOME was in a high-priced gate-guarded community. No one was admitted unless their name was listed with the rent-a-cop at the gate.

"That keeps out door-to-door salesmen and Jehovah's Witnesses, but not an enterprising burglar," Yolanda said, as she turned the black Ford Taurus into the entrance drive to the enclave. "He could sign on with gardeners or a home cleaning service. Service people have ready access." She looked at Eric as they waited for the gate to lift. "It's not quite as safe as people think."

Eric read the directions aloud. Yolanda turned right and followed the road, talking all the while. "And there's the possibility of leaving a car on a nearby street and using the pedestrian gate. Simply wait for someone to enter or exit, run up, say you left your key at home, please hold the door."

"And either do the same when he's leaving, or leap the fence."

"Never mind leaping a fence. Kids often leave the pedestrian gate unlocked. Or an adult leaves it unlocked for them, rather than give them a key."

"Why not use a combination that has to be keyed in?"

"They actually have both, but people forget the combination, especially seniors."

They passed what appeared to Eric to be mansion after mansion, all on beautifully landscaped lots. Gardening crews were working on several yards, trimming shrubs, blowing leaves from flower beds, mowing. Eric wondered how much land each house stood on. As if reading his mind, Yolanda commented that most of the property was in front, for show. She doubted any had as much as half an acre of land, including the land on which the homes sat.

"Land is at a premium in soCal, especially near the ocean. When realtors describe 'pool sized yard,' they're not kidding. The yard is the size of a pool."

Eric laughed, primarily because Yolanda was revealing a side of herself he had not known existed. As they drew near Marilyn Pendergast's house, Eric pointed to the house numbers painted on the sidewalk ahead, on the left.

"Tuscan inspired," Yolanda said as she turned the sedan up the circular drive.

Eric did not know what she was talking about—the house or the elaborate garden—and told her so. That brought a laugh from Yolanda. Aside from the dramatic approach and the size of the houses, they were similar to most newer homes in southern California, with stucco siding and red tile roofs. Yolanda parked in front of one of three garages.

"Three garages? And she lives alone?"

Yolanda smirked. "How would you spend your money, if you had more than you needed?"

"I could think of more fun ways."

"Maybe not when you're seventy."

"Point taken. However, there's always a worthy charity."

"Point taken," Yolanda said.

As they walked around the driveway to the street, Eric said, "May I assume you don't live in a house like this?"

Yolanda laughed out loud, noisily and heartily. They went up several layers of wide, multicolored stone steps to a portico, and began to search for the entrance.

"It would take too long for a burglar to find the door. He'd have to use a window for sure." Eric said. He was feeling unusually good in Yolanda's company. Or was it because he knew he would be given some credit for this. Whatever, he told himself, peering into alcoves that sheltered windows but gave no hint of an entry.

Still searching for entry, they turned as they heard a door open and a voice call out to them. There stood Marilyn Pendergast, a fit and attractive older woman in tennis clothes. She stood in the open doorway holding a small black dog with pointed ears. A tall dog stood next to her and a slim, medium-sized dog was at her other side.

"Casper is my Irish Wolfhound," she said, pointing to the large dog. "Nadia is a whippet, and little one, Gregor, is a min-pin."

Eric stared at the min-pin. It looked like a shrunken Doberman Pincher, very much shrunken. Marilyn smiled at him, thinking he was hesitant due to the dogs, and assured Eric they not only won't bite they won't jump on him. She stepped inside to lead the way across a ceramic tile-floored entry. Yolanda preceded him and Eric closed the door. Then he looked up, up, and up.

"Twenty foot ceilings, honeybun." Marilyn tapped him on the arm. "I apologize. I shouldn't call you that. I happen to have 'a thing' for handsome young men. But you're not really a handsome young man, are you? You're an FBI agent."

Eric reddened and reddened more when he saw the broad smile on Yolanda's face.

"Twenty feet high?" Eric said, to cover his embarrassment.

"That's what I was told. I never measured to see if I was gypped a foot or two."

"What do you do when you get cobwebs up there?" Yolanda asked.

"The spiders wouldn't dare. If one is so criminal as to breach my home, my cleaning crew will need to use a substantial ladder, don't you think?"

Marilyn led them into the family room. The windows revealed the rear patio and it was, as Yolanda predicted, minuscule, certainly in contrast to the size of the house. The patio was fringed with about a foot of yard, fully planted with various blooming things Eric could not name. Definitely not a yard for big, active dog. A dog like Kyle had would get a concussion, if it chased a ball to the fence. But the patio was nicely furnished with a wrought iron dining set, a barbecue, and a few potted plants that sprouted white flowers.

The family room had a white stone-raised hearth and fire place on one short wall, surrounded with white book shelves. If Marilyn had books, she kept them elsewhere. The shelves held various exotic artifacts from trips Marilyn had taken over the years. The skeptic in Eric surmised she could have acquired them from trips to local area shops that sold handmade goods from other lands. He would have loved to ask the story behind the artifacts. He had never known anyone who could afford a house valued at two million dollars. Driving here, Yolanda told him the price she supposed for this house, adding that it was relatively cheap by comparison with other, larger ones in Turtle Rock. He was speechless. Yolanda found it entertaining to render him speechless. She went on to tell him if he wanted a one bedroom condo in Turtle Rock it probably would cost four hundred thousand. For one bedroom? Eric had stepped into another universe.

The dogs immediately settled down on what appeared to be designated places on the area rug. The area rug covered the section of the family room that had furniture; the rest was ceramic tile. Eric and Yolanda seated themselves on a semicircular, cocoa colored leather sofa. Marilyn took the recliner, cranked up the leg section, and used it to rest her feet.

"On the phone you said I may be able to help you with an investigation into senior fraud. Intriguing. Intrigue me more."

Yolanda began. "You sold—" The doorbell rang, followed immediately by the front door opening. A small, slightly-built man in his seventies stopped at the entrance to the room.

"I hope you don't mind," Marilyn said. "This is Oliver Chase, my significant other."

Eric recalled the name from his examination of files. Oliver was unlike Eric's idea of a commercial real estate developer—a huge, portly man with a florid face. With a twirled mustache, goatee, and silver hair,

Oliver appeared more like Eric's idea of a college professor.

He bowed slightly, walked over and gave Marilyn a kiss on the cheek, turned to Yolanda, then Eric, and shook hands with each. Then he took the matching recliner to Marilyn's.

Yolanda began again. "We understand you sold life insurance policies to Archer Life Settlements."

"Indeed we did," said Marilyn. "Both of us. We used the cash for our trip to Italy. Next trip will be Switzerland."

"I'm curious,." Eric said, glancing from Oliver to Marilyn. "How did you folks learn about these transactions?"

Marilyn's face brightened. "I read a front page news article in the New York Times. That was a few years ago." Oliver nodded agreement. "A retired financial planner boasted about acquiring a policy with a multimillion dollar death benefit, which he planned to sell. I think the article was called, 'Late in Life a Bonanza.' I thought, What a great idea!"

"We named each other as beneficiaries." Oliver's eyes twinkled as he grinned. "For about one month, until we sold the policies, Marilyn could have done away with me and pocketed $20 million."

"You could have done the same," Marilyn said, looking down with a pout, pretending to be miffed.

Oliver reached out an arm to grab Marilyn's hand. "You knew I would never do that. You know you're worth more to me alive."

Eric nodded. He was tempted to remind them about the insurable interest law, the requirement for an insured to be worth more alive than dead to the beneficiary. Instead, he asked, "How much were the premiums?" When he heard from Marilyn, then Oliver, that they paid a total of nine hundred thousand before the policies were sold, he asked about the source of those funds.

"Oh, we took out second loans on our homes," Marilyn said cheerily.

"What would you have done if the policies did not sell?'

Marilyn looked at Oliver. He shrugged.

"That happened to other seniors," Eric told them. "There are several lawsuits filed because of this—seniors who lost their homes when the policies did not sell and they had no way to repay the loans."

"Never suspected that could happen," said Oliver. "I guess we hit it lucky."

Yolanda's voice was soft but her question was blunt. "Did you know you were engaging in fraud?"

Oliver looked startled. Marilyn smiled warmly. "Goodness, no," she said. "How could this be illegal? A financial planner was doing it, and they know about these things. If it were illegal, would The Times run his story as front page news? I never saw any criticism of this after the story ran."

Oliver asked what made it fraud. Yolanda told him it was purchasing with the intent not to keep the policy. Purchasing to sell it to strangers. "Naming each other as beneficiaries was a ruse to deceive the insurers. Each of you did this, and each of you signed off on the sale."

Oliver looked distressed. "Are we criminals? Are we going to be indicted?"

Marilyn looked close to tears. "I've never done anything illegal in my life—other than a parking ticket. How were we supposed to know this was illegal? We were told it was a good investment. So far, it has been."

Yolanda assured them they would not be prosecuted. The relief showed on their faces.

When Eric asked how they knew who to contact to get this ball rolling, Oliver said it was simple enough, a newspaper ad. "Ergo, our trip to Italy."

Eric looked at Yolanda as if to say, "What did I tell you?" She nodded as if to say, "Good job."

# Chapter Thirty-Eight

CARLY WAS ASTONISHED when her attorney entered the court and took his seat beside her. He looked as if he had been awake all night. His eyes looked glazed. His face was gray. She wondered if he had spent the evening at a bar. Then Carly remembered his family emergency. "Is your family okay?" she whispered. Stanley nodded—the judge was waiting for him to begin—and Carly watched her attorney, short, squat, gray and balding, step before the jury box. He began by apologizing.

"Ladies and gentlemen, I know you are tired of hearing lawyers talk to you. And I'm tired. I want you to know that. But I would like you, please, to try to give me your attention because this is so important. Nothing is more important to Carly Daniels than what you do when you retire to deliberate. So, tired as we all are, please try to go through this with me."

Irwin Stanley turned to look at Carly. He allowed his gaze to linger, expecting the jury to do so, too. Carly gave a slight nod of her head in acknowledgment. He turned back to the jury.

"I believe the court will instruct you that in order to convict any of the defendants on conspiracy charges the government must prove beyond a reasonable doubt that each *separate* defendant *knowingly* and *voluntarily* joined in any criminal agreement, if there were any." Stanley paused to allow those words to sink in.

"I believe the court will say a defendant who simply knows about a conspiracy, or was present at a time or associated with members of a group—that is not enough. Even if he or she approved of it or did not object to it."

Carly was calm until she heard the last sentence. *Even if he or she approved of it or did not object to it?* Her headache spiked. Her stomach twisted in anguish. Why did Irwin Stanley suggest she knew about a conspiracy? Why did he not state, flat out, that she was completely ignorant of conspiracy and any fraud, if these existed? Why did he not implore the jury to consider there was no conspiracy that involved Carly in any way? She knew his first words were the most important part of anything he said. She felt too tired to listen to another lawyer drone on and on, and it was her life on the line. The jury might be too tired or too bored to pay attention past the first few sentences.

Her hands were shaking. Carly hid them below the table. She tried to calm herself by imagining she was walking the beach. That did not work. She tried to picture Ethan from birth and at various ages. She searched her memory for pictures of Ben, from the day she first saw her new baby brother. Nothing worked. This was the last pitch for her, and Irwin Stanley did not tell the jury that she knew nothing. Now he was describing the burden of proof. *It was over,* she thought. *There's nothing more to say; it's over.*

"The burden of the prosecution is to prove any of these defendants guilty. It's a basic principle, and Judge Easterly will instruct you about this later, that anyone who comes into a courtroom is presumed innocent. Carly Daniels is presumed innocent. And what that means is that unless, and until, the prosecution proves her guilty beyond a reasonable doubt, you must acquit her. You must let her walk out of the courtroom."

Irwin Stanley had walked to the defense table and rested his hand on a stack of papers. As he began to walk away, his hand tumbled the stack to the floor. Carly bent to pick up the papers.

"Let it go, Carly," he said loud enough to be heard by the jury. She returned to her chair wondering if he was clumsy or if, like the TV detective, Columbo, this was a ruse. *Nah,* she thought. *He is not that clever.*

Stanley walked slowly toward the jury, with each step making eye contact with each juror. "Now, proof beyond a reasonable doubt, as you will hear from Judge Easterly, is the highest burden of proof in the law. I like to think of it as a mountain that the prosecution has to climb before they can get a conviction. Being charged is not evidence that the defendants are guilty, and you cannot consider this against the defendants in any way. That's a very important instruction."

That statement was so important that Stanley paused, and repeated it before continuing. "Being charged is not evidence that a defendant is guilty." *Something I learned the hard way,* Carly thought. What if the jury believes the U.S. government would not charge me unless I was guilty?

Irwin Stanley asked the jury to contrast their power with the enormous power of the government, the numbers they brought to the raid of Archer Life Settlements, the numbers who investigated before and after the raid. "Inside this courtroom," he said, "you have the power to hold the government to that burden of proof. I'm asking you, exercise that power. Make them meet their burden of proof."

*I am one against so many,* Carly thought, worried that the vast numbers of people involved in the investigation would be conclusive to the jury. Irwin Stanley returned to the end of the jury box, allowing the jury full view of Carly as she sat there, trying not to reveal any emotion.

"The big questions are: One, whether Carly Daniels acted willfully, whether she intended to defraud the insurance companies, and whether she participated in a scheme to defraud. These are all elements of the crimes that she's charged with. And Judge Easterly is going to instruct you on that."

Walking more swiftly, Stanley returned to the defense table. He rested his right hand on another, much smaller stack of papers. "You've heard this from several witnesses—that Carly Daniels started work at Archer two years ago. And you heard many things said about Carly Daniels, primarily by Vito Capone. Let me turn for a few minutes to Capone, one of my favorite subjects.

"Mr. Capone talked about blood swapping. Vito Capone is a man who lied all of his life for money. He now has the opportunity, thanks to the deal the government made with him, to lie in exchange for his freedom. And believe me, he is making the most of the opportunity. Mr. French went over with you some of the lies he told on his bankruptcy petition. He sued his in-laws for a million dollars for a phony injury. He sold one of his policies twice, once to Archer and once to some viatical company in Florida, collected the money twice, and then tried to say the other company cheated him. And he went so far as to write to the insurance commissioner in Florida, complaining of being cheated. I mean, this guy will do anything. But I want to focus on the lies he told in this case. From the witness stand, he told you— and I'll never forget the word that he used over and over. He told you that Carly Daniels 'educated' him on how to switch the Social Security number on his insurance application."

*Why is he reminding the jury of this?* Carly could not believe what she was hearing. This was her lawyer and her life on the line.

"Now, Capone told you he didn't talk to Carly for the first time until two years ago. Of course not. She did not work at Archer prior to that time. So we showed him a couple of applications from 1995 and 1996 where he switched the last four digits of his Social Security number. Well, he had a story about that. He had been switching—this is his story. Remember? He had been switching the last four digits of his Social Security number by 'innocent mistake' ever since he was a child. But Carly told him to switch all eight digits. Okay? That was the first story that he told you."

Stanley smacked the pile of exhibits. Two jurors jumped in their seats, startled, no doubt awakened by the sudden noise. Stanley went on. "Well, there was a problem with that, which is: He had an Allstate life insurance application dated nine months before Carly Daniels was hired by Archer. At least nine months before he ever could have spoken to her. Nine months before he knew she existed." Stanley tapped the stack of exhibits.

"In that application he switched all eight digits. Here is that Allstate application." Irwin Stanley lifted the application, walked to the jury box and held it up so that the cover page faced the jury. "This is from before Mr. Capone ever spoke a word to Carly Daniels. And if you look at the Social Security number, he switched all eight digits."

Irwin Stanley returned to the defense table, put the application face-down on the table, starting a new pile, and withdrew another application from the stack.

"Here is his Prudential policy, issued after he claims he first talked with Carly Daniels. You'll notice that he used exactly the same Social Security number as on the Allstate application. So his story about being 'educated' by Carly Daniels on the Social Security numbers was a total lie. He switched all eight digits before he ever talked to Carly Daniels, and he switched all eight digits in exactly the same way after he first talked with Carly Daniels."

Stanley placed the Prudential application on top of the Allstate application and turned to the jury. "And he lied about something else, too. Remember he told you that Carly Daniels educated him—his word—to put 'owner restaurant' as his occupation on these insurance applications? Well, we showed him three applications—I'll show them to you, too—that he filled out before he ever talked to Carly Daniels. Three applications where he put the same occupation, with minor variations. The first is the Allstate Application I just showed you. This was from *before* he ever talked to Carly Daniels. He lists as his occupation 'owner restaurant.'"

Carly looked up at Stanley. She hoped he could see the gratitude in her eyes. He was making the case for her innocence or, at least, a case against Capone telling the truth about her. That was reasonable doubt, was it not?

"Capone got on that witness stand," Stanley pointed, "took an oath, and told you that Carly Daniels 'educated' him to do that. I told you I had three. Here's a second one, a Massachusetts General application. Capone submitted this more than a year before he ever spoke to Carly Daniels. He lists as his occupation, 'owner restaurant.' Here's a CNA application he submitted almost a year before he first spoke with Ms. Daniels. And he lists as his occupation, a little variation this time, 'proprietor restaurant.'"

Irwin Stanley walked the length of the jury box, making eye contact with each juror as he spoke. "So he got on that witness stand,

and he told you that Carly Daniels educated him on how to lie about his Social Security number and how to lie about his occupation. That itself was a lie. It was a lie that he told on the witness stand under oath. But, of course, Capone's big lie, the one that they brought him in here to tell, was about swapping blood."

He walked back to the defense table, walked behind Carly, and rested his hands on her shoulders. "And I want to talk with you a little bit about that one. The first story he tells is to the grand jury that Carly Daniels told him to talk with Sean Beasley but he got scared and didn't meet with Beasley. This is the same Beasley, of course, that he's taking the taxi with and having lunch with. But he's scared of him back then. And that Carly told him later that Archer paid Beasley to take care of the blood test. That's the story he told under oath to the grand jury."

Irwin Stanley walked slowly back to the jury. "Well, that story was obviously false. And part of the reason you know it's false is that Vito Capone wrote a letter to US Life, which is Government's Exhibit 20-S. In his letter he made a big production that they were doubting the veracity of his blood test. So obviously he's got some involvement, okay? So the story just doesn't hold up. Then Capone comes in here and he's got a new story on the blood tests. Now, keep in mind, he's got to keep the prosecutors happy, that's how he stays out of jail. So it has to involve Carly Daniels somehow. Okay? That's the bottom line."

He turned and slowly walked the other way. "His new story is there were two blood tests because, remember, he got two policies, one from Prudential and one from US Life. And he says there were two blood tests. Okay? And he says they were a week or two apart, and on one blood test he used his brother, Angelo, to stand in for him and that Carly told him that the other one would be taken care of through Beasley. Now, there is still a problem with that story, because Beasley, of course, even when he came in to testify, denied switching any blood for Capone. But at least it explains that letter Capone wrote to US Life. Now we have two blood tests. For one, he used his brother, Angelo, and complained about US Life doubting his veracity and so forth. But for the other one Carly Daniels helped him."

Stanley walked back to the defense table and lifted the next exhibit from his pile. "Well, after Mr. Capone testified, I decided I would subpoena the blood test records from Prudential for that other policy. And it turns out that the blood test for that other policy was performed by the same examiner on the same day as the blood test for the US Life policy. And I'll show you the two documents."

He held up a page. "First, I'm going to show you the US Life blood examination. This is Government's Exhibit 20-C, which the government put into evidence." He walked toward the jury with the page. "And if you look down at the bottom, you'll see it is dated and witnessed. Okay? That's the U.S. Life."

Irwin Stanley walked back to the defense table, and took another page from his stack. "Here is the one, Defendants' Exhibit 42, that I subpoenaed from Prudential and which I put into evidence yesterday. It's a little hard to make out." He returned to the jury with the page.

"If you look down at the bottom of this one, you see that this other blood test, the Prudential one, is witnessed by the *same* paramedic and on the *exact same date*. So Capone's story about the blood test, even his new story, the one that he finally settled on here in court, was just false. There weren't two blood tests, one with his brother and one with Beasley somehow connected to Carly Daniels. There was one blood test on one day by D.C. Rodriguez. The results went to two companies. Vito Capone had his brother, Angelo, stand in for that blood test, and Sean Beasley had nothing to do with it. And Carly Daniels had nothing to do with it. That was a big lie that Vito Capone was brought in here to tell you."

Stanley returned to the defense table and placed the page on the stack. He turned toward the jury. "Now, I know you're tired, and I'm tired. I'm getting there." He smiled. A few jurors smiled, tiredly, Carly thought. Or perhaps it was out of politeness for his valiant effort.

"Most of what I've said, pretty much all of what I've said, bears primarily on the mail or wire fraud charges, and there's a reason for that. We also have money-laundering charges, but the bottom line is pretty much this: If you find Carly Daniels not guilty on the mail and wire fraud charges, you've got to find her not guilty on the money-laundering counts as well. And there's a simple reason for that. For all of the money-laundering counts, Judge Easterly will instruct you that the government has to prove that Carly Daniels knew that the money involved in the financial transactions was the proceeds of mail or wire fraud and that she intended to promote the carrying on of mail fraud or wire fraud. And so if you conclude, as I think you have to under the instructions that you're going to get, that Carly Daniels did not commit mail fraud or wire fraud, then you have to say that she did not engage in money laundering as well. I say that again. If you acquit Ms. Daniels of mail fraud and wire fraud, and I think you must, then you should acquit her as well of the money laundering, because the mail fraud and the wire fraud are, in effect, the foundation and the basis for the money-laundering counts.

Once again he walked slowly along the length of the jury box as he spoke. "The prosecution has not proven beyond a reasonable doubt that Carly Daniels acted with an intent to defraud or that she was part of a scheme to defraud. The prosecution just hasn't met that burden. This is a criminal case, and a woman's liberty is at stake, a young woman's liberty. This is—as I told you at the beginning—this is the most important moment in Carly Daniels's young life. Her future is in your hands, and all she asks of you, all I ask of you, is that you fulfill your oaths as jurors and hold the prosecution to its burden of proof beyond a reasonable doubt. Please focus on the questions that I highlighted for you at the beginning, and I think if you do those things, you will acquit Carly Daniels and let her go back to her young son. Thank you."

Judge Easterly called recess for lunch. Carly looked at Irwin Stanley. He had dark circles beneath his eyes. His face seemed to have taken on seams since they first met. He looked exhausted.

"Thank you. You did a good job," she told him.

"I hope the jury listened. And understood."

As soon as they left the court room, Stanley turned on his cell phone, walked off to a corner, and made a call. Carly wondered about the family emergency that had him rushing home yesterday. She waited for fifteen minutes but when he did not appear, Carly went outside to eat the sandwich she had in her purse.

☙

Court was in session. The judge called, "Mr. McGuire." The afternoon belonged to Tom McGuire and the prosecution's rebuttal.

McGuire began by saying to the judge, "Thank you, judge, very much."

*Very much?* That got Carly's attention. *Did he hope to influence the judge with his good manners?*

McGuire promised the jury to "make it as quick as I can." And that means, Carly knew, he would take all the time in the world. The jury would indulge him because they had no choice. Did they realize how unctuous he was?

McGuire eyeballed each juror. "But first I want to ask you a favor. Because I think I have some good points to make on rebuttal. And I'm not going over a lot of new things. It's in response to the arguments you heard. Please bear with me."

Carly was annoyed with everything about McGuire, his appearance, his manner of speaking, what he said, and that habit of a long pause in the middle of each sentence.

He began, "They deceived the investors. They deceived the insurance companies. That's undisputed." Wrong! Carly thought. *The real victims are the people who owned policies for years, and sold them because they were in need.*

McGuire continued. "The Archer brothers set up a company to deal in a business that began with a lie. Until Archer bought the policy from Vito Capone and his pals, the policy had no value because they never intended to keep it. Has the government made plea agreements with some of these viators? Yes, we have. But when it finally comes down to who sentences that person, it's not me. It's not the U.S. attorney office. It's the judge."

Carly felt like shouting, *Wrong! You're misleading the jury!* She had learned enough over these months to know the judge almost always followed the recommendation of prosecutors.

"Mr. French made a big thing that nobody has paid back any restitution," McGuire continued. "But that doesn't happen until you are sentenced."

Carly was weary of hearing McGuire go on and on with his half-truths. His words sounded like blah, blah, blah. It reminded Carly of a coffee mug in a Dana Point gift shop. It had a picture of a dog with its head to one side, trying to understand a stream of words spoken by a person. The words printed on the cup were, "Blah, blah, blah."

"The fact of the matter is the folks over there," McGuire pointed at the defendants, "would dance with the devil in order to turn a buck, and that's what this case is all about. Greed."

Finally McGuire thanked the jury and sat down. Carly turned to her lawyer. "Now it's over, except for the jury?" Irwin Stanley said it would be some time before the jury deliberated. First, the attorneys would argue before the judge about the wording of jury instructions the judge would deliver. This was very important, he told her. We want Easterly to tell them certain things that the prosecutors absolutely do not want. And they want the language of the instructions to point toward conviction.

"Once the judge decides, he'll call back the jury, give them instructions, and then send them to the jury room."

"Must I stay here all that time?"

"Go home. Sit on pins and needles, and pray, if you're so inclined. The jury could take hours, or they could take days. We'll be called back to court when the jury reaches a decision."

Carly drove home, struggling to concentrate on the cars around her, the road, the turns she needed to make. It was a familiar drive along the San Diego freeway but it did not seem familiar. She did not feel like Carly Daniels. She felt in a dream state. With little reason to believe the jury would absolve her, she felt an urgency to escape.

Carly no longer had faith in the system. What chance did she have to be acquitted, when she never imagined being charged with a crime, let alone multiple felonies?

Much as she tried to focus on the road and avoid the fears that plagued her, she felt drugged. This was a very real nightmare. Even if the jury found her not guilty, it would never be just a bad memory.

# Chapter Thirty-Nine

EACH DAY OF JURY deliberations Carly phoned her attorney. He could not tell her whether the delay was good or bad news. "You never know with juries."

Early on the fourth day Carly was preparing pancakes for breakfast when she dropped the spatula, startled by a terrified yowl from the front yard. She shut off the stove and rushed to the living room window in time to see a coyote prancing down the middle of the road, a neighbors' cat hanging limply from its jaws. *A bad omen,* Carly thought. She braced herself for worse news.

Her neighbors would do as so many others did, mount posters on light posts, computer-generated posters with a photo of their cat and a telephone number, and hope the wayward feline was simply hunting and would return in a week.

Once Ethan was on the school bus Carly planned to run next door to tell them their cat was … a coyote's filet minion? No, she thought. That's my craziness. Carly felt as if she was losing her sanity. Reality was worse than nightmares. Each day she forced herself to check the internet web site for the federal prisons, breaking off a crumb at a time—rules about visitors, telephone use, behavior. A crumb was all she could manage. Each time she visited the web site she heard steel doors clang.

After the school bus disappeared around the corner, Carly walked next door and rang the bell. There was no answer. No cars were in the driveway. Like her cottage, there was a single garage. Carly had forgotten that both husband and wife drove to work each day.

She was gathering tomatoes from the garden when her cell phone trilled. It was Irwin Stanley. Carly hesitated. It was unavoidable. She had no choice. Irwin Stanley was brusque. He told her the jury reached a verdict and she must be in the court room by eleven thirty.

Carly could not speak. Stanley filled the silence by asking, "Are you there?" She said, "Yes."

"One more thing," he said. "This is important. I mean it for your own good. Don't be stubborn. You want to influence the judge. Let him see you as fragile and feminine. Wear a blouse and skirt and flat shoes. Do not wear heels. Wear your hair loose, like a young girl. And be on time."

Her voice came out like a croak. "I'll be on time." Her hands were shaking as she closed her cell phone.

Carly knocked on Ben's door. She had promised to wake him when the verdict came in. As he headed for the shower, Carly told him what her lawyer said about not wearing a suit. He was furious.

"The s.o.b. expects a guilty verdict. Whatever the verdict, he is wrong. Damn wrong. Remember what Mom used to say? 'Go with pride.'"

Ben was right. Her mother was right. She would hold up her head, regardless of the verdict. Carly decided they could take her truck, her freedom, years of her life, but she would not allow them to take her dignity and her self-respect.

This court session should be brief. To be safe, Carly phoned Kyle to ask him to meet the school bus when Ethan came home if she did not phone him first, to tell him he was not needed. Then she took a quick shower and dressed in her black suit and a gray silk blouse. She did her makeup with care, adding mascara to assure no matter what happened she would not cry. She blow-dried her hair, which took more time now that it was long, and wound it into a French knot. She added her mother's pearl earrings, the dolphin pin, and slipped into heels.

When Carly stepped out of her bedroom, Ben was in the hall, leaning against the stair rail. He wore an oxford shirt and jeans.

"Waiting to catch me if I faint?"

"Nah," he said, without conviction.

"Let's go, bro. I'm ready for anything." She smiled at him, the first smile in a long time. They were walking out to the truck when Carly's phone trilled. She saw it was Blake. She answered with a simple, Hello.

"Just want to tell you, if we are convicted we plan to appeal. We'll cover your appeal, too."

"Okay. Thanks for calling."

Ben drove. The truck's motor was loud, the radio louder. Johnny Cash was singing "Folsom Prison Blues." Ben reached to change the station. Carly stopped him, saying, "Reality check."

The radio was background noise. Her head was filled with the echo of reporters who chased her whenever she appeared outside the court. "Why'd you do it, Carly? Why'd you do it?"

"I want you to sell my engagement ring. Pretend it was mom's. I forgot to declare it as an asset. I don't want them to know about it. I want the money for you and Ethan."

Ben grumbled. She could not stop, even though it upset him. "They'll probably take the truck. I have to make sure you have enough money to rent a car when you need it."

"I can get a fixer-upper for a few thousand. I know some guys who can help fix it."

"I keep worrying how to prepare Ethan. I was thinking to write to the warden, once I know which prison it will be. I'll ask for contact information for someone—an inmate." She paused. The word was difficult. "An inmate with whom I could correspond. Possibly someone with a child Ethan's age. Then we could all go to visit her, and Ethan will meet another child whose mother is there."

Ben was exiting the freeway and took the turn too sharply, quickly corrected, and was back on track.

"Whoa!" Carly said.

"It's this talk. Can't you shut up about this?"

"We can't escape it, Ben. If the court allows me two months to pre-pare, I need to use that time to make it easier for Ethan."

"I suppose."

"We can drive to the prison and back the first time, just to see the outside, and go to the visitors' room the next time, visit with the woman who will be my friend."

"God, how I hate this conversation."

"Me, too. But we have to plan. The visitors' room will be an ordeal for Ethan—many people, too much noise. There's no way to make that easier."

"His new MP3 player?"

"They don't allow visitors to bring anything with them, not even pictures."

Ben swore under his breath.

"I forgot to tell you—when Blake called he said they would file an appeal, if we're convicted. That could buy us more time. But I'm not sure I can go through with this again."

Ben shrugged.

When they entered the court room Carly saw Aidan and Blake at the defense tables with attorneys French and Stanley. They nodded at each other. When her attorney nodded, Carly was surprised he said nothing. She expected he would admonish her for wearing a suit. Ben joined Aidan's wife and the elderly couple at her other side. He never asked who they were. He did not care. The gallery began to fill with reporters.

Ben realized he was drumming his fingers on the arm of the chair. He stopped. *I am not as cool as I thought,* he told himself. If not for the air conditioning, he would be as lathered with sweat as he felt on the inside.

Carly, Aidan, and Blake sat stiffly and silent. Their attorneys stopped chatting and grew silent. Everyone waited. The court report-er took her seat. The judge's clerk entered. The judge was announced and slowly walked to the steps, again as slow as a groom going to the alter. He climbed and took his seat. The jury was called and they filed in. The bailiff announced the case. Carly no longer cringed when she heard, "The United States of America versus Carly Daniels."

The judge asked if they had reached a verdict. The foreman said, "Yes, but we want you to read a statement we prepared, first." He handed the statement and the verdict sheets to the bailiff. The bailiff brought them to Judge Easterly.

Easterly read the pages and frowned. He looked at the foreman, then at each juror.

"This is the final answer for each and every one of you?"

Each person was requested to respond. Each said it was.

"This is highly unusual." He called Aidan Archer. Aidan stood up, Mitchell French at his side. "The jury is unable to arrive at a verdict."

French did not sit down. He waited as Blake Archer was called. "The jury is unable to arrive at a verdict."

Carly was called. She rose from the chair to stand beside Irwin Stanley, four inches taller than her attorney.

"Not guilty on all counts."

Carly collapsed into her chair. There was no joy. She was too exhausted to do anything, say anything. Earlier, Ben expected her to faint, regardless of the verdict. How right he was. She felt light-headed and dizzy.

The judge banged his gavel. "Stay seated. I have to declare a mistrial for Aidan Archer and Blake Archer. This is the statement the jury wants read. 'Every juror believes the prosecution of this case is highly suspect due to what we learned about the case against Carly Daniels. Although we unanimously believe there is a great probability Aidan Archer and Blake Archer are guilty, we find insufficient proof to vote guilty beyond a reasonable doubt.'"

Judge Easterly officially declared a mistrial for Aidan and Blake Archer, and adjourned court.

Ben walked slowly toward Carly as if he, too, was stunned.

"Congrats, Sis." She looked up into his face, expecting a grin. He was so solemn it saddened her. She rose on her toes and kissed his cheek.

Over Ben's shoulder Carly saw Aidan and Blake shake hands with the lawyers and slap each other's back. Aiden's wife stood by, waiting her turn, then went into Aidan's arms. The few people in the gallery rushed from the court room.

"Media," Irwin Stanley said.

"What happens now?" Ben asked. Carly's mind was blank. She could not have spelled her name, if asked.

"You go home. It's over for you. As for the Archers, they'll be re-tried. Of course, the prosecutors will be in a pickle. They'll need other viators to testify."

He explained that those who testified at this trial will go before Judge Easterly for sentencing in accordance with their plea agreements. That meant they no longer would be obligated to testify at the retrial.

"Meaning," said Ben, "prosecutors will have to scrounge up a new set of liars."

Stanley ignored him. He wished Carly luck and left. Blake came over with his usual broad smile and gave her a hug.

"You're our good luck charm, Carly. Without you, who knows what would have happened? You'll be the first we hire when we start up again. And a fat raise to go with it."

Carly shook her head. "The future has been on hold too long. I can't think of anything right now. I just want to go home and catch up on sleep."

"I understand," Blake said. "It's been hard on all of us. I was almost driven to drink again. I was even tempted to look up my old drug supplier. But I don't want to end up in rehab again. That's what stopped me."

Carly was startled to hear this. None of the employees had ever mentioned Blake's past transgressions. Perhaps it was so long ago no one knew of it. She patted his arm as if to say, Good Boy, and hurried out with Ben to the truck.

# Chapter Forty

Eric was assigned to assist Kevin and Jenny with a mortgage fraud investigation. He looked for them but Kevin and Jennie were in the field. Eric returned to his cubicle, edgy. He could not concentrate unless he was engaged in a specific, time-defined task. Nicole-the-secretary stepped into his cubicle with a package. "This just came for you. Are you getting a dog or cat?"

Eric looked at the return address: Prenner Veterinary Clinic. He told her, "No." His glum tone discouraged her from staying to chat. He stared at the brown paper-wrapped package. He knew what it was. He had left it behind after dining with Kyle. Just a brief reminder of that dinner and his anger spiked. He stuck the package into his briefcase. He would take it home and either send it back to Kyle or chuck it.

His traced the edginess and sleeplessness, the problems with concentration to that last dinner with Kyle. He had to distract himself from those thoughts. For the first time Eric had no assignment other than the mortgage fraud. He had to look busy. He decided to read law news. He booted up the computer to check his email account with yahoo. His friends were scattered across the country. He could use a friendly message right now.

There was one, from Cheryl, the cute court reporter. She had attached the remaining transcripts. Eric did not ask for them, but they were here. He paused, trying to picture her. He decided to phone. Her email included her work and cell numbers. He tried the cell. She answered after two rings. He thanked her for the transcripts.

"Say, Cheryl, do you know a good jazz club, one that's not far? I'm new here."

"Sure. Steamer's Café in Fullerton."

"You've been there?"

"Lots of times. A good menu, too."

"Would you be interested in going again—with me?"

When Eric hung up, he was ready to whistle. In the event jazz did not appeal to Cheryl, he had planned to ask about reggae or country—whatever worked. Now he had a date, a place of his own, he was beginning to live life again.

His eyes fell on the monitor. The transcript awaited, nearly egging him to open it. He did, and began scrolling the pages, curious to learn what happened after he testified, whether it was significant when the Archer attorneys presented their defense.

Eric was mildly surprised to find it was not mentioned once in any closing statement. He scrolled backward, stopping after his testimony. *Holy crap,* he exclaimed when he saw two defense witnesses, neither of whom contributed anything. None of the outside attorneys they paid throughout the years? No expert witness? No one competent to address the issues?

Eric did not want to know more. He closed the email program, opened a search engine and began to read a law blog. Jennie peered around the edge of Eric's cubicle.

"You're here," she said with a bright smile. She stepped out and returned, dragging a chair.

"Mortgage fraud," he said, re-stacking a few boxes to make room for Jenny. Most of the Archer files were gone.

"Here's what we're looking at," Jennie told him, and handed him a folder. "The issue right now is mail and wire fraud. We know mortgage companies use USPS and private carriers like FedEx, and they use wire transfers. It's routine for them. Where we find mortgage fraud, we'll find grounds for mail and wire fraud charges."

"What is it you need me to do?"

"Find evidence of transfers. We looking to support a federal statute that prohibits the transfer of stolen goods. The statute also applies to non-goods. That means money, if the value is five thousand or more and the transferor or transferee knows the funds were stolen, converted or taken by fraud. Any questions?"

Eric asked for the relevant code. "You don't believe me?" Jenny looked aggrieved. Before he could answer she shrugged and gave him the information, "Okay, see for yourself. It's 18 U.S.C. §2324."

"I don't doubt you, Jennie. The reason I asked is this may apply to another case." He felt badly to upset her. She nodded, accepting his explanation, told him where to find the files seized from the mortgage company, and left to continue her own assignment.

Eric stared at his computer screen. He was right. Archer should not have been prosecuted by the feds; the charges belonged in state court. Yolanda was right. Archer was not innocent. But in their zeal to destroy Archer, the prosecutors completely missed a legitimate prosecution.

Eric decided to end this nagging concern by checking the code cited by Jennie, see it in black and white. Another blow: It did not apply to life insurance. Eric did not stop. He sensed he was on the right trail, finally. He continued searching the United States Code.

The next marker was a recent ruling from the First Circuit Court of Appeal. It described a company as "knowingly conducting and attempting to conduct financial transactions affecting interstate commerce involving the proceeds of unlawful activity." That fit Archer. He plugged in the citation, 18 U.S.C. section 1956(a)(1)(A)(I), added the word "viatical" and there it was—the answer he sought.

Years earlier federal prosecutors indicted and convicted a viatical company in southern Florida for running a Ponzi scam. The company purported to sell viatical investments but had few policies. The principals, their lawyers, their associates—all were convicted of securities fraud and numerous other violations under this exact statute.

It was not an exact fit to Archer, but Eric found a more recent case, one filed in the federal court in eastern California. Once again, securities fraud was the primary cause of action. This company sold viaticated life insurance as investments.

The problem was Archer never resold the policies to the public. Other than that, it worked. The predicate offense was committed by the insureds who clean-sheeted in order to acquire policies. The financial transaction was Archer's purchase of the policies. The interstate commerce angle was easy: the insureds were residents of many states. All that was missing was a way to dovetail federal law with McCarran-Ferguson. Eric needed something that explicitly referred to life insurance.

Eric added the words "life insurance" and searched the United States Code. He found it: Title 18 of the United States Code, section 1033, "Crimes by or affecting persons engaged in the business of insurance whose activities affect interstate commerce."

How did he miss it, in all this time? The words, "knowingly and with the intent to deceive," applied. Section 1033 was part of the omnibus anti-crime bill entitled the "Violent Crime Control and Law Enforcement Act of 1994. The purpose of 1033 was to provide a federal statutory basis for federal law enforcement agencies to *assist state insurance departments*. And this section was enacted at the behest of the National Association of Insurance Commissioners.

Eric was grinning. He found it. Finally. He actually found it.

If prosecutors used these sections of the code, the entire case could rest on the company's files. Without victims, Cutter and McGuire could have saved tens of thousands of taxpayer dollars spent to transport, lodge, and feed witnesses. Since testifying viators were not needed, they would not have earned "sweetheart deals." IRS would have been able to collect the unpaid taxes.

What about those sweetheart deals? Eric was curious. He logged onto PACER and went directly to the criminal courts. He had to look up each witness individually. No surprise. Prosecutors recommended downward departure and probation. No prison time. The judge rubber-stamped each recommendation. No one other than Hank Rodriguez was ordered to pay restitution. It was a measly sum compared to the total he pocketed and never reported to IRS.

The surprise came when Eric looked up Patricia Russell. Her thirty-four month sentence was reduced to eighteen months. A light sentence made lighter by the many hours she traveled the country to testify at trials. Eric went back to the transcript and scrolled until he found her testimony. He wanted to she what she did for the prosecutors to earn that reward.

Clever lady, he thought. She sure knew how to work them, saying, Yes, I'm guilty even though you said, Wow, even though you asked why I pled guilty. She sure did wow them, figuratively as well as literally.

Crime does pay, Eric thought. He was angry at the prosecutors, the judge, the entire system. And disgusted. Why did he feel angry and disgusted? He expected this. If he did not know better, Kyle was there to remind him, which is exactly what he did when they met for dinner after the trial. He did not notice Kyle carry a small package into the restaurant.

They ordered their dinners and the waiter left to place their orders. Kyle grinned and placed a package on the table. He pushed it across to Eric. It was wrapped in gift paper, a small package, book-sized. Curious, wondering why Kyle was giving him a gift, he tore open the wrapping. When he read the title, *Three Felonies a Day: How the Feds Target the Innocent,* curiosity changed to surprise, and surprise to outrage. He looked up at Kyle. Kyle continued to grin as he explained.

"I read a library copy and was greatly impressed. That's why I ordered a copy for you."

"And what am I supposed to do with this? I don't need a door stopper."

"Read the back of the book jacket, Eric."

Eric did so. The author, a civil liberties lawyer, referenced actual legal battles to show how prosecutors used seemingly innocuous behavior to pin federal crimes on various citizens.

"I picked this up to try to understand how such a thing could happen to Carly," Kyle said, "and, as you warned, could happen to me."

"Why give me a copy? I already know this."

Kyle said, "I learned the problem is far worse than anything I imagined. I realized there's absolutely nothing I can do or say to change things. For you, on the other hand, it might be inspirational."

"You wasted your money. Can you get a refund?"

"Keep the book, Eric. You have the knowledge, the training, and the values, a combination that means you can do things I could not do. You've already started on that road."

The waiter brought their dinners, set the plates before them, asked if there was anything else they wanted, and departed. Eric felt as if his body was shaking with anger. He knew it did not show. The anger was on the inside. Kyle did not understand how misguided he was. He did not understand how powerless Eric was. How could he reach him? Finally, he spoke.

"I may not be with the FBI much longer."

"Are you that fed up, Eric? Don't quit. The FBI, the whole system is in need of people like you."

Eric did not want to tell him what Yolanda and, undoubtedly, others higher up the chain of command, thought of him. Instead, he shifted in his seat, trying to figure out how to engage Kyle in an intellectual discussion. "Change comes so slowly it might not happen in our lifetimes. Consider the 1896 ruling of the Supreme Court. Note, this was decades after the Civil War. The Supreme Court declared racial segregation in schools and businesses to be the law of the land. It's a famous or, rather, infamous lawsuit—*Plessy v. Ferguson*. As a result, 'separate but equal' remained U.S. law until the 1954 Supreme Court decision in *Brown v. Board of Education*."

"Change has to start somewhere."

"Fifty-eight years, Kyle."

"I don't know history half as well as you, but I'll bet the 1896 case was not the first legal challenge. It probably started long before."

"The point is: What change occurred after *Brown?* States resisted integrating their schools—violent resistance. When Martin Luther King, Jr. was killed in 1968—fourteen years after the Supreme Court ruled in *Brown*—very little had changed. In fact, Barack Obama's parents, who were legally married in Hawaii a few years prior to King's death, could not travel to many states where miscegenation was considered a crime punishable with imprisonment."

Kyle continued to look eager. In his mild way he said it was his belief that change was slow or non-existent because too few people had the guts to do what was right; and too few had the guts to fight for what was right. "That's why you are needed, Eric."

"Now you're arguing with me?" Eric forced a laugh. "I guess there's a first for everything."

"I'm not arguing. I'm trying to persuade you. Don't give up. You may be the one to make things happen. Or together with others like you—you need to persuade others to work with you. Then you can bring about the change we need."

"Kyle, don't you get it? I'm a rookie. I have no power, no influence, and little status at the FBI."

"That's modesty speaking. What you did for Carly—without you, she'd probably be in prison now."

"You're wrong there. That was not for Carly. I was doing my job. What I did—I told the court the facts. It happened to come up in the context of Carly, and it happened to help her. But I did not do this for her." Eric laid down his fork. He had lost his appetite.

Kyle called him a modest hero. Eric tried again to tell him he had neither greater power nor influence than Kyle or any other citizen.

Kyle, grinning, said Eric was a hero. "You're a hero in my book and I'm sure you are in Carly's book, and her brother's, and..."

"I am not a hero," Eric said sharply. "Do me a big, big favor, Kyle. Don't say that again. Don't even think it. I want this to be the last time we discuss this. I am not cut out of hero cloth." Eric pushed his plate away. The waiter came over and Kyle agreed that he was done, as well. Neither had finished their dinner.

Kyle looked wounded but said nothing. They finished their wine without another word until Kyle, looking at Eric, said, "Want dessert? I'll tell you another box turtle story."

Eric smiled wanly. He did not have the energy to tell Kyle he appreciated the effort. He felt too miserable. He wanted to tell Kyle how low on the totem pole he was at the FBI, lower than before, due to his testimony. He said nothing. Kyle would feel badly for him, but he could not help.

They did not order dessert. They left the restaurant shortly after, and Eric declined a walk along the dock at Dana Point harbor. Driving back to the hotel, he kept thinking, Hero or Wash-up?

More than two weeks had passed, weeks in which he was haunted with questions. Near the top of the list was the question, Why did he feel resentful of Kyle? Kyle did not trap him into doing or saying anything. His testimony was exactly as he told Kyle. He was doing his job.

∽

The day Eric moved into his own apartment he taped his beloved Castanada quote to the inside of a kitchen cabinet. It would go near a desk, when he owned a desk. He had a mattress on the bedroom floor, his clothes either hanging in a closet or folded in a suitcase, and he drank his morning coffee or ate his dinner standing at the kitchen counter. At least once a day, while standing in the kitchen, he read the quote: "Before you embark on any path ask the question: Does this path have a heart? If the answer is no, you will know it, and then you must choose another path."

Eric's thoughts drifted to Robert Fitzpatrick's downfall at the hands of powerful politicians and FBI officials—and this despite the success of Fitzpatrick's prior assignment, the ABSCAM investigation, which resulted in the convictions of six congressmen and a powerful senator. Now Eric was in the cross hairs of powerful, unnamed enemies, probably including congressmen. He thought about Duke Cunningham and wondered why it took an investigative journalist to expose Duke Cunningham's many years of corruption. How did a journalist do what the FBI could not? That insatiable curiosity, which got him in trouble when he testified, was not abated. Eric looked online for the story-behind-the story. He found it, at the web site of *The American Journalism Review.*

The journalist, Marcus Stern, worked for Copley News Service. Without ever leaving his desk and by doing searches on Google and LexisNexis, he uncovered property records of suspicious real estate deals between Cunningham and a defense contractor. If Stern found readily available documents, the transactions between Cunningham and the defense contractor were not a tightly guarded secret. Why did no investigation occur until after Stern's exposé?

Investigations by the FBI and the IRS led to an indictment, a guilty plea, an eight year prison sentence, and to other investigations and indictments, most notably lobbyist Jack Abramoff and powerhouse Senator Tom Delay.

"Light bulb going off," Eric said as he leaned back in his chair. Now he saw it, a role for him to play with the FBI—if he was not booted for his so-called transgression. There was a possibility now, due to the acclaim of Fitzpatrick's book, that things might be different. He might have a chance. He, Eric Price, might be the one to expose the next Duke Cunningham, Tom Delay, or Scott Bloch.

As he began to recite the Castanada quote to himself another quote sprang to mind, a quote from Satre he had not thought about since college: "Some men are born committed to action: they do not have a choice, they have been thrown on a path, at the end of that path, an act awaits them."

That was what Kyle was trying to tell him. Kyle, who annoyed him for months, harassing Eric with a barrage of phone calls. His anger at Kyle was misplaced. Kyle was true to himself, to his values, to his ethics, and he tried to do good for others. The boy Eric once admired was a man he admired. His eyes grew moist, remembering, realizing: Kyle was the friend he always had been.

That dinner. Eric walked off without the book and did not give it another thought until today. He did not answer when he saw incoming calls from Kyle. The last time Kyle tried to reach him and, again, Eric did not answer, Kyle left a message offering to help him find good second-hand furniture once he found a rental. He would take him to yard sales at upscale communities. Eric did not return the call.

Eric suddenly felt a huge emptiness. None of this was Kyle's fault. He took out his cell phone and stared at it. What would he say? Hey, Kyle, I'm a stray mutt who needs rescuing? He continued staring at Kyle's phone number, not knowing what to say. Maybe invite him to see his new, tiny, sparsely furnished apartment. He needed to break this impasse. He dialed Kyle's number.

Yolanda's head peered around the cubicle wall. When she saw he was on the phone, she signaled to him to hurry. He ended the call, telling Kyle he was rushed and would have to hang up immediately, but was it okay to meet at six o'clock for a drink? Usual place? Kyle agreed.

Walking to Yolanda's office, he was again filled with trepidation. Was she going to tell him he was booted? Or not yet booted but would be watched closely, she and others looking for additional signs of "a loose canon?" Was she going to warn him about proving he was—or was not—a team player? What future did he have here? Had he sacrificed the possibility of being accepted at the National Center for the Analysis of Violent Crime?

NCAVC, described on television as the Behavioral Analysis Unit, was intensely competitive. Preference was given to agents with at least eight years. To be considered, Eric would have to toe the company line for years. Could he last eight-plus years, if nothing improved? Would he be given the chance to last one more year?

The door to Yolanda's office was open. Yolanda stood behind her desk. He could not read her face. She did not signal him to shut the door. He was almost relieved. Without privacy, she would not bombard him with another lecture. Unsure of himself, he shut the door.

"I want to warn you, Eric, it could be years before any antitrust action begins. That's why I assigned you to mortgage fraud, but I do want you to continue working the antitrust angle."

Eric felt himself let go of the breath that cramped his chest. "I know we can't subpoena the information without cause, but is there a possibility life insurers would volunteer it?"

As he spoke, Eric walked toward the desk and sat down in one of the hard wooden chairs. "Doubtful, Eric. They should be motivated, since they are on the hook for millions in death benefits, but they're not likely to have a computer program to identify this information."

"If they all used the same computer program, we could have our techs design something to distribute. But my guess is they each have their own system."

Yolanda stared at him. Her expression was gentle. "You did good recognizing this. If the antitrust action comes to fruition—it will be your baby. Cheer up. You proved yourself to be a valuable member of the team."

"And I finally have my own apartment. I guess I should celebrate." He did not sound as if he would celebrate. He stood up to leave.

"Get some friends together and go out on the town. Take a few days off and go scuba diving. You earned it."

Eric looked up, startled. "You scuba dive?"

"I don't live in this office. It's my work, not my life."

Another lesson, Eric thought. He thanked her and walked back to his cubicle

# Chapter Forty-One

CARLY PICKED UP the newspaper from the front step as the school bus rumbled past the cottage. She carried it to the back door, out to the patio, sat down in one of the plastic lawn chairs and began to flip pages. She was looking for news she hoped not to find. Her spread sheets listed Marilyn Pendergast three times. It worried Carly that Marilyn might be charged with fraud.

If Marilyn was charged, she might sell this cottage to finance legal fees. Even if a buyer continued it as a rental, Carly and Ben would not be able to afford to live here, not with all the improvements Ben made. The rent could increase six hundred percent.

To her relief, there was nothing about seniors charged with fraud.

Carly returned to the first page. She skimmed headlines, all bad news, and turned the page. She avoided bad news. The trial was over but the sense of emerging from a coma lingered. She had to remind herself that life was returning to normal. Normal had new meaning. No longer an accused felon. Her son no longer fearful he would lose her. She was self-employed with irregular income and a growing business.

She skipped past the headline about prosecutors filing for a retrial of the Archer executives. What did Blake really want, when he drove up yesterday? Carly was in the front yard, weeding the flower garden. She stood up at the sound of his car and he jumped out, almost before the engine quieted, a big smile, an attempt to grab her in a hug but she squirmed away.

"Hey! I like your hair. I always told you to grow it long."

Her hair was pulled back into a rubber band. His eyes scanned her body. Carly wore shorts and a halter top. Anger flashed through her. She asked him to please go. He said she could not mean that—he came to ask her out to dinner.

"I don't want to see you again, Blake. I don't want to know you."

That was all she said. She did as her brother had done the first time Blake came to their street. She turned and walked into the cottage, closing the inside door before the screen door completed its travel.

Carly's thoughts stayed with Blake. She resented that he continued to haunt her. What she once believed were good feelings for him, Carly realized, were nothing but the remnants of a lifelong habit of excusing people for inexcusable behavior. Isn't that what she did with Scott, until he crossed an unforgivable line? Even now, she preferred to blame the alcohol. No, she knew better. She was learning. She had only to compare Scott with Kyle to know better. Kyle, whose birthday gift for Ethan was a tiny MP3 player to replace the bulky CD player.

A thump startled her. Ben, like a kid, jumping down the last few steps. He came to the back door and stood there, beaming, dressed in an oxford shirt and khakis. The mustache and beard were gone. Carly whistled.

"A hot date?" she asked.

"Yep. A date with neighbors of Marilyn. I'm headed there to give them a quote for enclosing their patio, put in a ceiling fan, a bar, the works. Just a minute." Ben went inside to the coffee pot, returned with his cup and a freshly baked muffin, and joined her on the patio. He placed the cup and the muffin on the table. Instead of sitting, he placed his hands on his hips, twisted one way, then the other.

"What do you think?" He stood there, grinning.

"You are one handsome guy."

"Do I look like an entrepreneur?"

Carly smiled. She thought he was joking.

"Really," he said as he sat down. He raised his cup and took a sip. "You're an entrepreneur. So am I. You are looking at the president of Nolan Remodeling, Inc."

"Ink?"

"I'm incorporated. And licensed. And insured."

"Wow. That's great. What brought this on?"

"Can't be a beach bum forever." Ben blushed.

"And?"

His voice lowered. "I needed to be able to care for Ethan without you, if things went south."

Carly's eyes filled with tears. She reached out and squeezed his arm.

"I really am an entrepreneur," Ben said, meeting her eyes. "I took courses at Saddleback Community. Some classes were mornings, others on the internet. Business courses. Courses about being an entrepreneur."

"When did all this happen?"

"The courses? While you were at court."

"That's how you kept it secret. But how did you manage with waiting tables and tending bar?"

"I cut back work hours. I began to plan a while ago, after meeting with Cutter. I thought I put aside enough earnings to cover." He scoffed at himself. "Not exactly. I had to do away with what are known as 'discretionary expenses.'"

"I had no idea."

"You had enough to worry about." Ben finished his coffee. He wiped his mouth with the paper napkin in which he had carried the muffin. "Ethan's school had my cell number. When I was in class, the cell was on vibrate."

Carly clapped her hands. "You thought of everything. I am so proud of you."

Ben grinned. "Can't start a business without financing. So I approached Marilyn to co-sign a loan. I brought my transcript to show her."

"Nervy of you! What did she say?"

"Say? She wasn't interested in the transcript. She was flattered. She took credit for inspiring me." Ben laughed and stood up. "Wish me luck. I'm off to meet Mr. and Mrs. Bigbucks."

Carly watched as Ben went indoors. "Jaunty," she thought, and began to fold the newspaper.

"One last thing," Ben said from the doorway. "The party?"

Ben wanted a celebration party. He had bugged her every day for the past week to set a date. He planned to invite all his friends, her friends, neighbors, the mailman—anyone who ever said a kind word about Carly, anyone who came to the bar and knew he was her brother and agreed to hire Carly to design a web site or brochures for their business. He added new reasons each time they discussed it.

She shook her head.

"Think of it this way, Carly. If we have a gala, I can show off the house. I have a scrapbook with before-and-after pictures. We can write off the expense as a business deduction, if it leads to business. So, what do you say? How about next Saturday?"

"I'm really not up to it."

"What, you have wounds? Scars? Did you forgot Mom's story about St. Peter?"

"I guess I did," she admitted.

Ben told her a party was a good way to get out of a funk, and she definitely was in a funk. He circled Saturday a week later on the calendar, and told her to keep the date in mind.

"People care, Carly. They'll be glad to help us celebrate. I bet everyone in Laguna will want to help us celebrate."

When she said nothing, he threatened a block party, asking the police to close off their road so everyone in town could come. His face lit up. His eyes sparkled. "Wow! That's a great idea, Carly. Let's invite everyone."

"We can't afford the food and drink," Carly protested.

"So we make it BYOB and pot luck. Everyone brings something. It's doable."

"I need more time. I don't feel in a party mood."

"You can get in a party mood. Stop thinking about what was. Think about what might be."

"Such as, Mister Positive?"

From that remark Ben knew he was reaching her, finally. "Lots of laughter and a boom box blaring and lots of food and drink. Let's do it. Next Saturday. From two in the afternoon to whenever. It's gonna happen. Your choice: hide in your room or join us."

He told her to buy something new and glamorous for the party, maybe a Hawaiian print dress. It was time to begin the rest of her life.

Carly shrugged, smiled, and took out her cell to begin phoning. She knew Marcia would not come without Phoebe, and specifically invited the Yorkie. When she phoned Allison, she told her to bring her husband and her baby girl. Carly asked each person to contact three others and invite anyone else who might care to come. She added Ben's ideas about pot luck and BYOB.

When she stepped into the veterinary clinic the following day, after delivering Ethan for "work," she invited Kyle. Of course Kyle knew about the party. Both Ethan and Ben had told him. Yes, he would come, definitely, wouldn't miss it for the world, and he thought it was a great idea, that Ben was a great brother to think of doing this.

As soon as Carly's truck drove out of the parking lot, Kyle picked up the phone and called Eric to invite him to a friend's party.

# Epilogue

THE UNITED STATES ATTORNEY is the representative not of an ordinary party to a controversy, but of a sovereignty whose obligation to govern impartially is as compelling as its obligation to govern at all; and whose interest, therefore, in a criminal prosecution is not that it shall win a case, but that justice shall be done. As such, he is in a peculiar and very definite sense the servant of the law, the twofold aim of which is that guilt shall not escape or innocence suffer. He may prosecute with earnestness and vigor—indeed, he should do so. But, while he may strike hard blows, he is not at liberty to strike foul ones. It is as much his duty to refrain from improper methods calculated to produce a wrongful conviction as it is to use every legitimate means to bring about a just one."

—*Berger v. United States,* 295 U.S. 78,88 (1935)

# A Few Words from the Author

THIS WORK OF FICTION was inspired by actual events. At the simplest, I knew dogs named Java and DeeOhGee, and I did meet a woman at the dog park who was raising a grandson who was autistic. She told me the boy did not speak a word until he was six years old. He began speaking after they adopted a mixed breed from the shelter.

As for the legal aspects, everything cited here—lawsuits, court rulings, news stories—are real; you can find them on the internet. Although opinions of characters in the book are theirs and not necessarily those of the author, what is written here about grand jury hearings is based on extensive research. To do your own, start at cato.org.

In some ways Accidental Felon was decades in the making. Many years ago I wanted to write about a real trial and a heroine lawyer, but was stymied by lack of knowledge. I wanted to write Susan Glass' story. Susan was a former social worker and new attorney who established a family law practice in Bridgeport, Connecticut. She was so new that she had no trial experience when she was approached by a nun who sought help for a young Hispanic man falsely accused of murder.

The nun was chaplain at a local prison. Several inmates told her they knew who was responsible for the murder, and this Hispanic man had nothing to do with it. The nun, who spoke Spanish, learned from the man that his young wife and two babies were without food or utilities, without his support.

After the nun approached Susan, they visited the young wife together—in a dangerous, subsidized housing project. Susan used her social work experience to get aid for the family. Together, Susan and the nun—who served as translator—traipsed the project for days, locating and interviewing. At trial, with the help of a judge who believed in justice and recognized Susan's inexperience, she successfully defended the young man. He was acquitted.

When I investigated, intending to write this story, I met with the assistant district attorney who prosecuted the young man. He told me, "It does not matter if he was actually innocent. He's probably guilty of something else, or will be. So we got him off the street."

I was shocked and depressingly aware of my ignorance. I was not competent to write the story. But decades later, with far greater knowledge, the prosecutorial misconduct that underlies Susan Glass' story prodded me to write Accidental Felon.

For readers who are lawyers and become irate that my tale includes a defense attorney who called a maintenance man as one of two defense witnesses, there are far worse true stories—defense attorneys who fell asleep during capital murder trials, resulting in clients sentenced to death; defense attorneys whose heads were stuffed with drugs or alcohol during trial; convicted defendants whose appeals ended up in the "circular file" when appellate courts decided the defense lawyer's nap during trial was not proof of ineffective assistance of counsel. For details, see www.InnocenceProject.org.

I know from hundreds of hours of reading the biggest problem is not defense attorneys but prosecutorial misconduct. Prosecutors have more power than judges—from start to finish. Prosecutors decide who to charge, what charges to bring, whether evidence in their possession is exculpatory and must be turned over to the defense or, if questionable, left in a drawer, and so on to the sentencing when judges usually rubber stamp the prosecutor's recommendation at sentencing.

Prosecutorial misconduct occurs daily throughout the nation, in state courts and federal courts. It will continue as long as there is no accountability, as long as judges and appeals courts seek excuses rather than justice, as long as we, you and I, choose to believe this is "the best system in the world" and ignore serious defects that one day might victimize an innocent loved one, a neighbor, a friend, a co-worker. Under our current system, no one is safe.

# Acknowledgements

THIS BOOK IS DEDICATED to three people whose lives crossed mine at critical junctures and whose positive influence endures to this day. The poetry of Dick Allen continues to nourish and inspire as did his personal encouragement when I was enrolled in creative writing classes he taught at the University of Bridgeport. He remembers me as a far better fiction writer than I recall after all these years, and once again inspired me to reach for the stars.

Norman Goroff's many "Normanisms" (e.g., "Today I am the best I can be today,"), our shared admiration of Viktor Frankl, love of Samoyeds and so much else are distinct memories despite the passage of years. He was an unusual as well as inspiring professor. Norman came into class, wrote a sentence on the board such as, "All people have an inherent right to dignity and self-respect," then sat on the outer edge of his desk, swinging his legs, looking into each face, waiting for discussion. With his black bushy beard and black, lively eyes, he looked to me like a Biblical scholar. Norman invited us to grade ourselves the first day of class—on a paper he passed around the room—explaining it was not his responsibility but ours whether we read the "suggested" material, whether we learned anything, whether we even attended class. He was challenging, stimulating, and caring, and I probably read more for that class—including following up footnotes in his handouts—than I did for any before or since.

If you think research is dull and analyzing the validity of research results a chore, you never met Ray Pichey, a cheerful, down-to-earth person who was scrupulous about his work. Fortunately for me, Ray recognized my interest and ability in research. He invited me to participate in a research project that brought social work graduate students into the prisons of Connecticut to interview inmates. As a result, we formed a more personal relationship as colleagues than if we remained professor-student.

I doubt Ray knew more than what he was told about a former inmate of Somers, the maximum security prison. When we visited Somers, this former inmate was an employee at the prison. He volunteered to guard me as we went through halls, into the cafeteria and other places, and he expressed concern for my safety by asking to sit in on interviews I conducted solo with inmates (I could not allow this). He must remain unnamed because I lost touch with him and never asked permission to reveal his story.

A huge man, perhaps six foot five and weighing close to three hundred pounds, when he was an inmate he had the opportunity to participate in a pilot program that assigned inmates to mentors in the business community. As a result, he learned computer programming and had work experience. After release, he enjoyed high-paying, prestigious employment. When he learned the mentor-inmate program no longer existed, in gratitude for how it changed his life and eager to extend that good fortune to others, he returned to the prison to attempt to recreate that program.

He confided to me that he wrote poetry. A closet poet, he never shared it with anyone but asked my opinion and entrusted me with the blue loose-leaf binder in which he stored his poems. I took it home to read, returning it later. The poems were excellent.

From Ray's invitation to pursue this unusual research project to this former inmate, my horizons were broadened and, over time, I followed the roads that previously were beyond my vision.

⌒

I located the story in southern California because I lived there for many years and loved it; this was an opportunity to revisit my memories. I do not want any reader to consider the trial to be a reflection on California's federal judges, many of whom are superior to those of other states. For example, U.S. District Court Judge Cormac Carney of Santa Ana, the courthouse that is the locale for the Archer trial, had the courage to toss out convictions against the principals of Broadcom, after he reviewed evidence of numerous instances of prosecutorial misconduct.

As a writer who had done nonfiction for many years it was a struggle to return to fiction and to turn this story into something I dare present to readers. It helped immeasurably to have the advice and encouragement of a number of writer and publishing friends: Kathy Rapp, Joseph Harris in the U.K., Dick Margolis, Alan Canton, Patricia Bell, Steve Litt, Andrew Chapman, Dave Marx, and William L. Warner, M.D.

Special thanks to Dr. Julio Morales Jr., professor emeritus, the University of Connecticut Graduate School for Social Work, who contributed more to improving this novel than any other individual.

I greatly appreciate the contributions of attorney Alan Anderson of Minnesota and Michael Pasano of Florida, each of whom addressed specific legal questions I posed and corrected mistakes I would have made but for their help. If there are other legal errors, the fault is entirely mine.

Yuri Martsinovsky of the Canadian-based company, Deep Software, Inc. (www.deep-software.com) provided the information for Eric's testimony. Other companies were asked similar questions but their representatives either did not know enough about their own technology or their technology was not as efficient as Deep Software.

∽

Gloria Wolk is a member of Investigative Reporters and Editors, author of three nonfiction books and editor of a legal text. She lives in Raleigh, North Carolina. She has two websites, where readers can find her email address: www.Viatical-Expert.net and www.AccidentalFelon.net.